For the Love of Quinn

Now and Forever
Part 2

Tammy Dennings Maggy

ISBN: 0-9861543-7-7
ISBN-13: 978-0-9861543-7-9

DEDICATION

This book is dedicated in loving memory to John McInerney, who encouraged me to follow my dreams no matter what anyone else thought. Win or lose, it would always be my choice. Thanks for everything, Dad*! Semper Fi!*

I'd like to thank all who stood by me during the writing of the original version of this story. It took a year to write, a year to get published, and now here it is again six years later, the way I'd envisioned.

CHAPTER 1

"I hate this fucking town, Jake!" Iris angrily paced across the kitchen floor with her fists clenched.

"Calm down, Iris. We'll be out of here at the end of May, and we can start all over."

"Easy for you to say. You're not the one being investigated by the government. We'll be lucky to be able to rent a house month to month in Greenville. God knows if we'll ever be able to qualify for a loan to buy one."

"It's not that bad; it's an audit. Just take in your returns and receipts and be done with it."

"You don't get it. My brother-in-law, Aaron filed all of our tax returns. He had to fudge them a bit to make them come out in my favor. I didn't want to work at any of the Laundromats that my parents owned, or for my father's other 'not so legal' businesses. I wanted to make it on my own, but my folks still insisted on sending me money every month to help with expenses. Aaron handled the books for my parents so he was usually the one to make out the checks that were sent to me. I left all the income tax stuff in his hands. I just signed the returns when they were done. "

"What the hell do you mean by 'not so legal'?" *Holy shit!* What else had she been hiding from him?

"Well, my ex was into all sorts of shady stuff. The bills were always paid, and we had extra money when we needed it from him and from my parents, so I didn't ask questions. I didn't claim a lot of it as income either. So, Aaron had to come up with creative ways to explain that and some of the other things we'd been claiming as business expenses."

"Jesus Christ, Iris! All this time you've led me to believe you're struggling and you've been rolling in cash. Sounds to me like your family has been taking the money and laundering it through their legit businesses. What the hell made you think that shit was okay to do?"

"Hey, don't get all high and mighty with me. I had the kids to take care of and I didn't care where the money came from. They were my priority."

He closed his eyes. "Don't you think you could've told me about this before now?" There was no way in hell he was going to go to jail for something her family had done.

"We've never had to worry about the IRS before. Aaron always took care of everything. It all looked good on paper, but since Quinn came into the picture, there's been all sorts of investigating going on. Now there are cops coming into work asking questions about whether or not I knew about my ex dealing drugs or my Daddy running moonshine. There hasn't been a week gone by since we were in Vegas that there hasn't been someone looking into the businesses and the taxes, how I raise my kids, even trying to nail Aaron for tax fraud. It's all been a nightmare!"

"I told you to back off Quinn, but you wouldn't listen. You had to keep digging around in my stuff and e-mailing her husband left and right. Yeah, I know all about those e-mails to Jackson, Iris." Jacob threw her paperwork across the table. He was so disgusted with her.

She practically snarled at him then, "I. Want. Her. *Out* of our lives, Jake! With her still in the picture we can't go forward. I don't think I can ever—"

"Trust me? Yeah, I get that!"

"Well, what do you expect? Every time I turned around you were cheating on me. First it was the old girlfriend from Vegas you *had* to spend the weekend with to see if it was really over between you. Then it was another hoochy online you kept cybering with even when I was asleep in the other room. And then there's Quinn who seems to have a hold over you I can't get through. I can't take it anymore!"

"She broke it off with me. It's over." But not in his heart. Not in his soul, not ever.

"*She* broke it off? I thought you did?"

"Same end result, isn't it? You made sure of that!"

"Hey! You asked me to marry you, Jake. I thought that meant something."

Jacob's mind temporarily blanked with disbelief. She really was delusional. "I *didn't* ask you to marry me. You just assumed I was going to ask you because of the ring. The ring you found snooping around in my *locked* desk drawer! For Christ's sake, Iris, the ring didn't even fit you."

She turned very pale. "What are you saying?"

"Cut the bullshit!" He immediately regretted yelling at her and tried to calm down before he said anything else. "It doesn't matter anymore. You asked me to marry you and I said yes. You're getting your wedding next year. What more do you want from me?"

"I want you to love me like you love her." The tears in her eyes finally spilled over and ran down her cheeks. "I want you to call out for me and reach for me in your sleep and not her."

He closed his eyes and took a deep breath. He didn't want to keep hurting her like this. Jacob wished he'd be able to give her everything her heart desired, that he'd be able to do as she asked and give their love a chance, but he couldn't. "I don't know why this is happening to us and if we'd met at another time or place maybe things would be different. I can't let her go, Iris. I told you that all along. I do love you, but I'll never be in love with you or love you the way I love her. I'm sorry. I just can't."

She wiped the tears from her face and nodded. "Where do we go from here? You can't let her go? Well, I can't let *you* go. You are my whole world. Can *she* say that? Seems to me that she has it pretty damn good with two men fighting over her, and she isn't even divorced yet."

"I know it looks that way, but I'm not fighting for her." Jake sat down at the kitchen table and put his head in his hands. He heard the chair next to him slide on the floor as Iris sat down. "She doesn't deserve a mess like me, and neither do you. You deserve someone who can give you their whole heart. All I've been able to do is give you heartache."

"That's not true." She pulled his hands away from his face and made him look at her. "If you forget about all the shit with Quinn, you've given me a lot of happiness. I think it's enough to fight for, and I'm willing to give it one more chance. Come with me to Greenville for spring break with the kids. Let's look for a place to live and move forward. You said yourself over and over that Quinn is better off with that billionaire. Well, if you love her so much, let her go. When you do that, maybe you'll see that you can be happy with me."

Jacob gently squeezed her hands. "I'll go to Greenville to help you look for houses, but once we get back here, I'm going to stay with a friend from work for a while. I need to think this all through, on my own, without you and the kids around."

Her eyes narrowed and she pulled her hands out of his reach. "If that's what you think you need to do, then go for it." She got up from the table and walked down the hallway toward their bedroom. She called out to him as she reached the door, "I know as soon as you lay your eyes on Greenville, you'll change your mind."

I wish I could believe that but my heart and soul will never be happy without Quinn.

After pulling another long night in surgery, Quinn was really looking forward to being able to sleep at least the next eight hours in her own bed. There was nothing like your own pillow to curl up to when you were bone weary. The emergencies had rolled in all night long and four of those ended up on her surgery table—two Great Danes with bloat from the same household, no less, a Pit bull with a knife buried in its back nearly severing the spinal cord, and an English Bulldog who went into labor two days before its scheduled C-section. Of course she couldn't deliver on her own, so eight puppies later she was resting comfortably while Quinn's technician watched the pups nursing hungrily. All in all it was a great night to lose herself and forget the rest of the world. She got four hours of sleep at the clinic and then covered another eight hours for Sarah. Poor thing was out with the flu and sounded like shit on the phone.

She finally pulled into her winding driveway at 6:30 p.m., and her eyes refused to keep open any longer. Her body craved sleep but fear of what she'd encounter when she dropped off kept her awake. For the last week she'd been plagued with horrible dreams, the night terror type where she kept chasing after someone who'd always be out of her reach. She kept yelling for them, but she'd lost her voice.

Quinn always woke up with her heart racing, tears streaming down her face, and sometimes screaming.

She wanted the other dreams back. The ones with the island getaway with lots of sun, sand, and the ocean, and Jake. They'd spend all day and all night together learning about each other, laughing and loving until they fell asleep in each other's arms. Quinn never wanted to leave those arms, but something always pulled her back to this reality and her broken heart.

Sarah had been trying to get her to go see a therapist to help sort through all of those feelings and the dreams. She needed to go for her own sanity. Sarah was right, of course, but Quinn kept putting it off. Even the death of one of her mentors hadn't been enough for her to get help for her own depression and suicidal thoughts.

Instead she threw herself into her work and stayed out of the house as much as possible. She had very little contact with Jackson if she could help it. If she wasn't at home, his mother couldn't reach her either. Man, that woman would not let Quinn be! She kept prying and wanted to know why she wasn't taking care of her son the way he needed. Of course the last time she'd talked to her, Quinn asked her if she called up all of her son's mistresses and asked them why *they* weren't taking care of his needs. That shut her up, but she still stalked Quinn on Facebook. She guessed it was time to block her once and for all, but she had to admit to herself she did enjoy getting the other woman all riled up.

With the hectic schedule she'd worked over the last week, Jackson had suggested she stay at the house in Oakland so she didn't have such a long drive when she was tired after the marathon shifts. Quinn really didn't want to, but it made the most sense. The commute to the Bay House was a bitch on a regular day, let alone after a forty-eight hour shift. He'd stayed out of the master bedroom and kept to himself in the guest bedrooms. The arrangement appeared to work out for both of them. They didn't have much contact with each other because of the hours she spent at the veterinary hospital, and that was fine with her. The added privacy allowed her to come and go as she pleased without any more fighting. The only person on her mind the last couple hours had been Steve. She wanted to call him before she went to bed. She missed his voice, and most of all she missed his arms around her.

She pulled the Sky into the empty garage and closed the door behind her. Jackson's Mustang was not in its spot. *Big surprise there.* She thought he'd told her that he had to work today, but who the hell knew the truth anymore? And even if he was scheduled to work, he would be out most of the night with any one of the bimbos he'd been tapping.

Quinn entered the house through the kitchen and her jaw dropped. Two days' worth of dishes had been left stacked up on the counter and the sink. Leave it to Jackson to let it all go until she broke down and did it. She threw her things down on the kitchen table and dove in on the mess. She opened up the dishwasher to find it empty. *Thank the Goddess for small favors!*

She flipped on the television, ran through some of the shows she had saved to the DVR, and started up last week's episode of *Supernatural.* She loved those Winchester boys. She sorted through the plates, silverware, and glasses stacked all over and received another surprise—two filthy wine glasses, and one with hot pink lipstick.

Fucking bastard!

Now he'd stooped to entertain his whores in her house? Not on her life! They had agreed neither one of them would bring "dates" back to the house. He'd never done it before so after her initial shock wore off, she let her anger spill over. He'd been the one to convince her to stay in the house pretending to be concerned for her welfare. *What a crock!*

She slammed the dishwasher door closed, pushed the button to start up the cycle, and decided she'd lost her appetite. *Might as well go upstairs, shower, and go to bed.* She had to be rested before she confronted Jackson. Quinn peered into the larger of their two guest rooms where Jackson had moved into right after she'd returned from Vegas, and it was a total disaster, as she had expected. She slammed that door shut and stomped upstairs.

She opened the door to her bedroom to find it looked like a tornado hit it. There were clothes strewn all over the place— Jackson's, not hers—more wine glasses on the nightstands as well as a nearly empty bottle of wine, and the sheets in a tangled heap. *This night just keeps getting better and better!*

She pulled off her scrubs, threw them into the overflowing laundry hamper, and pulled out a tank top and shorts from her dresser to make herself comfortable. Quinn knew she wouldn't be able to sleep in this mess and decided to at least make a dent in it. She pulled back the covers and found them damp, reeking of cum and someone's cheap-ass perfume.

Now he'd done it. This was the last straw. She stayed at work making money to pay off the bills he racked up, and he'd brought his boss here to fuck, in *her bed*! He didn't even have the decency to use the other guest bedroom.

Her cell phone buzzed with an alert from her Facebook page. Derek had sent her a message asking her to let everyone know how she was doing. Everyone was worried. *Okay, here it goes.*

Status update: Came home after working a 48-hour shift to find that Jack has been entertaining his uhhh, companions, in MY BED. TODAY!! Will be temporarily unavailable as I have to get the trash and filth out of my house!

She added a follow up message to that status, asking if anyone knew the fastest way to get rid of cum-soaked sheets and the stench of cheap-ass perfume. That should get some tongues wagging and absolutely mortify her mother-in-law. A second follow-up message let them all know what she was going to do. *BBQ anyone?*

She pulled off the sheets, pillows, and the comforter and threw them out the patio windows down to the deck below, right next to the fire pit. She went back downstairs to the garage and hauled out all the cleaning supplies—bucket, mop, sponges, and lots of bleach. Next stop the cabinet where they kept the barbecue pit supplies. *Now where was the lighter fluid?*

Derek was beside himself when he read Quinn's Facebook status update. "Goddamn it! I'm going to kill Jackson! This is low, even for him. Bringing his broads home and screwing them in Quinn's bed. Does he think she's just going to keep taking this from him and do nothing?"

He wasn't going to let Jackson get away with this shit. It was time to help Quinn whether she wanted it or not. He grabbed his cell off his belt and scrolled through his contacts. He hoped Steve wasn't still out of town. It rang twice, and then the familiar deep voice greeted him.

"Derek! I was just going to call you. I'd like to get you to do some more artwork for the casinos. The fire and ice theme was a big hit, and my business partners want more of the same."

"Steve, that sounds fantastic, but there's something else I need to talk to you about. It's Quinn. She finally sent me a message through Facebook. Looks like Jackson brought his current bimbo home and slept with her in *Quinn's* bed. She found the evidence all over the house. She just got off a forty-eight hour shift, and I'm worried about her. I don't think she's been eating well, let alone sleeping.

"I know. I've left her messages daily for the last week since she'd told me she'd decided to stay at the house in Oakland. Once in a while she would send off a text to me saying she misses us here in Vegas and when she gets a chance to breathe she'll call. I've been trying to give her the space she needs, but I'm worried, too. I've asked some of my Oakland PD buddies to check in on her. Maybe I'll call them now and give them a head's up with this latest development."

Derek felt a little better, but something else nagged at him about the whole thing. It wasn't like his sister to blow people off this way, busy or not. She'd always had time for her friends and family. He was scared that she was pulling away and trying to hide whatever she was going through from all of them. "Thanks, Steve. Hopefully we're just being overly protective, but I'll deal with her yelling at me about it later as long as she's all right."

"I'll let you know if I find out anything."

Holy shit! He thought Quinn wasn't going to be home until the following night. Maybe she would be too tired to rip into him tonight about the mess, like she'd been for the last few weeks. *Might as well face the music.* He closed the garage door and entered the kitchen where he was immediately assaulted by the smell of bleach and smoke. *What the hell?* It looked like Quinn had been on a cleaning rampage. The house appeared spotless. He was really going to catch it now.

He heard the stereo blasting from the bedroom upstairs. What was she doing up there at two thirty in the morning? And where was the smoke smell coming from? He looked out onto the patio and saw the remnants of a fire still glowing in the barbecue pit. That couldn't be a good sign. "Quinn?" He ran up the stairs two at a time and got his ears blown out with the strains of "Help Me Rhonda" and Quinn singing right along with it.

Okay, he never thought he would say this about her, but she scared the shit out of him seeing her this way, on her hands and knees scrubbing the tile floors with *his* toothbrush! The bleach overwhelmed his nostrils and he gagged. *What the hell?* "Quinn? What are you doing?"

She looked up at him and he had to step back. She was sobbing, and her makeup ran all down her face. She was really scaring him now. Never had he seen her in this state. "Gotta scrub my house. It's filthy." Then she sang again but changed the words just a bit: "get him out of my heart."

"Quinn, the house looks great. You've really outdone yourself." Jackson noticed she'd stripped the bed completely. *Oh no, she didn't put all of it in the pit did she?* "Give me the brush and come to bed—"

"Don't you fucking touch me!" She threw his toothbrush at him, narrowly missing his head.

"Baby?" He stepped closer to her and tried to help her up off of the floor. Her hands were so red and raw from the bleach water. He thought they could be burned.

He had to get her to a doctor.

"Don't you dare call me 'baby'! You bring your trashy whores home to fuck in *my* bed? You stay away from me!" She just went back to scrubbing with an actual scrub brush and singing. He couldn't leave her that way.

He dialed 911 and requested an ambulance. She needed professional help and fast.

Within ten minutes several police cars and an ambulance lined up in their driveway. Jackson recognized a few of the officers as friends of Quinn's, and relief washed over him. Maybe she would listen to them and let the paramedics fix up her hands and her knees.

Officer Frank Samuels was the one who got her to listen to reason. "Quinn, you have to let Jenny finish putting the dressings on your hands and your knees. I think you've burned yourself pretty badly with the bleach. Atta girl." He helped her up so she could sit on the bathtub, and the paramedic named Jenny got right to work. Frank rose up and nodded for Jackson to meet him in the hallway.

"Thank you for coming so fast. I couldn't get her to snap out of it."

Frank pulled him away from the others and spoke really low, "Cut the bullshit, Jack. We all know you've been running around on Quinn for years. For the life of me I don't know why she's stayed with you, but I sure as hell am not going to leave her in this house with you any longer. The paramedics are taking her to Alta Bates where she'll get the attention she needs. And just so you know, if I find out you had anything at all to do with this…" He stopped and just glared at Jackson. "You just get on the phone and call her family. They'll want to be here for her."

"Hey! I just got home and found her like this. She's been off her rocker for months." Frank started toward him, and he figured it was time to shut up. He wasn't going to get anywhere with the cop at all. "Okay, I'll call her sister. I'm sure she'll be on the first flight out of Detroit."

Frank dismissed him with a wave as he walked away. He pulled his cell out of his pocket and furiously punched at the screen. He'd walked far enough down the hall to prevent Jackson from overhearing his end of the conversation but he did hear Quinn's name. *Who the hell would he be calling at this hour?*

* * * *

CHAPTER 2

"Thanks for taking care of her, Frank. We should arrive at Oakland International around 5:00 a.m. Don't worry about her sister and mother. I'll make sure they get out here."

Steve's hands shook as he hung up. He should've been out there sooner. He should have made her promise she'd stay at the house on Treasure Island until he returned to California to join her. *Goddamn it!* Steve threw his coffee mug against the wall, and it shatters into several pieces. The buzzing of his phone brought his focus back to what he needed to do.

"Derek? Can you be ready in a half hour to fly to Oakland?" He added a few more things to his rollaway. He always kept one packed just in case for sudden business trips, but he never thought he would have to pack like this to sit at Quinn's bedside.

"I'm ready now and down in your lobby. I just got off the phone with Randi. They can't get a flight out until the afternoon. She said Ma is struggling to hold it together."

"Let me take care of everything. You just have them sit tight. I have a car en route to pick them up now. They'll fly out of Detroit Metro and be here by 8:00 a.m. at the latest. I'm sending one of my planes for them, and you and I will be flying out on the other. I'm on my way down now." Tears blurred his vision. "What if we're too late this time, Derek? What if she doesn't bounce back from this? I should've insisted she get professional help when she broke down in February." His stomach cramped hard enough to double him over.

"Stop it. We don't even know how bad it is yet. I know you love her, dude. But we have to be strong for her. I don't want to even think about my life or the world without her in it."

Steve closed his rollaway and headed for the elevators. "Neither do I, Derek. Neither do I." *A life without Quinn was not worth living.*

"I fucking hate hospitals." Jackson paced around the lounge he and his parents had been waiting in since they'd arrived over two hours before.

"Well, they're no picnic for the patients either, Jack, so you might as well sit down and shut up. The doctors will let us know what's going on with your wife as soon as they can."

"Thanks, Dad. I couldn't have figured that out without your help."

"No need to get all pissy. We're all worried about Quinn. What the hell was she doing cleaning the house at two in the morning? Didn't she work a forty-eight hour shift or something crazy like that? And where the hell were you?"

Jackson glared at his father. He was always pointing out the obvious and never passed up a chance to make him feel like everything was his fault. "None of your fucking business."

"Stop it, the both of you. We all know Quinn hasn't been herself for months. No wonder, too, with all the trips to Vegas to visit her brother and that mobster."

"Mom!" *Christ, here we go again.* Not that he didn't agree with her, but he was in no mood to have his personal life the subject of hospital gossip.

"I'm just saying if you did your job as a husband instead of running around with every bimbo that said hello to you ever, then maybe Quinn wouldn't be running around with Eischer. Oh, and don't get me started on that brother of hers, covered head to toe in tattoos. He's nothing more than a common street thug. I hid all the silverware the last time he came to visit. He's just plain creepy."

"Oh, quit acting like you care about anything other than the inheritance. You only liked having Quinn as a daughter-in-law because you thought you were going to get free veterinary care for you and all of your friends. When Grandma cut everyone but Quinn out of the will, you had a new reason to ensure she stayed a Hollis. It's all about money with you both."

His mother rolled her eyes. "Oh, don't be so melodramatic. You want the money just as much as we do. Don't tell me you wouldn't love to be free of your ball and chain so you could run around and do as you please."

"Well, that can easily be arranged."

The three of them turned and looked at the doorway to the waiting room to see who'd spoken. It was none other than the "mobster" himself, Steve Eischer, and Quinn's brother Derek. Both looked like they were going to bust some skulls, starting with his.

"You want out of your marriage, Jack? I want you out of Quinn's life altogether. It sounds like a win-win situation to me."

"Not gonna happen, Eischer. She's had every chance to leave me for you, and yet she still stays. Why do you think that is?"

Steve wanted to smash that self-satisfied grin right off of his face, but instead he kept his cool. He wasn't there to beat the shit out of him. He was there for Quinn. But Derek had other ideas. He walked calmly into the room and right up to Jackson, nose to nose until he'd backed the man up against the wall.

"You step away from my son, you thug, or I will have you thrown in jail with the other riff raff." Mrs. Hollis was on her feet with her hands on her hips and her face the color of a ripened tomato.

"I wouldn't be so sure of that, Mrs. Hollis. You go ahead and call OPD. Let's see how many will respond to your call to save Jack. I'm willing to bet that Officer Samuels has filled them all in on what has happened to Quinn."

She spun around to glare at Steve, and he almost laughed. She really thought she could intimidate just about anyone with that face of hers. "I'm sure you already bribed the police into bullying Jackson, haven't you? Until you came into the picture, Quinn was happy being married to my son. Now she's covered in tattoos, multiple piercing in her ears, and running off sleeping in your bed."

That was just too much for him to take. Steve burst out laughing and had to lean against the wall for support. Derek's laughter joined his. "Now I know where your son gets his delusions. Quinn has been dying inside being married to your son and a part of your family. You don't give a shit about her at all. You just want to get your hands on Grandma Hollis's fortune."

The three of them looked at each other and then back to Steve. All were at least three shades of pale lighter than they were when he'd arrived. Mr. Hollis was the first to find his voice. "How, how did you find out about that? That's personal family business."

"Does it really matter how I found out? All you need to know is I hold all the cards here. I won't sit back and let this go on any longer. As soon as Quinn is released into the care of her family, I'll make sure you're all out of her life for good."

"How dare you!" Mrs. Hollis was one pretentious broad. He had to give her that much but even that turned into a stretch for him the longer he had to share space with her and her family.

He pretended to ignore her and glanced at his watch. "Well, it's nearly 6:00 a.m. now. Quinn's mother and sister will be landing at Oakland International in less than two hours. I recommend the three of you be gone well before they get here. I have a sneaky suspicion that Mrs. Quartermarsh isn't going to be as polite as I've been with you. Come on, Derek. Quinn's doctor offered his office to us so that we can wait to see him after he's examined her."

Jackson couldn't leave well enough alone. "If the doctor has anything to say, he'll say it to me first. I'm her husband and her legal next of kin."

He really should've kept his mouth shut. Steve flew across the room and smashed his fist into Jackson's mouth. *Goddamn!* That hurt his hand, but it was well worth seeing that piece of trash on the ground and bleeding. "Just so you know, Quinn had a new will drawn up. She named her sister and Derek as advocates for her in case she was incapacitated and unable to make her own medical decisions, and she completely cut *you* out of everything. I had my lawyers draw it up for her the last time she was in Vegas. They sent a copy of it to the hospital so you don't have any authority over *anyone* here."

Derek walked with Steve down the hall with a huge smile on his face. "Damn, Steve! You got one hell of a right cross! Remind me to never get on your bad side." He looked down at his hand, which was starting to swell. "Maybe we can ask one of the nurses to get you some ice for your hand."

"Naw, I would rather feel the pain in my hand than what I am feeling inside worrying about our girl."

"I hear ya, dude." Derek looked back at the Hollis family still sitting in the waiting room with stunned expressions on their faces. "I didn't know Quinn had named me as one of her advocates. Before today, I would've felt really uncomfortable with that responsibility."

Steve put his arm around Derek's shoulder as they walked toward the doctor's office. "She trusts you with her life, and so do I. She didn't even think twice about it. When David asked her who she wanted she named you and Miranda right off."

"I don't know how to thank you for all that you've done for her and for our family, Steve. You've been the best thing that has ever happened to her. I just wish that she…"

"I know she loves me. She's told me as much every time we're together. She's my perfect match in every way, but her heart longs to be with Jake. I've accepted that right from the start."

"But she wouldn't be in here if she would just let herself fall in love with you and forget all about Hartley."

"We're in love with each other. It's just a different kind of love. It's a love that neither one of us will ever let go. We need each other. As you know very well, before she came into my life I was completely married to my job. She reminded me that there is a hell of a lot of living to do outside of all of my business meetings. No matter what she decides to do or who she chooses to spend the rest of her life with, I know I'll always have a place in her heart. I have no intention of losing the friendship we have. No one can ever take that away, not even Jake."

"I won't let him near her again." His body tensed up under Steve's arm.

"He loves her, Derek. He just doesn't think that he deserves her. I'm hoping he'll come to his senses soon and ask Quinn to forgive him."

"Why would you want to put her through that pain again?"

"If my hunch about them is right, we haven't seen the end of their love affair."

She heard the sound of the waves crash on the beach outside her room. A soft breeze swirled through the open patio doors and brought her the rest of the way out of her dream. She didn't immediately recognize where she was, but for some reason it didn't bother her. The silky sheets caressed her skin as she rolled over to get out of the bed. Her eyes snapped open as she realized she was naked. *What the hell?*

"Good morning, baby doll."

Jake! Her heart strummed wildly, and she couldn't believe he was standing there out on the patio. The breeze tossed his hair around his shoulders and the sun caused his already tanned skin appear to glow. "I, how did I get here? And where are my clothes?"

"I've missed you, Quinn. I've been waiting here on our island hoping you'd come back to me." He walked into the room and over to the bed. "I was asleep and dreaming of making love to you, at least I thought I was dreaming. You just appeared in my arms and—"

She pushed the covers off and threw herself into his arms. "Don't let me go back, Jake. I never want to leave you again."

He held her tight against his bare chest. His heart beat in sync with hers. She didn't understand how they were finally together on the island she'd dreamt of over and over again, but she didn't care. She could finally touch him, kiss him, and make love to him again and again.

"Baby, we don't have much time left. You'll have to go back. It's not our time to be together yet."

She couldn't believe what he'd just said. "I don't understand. Don't you want me to be with you?"

His eyes filled with tears. "Of course I do. My life is so empty without you, but if you stay too long here with me, you'll be lost forever to the other people in your life who love you, too. I won't let you give up all of them for me, Quinn."

"The doctors haven't given us any more information yet, Randi, but we expect to hear something soon. I left word at the admittance desk to send you up here where we're waiting. I'm not sure if Jackson and his parents are still in the waiting room or not, but I don't want you to have to see them at all. Tell your mother not to worry. I've made arrangements for everyone to be able to stay close by. See you soon."

"I take it that Ma is worrying about everything under the sun in order to not worry so much about Quinn?"

Steve laughed. "You could say that." He pictured her in the front passenger seat next to Nathan arguing with the GPS about the fastest route to the hospital from the airport. Steve had met Helen Quartermarsh the past summer when she came out to Vegas to visit with Derek for the Fourth of July. Quinn had surprised her by flying out as well, and Steve had invited Helen to stay at the hotel as his guest. She'd balked at first, but then relented when Derek reminded her how much she loved staying at the MGM. Fiercely protective of her children, Helen grilled him for well over an hour about his intentions toward her daughter. By the end of her interrogation they were both a bit drunk and had come to an understanding. Steve loved her daughter unconditionally and was determined to get her away from Jackson and his family if it took everything he had.

"Mr. Quartermarsh? Mr. Eischer?" Quinn's doctor had entered the room. Dr. Marshall walked right up to both of them and shook their hands. "We've completed our initial evaluation of Dr. Hollis, and there are a few things we need to clarify, if you don't mind."

Derek immediately took the lead. "We'll do the best we can. My sister has had a hell of a time the last couple of months and has been keeping things from us."

Atta boy! He knew he could count on Derek to take his role as his sister's medical advocate seriously.

Dr. Marshall nodded. "She was pretty coherent when she arrived even after all she went through tonight, and she answered a lot of our questions herself. The burns on her hands, knees, and legs were pretty painful for her so we had to give her a sedative along with her other pain meds to help her rest. Honestly, that's exactly what she needs. She's been really burning the candle at both ends and in the middle. I'm surprised she's made it through the last few months like this."

"What do you need to know, Doc?"

"Well, she kept calling out for a Jake. I take it that's not her husband or one of you?"

Derek's face reddened, but he kept it under control. "No. He's someone who pretty much destroyed her world in February. Long story short, he's now engaged to someone else."

21

"Ah. That was probably what started this round, too. We've reviewed her medical records from the hospital in Vegas, and we think that was just the tip of the iceberg for her. Who's Danny?"

Derek put his hands over his face and sat down quickly. "Oh God."

"He's our brother. He died twelve years ago now. Quinn broke down and nearly lost herself then, too. If it hadn't been for our cousin, Brigid I don't know what we would've done to help her." Miranda walked into the room with Helen. Both women embraced Derek as he stood to greet them. Helen then went over to Steve and hugged him tight, not saying a word. He didn't need any.

"Dr. Marshall, this is Quinn's mother, Helen Quartermarsh, and her sister, Miranda Hawkins." The doctor shook hands with both women and asked them to please sit so he could tell them more.

"Okay, all of this information confirms what we had suspected. Quinn has had to deal with some major mental and emotional traumas in her life. Unfortunately she chose to bury them instead of working through them, which brings us to what happened early this morning. Quinn has pushed herself beyond mental and physical exhaustion. Combine that with severe depression and her mind snapped. Now, when most people hear their loved one has suffered a nervous breakdown, they think the patient has lost their mind. That's not the case. What has happened here is Quinn's mind couldn't sustain another shock. It's protecting itself by powering down, so to speak. When her mind feels it can handle things again, it will. Until then, we just have to watch and wait."

Helen spoke up finally. "What about the burns on her hands? Will they heal, or does she have permanent damage? She's a gifted surgeon. Her hands are her livelihood."

"The burns will heal and leave only minimal scars that will fade over time. She hasn't caused any nerve or muscle damage with the hot bleach water she used to scrub her home."

Steve hadn't realized he'd been holding his breath until he heard himself exhale.

Helen squeezed him tighter. "Don't worry, Steve. Our girl is a fighter. She's gonna come back. You wait and see."

"I'll wait for her forever if I have to, Helen."

"Well, I'm glad Quinn has all of you to rally around her. I called in our staff psychiatrists to consult on her case. They're in agreement. We'll know more about how she's doing mentally once she wakes up."

Miranda posed the question Steve was afraid to ask. "You keep saying *when* she wakes up. Is she in some sort of coma? Why can't she just wake up now?"

"The sedative we gave her wore off about two hours ago. We've tried to wake her, but she continues to sleep and dream. We can tell this by her rapid eye movements, and she is talking off and on to someone in her dreams."

Derek looked up at the doctor with a defeated expression. "Jake?"

Dr. Marshall nodded. "We've got her in a private room now with strict instructions that visitors are limited to the four of you and anyone else you put on a list. The Hollis family created a scene earlier and threatened to sue the hospital, but our legal department smoothed everything over." He looked at Steve. "Quinn's request that Mr. Quartermarsh and Mrs. Hawkins be her medical advocates will be honored."

"When can we see her?" Helen stood up straighter and looked like she was ready for the worst to be thrown at her. To be honest, Steve wasn't sure that he was this time. She must have sensed that and gave him another reassuring squeeze.

"Follow me."

"I love you, Jacob Hartley."

"I love *you*, Quinn Lee Quartermarsh."

She laughed. "Oh, so now I go back to my maiden name, huh?"

Jacob had his arms wrapped around her from behind, and he rubbed his stubbly chin on her neck and bare shoulder. "Uh-huh, at least until you change it to Hartley."

She looked out at the waves crashing on the beach in front of their bungalow. The sun was setting, and the sky lit up with brilliant reds, oranges, and yellows. "This is where I want to get married. Just you and me and a minister or whoever can legally marry us."

He turned her so that she was facing him and then got down on one knee in the sand. "Quinn, will you be by my side in sickness and in health, during football and hockey seasons?"

She broke out into a fit of giggles remembering their many conversations about their dream proposals.

The corners of his mouth twitched as he appeared to struggle to keep a straight face as he continued. "Will you let me love you forever and ever? Can we fall asleep in each other's arms and wake up making love every morning? Quinn, my heart, my soul, will you marry me?"

"Yes, my love, my life. I will marry you."

* * * *

CHAPTER 3

Quinn looked so frail in that bed with her hands all bandaged, and an IV line going into her right arm. Steve felt helpless at that moment. He had unlimited resources, and yet he'd been unable to stop this from happening or protect her from another collapse. He'd failed as her knight in shining armor.

Miranda squeezed his hand and looked into his eyes. "Don't you dare."

"I can't help it, Randi. I was just with her two weeks ago. She spent a week with me on Treasure Island. She'd agreed to stay at my house there and let me push her divorce through. Then last week she called and told me she was going to be working a lot of extra shifts and would need more time before she could meet with the lawyers again. She was going to go back to her house in Oakland since it was closer to work. I tried to talk her out of it, but you know how she is."

Helen held Quinn's bandaged hands. "Yes, we do. She's just like her father: tough as nails and stubborn as a mule. But all of us are like that, including you, Stephen."

"Oh, now you're in trouble. She's called you Stephen." Miranda giggled. Quinn's giggle, and Steve couldn't help himself even though he wanted to cry.

"Well, I think I would be a bit more afraid if she started to refer to me as 'Mr. Eischer' like the two of you do when you're scolding me." Derek's laughter joined in, and Steve almost forgot why they were there.

Almost.

After the drama all of them had been through in the last eight hours, it was nice to laugh a little bit, and what surprised all of them was the smile that appeared on Quinn's face. "Yes, my love, my life. I will marry you."

Derek's eyes locked with Steve's. "She's there with Jake, isn't she?"

Miranda squeezed his hand tighter. "Quinn's been dreaming of the island paradise she and Jake used to fantasize about. She told me she didn't want to wake up from those dreams. Everything was so real, as if they'd been there before. She said that's where they'd fallen in love and promised to always find their way back to each other. When the alarm would go off, she'd be thrown back into this reality. Every fiber of her being yearned to stay there and never leave. She's gone there to be with him again."

Steve squeezed his eyes closed. "I'll be right back. I need a minute." He left the room and walked down the hall toward the chapel. He didn't get very far before the tears spilled over and he had to lean against the wall. *She might never come back from this, not if she thinks she's really with Jake.* He couldn't do this. He couldn't watch her slip away from him and life. He finally ended up in the chapel and sat in the back. No one else was there just Steve and God. "Please don't take her away from me. She's brought me so much happiness and got me to live life again. My world would no longer exist without her in it." He put his head in his hands and allowed the grief to wash over him.

Quinn knelt down in the sand next to Jacob. She held his face with both of her hands and got lost in his deep blue eyes once again. "You are my heart and soul. My life was so empty when we were apart. I never want to live that way again. Of course I'll marry you. You just try and stop me!" Her lips touched his, and she felt him melt into her, holding her tighter against his chest. His tongue slipped over hers, teasing and drawing her in deeper. Quinn could feel him slowly lowering her to the blanket they had laid out on the sand for a front row seat to watch the tide come in.

He untied the strings of her bikini top, tossed it aside on the blanket, and distracted with his mouth and tongue on her neck. Her hands trailed up and down his back, caressing his flexing muscles and the blue and red dueling dragons displayed there with talons and teeth bared and flames shooting out of their mouths and nostrils. This was in stark contrast to the very same dragons on her lower back. They were blue and red entwined, mating for life and loving each other forever. The fire between them burned as hot as it did when they fought, but when they came together to seal their bond, it turned magical. Now Jacob and Quinn had come together to seal their bond for life, and it was just as magical and explosive as it was for their dragons.

His lips continued down her body, igniting wave after wave of passion flooding through her. He sucked hard on first one nipple and then the other before making his way down her stomach, his fingers untying the strings that held her bottoms in place. He tossed those aside as he settled between her legs.

Her chest rose and fell rapidly, anticipating the touch of his tongue on her clit. He glanced up at her and smiled, grabbing her thighs as his lips found the nubbin and sucked hard. She raised her hips up off of the blanket and cried out, but he held her right where he wanted her, flicking and sucking her clit until the blanket became drenched beneath her.

"Jake, it's too much. I…can't."

He slipped his trunks off and returned to lie on the blanket with her, face to face. "I can't wait any longer either. I need you, Quinn." He pulled her right leg up around his waist as he entered her. "Baby, you feel so good."

His tongue teased hers as they moved against one another, enjoying the feel of their bodies entwined, touching, tasting, sharing everything they had with each other. He rolled over onto his back, pulling Quinn on top of him, continuing to thrust deep inside her. She sat up and coaxed him with her. His hands slid up and down her back, and his fingertips tenderly touched the mating dragons. "This is how we are, and how we'll always be. Forever."
"Promise?" She stared deep into his eyes, wanting him to say it, but afraid to hear it just the same. This was where she wanted and needed to be, but something wasn't quite right.

"I promise you one day we'll have our forever." He thrust into her harder as she clung to him, letting their bodies take them over into the magical abyss.

"I'll take the first shift with her. You and Randi go with Steve to the hotel and get some rest. I promise I'll call you if there are any changes, but you heard the doctors. She'll wake up when she's ready, and it most likely won't be tonight."

"Derek's right, Ma. We won't do her any good if all of us are dead on our feet when she does wake up."

Helen shook her head and held her ground.

He smiled. He didn't expect anything less from her. "I promise I'll call you back here if anything happens."

"You've been up dealing with this stuff longer than we have, Derek. If anyone should go to the hotel for some rest, it's you and Steve."

His eyes locked with Steve's. "Are you going to give me a hard time, too, or are you going to take my family to the Marriott and get some rest yourself? You know you'll be one of the first people Quinn will ask to see when she comes out of this. You don't want to scare the shit out of her, do you?"

Steve laughed hard. "You got a point there. You know she'll be pissed at us for running ourselves into the ground because of her. Honestly, that may be part of the problem. She buries everything because she doesn't want to be a burden. The best thing we can do for her is to take care of ourselves and be here for her when she comes back to us."

After making him swear he would call them if anything at all happened, no matter what the time, they'd finally left him alone with Quinn. He sat on the bed next to her and took her bandaged hand into his. "Did I ever tell you I thank the Goddess every single day you walked into my shop all those years ago? I thought you were the most beautiful woman I had ever seen. Oh, and don't go arguing with me that you weren't beautiful then. I never saw 'the fat chick' as you called yourself. I was drawn in by those eyes of yours and right to your heart. This bootylicious body you have now just happened to catch up with your inner you. You've always been this way to me.

"I felt a pull on my heart that day I'd never felt with anyone. There always been a deep connection between you and me. It's almost like we were separated at birth." He remembered the day she introduced him to the rest of the family. After so many years being all alone in the world, he finally felt like he was home. Quinn gave him that, and he was terrified he was going to lose her. "Please, don't leave me now. There's so much more that I want to share with you and the rest of our family.

"Who's going to help me find the love of my life? Who's going to smoke a cigar with me when my first child is born? Who's going to get up on stage with me even though she's scared shitless and end up stealing the show?" He knew he was being selfish, but he needed her in his life. "I love you and I want you to be happy. If Jake is who you want, I'll do whatever it takes to bring him back into your life here with us, not in your dream world."

Her fingers tightened around his. *She'd heard him!* "Come back, Quinn."

His phone rang. He'd already asked if they'd be able to use cell phones in her room and had been given the okay, but he still felt like he was going to get into trouble. He looked at the caller ID. It was Eric Hartley, just the man he needed to talk to at that moment.

"Hey, Eric. Sorry we haven't called you, but it's been a hell of a day let me tell you."

"I sort of figured that, but I couldn't wait any longer. I've been worried sick about her, and so have the guys in the shop. Any news yet?"

"Well, besides the chemical burns on her hands and legs from the bleach, the doctors said basically it's exhaustion and that she's suffered a nervous breakdown. She's buried so much pain in her life from childhood on that finally her mind couldn't deal with it. They said when she's ready, her brain will reboot and let her wake up."

"What do you mean? Is she in some sort of coma?"

"Not exactly. She's asleep and dreaming. Randi said Quinn told her she's been having dreams of a tropical island she used to fantasize about with your brother. We think she's there now in her mind. Sometimes she starts talking to him, and it's a bit unnerving when it happens."

"I'm so sorry, D. Is there anything we can do for you and the family?"

"Well, even though this kills me to say it, I think the only person who can bring her out of this is Jake. Will you see if you can get him to fly out here? If it's a money issue, tell him we have it covered. He just needs to be on the next available flight."

"I'm not sure he'll even listen to me right now. He's shut himself off from us, too. I have a bad feeling that part of it is that bitch, Iris. I know she's hiding e-mails from me and erasing voice mail on his phone." Eric took a deep breath and let it out slowly. "Maredyth may be able to get through to him or my ultimate weapon."

"Your Mother?"

Eric laughed. "You better believe it, brotha! If anyone can get him to come to his senses, it's her." He got really quiet for a second and Derek thought he'd lost the connection, but he spoke softly now, tentatively, like he was going to ask him something he was afraid to know the answer to. "D, is there a possibility she won't come out of this?"

"Yeah. If she convinces herself the only place where she can be with Jake is on her dream island, she'll simply stay there and never come back to us."

"Oh God, this is a nightmare. I promise I'll do what I can. I'll call you or Steve to let you know if we can get through to him."

"Thanks, Eric." Derek placed his phone on her night stand, kicked off his shoes, and crawled into bed with her, careful not to get tangled up with her IV line. She turned slightly so her head rested on his shoulder, mumbling in her sleep, and then she spoke clearly. "Don't worry, I won't let Freddie Kruger getcha, Danny, but you have to stop hogging the covers."

"Okay, honey." Derek was not sure what scared him more, hearing her talk to Jake or to her dead brother.

"Danny? How the hell did you get here?" Quinn didn't understand what was happening. "Where's Jake?"

Her brother looked at her with the same blue-green eyes she had, and Quinn's stomach dropped. She'd been through this before. He had been the one to tell her she had to leave before. "I can't do it again. Please don't ask me to leave him again."

"You can't stay here with him, Quinn. It's not your time to be together yet."

She pulled away from him. "You don't know what you're talking about. How can it not be our time to be together? We found each other again, Danny. You and Lady Fate promised if we chose to go back to our other lives, we would be together forever."

"No. This isn't real. If you stay here too long you won't be able to go back." He turned her around so she had to look him in the eyes again. "Are you going to break the promise you made to me when I left you?"

Quinn shook her head over and over. "That's not fair. You don't know what I've gone through since you died. I was beginning to think that I would never be happy again and then I met—"

"Steve."

"And Jake. I met him first here on this island. I know it. That's why it's so familiar and everything with us has been déjà vu. We've lived it before and you were here!"

He nodded. "I couldn't tell you all you would go through to find each other again. You had to make your own choices but the two of you are so damn stubborn. The Three allowed us to intervene again. You have to choose to go back for yourself and for them."

"How can I choose between them? I love them both. I need them both."

"It's not just the two men of your heart. If you stay here, you'll lose Steve forever, and he'll be devastated. You mean more to him than his own life, Quinn. And then there's Derek, Randi, our nephews, and Ma. If you stay here with the Jake in your mind, Jacob Hartley in the real world will finally find a way to kill himself."

"Stop it, Danny!" She tried to cover her ears with her hands, but he held her arms down at her side, making her listen to him.

"Quinn, remember how you felt when I died? Do you want all of these people to go through that, too? You are a huge part of all of their lives, and mine. You promised me that you would carry on my legacy: my music, my love of life. Without you, Derek will stop playing with his band, and he'll lose the desire to create his beautiful artwork. Without you, Ma will stop traveling and enjoying life. Without you, Randi will never follow her dream of opening her own restaurant with Robb and Brigid. Without you, Steve will go back to being totally married to his work and never let anyone get close to him again. He'll just give up and die alone. Without you in the world, Jake will blame himself for your death, and he'll get on that motorcycle of his and—"

Her body shuddered as the sobs tore through her body. Danny's face softened, and he pulled her close, his tattooed arms holding her tight. "You have to go back, honey. I promise you that you'll have a little more time here with your Jake, but when it's time, you both will have to leave."

"Will we be able to say goodbye to each other? He's just not going to disappear on me again, will he?"

He hugged her tighter and then pulled back to look at her again. He closed his eyes and nodded. He kissed her on both cheeks. "You'll be able to say goodbye, just like the last time. I promise it won't take so long for you to find each other again. I'll make sure of it. I am one of your Guardians after all."

"Do you have to go now, Danny?"

"Yes, baby girl. It's time, but I'll always be right here." He put his hand over her heart. "You are not going through any of this alone. Why don't you lie down for a bit? When you wake up, Jake will be back here with you." He guided her toward the bed. "I love you."

She hugged him tight once again. "I love you, too, Danny."

Eric couldn't believe he'd spent the last two hours telling Maredyth everything he knew about Jake and Quinn's relationship: the connection between them right from the start, Jake being so obsessed with her that he practically stalked her on Facebook before he got the nerve up to send her a friend request, the flirtation, and the online affair.

"You know, what I don't get is why he would stay with Iris when he had such a wonderful woman ready and willing to be with him. What the hell was he thinking?"

"Mare, I've been trying to wrap my mind around it myself. I've known Quinn for nearly nine years now. She's the most genuine person I've ever met. I think Jake got it in his head he didn't deserve her and that maybe she was in love with the fantasy they created and not him."

"Oh, that's the crap with Julia that made him think that way. He admitted to me he was trying to kill himself on that motorcycle ten years ago because of *her*."

Eric sighed. "I know. And I thought he would never do that shit to someone else, considering what Julia had done to him. And yet, he crushed Quinn just the same. I had to be the one to tell her that Jake had proposed to Iris, Mare. I'll never forget the look on her face when she saw those damn pictures of their rings on Facebook." He dropped the bomb that Jacob had actually been on the phone with Quinn for over an hour that afternoon, promising to get out to Las Vegas to be with her as soon as he could get away.

"Oh, my God, Eric! He didn't have the nerve to tell her himself?"

"No. I found out later he thought she would be better off with Steve. He thought he couldn't compete with him and what he could give her, so he let her go and decided to stay with Iris. I'll admit that he genuinely cares for her and maybe even loves her, but it's nothing like what he feels for Quinn."

"Do you think that Jake really loves her?"

"Yes. He's only with Iris because he doesn't want to be alone. He's so messed up. He thinks he doesn't deserve to be with Quinn. He's got a death wish now." Eric had a hard time telling Maredyth about Jacob letting Derek beat him up and more or less begging him to live up to his promise to kill him if he ever hurt Quinn.

"Maybe it's time Jake learns what he's done to her and faces the music. We can't protect him anymore."

"I'm not protecting him. I was trying to protect her. Since Julia broke his heart, he's been a love-them-and-leave-them kind of guy."

"Yeah, well, look where that got you. They still fell for each other, and now both of them are a mess."

"I know. I know. Will you please help? I've been sending e-mail after e-mail and getting no response. He's not been on Facebook for some time now. Iris has been playing his games, reading his e-mails, and the bitch has been intercepting voicemails, too. I was hoping that either you or Ma could get through to him."

"Count me in, and you know Ma will help any way she can."

"We have to act fast before they set a wedding date or elope."

"Bite your tongue, little brother! Jake won't marry Iris if I have anything to say about it. As for getting him to accept Quinn does love him, that's going to be harder, but I'll give it my best shot. Do you have Steve's number?"

He didn't want to be around Iris at all at that moment. Jake needed to think, but he couldn't turn his mind off. He pulled the extra pillows and blankets out of the hall closet and walked down to the spare room. The kids were staying with their dad this last weekend before they were to head out to Greenville for spring break.

At least there was something good that came out of tonight. There was an extra bed he could bunk in.

Iris had gone straight to bed after their argument. He couldn't say he blamed her. Nothing like being reminded that your fiancé was in love with someone else and would never give his heart to you. The whole thing had really blown up. Jake had crushed Quinn, and now he was destroying Iris's life. Why the hell either of them would want to be with him was beyond what his mind could comprehend.

He jumped at the sound of his phone ringing on the night stand. He would give anything for the person on the other end to be Quinn. No such luck. "Hey Mare, what's up?"

"Oh, good. You're still up, and I don't have to leave a long drawn-out message on your voice mail that you may not get."

He rolled his eyes. "Maredyth, please don't go there. It's not been a great night around here."

"It's not been all that great around here either. I just got off the phone with Eric."

"What's wrong? I would think that since I wasn't in Vegas for him to clean up after, his life would be all peachy now."

"He isn't the one who is in trouble. It's Quinn."

The room spun around him and he sat down hard on the bed. "What, what's happened to her?"

"She's in the hospital. It's bad, Jake."

"I don't understand. Tell me what happened. And why didn't Eric call me himself?"

"He did try to call you. He's left several messages on your voice mail and sent you e-mails. Obviously someone has been intercepting them."

Fuck! Iris had promised she hadn't been intercepting messages from his family. Jacob couldn't ignore it any longer, and he had no one to blame but himself. "I can't deal with that part right now, Mare." His voice cracked as the tears blurred his vision. "What happened to Quinn?"

"I don't have all the details, but I looked at her profile on Facebook myself and she's posted some really sad, lost things since she found out about your engagement. She's been throwing herself into her work and isolating herself from her family and friends. Anyway, she came home the other night and found evidence that her husband was screwing around, in her house, in *her* bed."

"How the hell did she end up in the hospital?" His stomach clenched along with his jaw. "Jackson didn't hurt her, did he?"

"Not physically, Jake. His stunt just pushed her over the edge. She posted on Facebook what she found and then said she was going to clean the filth out of her house. And that's exactly what she did."

"Mare, I still don't understand. Just tell me."

"Hold on and let me get everything out. You need to hear it all, Jake. You're the one who set this all in motion."

"You're scaring me. Please, tell me." Jacob closed his eyes and clutched the bedding, waiting for her to tell him the worst.

"She got home and found wine glasses in the sink, and then her bed was unmade, with evidence that someone had sex in there and it was reeking of someone else's perfume. She stripped the bed and burned that stuff in her barbecue pit and then started to bleach and scrub the house from top to bottom. Hubby came home to find her scrubbing the floor, crying and singing "Help Me Rhonda" at 2:30 a.m. She was screaming at him to leave her alone and wouldn't stop, so he called an ambulance. She's been in the hospital for almost two days now and they can't wake her up."

The sobs tore through him, and he couldn't breathe. "What, what did her doctors say happened?"

"Jake, her heart is broken. Her whole world came crashing down yet again that night, and her mind couldn't take it. It shut down. She hasn't been sleeping or eating well at all. They're calling it severe exhaustion and a mental breakdown. Steve, Derek and Quinn's sister and mother have been there at her side the whole time so far. Her husband and his family were there causing a ruckus, but Steve made sure they got thrown out or something. Anyway, Derek thinks you're the only one who could bring her out of this, and he asked Eric to find a way to tell you what was going on."

"What am I supposed to do? She's better off without me in her life. I'll only hurt her."

"Excuse me? What the hell do you think is going on right now without you in her life? She's bad enough that a man who wanted to kill you for hurting her is asking you to come and bring her back to them. Are you just going to keep hurting her and punishing yourself because you think you don't deserve to be happy?"

"I created this mess, and I deserve everything that's being thrown at me. Quinn has so many people there who will help her get over me. Steve loves her and will protect her from Jackson."

"Jake, listen to what you're saying. Steve is at her side right now and she's still locked in her mind. What the hell does that tell you?"

"I can't go back into her life, Maredyth. Each time I did, I hurt her more. I can't live with that."

"Stop talking like that and listen to me. You need to get away from Iris and her kids. Why don't you go visit Ma for the next couple of days and really think things through? Iris can't mess with your phone or your e-mails when you're there. You'll be able to log into that e-mail account you had Quinn set up for you last year. I bet any money she kept writing to you even after she found out about your engagement. I know I would."

"We're supposed to go to Greenville for spring break and look for a house in a week. I guess I can spend time with Ma before we head out."

Maredyth sighed. She sounded disappointed with him, but that was the story of his life. Jacob hadn't been able to please anyone in his family for quite some time, except their mother. Maredyth was right. He needed to get away and be somewhere he could think clearly.

"Okay, I'll head out for Ma's tomorrow morning. Will you let me know what happens to Quinn?"

"Are you sure you want to know? I have Steve's number. You can call him and find out for yourself and maybe take him up on his offer to help you get back into Quinn's life."

He closed his eyes tight. He remembered Steve telling him to take a chance. What did he have to lose? "What's the number?"

* * * *

Chapter 4

"Jacob! I'm so happy to see you." His mother bear-hugged him as soon as he walked in the door. His nose picked up the aroma of one of his favorite meals baking in the oven.

"Is that lasagna all for me?" He thought Maredyth must have called her to tell her he was coming. "Oh, and garlic bread? You didn't have to do that, but I am so glad you did!" He kissed both of her cheeks and hugged her again.

She held him at arm's length and inspected him from head to toe. "Jacob, you haven't been sleeping or eating like you should. Doesn't that girl you live with take care of you?"

"Her name is Iris, Ma, and I can take care of myself." He dropped his bags down on the floor and let her lead him over to the couch. "I've been going through a hell of a lot and I needed somewhere safe to rest my mind a bit."

"This is your home. You should always feel safe here with me. That's what mothers are for even after their babies grow up to find the loves of their lives." She stared deep into his eyes. "Tell me what's happened to hurt you so?"

Her soft Polish accent warmed his heart but he couldn't bring himself to open up. "I'm not quite ready to talk about that yet, maybe after dinner. How have you been?"

She tilted her head to the side and sized him up. Her mother's intuition kicked up a notch but she held her tongue. She wouldn't press him further. She'd let him tell her in his own time. "Okay, my son. When you're ready to tell me about this beautiful woman who has your heart, I'll listen." That was how Katrina Hartley got all of her kids to open up to her, all in their own time, and using their favorite meal as incentive. Of course, having siblings who liked to rat him out left and right helped to keep her informed.

"So you know about Quinn?"

"Yes. Your brother and sister have told me about her and the affect you two have on each other. To be perfectly honest, I've been worried about you. She must be a very special woman to have such a hold over your heart."

He couldn't help but smile at his mother. She was going to get him to talk about Quinn now whether he wanted to or not. "When I first saw her and looked into her eyes, I felt like I was hit by lightning."

His mother chuckled knowingly. "Yes! That's what I felt for your father. How does Eric say it, thunderstruck?"

"That's it. From that moment on I wanted her. I've obsessed over her body, her eyes, her voice. How it would feel to hold her in my arms and kiss her. I saw us growing old together with lots of kids. I felt all of this that one moment getting lost in her eyes, blue-green like the ocean."

"You told her this?" His mother got up to take the lasagna out of the oven to allow it to settle and cool before she cut it into pieces. "Did she feel the same for you?"

"Yes. After seeing her in Vegas, I found her online and we started talking to each other, building up a friendship, and then suddenly it was more than that. The innocent flirtations started to get more involved. We would fantasize about being together, and finally we admitted we were in love with each other."

"I don't understand. How is it you're in love with this woman and you are going to marry Iris?"

"It's a long story, Ma."

"Hey, I've all the time in the world. Come on, let's cut the lasagna and you start your story." She got up and shuffled back into the kitchen. She didn't wait for him to answer her. She expected him to just get his butt in there with her and tell her everything, which was exactly what he was going to do.

He confessed it all to his mother, and she took it all in with a soft smile on her face and tears in her eyes. She told him his story reminded her of her courtship with his father. They'd had to overcome a lot of obstacles to be together and they'd ended up being

38

married for forty years before he passed away. Jacob felt so much better talking the whole thing out and having someone just listen to him.

"You need to read those e-mails she sent to you. You have to know how she feels about everything. Maybe you'll get the answers you seek."

"I can't read them. I'm afraid to find out that she hates me now. I've caused her so much pain." Tears burned his eyes and blurred his vision.

"Are you more afraid she hates you or that she still loves you and you continue to tear her heart out by staying away?"

He looked at his mother and shook his head. She had a good point. He didn't know what he was more afraid of learning. "Both."

"Then let me read them. I'll tell you what I think and then you decide if you'll read them now or later. Yes?" She started to clear the dishes, but he stopped her and took over.

"I'll take care of these after I set you up on your computer." He hugged her again. "Thank you."

"Oh, don't thank me. I promised your sister I'd get all the dirt!" She laughed and held him close, her hand over his heart. "I know you are afraid of what you might learn, but that is how we get through life. We make mistakes and learn from them so we become better people. Don't worry, after I read some of them, I'll give you my honest opinion." She kissed his cheeks and then went to boot up her computer.

He followed her out to the living room and entered his login information to the e-mail account Quinn had set up for him a while ago. It had been meant as a safe place where they could communicate with each other and no one else would have access to it. After he'd accepted Iris's proposal, he had deliberately stayed away from the account. He'd tried to convince himself it had been because he needed to let her go and move on with Iris, but that wasn't the case. He'd been too afraid of what he might find out by reading them.

"There you go. I'll leave you to this, and I'll finish up in the kitchen. Do you want some coffee?"

Katrina put on her reading glasses and peered over them at her son. "It looks like your lady love has written a lot. Better put on a whole pot. I'm going to be here a while."

Jacob did as she asked and took her a steaming cup of it prepared as she liked it with a splash of cream and sugar. She was engrossed in Quinn's words and barely noticed he'd brought her the coffee. He went back into the kitchen to finish up the dishes and put away all the food. When he'd run out of things to do, he returned to check on her progress.

He stood next to her, but his fear and anxiety prevented him from looking at the screen. Instead he watched her reactions to what she read. She placed her hand over her heart and mumbled Polish endearments to herself. He understood enough of the terms to recognize "poor child" and "my heart breaks for you." She finally noticed him standing at her side. "You have to read these. If not all of them, at least read this one where she says goodbye." She got up and pointed to the seat. "Now."

"Ma, please. I don't know if I can do it." The grip on his heart tightened, and his stomach churned and revolted. He still did as she said and sat in her chair. She hugged him, kissed the top of his head, and left him alone with what he had done to Quinn.

He skimmed through them to the one his mother had pulled up in a separate window. It looked like it was the one that she wrote to him right after she found out about the engagement.

From: Quinn Lee Hollis
To: Jacob Hartley
Date: February 19, 9:42AM
Subject: What the hell happened?

Jake,
After we talked on February 18th, four days after Valentine's Day, I was so excited. I'd told you I was leaving Jackson and could finally be free to see if we could have a life together. You promised you would come out and see me and told me you loved me. Little did I know that was just the tip of the iceberg of lies you've told me over the last several months.

I still couldn't believe it, so I had to look for myself. I pulled up your profile page on Facebook and saw it for my own eyes again. "Engaged to Iris Campbell Moore." WTF?!!!

Was that your Valentine's gift to Iris? Having an hour long phone sex session with me four days after you ask her to marry you, telling me you love me over and over and then promising to come see me? Did you both laugh about that?

The stupid, fat girl believed everything you said—all the "I love yous" and "I want yous" and the fantasizing about being together, just fucking lies. Was it fun for you to hurt me this way? You had already asked her to marry you when we talked last. I could hear there was something wrong in your voice, but I thought you were just surprised that I was going to leave Jackson finally. Nope. You just kept lying to me, saying everything was fine just so you could get one more kinky session and maybe more pictures out of me.

I can't believe I fell for all of your shit. Asking me if I would leave Jackson and Steve for you and telling me you would have no problem leaving Iris for me, and all along knowing you were going to marry her. I asked you point-blank several times, and you said you were NOT going to marry her. Why didn't you just tell me? Why keep up the charade? Why send me text messages saying "U don't know how bad I want to show up in Cali to take you away?" What purpose did all of that serve except to keep me holding on to any hope that we would be together? What a fucking crock!

Man, I wish I never would've started anything with you. All it did was break my heart further. Both you and Iris knew how broken I was inside over my marriage falling apart and how badly I felt about not being able to love Steve the way he loved me, and still you did this shit to me. Did you mean ANYTHING you said to me, EVER? Was it all lies? How many other people have you done this to? Pull them in and get them to trust you with deep secrets they've never told anyone about and then crush them? Promise them over and over again that what you feel for each other is real and then drop them without warning or even goodbye? You had the fucking nerve to say you wanted to have kids with me, knowing full well it was something I had given up long ago because Jackson and I haven't had any kids since the miscarriage seven years ago. You were even cruel enough to say you wanted the whole thing with me, kids and marriage. What kind of person does that to another human being?

Did you share all of the pictures I sent to you with her? Must have been a lot of laughs and mean, cruel jokes at my expense. Doesn't seem fair that I'm the one left behind and you get to keep going on as usual, as if you did nothing wrong. It's all someone else's fault now, isn't it? You get happily ever after and I get shit upon. Fucking fantastic.

I hope one day soon you get to read this and know how badly you hurt me. Maybe it will help you to not do this sort of thing again and hurt anyone else. But I know I'm just kidding myself. You won't come to this e-mail addy again ever because then you would have to man up and take responsibility for what you did and what you've done. You keep doing this sort of thing over and over again and yet, Iris keeps holding on to you. Right now, I don't know who the bigger fool is: me or her.

Both of us believed you when you said you loved us and wanted some kind of future together. I didn't want to control your every move or change who you are, that's who I fell in love with. Iris wants to change you and keep a tight leash on you. I guess that's what you really want, an abusive controlling partner. Well, I'm not that, honey. I wanted to give you the world and experience it all with you, but you threw it all away after you hung up with me never telling me you chose her. I gave you every opportunity to tell me it was over and to stop this, and you kept reassuring me you still wanted me. You kept sending me texts when you were at work and after Iris left in the mornings. You kept promising me the moon and all along the same to her.

Well, I'll give you what you never gave me. Good-bye Jake. I hope you find all you want in life and a partner or partners to share it all with. I just wish you had the decency to tell me yourself that you decided to marry Iris. It still would have hurt like hell, but I only wanted you to be happy. Now, finding out this way was huge slap in the face, and I could care less if you end up married or not.

Karma is a bitch: You made your choice and you deserve all that comes with that.

Quinn

Jacob closed his eyes and allowed every word to sink in. So much had happened to them both that put them on separate paths. Why hadn't he trusted Quinn wanted him and just fly out to Las Vegas to be with her on Valentine's Day? None of this would've happened, and he would have her with him now. There was another e-mail that caught his eye and he clicked on it to read. It was dated a week ago.

Jake,
I don't know why I keep writing to you here. You've not read any of the e-mails I've sent to you, but I feel the need to reach out to you still. I know in my head that you're moving on with Iris and that you'll be moving to North Carolina soon to start your new life together, but my heart just won't accept it.
I find myself lost in my dream world all the time. There I get to kiss you, touch you, and see your smile. We walk on beaches hand in hand and make love all night long. Those dreams are more real to me than my everyday life. I never want to wake up from them, but then the dawn comes, the alarms go off, and I'm

hurled back into reality. I can still feel your lips on mine when I wake up, and then everything crashes in on me. You're not there. You never were and you never will be. I can't stop the tears. They fall nonstop. I can't eat, I can't concentrate on my work. I just want you.

If this is how my life is going to be like without you in it, I don't want it anymore. I want to stay in that dream world with you forever and never wake up again.

I just don't understand what happened. I thought you loved me. I thought you wanted me. You've been chasing me for such a long time, and I finally let myself go to accept that you loved me. Then you were gone. Was it my relationship with Steve that sent you away? I told you I loved him dearly, but I was never in love with him like I am with you. He's my knight in shining armor, but I can't give him what he wants either. He loves me unconditionally, and that's a great comfort, but it's your love I want. It's your love that I need to make me whole again.

Without you, I'm hopelessly broken. I can't believe that it was all a lie. I won't believe you said all those things just to get what you wanted in order to toss me aside when you were done.

I tried to let you go and start making a life with Steve. He does make me happy, until I fall asleep and there you are. Then the sun comes up and you leave me again. Steve tries to give me everything I need, and I do feel safe and loved when I'm with him. It's just not the same. A part of me is still missing. A part of me that will only belong to you. Without you, I can't be whole. There is no one else who'll be able to complete me, ever. I'm going to stop looking and go back to my dream world where you're there, arms open, waiting to take me away…

Forever,
Quinn

He couldn't read any more. This was what she was going through right then in the hospital. She had given up. This wasn't supposed to happen this way. She was supposed to let Steve take care of her and forget about him. Jacob kept his eyes shut tight and shook his head over and over again. "Don't do this, Quinn. Don't give up your life for me. I'm not worth it."

He didn't hear Katrina come back into the room and stand behind him. He felt her embrace him tightly like when he was a boy crying when one of their pets had died. He was feeling that same pain with these e-mails from Quinn.

"You really love her, Jacob?"

He nodded and kept silent. His throat constricted and he was having a little trouble breathing.

"I ripped her heart out, Ma. She thinks I lied to her and never meant the things I told her. She thinks I don't love her, that I never did."

"Did you lie to her?"

"No! I never thought I could say those things to anyone again after Julia and then my accident, but Quinn brought it all out of me. When I talked to her, I felt alive and happy." Jacob let out a little hoarse laugh. "And I feel a lot of lust for her, too!"

That brought another knowing smile to his mother's face.

"I want to be with her all the time. I can't eat, sleep, or anything."

She looked him hard in the eyes and asked the million dollar question, "Then why are you with Iris?"

"What if Quinn finds out she doesn't really love me but the fantasy that we created? I don't want to be rejected and alone again, Ma. It hurts too much."

"Oh, my sweet Jacob, a love like you and Quinn feel for each other doesn't just go away because your heart breaks. It's always there, waiting for the chance to come out and bloom again. Your hearts are broken because you love each other so deeply. Just like your father and me."

"I don't know what to do." He looked into his mother's face and saw the love she still had for his father rushing out at him. That was the kind of love that he wanted and needed. Jacob knew he would never have that love with Iris because it was exactly what he wanted and needed with Quinn. .

"Yes, you do. Listen to your heart, Jacob. It'll never steer you wrong. It wants to be whole again." She kissed him on the forehead. "Come, your bedroom is ready. It's time you got some sleep."

Jacob held Quinn's hand as they walked along the beach together. They both knew their time on the island was coming to an end, and neither of them wanted to go.

"Danny said all of this isn't real. It's not our time to be together yet, and if I don't go back, the lives of the people I care about will change forever, and you'll finally find a way to kill yourself. What did he mean by that?"

Jacob stopped walking and pulled her to him. For the first time she noticed the bruises on his face. She touched his cheek where the deep purple spot grew right before her eyes. "It's nothing. Derek was just protecting you. I wanted him to do what he promised and kill me. I couldn't live with what I'd done to you."

"All of that doesn't matter anymore. We found each other here so we can find each other again when I go back. Right?"

His silence frightened her more than the thought they had so little time left together in their dream world.

"I'm scared that you won't want me anymore. I hurt you so badly, Quinn. You're here on this island because you collapsed and broke with reality. Because of me you stayed with Jackson. Because of me you wouldn't let yourself fall in love with Steve and be happy." He started to cry. "I can't live without you. You're my life, my soul, my everything."

He fell to his knees in the sand, and Quinn went right with him, holding him tight and letting him cry it all out. He clung to her. "I'll always love you, Jacob Hartley, through all of the tears and the pain, through all of the good times and bad. I will live for you. I will go back *for you*."

"Promise?"

She wiped the tears from his face and kissed him softly. "I promise you forever, Jake. Don't stay away from me because you're afraid I won't want you anymore. Please find me again. Take a chance on us. I can't live without you either. You're *my* everything."

Quinn could feel she was slipping away from him. Jacob held her tighter. "Don't go yet, Quinn. Give me just a few more hours with you. I want to make love to you one more time. I want to fall asleep with you in my arms knowing that we'll find each other again."

She stood and helped him up from the sand. "I'm yours now and forever, Jake."

* * * *

CHAPTER 5

Helen suggested they stop and pick up a couple of breakfast sandwiches for Derek on their way to the hospital. Even though they were worried out of their minds about Quinn, the three of them managed to get some sleep but barely touched their own breakfasts. Derek had called first thing that morning to give them an update on how she'd done overnight. Steve could tell by his voice that something had happened that scared the shit out of him. He wouldn't go into it over the phone, but he promised to tell them about it after they arrived.

Steve did get a surprise after he spoke with Derek, a call from Jacob and Eric's sister Maredyth. Apparently, Derek had finally realized Jake might be the only person who could bring Quinn back, and he'd asked Eric to try to get word to him about Quinn. Maredyth told Steve that she'd been able to reach Jake and of course he was devastated over the news about Quinn. Unfortunately, he still believed she was better off without him in her life, but she did have one ace up her sleeve. Jake had agreed to stay the week with their mother. She thought without any interference from Iris, he'd be able to think clearly and read all of the e-mails Quinn had sent to him since February. Hopefully, Jake would come to his senses and they would hear from him soon.

While Helen sat up front chatting away with Nathan, Steve took the opportunity to tell Miranda about the call from Maredyth. "I agree with Derek. I think Jake is the only one who might be able to pull Quinn out of this. If his family can knock some sense into him, I'll fly him out here."

"Even though I'm just as mad at Jake for hurting her in the first place, I agree with both of you. Maybe seeing her this way will make it all real for him. I tell you, I would've given anything to pop him in the mouth myself. I told him all about what she'd been through in her life and made him promise me he wouldn't do the same shit to her. What was he thinking?"

"He misunderstood our relationship. He thinks she's better off with me, and all she has to do is let herself fall in love with me to live happily ever after."

Miranda squeezed Steve's hand tight. "All of us thought she could finally have her happily ever after with you and told him as much. You can't blame him for believing it. The rest of us are just as much to blame here."

"I would give all that I have and all that I am if it would mean she would be happy with me as my wife…" His chest tightened, and he had to take a moment until he could breathe.

"Did you ever tell her that?"

"Yes. I told her there would never be anyone else for me. I remember the look on her face that day. It was so sad. She felt guilty for not loving me the way she thought I deserved to be loved, guilty that she couldn't give her whole heart to me."

"Good lord, it's a theme with those two, isn't it?"

"What do you mean?"

"Jake and Quinn both have been hurt so badly in the past by people they thought loved them that they can't trust their hearts when love finds them again. They second-guess it and end up being miserable. Quinn did it when she married Jackson. Jake is doing it now with Iris." She crossed her arms over her chest and took a deep breath, "You and I should have hooked up in Vegas."

She looked at him with that wicked grin. He held his breath. He stared at her and then doubled over with laughter.

"What's funny about that, Mr. Eischer?" She laughed right along with him.

"Well, it would have made things a lot less complicated." He took her hand back into his. "I would've still fallen in love with Quinn. My heart will always belong to her and whatever time I get with her I cherish. Just like I told Derek yesterday, the heart wants what the heart wants. Her heart wants and needs Jake. I've accepted that, and I'll do what I can to bring them together. What happens from there on in is up to them. No matter what, I'll always be there for Quinn."

Miranda looked at Steve and smiled again. "Thank you for that. I don't know what we would've done if you'd never come into our lives. I do know you're the only person who Quinn has ever turned to for help, not me, not Derek, not my parents, not even Danny when he was alive. That should tell you something."

"It does. And I love her all the more for it."

Nathan pulled up to the hospital entrance and assisted Helen out of the car, which made her smile. If Steve didn't know better, he'd think that Mrs. Quartermarsh had a little crush on Nathan. Miranda noticed it, too, and giggled. "Come on. Derek's got to be starving by now, and I want to hear what happened with Quinn that he couldn't talk about over the phone."

"That's right, she was talking to Danny, telling him she would protect him from Freddie Krueger, but he had to stop hogging the covers." Derek noticed the smile on Miranda's face. "What am I missing here?"

"Danny begged Quinn to let him watch a *Nightmare on Elm Street* marathon one weekend when our parents were out of town. He had nightmares for the next two weeks and kept slipping into Quinn's bed for protection. He was around seven years old then, and Quinn was eighteen. She left for college the next year, and he wouldn't watch any of those movies again unless she was home for a visit."

"I guess me crawling into bed to hold her for a bit set that memory in motion, but not the stuff that came later."

All three of them stared at Derek, waiting for him to go on.

"She asked Danny what the hell he was doing there and where had Jake gone. Then I think she was arguing with him about coming back to us. She didn't want to leave Jake, but I think Danny told her it wasn't their time yet. Quinn kept asking how it couldn't be their time when they were together there."

Steve took one of Quinn's bandaged hands into his and traced over the material with his thumb. "Did she talk to Jake again or was it just Danny?"

Derek closed his eyes to hold back the tears. He didn't want his mother to see him break down. He needed to be strong for her. "Yeah. She cried a lot during that time. I think they were talking about what Danny told her, that they didn't have much time left. She asked Jake if he was trying to kill himself in the real world."

Miranda's eyes flew open. "How the hell does she know that? Do you think Danny was really there with her and told her all of this?"

"What do you mean? Has this Jake been trying to hurt himself?" Helen paled, and Derek got up to help her back to one of the chairs.

He looked at Steve and Miranda, and they both nodded for him to continue. "After Quinn found out he was engaged to someone else, she wouldn't believe it at first. I had to show her the evidence on Facebook, and ultimately she did confront him about it over the phone. We were so concerned over how badly she was handling all of this we didn't realize what was happening with Jake. He'd been riding his motorcycle without his helmet and had several near misses in Chicago. He came out here a few weeks ago and——"

"And what, Derek?"

"I smashed his face in a few times. He asked me to kill him, Ma. He wanted me to keep hitting him so he didn't have to feel the pain of losing her anymore. God help me, I wanted to kill him for hurting Quinn."

She touched his face softly. "So you don't feel that way anymore?"

"I don't know what I feel now. I just want Quinn to come back. If Jake can help her to do that, then I'll *drag* him back here myself."

"Well, his sister Maredyth called me this morning. She told Jake what happened to Quinn, and I guess he broke down, too. He has my number, and I hope that he takes me up on my offer to help him get Quinn back."

"I would think that if he truly loved her like you all say he does, he would move heaven and earth to be at her side right now. I don't understand half of what's going on between them, but if Jake is the only one that can bring my daughter back, he's going to have me to answer to if he stays away much longer."

Derek smiled and squeezed his mother's hand.

Steve looked startled and looked down at Quinn, who started to cry softly. "I'm yours now and forever, Jake."

Helen got up from the chair and took Quinn's other hand. "It's okay, baby. Jake loves you and will find you again if you come back. Please, Quinn, come back to us." She looked at Steve. "What made you look at her like that?"

"She squeezed my hand, hard. I thought she was telling me that she heard me about helping Jake." Quinn squeezed his hand hard again, and this time they all saw her do it because she lifted her hand up a little off the bed as she squeezed. Steve leaned over and kissed her. "I promise you, Quinn. I'll help Jake find you again. Come back, darlin'. How can I be your knight in shining armor if you're gone?"

He couldn't believe how good it felt to be able to fall asleep in his old room. Maybe it was the smell of the fabric softener still in the pillow cases and sheets, but the tension in Jacob's body melted away. He just wanted to sleep and maybe dream of Quinn.

Reading all of the e-mails that night broke his heart, but the last one he read got him thinking. If Quinn was dreaming of their tropical island, maybe he could dream of it, too. They could be together for a little while and just let all of the crap in this world go. No Iris. No Jackson. No Steve. It would just be the two of them loving each other on the beach.

His mother thought after he got a good night's sleep he would know what to do. Honestly, he already knew what he wanted to do. He wanted Quinn. He just needed to figure out how to get to her and make her understand that he'd never meant to hurt her this way. If there was any chance she would forgive him, he had to take it. Now he had to figure out how he was going to break things off with Iris.

Jacob's eyes couldn't stay open any longer. His mind and body drifted off and brought him closer to being with Quinn. .

"I am yours now and forever, Jake." Quinn stood up and helped him get up from the sand. It took Jacob a moment to figure out where he was. He'd done it. He was really there with her.

"Quinn, we don't have much time."

"I know, baby. Let's go back to our bungalow and make love one more time. We'll fall asleep in each other's arms just like you wanted."

They walked just a short distance down the beach to their bungalow. It was exactly as they'd fantasized, especially the king-size bed with the silk sheets and pillows. He reached down and touched the bedding. It felt real, and so did Quinn's hand.

"Baby doll, I don't know how this happened, but one minute I was falling asleep in my old room at my mother's house thinking about you, and the next thing I knew I was here."

Quinn laughed and put her arms around him. "I know exactly how you feel. Just go with it, Jake. I don't know how we are really able to be together right now or why."

This was it. This was his way to be with her forever. "Then let's not go back. Let's stay here forever, together." He held her against his chest. He was afraid to let her go. Afraid of what she was going to tell him.

She started to cry. "Danny told me if I stay here with you, everyone I love will be lost. If you stay here with me, you would die in the real world like I would. We can't do that to our families."

"But if we go back I'll lose you again. I don't know if I can—"

"No! You promised me on the beach that you wouldn't be afraid to find me. Do whatever it takes to get back to me, Jake. Even if you think I'll tell you to fuck off, take a chance. Our hearts are meant to be together. You told me that. Don't you believe that anymore?" She held his face in her hands and searched his eyes. "I love you. I've always loved you. Without you I am lost. Please, Jake, make love to me one more time. We will be together again. I promise."

Those damn eyes that haunted his dreams every single night since they first saw each other pulled him right in and erased all his doubts and fears. "I love you, too, baby doll. I promise I'll fight for you when we go back. I'll never stop fighting for you, Quinn." Jacob scooped her up into his arms, carried her over to the bed, and draped her on the pillows. She reached for him, pulling him to her as their lips touched.

She pulled Jacob down toward her on the bed. His lips touched hers so softly, like he wasn't sure she was real. He touched her face with his fingertips, tracing all along her jawline, and kept his eyes locked with hers. "I never stopped loving you, Quinn."

"I know, baby." Her arms encircled Jacob's body as his mouth covered hers, no longer tentative but more possessive. Jake was finally taking what had been his all along. Her tongue slipped over his, teasing, tasting, drawing him in deeper, and then followed his lead as he did the same to her.

His hands slid up her thighs, pushing the hem of her sundress higher and higher until he reached the top of her hips. His thumbs hooked her thong and started to slide it off of her body. Jake's lips left Quinn's just long enough to quickly break her thong away and then drop it on the floor. She sat up, and he kissed her again before sliding her dress the rest of the way up and off over her head.

Now they were both kneeling on the bed, and she slipped her hands into his swim trunks, easing them over his hips and down his legs. He pulled her back up, crushing her chest against his as he ran his tongue and lips down her neck to the cleft between her tits and back up again to kiss her deeply. He eased her back onto the bed under him as he wiggled the rest of the way out of his trunks.

Quinn loved the way his skin felt against hers, the way the muscles of his arms flexed under her fingertips as he moved her legs up over his hips, pulling her as close to him as possible before he thrust his cock into her. Quinn arched her back as a powerful orgasm took hold of her. Jake slid his hands up her arms, lacing his fingers with hers, pinning her hands up next to her head. He continued to enter her slowly and deliberately, drawing out their lovemaking for as long as possible.

Quinn's body continued to respond to his every move and caress. Each orgasm built upon the previous one to the point where she could no longer control her body, and Jake was right there with her.

"Quinn, I can't, I can't hold back any longer. You feel so good. Take me with you, baby doll."

And just like that, her body responded to his every wish, every demand. Every single muscle of her body contracted hard, including the ones surrounding Jake's cock deep inside of her. Quinn arched her back again and nearly threw Jake off of her, but he held her hands tight against the bed, riding their final climax together.

He collapsed on top of her, both of them out of breath, hearts pounding. They slowly untangled their bodies so they were lying on their sides facing each other. Jacob smiled at Quinn and held her close. "I want to hold you until we have to go. I want to remember all of this, but I'm afraid that as soon as I wake up on the other side, it'll just be a fuzzy, happy memory. What if I don't make the right choice, Quinn? What if I let my fear take over again?"

"Shh, don't second guess yourself. Trust your heart. I do. I trust that you'll come for me. You'll fight for me. The love we have is too great, too powerful to ignore any longer. Lady Fate promised we would be together in this life time. Danny helped me to remember that."

"We were here before, weren't we?"

She nodded. "I don't remember all of it, but Danny said it will all come back to us when the time's right. He's one of our Guardians. He won't let us stay away from each other any longer."

Jacob lay on his back and pulled her close to him so her head rested on his shoulder. He tipped her chin up so she looked into his eyes again before he kissed her tenderly one last time. "You're my always and forever, and I'm never going to let you go again."

Quinn noticed they were slipping away from each other now. "Promise?"

"Forever. I promise you forever and ever, my love."

Quinn squeezed his hand so hard the last time Steve thought she was going to pull him right in with her. Then he noticed the flush starting on her cheeks, traveling slowly down her neck. Steve had watched that happen to her on many occasions and he knew exactly what was happening. She was with Jake all right.

He looked over at Helen who held tightly to Quinn's other hand. The look on her face told Steve he wasn't the only one whose fingers were nearly crushed in her grip. "Why is she starting to get all flushed? What's happening to her?"

At that moment Quinn arched her back and turned her face toward Steve, gripping his hand tight once again. "Jake. Jake." Her breathing quickened, and her body started to shake. Steve got into bed with her and held her tight to his body.

Helen stood up quickly and started to panic. Her voice rose another octave. "What's happening, Steve? Where's the call button? We need the doctor!"

Miranda took one look at her sister in the bed with Steve and smiled. "No, Ma. We don't need a doctor." She giggled behind her hands over her mouth. Derek's eyes flew open then slammed shut.

"Miranda Lee, what the hell is so funny? Your sister is having some sort of seizure, and you get fits of the giggles?" She looked at the three of them with smiles on their faces like they had all lost their minds. "Will one of you please tell me what is going on?"

Miranda got her giggles under control, barely, and tried to tell her mother what they were witnessing. "Uh, hmm, Ma, she's not having a seizure per se. Oh hell. She's having an orgasm, several of them by the looks of it." Then the giggles burst out again. "I'm sorry, but I can't stop." Miranda wiped the tears from her eyes.

Helen looked at Steve in bed with her eldest daughter who was starting to moan and shake again. "How do you know that's what's happening to her?"

He smiled and kissed Quinn on the forehead, letting her ride out the last climax she was experiencing. "I've been through this a few times with her before, more than a few actually." Steve held Helen's gaze for a few moments before he answered her unspoken question, "No, I don't believe this means she is choosing to stay there with Jake."

Helen looked at all of them and back to Quinn. Relief washed over her face as the giggles hit her, too. "Well, at least we know she's enjoying herself over there."

"Ma!" Derek and Miranda both stared at their mother with their eyes wide. .

"Come on, you two. Let's leave Steve alone with your sister. With all this racket going on in here, the nurses will end up throwing us all out. Besides, I could use a cup of hot tea and maybe we should get something for Nathan."

Miranda looked back at Steve and winked. "Oh, now aren't you the cougar!"

Helen laughed. "Hey, I may be getting up there, but I ain't dead!"

Derek put his hands over his ears. "Too much information, Ma!"

"Oh stop. I've been talking to him about your cousin Samantha. I think Nathan would be a perfect match for her. She needs a strong, handsome man in her life instead of pining away for the one who keeps breaking her heart."

"Good call, Ma. Sammi is ready to move on and Nathan is just the man for the job."

"Do you two ever stop trying to hook people up?"

"You just hush. I'll have you know we've been working behind the scenes to get you and Sarah together. You don't have to thank us."

As the three of them made it down the hallway, Quinn's body relaxed in Steve's arms. She snuggled up against him with her head on his shoulder and her hand over his heart. "Trust your heart, Jacob. I do."

Steve's heart went out to her. "He does love you, Quinn. He's just scared that he's hurt you too badly to be able to come back. Tell him, baby. Tell him to fight for you."

She held him tighter and tilted her face up toward his. Her eyes were closed, lost in her dream still, but he knew she was looking into Jacob's eyes, making her case. "I trust you'll come for me. You'll fight for me. The love we have is too great, too powerful to ignore any longer."

Steve touched her face with the palm of his hand. Her cheeks were still rosy and warm. He couldn't help himself. She was so beautiful with her face turned up toward him. "I love you, Quinn. Please come back, darlin'." He kissed her, and she started to kiss him back.

Her hand slowly slid up his chest, his neck, and then cradled the back of his head as she molded her body into his. Her tongue followed Steve's slowly and then with more purpose. He pulled back from her in surprise. Was she coming back to him? He kissed her again, and she definitely kissed back and pulled him closer to her, her tongue leading the tango that weakened him to his very core. He broke the kiss again to search her face. Her eyes fluttered open. "Jake?"

"No, darlin'. It's Steve." He couldn't stop the tears from rolling down his face now. She was back!

She touched his face, gently wiping away the tears still falling down his stubble-covered chin. "Steve? How did you get here?" She blinked a few more times. "Why are you crying, baby? Aren't we home yet?"

"Not yet. You've been gone a long time. I've missed you." Steve kissed her again and held her tight. He couldn't believe she was awake and talking to him.

She treated him with the smile he loved so much. "I've missed you, too. How long was I at the beach?"

"Is that where you've been hiding from me?" Steve wanted to keep her talking for as long as possible. He didn't know if this would last or she would drop off again. His heart pounded with the combination of fear and sheer joy that she was in his arms, smiling at him once again.

"No, I wasn't hiding from you. I was just so tired, and I wished to be on my tropical island. I woke up one morning in my dream bungalow. I don't know how I got there, but it was so peaceful and relaxing. I wish you could have been there with me, but I wasn't alone."

Steve looked up and noticed the others had slipped into the room quietly while Quinn was talking. No one wanted to interrupt her. It was just so good to hear her voice. Derek walked over to her bedside and took her hand. "Hey, hot stuff! Who was there on your island with you?"

"It's all a bit fuzzy now. I remember seeing Danny at one point, but I spent most of my time with someone else." She caught the looks exchanged between everyone. "What are you guys not telling me? Randi?"

Miranda looked at Steve, and he nodded. She needed to know. "You talked a lot in your sleep. We knew you were talking to Danny, but most of the time you were with Jake. You did more than talk."

Quinn's eyes widened, and she giggled. "Well, that would explain why my panties are soaked!"

"Oh, my God! Your father and I didn't raise you two to be such potty mouths!" But Helen didn't fool Steve. Potty mouth or not, she was thrilled to have her daughter back.

Quinn looked back up to him. "I heard you, Steve. I knew when it was time to come back because I heard your voice calling to me. I felt you kiss me. Danny said that if I didn't come back…"

"You don't have to explain. We heard enough of your side of the conversations to know. You mean the world to me, to all of us. I don't know what I would have done if you left this world forever, Quinn. Hey, how about I take you to another beach when you're feeling up to it? How's Maui sound?"

Quinn looked at all of them surrounding her bed and shook her head. "As much as I would love to go away and be alone with you on Maui, I can't, at least not now. I can't keep running away from my life, Steve, even if it is with you." She kissed him softly and smiled again. "It's time I take back control of my life. I can't do it alone anymore. I need therapy and a lot of it."

"And that's where I come in." One of her doctors entered the room, obviously thrilled to see she was awake. "Welcome back, Quinn." She walked to the bedside and held out her hand. "I'm Dr. Karla Johnson, and I'm going to help you find yourself again."

* * * *

CHAPTER 6

He woke up back in his old room. The touch of her soft lips on his and the feel of her body molded to his own were so real. Her scent still filled his nostrils, and he longed to taste her once again. Jacob knew without a doubt he loved her with his whole mind, body, and soul. His mother was right. He *did* know what he was going to do.

He was going to fight for her. Fight for them. Fight for their forever.

"Welcome home, Jakey."

"Pop? How…I don't understand."

"I don't have much time. Your mother will be up and about spoiling you with breakfast in bed. Let her do it for you. It brings her great joy to take care of you kids."

"I will. How are you here now? Am I still dreaming?"

His father, Michael Hartley shook his head. "You're wide awake and in the here and now. The Three felt it was time we intervened to be sure you get back on track with your soul mate. The two of you have put us through the ringer. Danny and I have our hands full with the lot of you!"

"Danny. Quinn's brother?"

"The very same. He's been with Quinn on the Island and helped her see she couldn't stay there with you. Both of you chose to find each other here in this realm. I'm so sorry it's taken so long and both of you had to go through so much pain."

He shrugged. "It's not your fault. I've made some bad choices but I'm going to change all of that. I'm going to take Steve up on his offer and win Quinn's heart again."

"Good. The two of you will need the love of all of your friends and family as there are some dark things coming your way. You'll need to lean on each other to get through it. I can't tell you more than that. Promise me you'll hold on to your love for Quinn and never let go, no matter who or what gets in the way."

"I promise."

His father leaned over and kissed him on the forehead like he used to do when he was very young. "I'll always be with you, Jakey. I want you to know I couldn't be more proud of you. Stand your ground and fight for the one you love. It worked for your mother and me."

He clutched his father's hands in his until he faded away. "I promise, Pop. I won't let you down."

The aroma of fresh brewed coffee caught his attention, and he was sure his mother had an omelet on that stove waiting for him to get up and greet the day. He smiled. He had spent all of these months trying to avoid coming back home admitting he failed, and here he was. This was exactly what he needed all along to help him refocus and find his way again.

"Jacob? Are you up yet, my son?"

"Yeah, Ma. Come on in." She pushed the door open using the tray covered with a pot of coffee, a huge omelet and a side bowl of berries.

"I brought you your favorite breakfast to help you start your day." *Just like Pop said she would.*

He looked up at her and smiled. "I'm going to fight for her, Ma. I'm going to beg her to forgive me and to give us one more chance. She told me in my dream last night to fight for her even if she told me to fuck off. That's exactly what I'm going to do."

"Good. I have news for you, too. Your sister called. Quinn woke up this morning."

Jacob's heart skipped a few beats. She'd come back to the world like she said she would, for him. "Is she all right?"

"Maredyth said Quinn will be in the hospital for at least a couple more days and then a lot of therapy. She wanted me to tell you Steve is waiting for your call to claim what's already yours, what's still yours. She said you would know what that means." She smiled at her son with tears in her eyes. "If your father and I had such a person in our lives moving heaven and earth to give us the chance to be together, we would have jumped at it and had another ten years together."

"Really? I didn't know you and Pop had such a hard time getting together."

"Oh, do you think you corner the market on heartbreak? I was promised to another because of an arranged marriage. My parents promised my hand to a man I had never met here in America so that I could get a better life. Your father was a Marine stationed in West Germany when I first saw him. So handsome in his dress blues. I couldn't keep my eyes off of him, and he was watching me, too." She sighed deeply and sat on the bed to continue, "Eat up, Jacob, before it gets cold."

"Yes, Ma." He did as he was told and listened to her tell how his father followed her around the square for a little bit after a memorial ceremony to celebrate the seventh anniversary of the end of the war and the end of the Nazi regime. She hung back from her friends so she could "accidentally" bump into him pretending to be looking at her guide book. "Smooth move, Ma."

"Oh, you hush. It worked. I dropped my umbrella and your father picked it up for me. Our fingertips touched when he gave it to me, and we froze staring into each other's eyes. It was magical."

"Thunderstruck."

Katrina's face glowed with the memory of how they first met. Jacob knew exactly how they both felt and how she still felt about her husband. "Yes. Thunderstruck. From that moment on we spent every chance we could together for the next two weeks. I fell head over heels in love with him and he with me. Unfortunately my betrothed couldn't care less. He came to claim me at the end of my mini-vacation. I refused to go with him, and he threatened to send me back to Poland and disgrace my family. He said he would demand all the money back that he paid for me since I was breaking a contract. He was a powerful man, or so I thought. He pretended to be a rich man who would take care of my family once we were married. What a joke. As soon as he had me here, married to him and in his bed, his true colors came out. He was a violent man who liked to use his words and fists to keep me in line."

"Why didn't you tell us this before?"

"It wasn't important. I gladly went through all of it because I knew that one day your father, Sgt. Michael Hartley of the United States Marine Corps, would find me again, and we'd have our happily ever after."

"How'd you know that?"

"He told me so the last night we were together. He said he'd never give up until he found me again and made me his bride." She sighed again. "He never gave up looking for me either. At first, my family wouldn't give him any information about me. They were afraid my husband wouldn't send them the money he promised to help them come to America, too. After three years, when no money came to them, they knew that they'd made a big mistake. My sister contacted your father and gave him my address."

"Did he find you?"

"No. We had moved around a lot. You see, I was married to what you would call a grifter. He went from town to town cheating people with cheap carnival games. That's right, Jacob. Your mother was a carnie!"

"Ma! Stop pulling my leg. You were *not* a carnie!" Jacob couldn't believe she was telling him this story, but she wasn't laughing. "You're serious?"

"Of course, I'm serious. We traveled from town to town, never staying in one place for longer than four days. I missed my Marine who made me smile. I dreamed of him night after night. I wished the man who shared my bed was Michael. I prayed for him to come in and rescue me. One day I looked up at the concession stand I was running and there he was."

"He finally found you? How?"

"One of the other carnies mailed a letter for me to my family without my husband's knowledge. My sister got word to your father, and he followed the carnival for two weeks before he caught up to us. I was so happy when I saw him! I decided to run away that very night to be with him, but my husband had other plans."

"What do you mean he had other plans? Did he hurt you again? Or Pop?"

"If you stop asking so many questions, I'll tell you!" She slapped his arm playfully. "He had every intention of hurting the both of us, but it backfired on him. He ended up getting caught in his own trap and was killed in the fire he set. He died six years after we were married."

Jacob didn't understand. He thought she said they would have had another ten years together. She saw the question form in his eyes and continued with her story.

"Not all of the carnies believed my husband had set the fire himself. They knew your father and I were in love and had planned on leaving together, so they told the police it was your father who set the fire. He had to spend nearly four years in jail for something he didn't do until finally he cleared his name. We were married the very next week. That was on Valentine's Day, 1962. October that year your sister was born."

"Did you or Pop ever think either one of you would be better off without each other? Did you ever doubt what you felt?" Those doubts tried to creep back into his head again. He worried Quinn wouldn't want him when he went for her, that she would choose to stay with Steve who had been with her this whole time.

"Oh, yes. I thought your father would be better off marrying someone who didn't come with so much baggage, someone who wasn't already married. I wanted nothing more than to see him happy, but he said no one else would make him happy. He told me I was his heart and soul and he just couldn't see his life or any future without me. I felt the same." She touched Jacob's face with the palm of her hand. "My son, you and Quinn share the same kind of love for each other. Don't let another day go by without you doing everything in your power to get her back. You owe it to yourself and to her to see if this love you have between you will overcome the pain you've been suffering through. I think it can, and so does this Steve. He loves her like you do, but he can see that you are what her heart calls for. Why can't you?"

"I'm beginning to let myself believe it, Ma. There are a few things I have to tie up with Iris before I can move forward with Quinn."

"You have to be honest with Iris. She does love you, but not the way your heart craves. She's like that Julia Santos, wanting to change you to someone you're not and controlling everything in your life so you fit into her world. I'm afraid for you if you stay with her, Jacob. I'm afraid I'll lose my son forever."

Now he understood why the family had been so against him being with Iris. He couldn't see what was happening because he was so distracted over losing Quinn. They could see him going down the same path that had led him to nearly dying ten years ago, and they couldn't put themselves through it again. "Don't worry, Ma. I know what I have to do. I'm not going anywhere. You're stuck with me!"

"You've made me very happy today, Jacob. Not only did you wake up with a smile on your face and the twinkle back in your eyes, you now have a purpose once again. Will you still make the trip to Greenville with Iris to visit with her family?"

"Yes. I don't want to just spring all of this on her. I want to be sure she's all set with the move and all before I leave. She'll need her family now to help get her through the move, cancelling the wedding and everything."

"She's been having all sorts of problems with her family lately, I hear. You won't be dragged down with them, will you?"

Eric must have told her about all the legal problems that Iris and her family were going through. "No. Iris brought all of that on herself. I told her to leave Quinn alone, but she wouldn't listen. Now Steve has tipped the various government agencies off to all the shenanigans they've been doing. I'm sure you figured out Steve is a very powerful man. He has connections all over the world. I wouldn't want him as an enemy."

"I agree. It's good to have friends in high places, and ones who know your heart even when you don't."

"You know, before I could only see him as my rival for Quinn's heart. Now it's different. I am starting to see him as a true friend. I'm going to have to get used to him being around a lot because there's no way Quinn will ever cut him out of her life, nor should she."

"Good for you for seeing him that way. I've liked him right from the moment Eric started working for him. I'm glad I don't have to pick sides between you two. You know he's really quite handsome with those green eyes."

"Oh, now don't you start, too!" She giggled like a teenager, and that made Jacob laugh more. It felt great to laugh and feel good about his future for a change. A future he hoped would include Quinn by his side.

Steve was so relieved Quinn was awake but reluctant to leave her alone with Dr. Johnson. Out in the hall, Helen took his hand and gave it a squeeze. "It's okay, Steve. She's not going to slip away again. She's back."

"I know. It's just that I was so scared we were going to lose her. I can't believe she woke up after I kissed her. I thought I'd fallen asleep in bed with her and was dreaming."

Derek was down the hall a ways on his cell phone and was walking swiftly toward them. "I called Eric to let them know Quinn was awake. He'll get word to Jake and everyone else in Vegas. Sarah is on her way and should be here within the next twenty minutes or so." He was beaming now. "I'm so happy Quinn's back. I feel like I can breathe again."

"And that smile wouldn't be because Sarah is on her way here now, would it?" Miranda was relentless. Helen raised her eyebrows. "Oh, my bad. Maybe you should thank us now for getting the two of you together. Lord knows if we left it up to the two of you, you'd still be at the flirty aloof stage."

Steve excused himself from the family ribbing to make his own call to another member of the Hartley family. He had called Maredyth as soon as Dr. Johnson asked them to give her a few moments with Quinn alone. She promised she would call her mother and let her know what was going on, but Steve wanted to talk to Jacob himself. He had told Maredyth he would wait for him to call, but he thought it was time to give him another nudge. He dialed the cell number he'd found on Quinn's phone, stored under his screen name of Michelangelo, no less.

"Hello?

"Jake, it's Steve. I wanted to let you know myself that Quinn woke up today, and she's going to be taking medical leave to start intensive therapy. You may not know it, but you're the reason she came back to us."

"I dreamt of her last night and our island. It was so real."

"I'm sure it was for the both of you." Steve decided to let Quinn tell him that story herself at another time. "I think it's high time you stop this crap with Iris and claim what's yours, Jake."

"What if she turns me away?"

"Keep after her until she says yes. She's mad as hell at you right now, but that's because she loves you. I meant what I said. I'll do everything I can to bring you two together. So all you need to do is call me anytime, and I can have a car for you within an hour to take you to the airport."

"Why are you doing this?"

"She's my life. I want her to have it all, and you're it."

"I can never repay you for this, Steve."

"Yes, you can. Make her happy. Fulfill the fantasies that you two have had together and will still have together."

Steve gave Jacob all the numbers for his people in Chicago who would help him move his things out of Iris's house and to southern California to live with his sister. Jacob agreed that moving to California would be a great way for him to start over and get as far from Iris as he could. He didn't want anything or anyone interfering with asking Quinn to take him back.

Iris looked out the bay window to the porch where Jacob had been sitting just about every single day since they arrived in Greenville. He just sat there staring off into the distance, alone. If any of them went out there with him, he made some excuse to leave and be alone somewhere else. He'd been that way ever since he got back from the visit with his mother. He wouldn't tell her what happened there, but there was something different about him, and it scared the shit out of her. It felt like she was losing him, like she had already lost him and he was just biding his time until he told her it was over.

"What's wrong with that boy? You'd think he would be happy that y'all found a house to be able to move into out here."

Iris shrugged in response to her mother's question. "He's got a lot on his mind. His mom's been sick and he got to spend a little time with her before we came down. I think he wishes he would have stayed home with her."

Her sister, Jacqui, snorted. "He's still talking to that woman?"

"No. She broke it off, so he says."

"What? She did? I thought she was the one chasing after him, trying to take him from you. I still want to kick her ass."

"You can try, but you won't get very far. She's got all sorts of folks around protecting her, and she's got connections high up in government out here. You need to lay low, Jacqui, otherwise you may be looking at more Feds on your doorstep. She also has some rich dude in Vegas protecting her. I think he has mob connections. I don't want y'all doing nothing. Let me handle Jake. It will all be fine once we're married."

Jacqui wasn't convinced. "I still don't trust him yet myself, but hey, it's your life."

"His family still ticked at you about how you announced the engagement? I would think they'd be mighty happy to know their son was marrying you." Leave it to her mother to try to make her feel a little better about that fiasco.

"Yeah, his brother is completely out of the picture now. His mom is nice enough when I talk to her, and his sister, well, she's polite, but that's it."

"I overheard him on the phone talking to the folks at the hospital where you both work. I think he's planning to go back early without you. If I were you, I would send someone with him to watch and keep him in line." Jacqui was really getting on Iris's last nerve right then.

"He's not one of the kids, Jacqui! I can't watch him every second of every day."

"Yeah, and look where that gotcha. Your man is in love with another woman!"

"Shut your mouth, Jacqui! He wouldn't have asked Iris to marry him if he didn't love her."

Jacqui crossed her arms over her chest and stared at Iris. She was going to have to come clean about this eventually. *Might as well bite the bullet.* "Ma, he didn't actually ask me. I found an engagement ring in his desk drawer that he left unlocked one day. I don't know how long he'd had it, but I thought he got it for me. So I went out and got him a ring, too. I wanted to surprise him."

"Oh, Iris, what have you done?"

"I'm trying to hold onto the one man who ever treated me with any decency. I love him."

Her mother looked out at Jacob slowly moving the porch swing and looking out at the setting sun. "Maybe you need to give him a choice. Marry you before y'all move down here, or it's over. That will light a fire under him one way or another."

"What if he turns me down?"

"Well, then you've been wasting your time with him the last year. He'll never love you the way you want. You will both just be miserable and end up hating each other in the end."

"Send Aaron with him. He can pack up the house while you finish your visit here and let me help you find a wedding dress."

Quinn stood in front of the window and studied the garden below. Dr. Johnson's reception area had the best view. She wondered if it had been planned that way. It helped her relax looking out at the birds flying between the trees, and all the colors of the flowers were bright and cheerful. She'd been watching the gardeners work in the flowerbeds every day for the last four weeks, and she had started to look forward to it. Now that her daily sessions were coming to an end, a touch of sadness drifted through her. Maybe she would try garden at the Bay House or just put up some flower boxes to start. She made up her mind to ask Steve what he thought the next time she talked to him, hopefully tonight. He'd been so busy with the construction of the new mall complex in Vegas. No matter, eventually they would get to talk to each other.

Karla peeked out of her office. "I had a feeling you would be here early today! Sorry to keep you waiting, Quinn. I was just finishing up a phone consultation with a patient who's out of town on vacation. Come on in."

She sat down in the overstuffed chair opposite Quinn, who preferred to sit on the loveseat. "Are you still having dreams about your tropical island with Jake?"

"Not since I was in the hospital. I dream of other things, like going to Maui with Steve."

Karla smiled brightly at her. "Sounds like a perfect spot to dream about."

"He still wants to take me there when I feel up to it. I don't see it happening for a while, though. He's so swamped with the construction projects right now. We're lucky to get a half hour to talk on the phone. That won't be forever though. He makes sure he takes time off now."

"Does it bother you that you aren't dreaming of the island with Jake? That you're losing the connection you had with him for so long?"

She looked at Karla and shrugged. "Honestly, I'm not sure. I'm not in a panic now when I first wake up. I don't want to just go to sleep and stay on the island with Jake and never come back again. I thought at first maybe I was letting go of that because I was giving my heart over to Steve."

"Do you think that's what you're doing, finally giving Steve the part of your heart that belongs to Jake?"

"No. I think I'm taking your advice and starting to let Jake go. I can't keep holding on to the fantasy of what may happen if he ever decides he wants to be with me. It just hurts too much to do that and to have each day pass by that he doesn't come for me. I've given myself permission to let him go. If we're supposed to be together, he will come back. He'll find me. But I'm not going to keep putting my life on hold and keep waiting for the chance that Jake will come back. I actually let Jake go the last night we were on our island together."

"Have you been seeing a lot of Steve since you moved back into the Bay House after leaving the hospital?"

Quinn smiled and nodded. "He was able to stay with me a full two weeks before he had to go back to Vegas."

"How did you feel when he had to leave this time? Was it anything like before your breakdown? I remember you telling me *that* time he had to go back to attend to business matters you felt lost and alone after you had seen him off at the airport."

"Yeah. I had a hell of a time keeping it together for my driver, Nathan. He saw right through me. I made him promise he wouldn't tell Steve how I was falling apart. I didn't want him to feel guilty for having to leave. That was not how I wanted our relationship to go forward. We both needed to get back to our careers, and then we would see each other when we could."

"So how was it this time when he had to go?"

"Oh, I missed him terribly that first night!" Quinn winked at her and giggled like a teenager. Karla laughed right along with her. She knew exactly what Quinn meant. She had told her that she and Steve had a very active sex life when they were together. Karla had even teased her and said she was a bit jealous. "When I got home from the airport, I put on one of his dress shirts that still smelled like him and I slept like a baby."

"He makes you feel safe and loved so it's very understandable that you would miss him terribly when you are apart from him."

"That's it exactly, but why can't I just be in love with him all of the way? He's smoking hot, satisfies my every need and desire sexually, helps me feel like I can do just about anything in my life like get a tattoo or sing in front of tons of people. Steve knows me better than I know myself at times. But I just don't understand why."

"You still feel like you can't give everything to him, your whole heart?"

Quinn nodded and her eyes filled with tears. "He's made me the happiest I've been in such a long time, right from the moment we met. Why can't that be enough? I wanted it to be so badly that I practically threw myself at him before I was hospitalized, and he still reminded me that it was too soon after what I had gone through with Jake."

"Steve knows your heart yearns for Jake, and he wants you to pursue that. How does that make you feel when he keeps pointing that out to you?"

"Pissed off. It's like he doesn't want to fight for me and the love we feel for each other. Basically, in everything else, he's my champion, my knight in shining armor. But with Jake, I feel like Steve is pushing me toward something that will rip my heart out again just so he can save me in the end."

Oh, my God.

Quinn was stunned. She couldn't believe she'd said that. Was that really how she felt? She covered her mouth and looked at Karla in shock. "That's a horrible thing to say about someone who says I'm the love of his life and who makes me feel that way every single time he touches me."

"No, Quinn, it's how you feel right now. Anger is not a bad thing here. You need to feel that and not bury it. It may not seem rational to you to feel pissed off at Steve for pushing you toward Jake, but it is still how you feel. Don't dismiss it."

"I do love him. In fact I have been *in love* with Steve right from the start, but something nags at me like we won't be able to ever truly give each other everything. I have my career, and so does he. My heart is split in two. If only I knew for sure that Jake didn't love me and it was all a fantasy, a lie, maybe I could let myself go completely with Steve."

Karla leaned forward in her chair and stared deep into her eyes. "It's been my experience, Quinn, that when there is such a strong bond between people it's there for a reason. They may not be each other's always and forever as you mentioned before, but they're great loves just the same. Steve is a great love for you as you are for him. And Jake is another one for you, but he's even more. He's your soul mate."

"Karla! You're just like Steve. How do you know Jake is my soul mate? What is it about him that makes both of you see him that way?"

She reached over and took both of Quinn's hands into her own. "It's in your eyes when you talk of him. Your cheeks flush and your pupils dilate. Those are all classic animalistic cues that you've found your mate. When you talk of Steve, your eyes are happy and they soften, and you are relaxed, like you are at home and safe."

"I don't understand. Sounds like everyone else can tell Jake and I need to be together but the two of us. If it's meant to be, why is it so hard?"

"I don't know. Let me ask you this. If you were to marry Steve and move forward with your life together, what would happen if Jake came for you?"

Quinn's cheeks and neck started to burn with the flush that passed through her. "I don't know."

"Your body language told me differently."

"What if Steve is my true love and I hurt him so badly by pushing him aside for someone who'll flake out on me? Then where the hell would I be?"

"Maybe that's where you should start. Alone, without Steve or Jake or even Jackson around. Is it really so bad to be alone for a while?"

"I just started to find myself again when I dropped all that weight."

"And you went right into falling in love with two men."

"So you think I should try to be alone away from all of them?"

"Yes. Give yourself a weekend to start, just for you. Do your baking or crafts or just read a good book. No Steve contact, no day dreaming about Jake. No hassles from Jackson."

Quinn didn't want to think of cutting herself off from Steve so she changed the subject. "I'm still going through with the divorce as planned, filing on June twentieth."

"Good, but you still have unresolved issues with Jackson, too."

"Like I want to put my fist through his teeth?"

Karla sat back in her chair and laughed the loud, bawdy laugh Quinn had found endearing the day they met. "Yeah, that's one of the issues! The two of you used to be friends. I think that's why you kept holding on and not finalizing the divorce. You already admitted that you couldn't care less about the inheritance and you really didn't think his grandmother would hold you to the promise you made any longer. She was your friend, and I'm sure she'd want you to be happy."

Quinn closed her eyes and took a deep cleansing breath like Karla had taught her to do to help relax. "You know, I think I just don't want to admit I failed, that I took a great friendship and let it die. Jack and I were great friends at first. I guess I just wanted someone to love me so badly that I twisted that friendship into something more than it was."

"I think you should take Jackson up on his offer to go with him to Disneyland."

"What? You just told me that I should take time to be alone without men in my life. Now you want me to spend time with Jackson? Are you fucking insane?"

"Not at all. If you two can't even get along for a week at your favorite place on Earth, then you'll absolutely know it is over between you and you can release yourself from all the guilt you feel over the marriage failing."

"Why should I put myself in that situation again? I've been living in the Bay House since before I went into the hospital. Now you want me to go back to that?"

"Not to the Oakland Hills house, but to Disney, an impartial environment where you don't have any other issues like dishes, laundry, lawn care, your jobs, etc. interfering. At one of our other sessions you said that this trip to Disney was an annual event that you plan with several other couples. This could be your way to ease back into your social circle and tell them you and Jackson are splitting up."

"This could end up in disaster." Quinn was really sick to her stomach over the thought of having to spend any time at all with Jackson again.

"True, but it can also free your mind finally of Jackson and his family. I'm not saying stay in the same bed or even the same room. Just go there, plan excursions together and see how it goes. You can always rent a car and leave at any time. Or drive down in separate cars. Look at it as a group vacation and not one with your soon to be ex."

"That's true. It would be great to see our friends again. Besides, this is the first time that Jackson has taken an active interest in planning the trip and is paying for it all, too."

"There you go. At our last couples' session, he was genuinely concerned about you."

"I don't doubt that. He needs me for his inheritance."

"I think it's more than that. He cares for you, Quinn. At least a part of him does. Why else would he volunteer to go to counseling with you now when he's refused to do it in the past? If he was doing this just to make sure he got his inheritance, don't you think he would have agreed to these sessions sooner?"

"Hell if I know. I think he's up to something no good. He's looking for some angle to make himself look better if I choose to divorce him. Well, I have. June twentieth the papers will be filed whether or not I am in Anaheim with Jackson."

"That's only two weeks away. A lot of things could happen between now and then."

Yeah, like Jacob could come to his senses and move heaven and earth to win her back again. Quinn missed him so much, but Karla was right. She had to let him go to know whether or not he was really hers to begin with. "I'm just going to take one day at a time, Karla. Let the chips fall as they may."

* * * *

CHAPTER 7

"Jack, why do you always have to do this? I'm not a mind reader. What the hell do you want from me?" They were walking out of California Adventure after being there for just a couple of hours after lunch.

"I want you to stop harping on me and just try to have some fun for Christ's sake! You're the one who loves to sit by the pool. I thought you would want to do that this afternoon since I'm not feeling all that great."

"So you want me to entertain myself by the pool so you can go play with your buddies on the computer?" He had spent practically the entire day checking his e-mails from his phone. He couldn't leave it alone for more than fifteen minutes. Quinn was so tired of him doing this to her. She could have stayed home and found other ways to occupy her time. Why waste all this money on a vacation that was supposed to help them find the friendship they used to have if they were going to spend most of it apart? It was just stupid.

She'd trusted him to confirm all the trip details. Unfortunately, there had been a mix up with their reservations and they'd booked them in the same suite. The hotel manager promised to notify her as soon as another room became available, but at least for the time being she had to share amenities with Jackson. It really wasn't as bad as it could've been. They had two king sized beds and a kitchenette. Their friends would arrive the next day and they'd spend more time out of the room than in it.

Or so she'd thought.

"No. I'm not getting on the computer. I'm tired, and my gut feels like it's on fire. I'm sorry that our plans aren't going the way we expected, but I can't help it. I'm going back to the room to see if a nap will help. Maybe I'll feel up to the fireworks tonight. If not, there is no reason that you should miss out on anything. You can go with Bill and Connie. They should be arriving in a couple of hours, and they were so excited when I told them you were coming this year. Janice and the kids are hanging out by the pool today, but maybe the Greens will go park-hopping with you."

She had to struggle to keep up with his brisk pace. His stride was much longer than hers, and he always liked to walk ahead of her. Quinn hated it. It made her feel like one of those women who were required to follow so many steps behind their husbands. Fucking bullshit if you ask her, just like what Jackson was trying to pull on her now. "Fine. You go back to bed, and I'll entertain myself just like at home."

"You always have to get that last dig in there, don't you, Quinn?" Jackson turned and kept walking away toward the room, not waiting for her answer. Good thing, too. Quinn had some choice swear words to throw out there, but since there were so many kids at the pool, it was probably a good idea she held her tongue. One thing this trip had shown her was that their marriage was definitely over. It was time to stop feeling guilty over that whole mess. At this point, she wasn't sure she wanted to hang out with people who were actually Jackson's friends from before they were married. She'd never felt particularly close to any of them.

She walked up to the soda machines, trying to figure out if she wanted a Pepsi or Mountain Dew, and the hairs on the back of her neck stood up. She'd been feeling that same sensation all day long, like someone was watching her. She spun around and came face to face with the one person who she thought she would never see again.

Jacob Hartley.

"Hello, Quinn."

Oh, my God. Her stomach dropped. A sensation of dizziness clouded her brain and threatened to knock her off balance. He was really standing there in front of her as if nothing had happened between them. As if he'd never torn out her heart and smashed it to pieces. The sudden dryness of her throat prevented her from speaking right away. When she finally found her voice, it sounded foreign to her ears as if she'd spoken under water. "What the hell are you doing here, Jake?"

"I needed to see you in person. There's so much I want to tell you. Can we go somewhere and talk? Please, Quinn. I love you. I want to be with you if you'll still have me." He reached out for her hand, but she pulled away from him and shook her head.

"How the hell do you think you're going to be with me when you're planning your wedding with Iris?"

Jacob flinched as if she had slapped him. "Please let me explain—"

"I don't give a fuck anymore, Jake. She's your ball and chain now." She moved to walk away from him, but he shifted position to block her escape. God, she wanted to punch him in the mouth for showing up there and making her feel everything all over again.

"Quinn, just give me a few minutes. I'll get you the Pepsi, and we can sit out here at the pool so you don't have to be alone with me."

Okay, so she was a sucker for him still. No harm in listening to what he had to say. It didn't mean she would believe him. But damn, he still looked hot in person with his muscles rippling under his tight T-shirt. He'd let his hair grow out passed his shoulders, and it was lighter from the sun. His eyes were so blue, especially with his tan. *Focus, Quinn! Don't let him suck you in again.*

Jacob led her over to a table in the shade. It wasn't all that quiet with the number of kids running around and swimming, so they had to sit close in order to hear each other speaking. He focused his eyes on hers, and she struggled to keep focused. "Quinn, I never stopped thinking about you and what you told me the last time we talked. When you said you were going to leave Jackson for me, I felt like someone punched me in the gut. I realized I'd made a horrible mistake by agreeing to marry Iris. It's just that I was scared, and I didn't want to be alone. I wasn't sure if you would ever be able to leave your husband. You had the chance before with Steve in Vegas, and you still stayed with Jack. I didn't think I had a chance."

"What I have with Steve is different. We give each other what we both need when we're together, and it's worked for us. He's never messed with my head. But with you, goddamn it! Do you think you were the only one who was scared? I trusted you and believed you when you told me you loved me. You said you had no problem leaving Iris for me. I felt safe and willing to take a leap of faith that what we felt was real."

"I was afraid what we felt for each other wouldn't carry over to the real world if we got the chance to be together. So I went ahead and told Iris I would marry her. I know it was the easy way out, and I'm sorry. But I'm here now. I want to see if that heat is still between us, find that spark that we can build on."

"I don't…"

He reached under the table for her hand. "I was in Downtown Disney today when you walked by with Jack. I wanted to chase after you then, but instead I held back and watched the two of you together. At times you looked like you had some fun together, but the smile on your face never made it to your eyes." He squeezed her hand tighter. "Baby, my heart has been pounding being so close to you and not being able to touch you until now."

Quinn struggled to keep her composure. "What do you want from me?"

Jacob's eyes softened, and he leaned in to whisper in her ear, "I want nothing more than to take your face in my hands and kiss you, make you melt and then take you back to my room at the hotel next door and make love to you."

She was so stunned that he was there in the first place that she forgot all the stuff she'd wanted to confront him about. When he took her hand, she nearly came out of her skin. Why was he doing this to her? Why play with her emotions and her heart this way? Why do this just to throw her out again? Quinn lost the battle, and her eyes filled with tears.

She attempted to remove her hand from his, but he held tight and whispered, "Please, baby. Don't pull away. I know I hurt you. I know I was an ass and ruined all that we had, but give me another chance."

He reached up with his other hand, lifted her chin, and wiped away a tear that rolled down her face. He smiled, leaned in, and kissed her. "I love you so much, Quinn. I can't let you go without knowing how you feel about me now. Please give me a couple of hours, and let's see where this can go."

She was stunned that first of all he'd just fucking kissed her and now she couldn't feel her feet. Secondly, she completely forgot about Jackson asleep in their room just fifty yards away. If he would wake up and see her kissing Jake, well, that would be the start of a huge scene, and she was in no mood to have another fight with him. But the most overwhelming feeling running through her was the urge to slap Jacob and then fuck him silly.

She looked down at the table a few seconds to get her bearings and think about what she wanted to say to him. "Why should I trust you again, Jake? It's been nearly four months since our last conversation and several e-mails I sent to you asking you if we were over and you really chose Iris. Not one peep from you. I finally go forward with my life and start to get over you, and here you are in the place where Jackson and I have had the most fun together in the past. Now you want me to abandon him and our friends to go fuck you for a few hours."

She finally found the nerve to look into his eyes, but her voice wavered. "What's gonna happen when you get your two hours, and you're done with me? Are you gonna tell me you love me over and over, kiss me goodbye at the door with promises that you'll contact me later tonight or tomorrow and then nothing? I won't wait and stare at the phone for hours on end afraid to fall asleep and miss your call or text. I just can't do it. I won't set myself up to be rejected by you again." And she sure as hell wasn't going to tell him just how soon she would be free of Jackson once and for all, at least not yet. Not until she figured out what the hell he wanted with her.

His eyes welled up. She thought he was faking it, but it was working on her. "You have every right to be mad. I did tell you those things and then just stopped. I let Iris take over everything and control it all and didn't fight back. A couple days after we talked last, she came to me again screaming that you were sending all sorts of texts and phone messages still and they were the restricted ones. I asked her this time how the fuck she knew it was you if the texts were from a restricted number. Why did she automatically assume it was you? She just stared at me stuttering and stammering and then said that you had sent letters to her. She'd pulled out some papers from her desk and waved them around in my face as proof. I knew right there that she'd made it all up again. You had promised you would never do that to me.

"She also admitted she's tried to get my phone records to be able to tell who I was talking to and texting all the time. Her kids had told her that I had called someone in the afternoon one day telling them I would call them back after I ran an errand. Fucking shits! They were ticked at me for not letting them play with my Xbox as much as they wanted, so they lied knowing it would send Iris on a rampage again."

Jacob told Quinn that he finally did admit to Iris that he was the one initiating all of the contact between them. He explained how Iris had flipped out and kept threatening to try to ruin her, even though he had warned her that Quinn had powerful friends that would make life difficult for her and the rest of her family.

She wasn't buying all of his story. She thought he was making some of it up to get on her good side. *What the hell?* It sounded great so she encouraged him to continue. "Well, what did she say to that?"

"She got really pale and quiet. I thought she was gonna start throwing shit or something, but she just sat down at the kitchen table and asked me to explain. I told her you didn't go into specifics, but since you had police officer family and friends and knew people in government out here, she could find herself without a job, child protective services down her throat, kids in juvie, and perhaps herself in jail for harassment and stalking."

"Huh. So did her little brain grasp the concept that I could do more damage to her than she could ever do to me?"

"Don't be mean, Quinn. She isn't stupid."

"Like hell she isn't. You've cheated on her how many times, and she thinks that she can control everything about you and then live together happily ever after. Where did that get her? You're here chasing after me again, and I'm sure you'll find some way to let Iris believe it's all my fault this time, too!"

Quinn yanked her hand free from his. She gripped her Pepsi to stop her hands from shaking. Why the hell was he really there? Why the hell was she still sitting there listening to him?

"I told her I needed time away from her to think things through. Maybe we were rushing into the engagement and marriage. I told her I'd fallen in love with you and I didn't know what I wanted anymore. She just sat there staring at me, not saying a word for a long time. Her face went from being pale to all blotchy and red. Then she asked me what I was going to do. I told her I wanted to visit Maredyth and the kids, maybe go to Disney with them. Get my mind off things for a bit and try to figure out what I wanted to do."

"Did she believe you?" If she knew Iris, there was no way in hell she believed he was coming out here to see his family.

"What do you mean?"

"Did she believe you were going to come out here to California just to be with your family? Or did she figure out you were trying to see me? I can't believe she agreed to all of this without any fight."

"Well, I did catch her online trying to find out how to find you and Jack and making sure I wasn't going to Oakland. She was so pissed when she couldn't find any reservation for flights or rental cars under my name through the travel sites I usually book things through. She kept asking me for a copy of my itinerary just in case there was an emergency. She sulked when I wouldn't give her any information and stepped up her efforts to stalk you and find something she could hurt you with. She threatened to make your relationship with Steve public."

Quinn laughed. "It is public knowledge, you know. We've been filmed together in Vegas, Michigan, and here in California. Who cares?"

"Exactly! She called a few news outlets to give them the 'scoop' about your affair, and they laughed at her. I finally had to remind her of Steve's promise to ruin her life, and then she stopped doing that. She tried to send messages to you and Jack through Facebook but you have her blocked. Jack didn't, but he told her to fuck off too. That put an end to her messing with things at that time."

"Wait, so Jack knows you were coming out here to visit your family?" *Is that why he's acting all strange and sick all of a sudden? Just what the fuck is going on?*

"I don't think so." He filled her in on how Iris had been corresponding with Jackson back in March, telling him that he needed to watch his back and keep a leash on her. After that, the messages between them seemed to stop. "As far as I know, she didn't tell him about my travel plans."

"Jake, I thought for sure you'd try to contact me at some point and explain what the hell had her in such a tirade. Days and weeks flew by and not one word from you. I finally had to accept the fact that you wanted to be with Iris instead of me."

He smiled a little, leaned over, and kissed her again before she could stop him. *God, his lips are so soft.* She wanted to kiss him again and suck on his tongue, but she had to behave.

"Come with me now. Be with me for the next couple of hours. Jack will be asleep for a bit and he can call your cell when he's up.

Right?" His eyes sparkled when he smiled. *Fuck!* He had her all wound up in knots, and she really did want to be with him.

"You still didn't answer my question. Why should I trust you again? I begged you to tell me we were over and not one word from you. I had no way of knowing if your silence meant it was over or if you just weren't able to contact me. You had me set up that stupid e-mail account for you, and you never read anything in there. It was only a place where I could send you the pictures you wanted. And what did I get out of it all? Dumped without even so much as a 'nice knowing ya.'"

"Things had become so complicated and out of control. I wanted to contact you, but I couldn't get a break from Iris. Since February she's been watching every single thing I do and monitoring every call. I couldn't access the account you set up. I couldn't even go to Vegas to patch things up with Eric without her tagging along. Please know I never stopped thinking about you, wanting you, obsessing over you. I want and need to make this up to you. Give me this time to show you how much I love you, Quinn. Give *us* this time to see if we want to be with each other.

"I know I have no right to ask you to do this or to trust me, but we have a chance to see if we can be anything more than a fantasy. I need to know that our time on that island was real and not all an illusion. Please, baby doll. Now that I have you here in person, right next to me, I don't know if I can stay away. I need to hold you, kiss you. Make love to you. Aw, hell. I wanna fuck your brains out."

That got her laughing. They had always talked that way. "Promise?"

He inhaled sharply and swallowed hard before he answered her.

Quinn held her own breath. She was so afraid he was going to change his mind, but then she saw the look of relief come over his face.

"I promise." He stood up and reached out for her hand. "Come with me and be my forever lover like we've fantasized about, but only better."

She rolled her eyes, shook her head a little, and smiled. She put her hand in his and let him help her up from the bench and right into his arms. She forgot about everyone else and Jackson asleep down the way. He led her to the stairs of the hotel next to the one where she was currently staying. He opened the door to a room on the fourth floor that was filled with candles, a bed covered in pillows, and a bucket of chilling champagne. She raised an eyebrow, and he smiled and shrugged. "I was hoping you would say yes."

He closed the door behind them after securing the Do Not Disturb sign on the door knob. He gathered her beach bag from her and placed it on the table near the television. The candles cast a soft glow about the room, and the light danced in his eyes as he crossed the room back to her. Quinn hadn't moved from the door. She leaned against it, watching him slowly walk back to her. He drew in close and practically pinned her against the door. There was no turning back as he reached up and took her face in both of his hands and kissed her tenderly at first. Then his tongue found hers, and it was all over. Quinn melted into him, slipping her arms around his neck. He held her tightly around her waist and moved her over to the bed.

His hands moved over her back, over her waist, and down to her ass. She could tell he loved her ass as his hands cupped each cheek and he pulled her even closer to him, nibbling on her lower lip.

She moaned and her arms tightened around his shoulders as the back of her legs hit the bed.

He eased her down and under him. His lips pulled away from hers and trailed down her chin and neck until he reached the top of her breasts peeking through her tank top. "Baby, I want to see your beautiful tits."

His hands were already ahead of hers and under her shirt unhooking her bra while she lifted off her top. He freed her breasts in a flash and hovered over them a second just looking at them. He was making her feel really self-conscious about it, and she must have blushed because he kissed both of them and slid back up to look her in the eyes. "The girls are more beautiful in person than in your pictures."

"Stop being silly and kiss me again." She pulled him closer as his mouth crushed hers. Quinn's nipples were rock-hard and rubbing against his shirt. Her hands moved down his back and under his shirt. Her hands flat against his hot skin.

Jacob pulled his shirt off and had his mouth back on hers before she could catch her breath. God, she loved his tongue! She arched her back as his mouth trailed down her neck and back to her tits. Quinn had been dreaming of this moment for such a long time, and her cunt quivered with need to be filled by him. The first orgasms rippled through her as his tongue circled her right nipple for the third time. *Fuck!* He was driving her absolutely wild. "Do you love my nipples, Jake?"

His answer was to pinch the left nipple as he popped the right into his mouth and sucked hard, eliciting another long drawn out moan from her. "Baby, I don't know if I can take much more of this. I need you inside me, Jake."

He looked up at her and smiled wickedly. "Oh, I'll be inside you, baby doll. My cock is so hard right now, and it wants to fuck your pussy so bad. That will have to wait, because I'm gonna taste you first. Are ya ready for me?" He tore at her jean shorts, nearly ripping the button and zipper out of them before sliding them and her soaking wet panties off and on to the floor.

Before she knew it, he had her hips in his hands, pulling her toward the end of the bed so he could kneel on the floor between her legs. He grabbed a pillow and put it under her ass to prop her up and spread her legs wide. "Oh, baby, you're so wet. I need to taste that sweet nectar." His tongue ran the full length of her outer lips. His tongue pressed deeper to find her clit and sucked on it. She jumped as his lips sealed around her swollen flesh.

He chuckled against her pussy before he thrust his tongue inside to get a full shot of the cum that flowed freely out of her. Quinn's thighs quivered, and she was nearly breathless from the passion flowing through her body.

"Jake, don't. mmmmmm. Don't stop." The words caught in her throat as she stifled a scream. He had buried his face in her cunt and was licking and sucking with such frenzy she became light headed. The man could eat pussy better than any lover she'd ever had, including Steve. She felt his tongue snake lower and circle her anus. He thrust two fingers into her pussy, getting them well lubed while he fucked her with them. God, his cock had to be rock-hard now. She wanted to suck on it, but he had her so in knots right then she couldn't concentrate on that if she tried.

Now those lubed fingers traced around her anus. His mouth returned to her clit. His finger slowly entered her ass and set off another wave of ecstasy racing through her. The pillow under her was soaked, but neither of them cared. Jacob was so into eating her out and finger fucking her ass, and she didn't want him to stop, but then Quinn remembered his cock had not been tended to.

As if reading her mind, he stood up and stepped out of his shorts. His cock stood at attention and pre-cum dripped at the tip. Quinn attempted to sit up, but he was fast on top of her. "Just where do you think you're going?" With his knees, he shoved her legs further apart. The head of his cock knocked at her entrance, teasing her, driving her closer and closer to another orgasm.

She whimpered and then he was inside of her, all the way in one slow thrust. He stayed that way for a moment, locking eyes with hers. They moved together, grinding their pelvises when they met to try to get closer to each other with each thrust. He urged her to move faster, and she locked her legs around him as he slammed her pussy over and over. Her nails raked down his back, not enough to draw blood, but enough to dig in and drive him harder. Her thighs tightened around him as she rode through another orgasm, then he suddenly pulled out.

Quinn knew what he wanted now. She smiled and rolled over onto her stomach. He grabbed her hips and pulled her up and onto his cock. She cried out his name as he entered her, not caring that there were families walking around outside the door, not caring that Jackson was across the pool area in another hotel fast asleep. All she wanted and all she felt right at that moment was Jacob. His cock felt so good buried deep inside her cunt. It belonged there, and she didn't want anything else. She didn't want anyone else. She knew in that instant that she was still hopelessly in love with this man.

He had to feel it, too. It was in the urgency in his thrusts. It was in his kisses. She felt it in the way he held her tight, as though he didn't want to miss any inch of her. She sensed he was getting close to coming. Quinn wanted him to come deep inside of her. Maybe, just maybe, there would be a miracle and she would get pregnant. She would finally be able to have a baby, Jacob's baby. If she couldn't have him, she damn well would have his child.

"Fuck me, Jake. Fuck me harder."

"Quinn, oh God, I love you, baby. I love your pussy. So tight, so hot and wet for me."

His hands tightened around her hips, and his body tensed. She could feel him spurting inside of her. He filled her up, and then he collapsed on top of her, keeping his cock buried in her pussy as he rolled them over onto their sides. His arms were draped around her waist and her breasts. Quinn turned her face toward his and kissed him deeply. "Baby, why are you crying?"

"I'm so happy you didn't turn me away today. You don't know how frightened I was that you no longer loved me. Now I know. I won't let you go again, Quinn. You're mine." He kissed her over both eyelids, her cheeks, and then her lips.

She turned against his body to face him as they embraced and shared another kiss, which left both of them breathless. "Promise?"

"Forever. I promise you forever."

"Don't say that unless you mean it, Jake. If all we have is right here and right now, then so be it. But please, don't promise me forever when you're not sure what you want." Now it was Quinn's turn to cry. She hated crying, especially over Jacob. She'd enough of that in the last few months, and she'd be damned if she was going to go there again. He had promised her forever before and then abandoned her. This time, she wanted to be in control.

He wiped the stray tears that had managed to escape from her lids. "Are those happy tears or sad? I don't want you to have any more sad tears because of me. I want to spend the rest of our lives making each other happy."

She'd heard all of this before. She'd prepared herself to let him go when she walked out of his room and back to her life. At least she'd been prepared when she'd walked in there with him. Now, after making love the way they had, with such urgency and such passion, her resolve had melted, and she didn't like it one bit. "I'm not sure what I feel right now. Being here with you is the happiest that I have been in a very long time. But in the end, it'll make me sad because no matter what I want here, it's ultimately your choice. I gave it all to you before, and you picked another. Now I gave you everything left I had buried deep inside my heart. If you tell me now that you want forever with me and later change your mind…that would be it for me. So forgive me if I don't just jump up and down excited that you say you want me forever again. We both have things to change in our lives to be with each other that way. Are you willing to do that?"

"Are you?"

"Goddamnit!" She pulled away from him, got up out of the bed and, grabbed his shirt to put on over her naked body. She didn't feel all that powerful if she was naked yelling at him. "Why do you do that? Why do you turn it around on me? Can't you just answer the question first without knowing what I'll do?"

He got up out of the bed and walked over to her. He took her hands in his and brought them up to his lips and kissed them. "I already broke things off with Iris. I moved out of her place and moved in with my sister down here."

Confusion muddled her brain. She hadn't noticed that he wasn't wearing the ring Iris had given him when they proposed to each other. She had been so flustered he was there in Anaheim that she didn't even look for it. "So you are no longer engaged or attached in any way?"

She thought he enjoyed her confusion a bit too much, but he didn't keep her waiting for very long. He folded his arms around her, pulling her close to his still fully naked, aroused body. "You're the only one I'm attached to now, especially with you in my shirt."

Damn! She'd forgotten that was one of his turn-ons. Well, what the hell? She still had another hour or so before she should check on Jackson. She steeled herself and concentrated on the questions they posed to each other. Had he just said he was attached to her? "What do you mean by that? Oh God, stop nibbling on my ear and answer me, please."

He rolled his eyes and pulled her over to the bed to sit down. He kissed her one more time and then he continued, "I want to keep pursuing you until your divorce is final and you're free of Jackson. I'll keep pursuing you until you marry me, and I'll pursue you every single day for the rest of our lives. *Forever.*"

"You do know that it will be several months before I can be free of him. Even with Steve's connections, I can't just snap my fingers and be divorced. I have to get certain things in motion before that happens, and just because we share a couple of hours of passion doesn't mean—" She couldn't get any more out before his mouth covered hers again and she got to suck on that marvelous tongue.

He rolled onto his back, taking her with him so she was now on top of him. He reached down and grabbed her ass, forcing her legs further apart so he could impale her on his glorious cock. This took her breath away, and she had to disengage from their kiss. She ground her clit into him, sending shock waves through both of their bodies. He tried to take control of the pace and move her faster, but she stopped him. She took control of his hands and eased them up to her tits under his shirt. She pulled off the shirt, threw it to the floor, and leaned into his hands. He squeezed her breasts as she balanced against them. "God, Quinn, your tits are so beautiful. Let me suck on them."

She bent over and placed her hands on either side of his head so her breasts hung down toward his face. In this position, she had better purchase and rode his cock harder. She enjoyed the sensation of his hands and mouth on her tits. He squeezed them together, put both nipples into his mouth at once, and suckled, gently at first but then with more urgency as Quinn's pace quickened on his cock.

He met her thrusts, and she barely held on. The orgasms racking her body nearly caused her pass out, but Jacob held on to her tightly, whispering over and over into her ear, "Let me have all of you, baby. Let go. I'm right here to catch you. I will and have always loved you."

The heat flashed through Quinn from the top of her head to her toes. Her body shuddered and shook as the explosion of fluid came out of her. Jacob's body trembled against hers, and he once again rolled them over onto their sides. This time they were both out of breath. Her legs were around his waist, and his cock was still buried inside of her, pulsing and emptying out more of his juices.

She shivered, and he moved her closer to him, kissing her softly. She smiled and touched his face with her fingertips, tracing his lips, moustache, goatee, eye brows, everything, trying to burn it all into her mind so she wouldn't forget any moment of their time together.

"Jake, I—"

"Shush now. We have a little more time alone, and I want to remember you just like this. Flushed, glowing, and in love with me. Don't try to deny it, baby. We belong to each other now, and there's nothing that will stand in our way. I will have you as my lover and my wife. I can't let you go again. Not after what we shared this afternoon."

"I've never denied I was still in love with you, Jake. You took so long to figure it out, but man, when you catch on, you really catch on! I don't know if I am going to be able to walk right after this."

He laughed. "Good. I want everyone to know you're mine."

"Jake, I'm still married."

"I'll wait for you for as long as it takes. I'm not going anywhere. I'm going to stay here with my sister and her family and help with her business. There are a couple hospitals looking for physical therapists.

If we play our cards right, I'll be able to make trips up to your neck of the woods to steal time alone with you. We can make this work, baby."

She untangled herself from him and sat up in the bed. Her head swam with the combination of joy and pain. "Do you know what today is?"

"June 19. Why?"

"It's my tenth wedding anniversary. I just spent the last one and a half hours with the love of my life, and he's not my husband. What kind of person does that make me?"

He moved to sit in front of her on the bed and took her hands again. *Goddess, he knows how to get me every time!* "It makes you a beautiful, sexy, loving person who finally found what she's been looking for her whole life. You found a kindred spirit, a life partner who loves you for who you are and who wants to spend every waking moment making love to you, and of course fucking your brains out whenever you need that, too."

She laughed once again. She threw her arms around him and squeezed him tight. "I love you, Jake. I want you to be my forever lover, but I'll not make you wait for me."

His fingers were on her lips to stop her from speaking any further. He shook his head, and the tears formed in his eyes again and fell down his cheeks freely. "I will *not* let you go. I'm absolutely sure you and I are supposed to be together and I'll wait for you for as long as it takes. So let's get you all showered and presentable so that you can go back to your room with Jackson. I know we can't just run off together now, but we can have some shower fun before you have to leave me. What do you say?"

She let him pull her up off of the bed and into his arms again but stopped him before he could turn her mind to jelly with that tongue of his. "Is this really happening, Jake? Did you choose me?" She hated the way her voice cracked with the question, but she couldn't help it. She struggled and tried not to break down. She wanted him so badly before and being with him right then and there made it all come flooding back. She'd never stopped loving him and wanting him. She just had to force herself to give him up because he hadn't picked her before. He chose the easy way out, and Quinn was so scared he was going to do it again now that they'd finally been able to be with each other.

"Yes, I choose you. My heart, mind, body, and soul are yours, if you'll have me." He took her face in his hands again and gently kissed the tears falling down her flushed cheeks then her lips four times and just held her. His heart pounded against her ear. "My heart physically hurt without you these last couple of months, and now, it's like it has come alive again. I'll fight for you until I can't fight anymore, but if you say we can't be together, I'll respect your decision and leave you alone. But, please don't ask me to do that, baby." Jacob made her look up into his eyes, and she was absolutely lost.

"I love you. I chose you right when we first met in Vegas, and it seems like I've been waiting my whole life for this moment with you. I am not about to turn you away. Now, how about that shower you promised?"

"Give me a minute and I'll have it all hot and steamy for us."

She didn't want him to stop holding her, but she let him go and picked up their clothes from around the room. Her panties were still very wet so she decided they were not going to go back on her body. She had a better idea. She put them under his pillow. *Let's see if he finds them tonight after I leave.* She silently dared him not to keep chasing her now. She found her beach bag and her phone and noticed there hadn't been any calls missed. Jackson must still be asleep. It had been nearly two hours away from him. He thought she'd be spending time by the pool and exploring with some of their old friends.

She was just going to keep letting him think that. She chastised herself for feeling any guilt over spending time with Jacob. Still the thought nagged at her that she'd spent her wedding anniversary in bed with another man. *Really romantic, huh?* She reminded herself the trip with Jackson was never intended to be a romantic one. It had been a means to an end. An end of their friendship and their marriage as she had instructed the lawyers to file the divorce papers first thing the following morning.

She hadn't noticed Jacob had come out of the bathroom until he was behind her and slipping his hands over her stomach. "What are ya thinking, babe?"

She leaned back into his embrace and turned her face to look up into his eyes. "I just don't want this all to end. You've made me so happy today, Jake. You came for me like you had promised. Will you really fight for me?"

He turned her around and led her toward the bathroom and the hot, steamy shower he had prepared for them. "You just try and stop me. You're my life now, and I won't let you go. You can count on that."

The small hotel bathroom was dark except for the light of several candles. Damn him, he'd thought of everything and every single trick in the book to romance her pants off. Not that he needed that. She was already naked and throwing herself at him. They stepped into the shower together, kissing, enjoying the feel of the water on their bodies and how slick their skin felt under their ever-exploring hands. Jacob grabbed the scrunchy, filled it with a vanilla-scented body wash, and lathered up Quinn's shoulders and back while he kept his mouth on hers. When she started to suck on his tongue, he gave her a surprise of her own. His hands were full of lather, so he dropped the scrunchy and trailed down her ass, spreading her cheeks. Quinn gasped as his fingers teased her anus, circling it several times before slipping inside up to his second knuckle. "I want to fuck your beautiful tight ass, baby. Are you ready for that tonight?"

She couldn't speak but only nodded. She trusted him completely and she knew he wouldn't hurt her. She just wanted to be with him as long as possible. She took the scrunchy he picked up off the shower floor, lathered up her hands, and started on his beautiful, fully erect cock. How the hell could he be ready to go so quickly? She reached down and stroked his balls then between his legs and trailed up to his ass and spread his cheeks a bit. That got him to chuckle and speed up lathering the rest of her body. Quinn could tell he wanted to fuck her ass so bad he could taste it. Hell, he had tasted it about an hour ago!

He turned her away from him so she could brace her hands against the shower wall while he bent her over a little bit at the waist. The head of his soapy cock slid between the cheeks of her ass, wanting to be inside her already, but not forcing himself on her. His soapy hands slid all over her lower back, gently tracing the mating dragon tattoo Derek had designed for her. He reached for another bottle next to the shampoo. A snap reached her ears and then a sudden cold sensation around her anus made her gasp.

"Soap won't be enough for this, honey. Relax." He squirted more lube over his cock and began to slowly guide the head of his cock inside her. There was just a slight moment of discomfort, but then she felt his hands on her hips and he gently reached around to find her clit. Quinn moaned as he seated himself in her ass all the way. He stopped and just held her close to him for a moment.

"Are you okay, baby doll?"

"Yes, baby, yessss. Fuck my ass, Jake."

More soap and thick cool lube slipped around her ass, and the hot water poured over them as he moved. Her body flushed from another orgasm that couldn't wait to flow out of her body. Cum ran down her thighs already as she shifted to meet his gentle thrusts, encouraging him to go a little harder and faster. "God, Quinn, your ass is so tight. You feel so good!" He covered her body while continuing to fuck her in the ass. His hands were on hers on the shower wall, and they kept moving and loving each other as if there was nothing else going on in the world.

Both of them forgot she had to leave him soon and go back to sleep in the same room with another man with whom she was not in love. Both of them forgot there were a lot of things standing in the way of them being together. Nothing mattered but their bodies locked together in that moment in time. He pulled her off the wall and up against him as he continued to come inside of her ass, his arms wrapped tightly across her tits. She clung to his arms, trying to keep steady as her knees threatened to buckle. She was afraid she was going to fall because the last orgasm took everything out of her.

Jacob shivered in spite of the hot shower and whispered hoarsely in her ear, "I love you, baby doll."

"Promise?"

"Forever. I promise you forever."

This time, she didn't pull away from him when he said that. She wanted to hear it over and over again. Quinn wanted to hear it at their wedding someday, but she was getting ahead of herself. First she had to get through the shower with him and get all the soap off before the water got any cooler. Then she had to find a way to tear herself away from her lover and go back to her snoring roommate. That's what she was to her now. She couldn't bring herself to think of him as her husband any longer. "I will hold you to that promise, Jake. But for now, can you pass the shampoo?"

"Only if you let me wash your hair for you."

"I think it would go faster if I did it myself, love. I am not sure I have another orgasm in me, but if you start washing my hair for me,

I'll start one and probably pass out from sheer ecstasy." Quinn couldn't help but giggle at the look on his face. "What, haven't you had an orgasmic hair washing before?"

"That would be the whole point now, wouldn't it? But if you insist on doing it yourself, can I at least play with the girls while you do it?" He raised and lowered his eyebrows like some sexual deviant, and Quinn slapped him in the arm before untangling from his embrace long enough to rinse off the remainder of the soap.

She tingled from head to toe now all because of him, and she wanted to cherish every single moment. "You need to get out of here so I can finish without distraction. Go on, get."

He grabbed her one more time and buried his face between her breasts and then reluctantly left her alone in the candlelit bathroom. Once her hair was rinsed, she stepped out of the shower as she went over what had happened that afternoon. She still couldn't believe he'd come for her and they'd finally made love. Wiping the steam from the mirror, she studied her reflection. She was actually glowing! Was this what it was like to be with someone who loved you as much as you loved them? Would this thing last?

Fuck it.

She was just going to see what happened. If they made it past tonight, she would worry about tomorrow then. She wrapped the large fluffy towels around her body. Thank God she'd dropped those last ten pounds before the trip. She felt really good about her body at the moment, and the love of her life loved every single inch of it. *Hm, for a hotel, the towels sure are large and fluffy.* She realized he had to have brought them in for tonight just for her. He was certainly hoping she would say yes.

Quinn was glad he had. And she was glad she'd said yes.

She walked out of the bathroom and found him stretched out on the bed, still quite naked, twirling her panties around on his finger. "What's this? A souvenir for me to remember you by?" He appeared to be struggling not to smile, but he couldn't stop it from forming in his eyes. "You know how I love it when your panties are drenched. And, honey, these are still very wet."

"You don't want them?"

"You just try to take them from me now." He put them back under his pillow and got up off the bed. He crossed the room so quickly that she stepped back when he reached for her and the towel.

"If only we had more time tonight, I would rip off that towel, toss you over my shoulder, and throw you back on the bed to continue fucking your brains out."

She dropped the towel at her feet and never took her eyes away from his. "Kiss me."

"But you have to go. Jack will be up soon and will be wondering where you are."

Quinn stepped closer so she was just inches away from him. His breath smelled of champagne. She wanted him and needed him to put all of his love into that one last kiss. "Kiss me, Jake. I need you to kiss me before I can leave here and go back to that room with him. Put your promise to me in this kiss, baby."

His eyes stay locked with hers, and his trembling fingers touched her arms, moving up, brushing against her breasts with his thumbs. Then his control broke. His hands cupped her face, and he brushed her damp hair back behind her ears as his lips touched hers, so softly at first she thought she was dreaming. But no, he had her right where he wanted her, right where Quinn wanted to be. His tongue gently probed through her eager lips to find its sparring partner. As soon as he found it, he brought both hands down around her waist and lifted her up so she was on tiptoe and had to put her arms around his neck to keep balance. Her hands ran through his hair while she enjoyed the hot pressure of his mouth on hers. He won the battle of their tongues, and he claimed his prize, sucking on her tongue, making her swoon.

He pulled back from the kiss and gazed into her eyes, still holding her close. Now it was his turn to ask her what she had asked him all afternoon. "Promise?"

"Forever, Jacob Hartley. I promise to love you forever." Before Quinn could say anything else, her phone rang. She knew by the ring tone it was Jackson wondering where she was and when she was going to get back. She guessed telling Jake about leaving Jackson would have to wait a little longer.

He let her go but kept his eyes locked on hers. "You'd better answer that."

She moved past him reluctantly and answered, "Hey, did you sleep well? I met up with a friend at the pool and we've been catching up." Jacob came up from behind, kissing her neck and distracting the hell out of her. "So, you want to order in or go out for dinner? Not feeling well? Maybe it was that burger you had this afternoon. No matter. I'll be there in a few. Bye."

She pulled on her shorts without her panties and reached for her bra. Jacob was already on that. "Need some help with this?"

She put out her hand and raised her eyebrows at him.

"Oh, all right. If you can get away later tonight, call me. I'll be up. Maybe we can spend some time together walking around in the moonlight in the hotel gardens?"

"I don't think that will happen tonight, love. Now that Jack's had a nap, he'll be up most of the night on and off flipping channels, but I'll see what I can do."

"Quinn, after what we shared this afternoon, I can't bear the thought of you being in his bed, giving yourself to him like you did with me."

She spun around and hugged him tight. "Shush. We've not had sex for fourteen months, and we haven't shared the same bed for the last six. Now that he's feeling like shit, there's no way he'll try anything tonight. There is no way in hell I could give myself to anyone like I have to you. You're the only one for me, Jake."

"And you're the only one for me. I'm so sorry it took this long for me to realize that. The thought that I could lose you forever, that kept me up for days on end. I'll be here for you always. Call me whenever you need me. No need to wait for any signal anymore. I already reprogrammed your phone with my new numbers. I left it under the name you had me stored under. I think it's appropriate for now, my Gwendolyn Rose."

The sparkle was back in his eyes now. Quinn knew that she had to leave right then or risk causing a scene with Jackson. She kissed Jacob one last time. "Dream of me, my Michelangelo."

He groaned against her breasts and kissed each one. "I have dreamt of you every single night since I first saw you at Saints and Sinners. Now my dreams are coming true, and I have more to dream about, a future and life with you. Now go, before I rip your clothes off again."

* * * *

CHAPTER 8

Steve planned to spend the afternoon in the club assisting the bartenders with the inventory. They were more than capable to complete it without him, but he needed to keep his mind busy. He knew Jacob was supposed to make his move with Quinn today, and his stomach had been in knots all afternoon worrying about it. Would Quinn really give him a chance after all this time and all she'd gone through over the last year and half with him? Would Jackson try to interfere? Would Jacob let his fears of rejection take over again?

Will Quinn completely forget about me once she has Jake back in her life?

His cell phone buzzed, indicating a new text message. He read the words on the screen and smiled. "She said YES!!! Spent last two hours together. More to come!"

Well, hot damn! He bet she'd given him a hard time at first, and Steve would've loved to see her deck Jacob for all he'd put her through. Of course, he'd hoped once she got that out of the way, she'd hear him out. The elevators opened up, and Steve sprinted to the club and nearly collided with Eric. "Jake text you, too?" The question was more or less mute by the look of Eric grinning from ear to ear.

"About fucking time, if you ask me! I've been pacing nonstop all day, waiting for him to let me know what was going on. Maredyth told me all the little things he'd planned in case she said yes. I've never seen him go all out like this. And it's all thanks to you."

"I just kept nudging him in the right direction and made sure he was at the right place at the right time. The rest of it was up to the two of them. Now, for the next stage in my plan to make sure things continue to go their way."

Walking back to the room she shared with her soon-to-be-ex-husband, Quinn's mind raced. She didn't want to spend another night in a room with Jackson, even if it had all been an innocent mix up with the reservations. So far their trip together had been nothing but strife. They'd been fighting for so long and living separate lives, neither one could pretend any longer. In her mind and her heart, her relationship with Jackson had ended before they'd celebrated their fifth anniversary.

Time for new beginnings and a new life.

She wanted to be with Jacob. She wanted to spend the entire night with him and wake up in his arms. She'd made it to their tenth anniversary, and as she promised Steve, she was going to finalize the divorce petition paperwork with the lawyers as soon as she got back to Oakland. She didn't think he would cause trouble since she'd planned to give up all claims on his entire inheritance. As he'd pointed out to her during their fights over their finances, fifty percent of everything, both debts *and* assets, belonged to her thanks to California law. Of course that wouldn't stop him from deciding to be nasty just to be nasty.

As Quinn reached the room, she hesitated at the door. Her hand shook, and she fumbled with the key card. Finally the damn thing flashed green and she entered the room. Jackson's snoring echoed throughout the room. *What the fuck?* She'd talked to him less than ten minutes ago and he'd sounded wide awake. The room reeked. He wasn't kidding that he didn't feel well. He must have some sort of food poisoning or intestinal bug. She sure as hell didn't want to get that. And of course he'd piled all of his stuff from the parks today on top of her bed.

Typical Jackson.

She moved into the bathroom and turned on the shower. Even though she had taken one already with Jacob, she thought it was better if she smelled like her own shampoo and conditioner and not like sex. She quickly scrubbed herself all over once again. No point in starting another fight with Jackson about who was still fooling around.

Quinn still couldn't believe she'd spent the last couple of hours with Jacob. She wasn't joking when she told him she wasn't sure she could walk right. The sensation of his cock inside her pussy and her ass sent new shockwaves through her body and her knees turned to jelly. She braced her hands against the shower walls and closed her eyes. Her heart yearned to be with him again and she vowed she'd trust her feelings this time and not let him go.

She heard the door to the bathroom open and Jackson mumbling something and vomiting. *Christ! This was the last thing either of us need on this trip!* "Jack, are you okay?" She peeked out around the shower curtain and saw him hovering over the toilet and holding on to the seat with white knuckles.

"I will be. It's almost over, I think, but you might not want to be in the same room with me tonight. It's really bad."

"I don't know if I can get another one tonight. The earliest I could move would be tomorrow afternoon, if they have a spot open up. Do you want me to try another hotel?"

"I don't know. I'm just warning you that I can barely stand myself tonight. You may want to see if you can hang out with your friends tomorrow or by the pool. I don't think I'll be good to go anywhere."

"Do you need a doctor? You really look bad." She followed him out of the bathroom, worried that he would fall.

He shuffled back to his bed and collapsed on top of it. "No, I just want to sleep. I feel a hell of a lot better than I did an hour ago. You should get out of here before you catch this thing."

Quinn's mind raced. Maybe she could spend a whole day with Jacob tomorrow out away from the hotel for a bit and then in the room as long as he wanted. "Janice is alone tonight with the kids. Carl won't be joining them until late tomorrow. She said they have a suite with a pullout. Maybe I can bunk with them? She did ask me if I wanted to have some girls' time after the kids were asleep."

"Whatever you want to do. No need for you to get a crappy night's sleep, too."

Quinn fished her cell out of her beach bag and rapidly scrolled through her contacts. Sure enough, he had updated his numbers. She chose the entry for his cell and pushed send. Her heart jumped into her throat when she heard his voice come over the line.

"Hello?"

"Hey, it's Quinn. Jack is really sick, and he's encouraging me to take you up on your offer of staying with you and the kids tonight." She hoped Jacob wouldn't think she'd lost her mind and would just go with her ruse.

His laughter tickled her ears and she turned her back toward Jackson to conceal her expression. "Baby, do you mean that you didn't get enough of me the first time and you want to come back for more?"

"That's right, *Janice*. Jack's miserable and doesn't want to ruin my vacation for me or the rest of the group. He'll probably be out most of the day tomorrow, too." She held her breath waiting for his answer.

"Grab some things for overnight and clothes for tomorrow. You may not need them. Depends on whether or not I let you get out of bed! Hurry back to me, baby doll."

Her heart fluttered and she couldn't stop a smile from spreading across her face. "I'll be down in a few minutes after I make sure Jack has everything he needs." She hung up and turned to Jackson to find him out cold again. She secured the Do Not Disturb sign on the door to prevent housekeeping from disturbing him before he was ready. She filled the ice bucket at the ice machine down the hall from the room, and raided the soda machine to stock up on Sprite for the mini refrigerator. Hopefully he'd feel better in the morning and be able to spend time with his friends.

She grabbed her overnight bag and stuffed her makeup in there with the rest of her toiletries. She grabbed another pair of shorts, tank tops, and underwear—the sexy stuff she'd purchased earlier in the day at one of the local boutiques on a whim. *At least someone is going to appreciate them while she was in Anaheim.* A wave of anxiety passed through her. She didn't understand why she'd be nervous about seeing Jacob again as she'd just left him. She shook her head. No. It wasn't Jacob who'd brought on this feeling, but Jackson. She knew he wasn't faking his illness, but something was off with him. From the mix up with their rooms, to his behavior all day at the parks, all of it nagged at her. He'd been acting suspiciously since they'd arrived. Her thoughts kept taking her to the idea he'd set all of this up in order to make her look bad in front of his friends. This was the Jackson she knew and not the one who showed up each week for their joint therapy sessions.

She called the front desk to remind them she was still in need of a room and asked they'd contact her, and not Jackson, as soon as they were able to accommodate her. Until then, she'd leave the rest of her things packed and locked in her roll away. She'd thought of taking it all with her to Jacob's room, but changed her mind. She'd wait to see how things played out over the next couple days.

Steve slung his arm around his senior bartender's shoulders and handed him a first class ticket to Anaheim.

"I don't understand. You want me to go spy on them?"

"Not exactly. I think it's time you spend some time with your family. Between you, Jake, and Maredyth, I'm hoping you can convince Quinn not to go back to the Bay Area with Jackson. Well, at the very least remind her that the Bay House is hers to share with Jake if they want to stay up there."

"You're giving them one of your houses?" Eric stared at Steve in disbelief. "You don't have to do that, you know."

"I had that one renovated specifically for Quinn. It's her house now, and there's no way she should ever feel she couldn't share it with your brother and make it their home. I'm not sure where she'll want to end up practicing after she comes off her medical leave, but at least she won't ever have to go back to her house in Oakland."

"What do you mean? Isn't she supposed to return with Jackson in a week? I thought they drove down there together at the suggestion of her therapist. I still think her doctor was off her rocker to suggest that, but I guess it's all part of letting go of the bullshit."

"That's where you come in. You keep her there for at least another week and leave the rest to me. Quinn had planned on moving the rest of her things out of her house when she returned from this trip, but I thought we'd give her a hand now. This was the only way we could get Jackson out of our way. I'm going to fly to Oakland with Derek and enlist Sarah's help to get her completely moved out of the Oakland house at the same time Jackson is served with the divorce papers in Anaheim."

"Oh, that is diabolical! I love it. Count me in."

"Good. Now go home and pack your bags for a two-week visit home. You deserve a little time off before you start your new job as my assistant."

"What?" Steve thought Eric was going to pass out there for a second. "Your assistant for what?"

"Everything. I think it's time I replaced Anthony. I'm getting older, and I need to make time for other things in my life. Quinn taught me that. Hell, if it wasn't for the Quartermarsh and Hartley families, I would've worked myself into an early grave already."

"Steve, I'm, I'm speechless."

"You've proven yourself on a daily basis with the club. I think you're the best person to help me continue to run my empire. And you've known me long enough to know when I see a sure thing, I go after it. I see you running one or more of my casinos on your own someday and loving every minute of it. You could help me build more of these clubs in all of them. What do you say?"

He stuttered and then smiled. "Oh, hell yes! I'm honored that you think I can do this, and I'll make you proud."

"You already have. Now let's get you to California and our couple moving in the right direction."

Steve's cell phone buzzed again. "She's on her way back to spend the night with me and for sure all of tomorrow. Jack's sick or something. Putting next stage into motion." He smiled and showed Eric the message.

"What is the next stage for him?"

"Now the fairy tale begins." Steve filled Eric in on what Jake had planned if Quinn were able to spend more time with him. Between Steve's connections, Jake's romantic side, and the magic of Disney, Quinn would be swept off of her feet.

Quinn practically ran to the stairwell that would take her to Jacob's room. She forced herself slow down and catch her breath. When she finally walked up to his door, she was surprised to find him standing there in the doorway, sipping a glass of champagne.

He reached out and took her overnight bag out of her hand and handed her his glass. Now that he had a free hand, he took hers and led her back into the room. The candles still burned, and he'd reset all the pillows, but this time he'd covered the bedspread with purple rose petals. A large bowl of strawberries sat on the night stand next to three cans of whipped cream.

Quinn lifted her eyebrows and gave him her best what-the-fuck look. Overwhelmed with his preparations, she kept silent.

He smiled and shrugged. "I told you I'd hoped you'd be with me tonight, and here you are."

She took her bag back from him, set it on the chair, and reached inside to pull out the leopard print teddy and panty set. His eyes nearly popped out of his head. "I brought you a surprise, too. Do you want me to model it for you?"

"Please." His voice was only a husky whisper, but conveyed the longing she felt for him in return. Quinn took a drink of his champagne and kissed him quickly before twisting out of his hands and escaping to the bathroom to change. He'd gone out of his way to make their night extra special and she wanted to do the same in return.

The bathroom was still warm from their shower, and she noticed new fluffy towels hung on the rack and even more rose petals over the floor. *Damn, he'd thought of everything!* She peeled off her clothes, folded them up, and placed them in the corner of the bathroom to take care of later. The soft, cool satin of the lingerie brushed over her nipples, and they immediately came to attention. The matching panties she'd purchased with the teddy slipped on quickly and accentuated her ass perfectly. There was a time not too long ago she would've been extremely self-conscious about wearing this for a lover, but not tonight. The push-up bra in the teddy brought her breasts up and together, making them appear even bigger. *Man, Jacob was going to faint when he saw them!* "Okay, close your eyes. I'm coming out."

When she stepped out of the bathroom, Quinn found him sitting on the edge of the bed, his eyes covered with both hands. She walked over to him and pulled his hands away. He kept his eyes closed. "Open your eyes, silly."

From his position her breasts ended up at his eye level. He let out a small gasp and looked up into her eyes. "Wow." He reached up and cupped her ass, pulling her closer so he could bury his face between her breasts. Her fingers slid from his shoulders to become entangled in his hair as his mouth found her throat. He knew that was a hot zone for her, and the inevitable happened. His hand moved to feel her brand new panties become drenched. His fingers quickly found the Velcro at her hips. He looked into her eyes and tore the panties away so they fell to the floor. "Yum."

He stood up and covered her mouth with his, crushing her tits to his chest with his embrace. Quinn sensed the desperation creeping back into their lovemaking, and she pushed him away a little bit. "Baby, slow down and let me catch my breath. We have all night."

"Are you really able to stay the whole night with me?" He sounded so vulnerable and unsure of himself. Her heart burst, and she just wanted to wrap him up in her arms and take away all the pain, all the uncertainty forever. She knew forever was a tall order, but at least she could try for that night.

"Yes, baby. We'll fall asleep in each other's arms and wake each other up making love, just like we fantasized over and over again. It's really happening." Now it was her turn to take his face into her hands, kiss him softly, and tease his tongue with her own until he gave in and brought his arms around her under the teddy. Quinn loved the way his hands felt on her skin. She pulled out of the kiss and moved her hands down his chest and abdomen, trailing down to the soft hairs below his belly button and the waistband of his boxers. She hooked her thumbs in the elastic and shoved them down his narrow hips, cupping his ass as she went lower. His body shuddered, and he sat back down on the bed so Quinn could ease off the boxers the rest of the way. "Lie back on the pillows, Jake." She kissed him deeply one more time and then he scooted back on to the pillows at the top of the king-sized bed.

She knelt on the bed and followed him as he slid up to the pillows. She crawled on her hands and knees, stalking him. Her tits bulged out of the top of the teddy, and he couldn't keep his eyes off of them. She crawled up his body, straddling his hips.

He sat up to catch her and pull her tight to him so he could once again bury his face between her breasts. His teeth tugged at the front of her teddy, loosening up the ties that held everything in place and at the same time reached up to pull down the straps. Now her breasts were free and he feasted on both nipples at once yet again.

Damn him! This wasn't what she'd had in mind for right then, but it felt so good she let him have a little fun before she pushed him back down onto the pillows.

He wouldn't go quietly. He grabbed the bottom of the teddy and pulled it up and over her head, attempting to tangle her arms up in it so he could take over. Quinn wasn't going to let him distract her from her mission. She tightened her thighs around his hips to get his attention. "Come on, lover, it's my turn to drive you wild."

"But I can't keep my hands off of you, babe." He gave her that little boy whiny voice on purpose, and she was having none of that.

She pulled his hands off of her body and pushed his arms over his head. In this position, her boobs hung down in his face and he wasted no time at all.

"Now I can get used to this position." He thrust his hips up, and his hard cock knocked to get into her pussy.

She sat up off of him so he couldn't enter her before she wanted him to. God, did she ever want him to, but she stuck with her original plan. She held his arms down over his head and slid down to kiss him, shoving her tongue into his eager, hot mouth. He'd been nibbling on strawberries and tasted sweet. She moved her hands down his arms, and he kept them there for the moment waiting to see what she'd planned to do next. She left his mouth, trailed kisses down his neck to his chest and teased his nipples with her tongue and teeth.

He brought his hands down and tangled his fingers in her hair, urging her lower. "I want to fuck you so bad, baby."

He watched her closely with eyes that sparkled in the candlelight. "Patience, lover. It's my turn to feast on you." With that, she slipped down and settled between his legs. She pushed them a little wider apart, making him laugh, and thrust his cock closer to her. She circled his throbbing shaft with both of her hands, squeezing it roughly, but wasn't complaining by the sounds and the moans of pleasure coming from him now.

She loved the feel of his cock in her hands, both soft and firm at the same time. The blood pulsed through it, making it jump against her fingers. She kissed the head and then took him into her mouth. His chest heaved and he gasped as she continued to take him all the way in and hold him there for a few beats before she slowly moved him back out. She swirled her tongue over the top of his cock as she popped him all the way out and then back in. With her other hand, she cupped both of his balls and massaged them while she sucked and licked his cock. She had him slick with her saliva and then he started to thrust against her, literally wanting to fuck her mouth. *What the hell?* She'd let him have his way. She tasted the pre-cum on her tongue. She grabbed his ass and got him to stop thrusting against her all the while keeping his entire cock in her mouth. She sucked hard on him, causing him to moan loudly.

"Goddamn, Quinn, I'm gonna explode." That was her cue to pop him back out and try something different. She took both tits and wrapped them around his cock tightly. Quinn opened her mouth and took in the head with each thrust of his dick through the cleft between her breasts.

"I, I can't stop, baby." His cum shot up into her mouth, and she managed to swallow most of it. Some escaped and coated her chest, making everything slick for his still hard, pulsing cock.

He reached for her and pulled her up his body, rolling them over so that she was on the bottom now. The rose petals clung to both of their bodies. She reached up and brushed some of them out of his hair as he looked down at her.

"You are so beautiful like this."

"What, covered in cum and flower petals?"

He chuckled then pulled her in tighter to him. "It's not the cum or the rose petals. You let down the walls and let me love you, all of you. I got to experience the wild, passionate, super-sexy woman that you've been keeping all locked up inside. Your face is radiant, and your eyes, your come-fuck-me eyes, I'm lost in them every time I look at you."

"So I guess you're happy I came back to spend the rest of the night with you?"

He pressed his forehead to hers and closed his eyes. "Happy doesn't describe all of what I'm feeling right now. I feel like I fell asleep after you left earlier and I'm dreaming all of this. I want to keep touching you, keep feeling your body against mine. If this is a dream, I don't ever want to wake up."

She felt the exact same way and couldn't believe she was there with him again. "It's not a dream. I'm right here with you. Can't you feel my heart pounding? I've never felt this way about anyone, *ever*, Jake. I mean that. No one has ever brought out all of this in me. You've had me in such knots for months now. I didn't know if I was coming or going, only that I wanted to be with you even for just one night. Whatever happened after that, then so be it."

Jacob shifted his body off of hers so they were now on their sides and face to face. He reached down to move one of her legs up to hook around his waist. "Were you going to leave earlier and not spend any more time with me?" The small catch in his voice didn't go unnoticed.

Oh God, he thinks I didn't want to be with him.

She traced his jawline with the fingertips of her left hand, and her right pressed against his back. He trembled under her touch. "I walked in here the first time thinking we would be together for a few hours and then part ways. I thought you were going to marry Iris and this was the only chance I was going to have to be with you and know if it was all fantasy or not. When you kissed me in this room, my resolve melted away. I wanted whatever you would give me. Then you told me you'd left her and you were here for me and that you were gonna fight for me…"

"I will fight. We belong together. *You* are my always and forever, and however long it takes, I'll wait for you." His mouth crushed hers, sealing his vow. The last bit of control she had inside broke away, and she clung to him, needing to be in his arms forever. He ended the kiss, and she couldn't speak. She stared deeply into his eyes as he shifted their bodies slightly and entered her quickly and fully. He just stayed that way, not moving, staring into her eyes, then he kissed her softly. "You are all that I want, all that I need." He started to move again, no longer desperate to prove they belonged together.

He just knew.

So did Quinn. Tears fell out of the corners of her eyes. Not sad tears. Happy tears. Tears of joy. This was what love was supposed to feel like. The bond between them was sealed, unbreakable. "Jake, Jake, mmmm. I love you so much, baby. I don't want anyone else. Just you." Even with the slow pace, an intense orgasm rolled through her body. Her pussy clenched around his cock, pulling at him, trying to keep them connected.

Jacob rolled them yet again so she was on top now. He sat up and cradled her in his arms so she could shift and wrap both of her legs around him, sitting in his lap and impaled on his cock. Quinn arched her back and pushed her tits toward him as her body took over and she moved against him. His lips were on her neck and then her breasts. His hands trailed down to grab her ass and help her move against him. She bit her lower lip as he parted her cheeks to find her anus again. He inserted one finger and then another, and she couldn't hold back any longer. "Jesus Christ, Jake. I can't, I can't stop my body."

"I don't want you to stop baby. Give it all to me."

Her body quaked, and she clung to him desperately. His hand trailed down between them, and he pulled her off of his cock again. Jacob reached for the bottle of lube next to them.

She gasped as the cool gel touched her anus and between the cheeks of her ass. He tipped her hips more toward him and then he entered her. Moving to lay her back on the bed, he kept his cock buried in her ass. He pulled her legs up to rest on his shoulders. Then his hands moved to her hips as he thrust harder, sending more shockwaves throughout Quinn's body. She clutched at the bedding, trying to hold on as he pounded his cock into her ass as deep as he could get.

"You love fucking my ass, Jake?"

He smiled and moved a little faster. That did it for her as yet another wave of orgasms hit her. "Jake, mmmmmm. Oh, *God!*"

"Yes, baby. I, I, Jesus Christ, I'm gonna come again." His breath came faster, and he clutched at her hips, digging in his nails as he went rigid. His cock softened as he pulled out of her, parting her legs so he could cover her body once again. Quinn held him close, covering his face with kisses.

"Open your eyes, Jake. Look at me."

He took a deep breath and did what she asked.

"We will be together. I promise. Technically, I've already left Jackson. We haven't lived in the same house since April."

Jacob looked puzzled. "Why are you here with him in Anaheim?"

"It's a bit complicated, but for now just know that it's all part of my plan to be free of him and his family completely. My lawyers are standing by for me to give them the go-ahead. I don't want to talk about all of it tonight. I just want to concentrate on you and me."

He rolled over onto his back and propped himself up on the pillows. "So do I. Come here, baby." She scooted up and back into his arms, settling her head onto his chest. "Now this is what I want, you falling asleep with your head on my chest after telling me that you'll be mine forever. Perfect way to end the day if you ask me."

She loved it when he laughed, especially when her head was on his chest. The rumble tickled her ear and made her smile. Quinn traced her fingertips along his chest and abs, enjoying just being with him. Now she felt like she could fall asleep. She wasn't afraid she would wake up and he would be gone. He'd promised her forever and this time she knew it was for real and not a fantasy. "I agree that it's the perfect end of the day, but the night is just getting started."

"That it is, baby doll. Are you hungry?" He kissed her quickly and slid his tongue over hers. "For food, that is?"

"Now that you mention it…" Quinn sat up and reached across him for the strawberries. She offered one to Jacob and settled back into his arms, nibbling on a berry of her own. "I haven't eaten since noon. What time is it, anyway?"

He covered up her eyes with both of his hands. "Do you really want to know what time it is, or are you trying to figure out how much time we have left together?"

"I don't want to think about leaving you yet, so don't get me obsessing over the time we have left. I was just curious if we still could order something in. I don't want to get dressed and go anywhere. I'm right where I want to be." She turned to bury her face in his neck as his arms tightened around her. "Don't let me go, baby."

"I won't ever do that again. I do, however, have to feed you at some point. I have more surprises for you, but you have to let me out of the bed for a few minutes to get them."

"Oh, all right." She smiled. "What more do you have hidden in this room?"

He slipped out of the bed and over to the cooler in the corner. *Why didn't I notice that before?*

He reached inside to pull out several small containers and a serving tray. Quinn started to get out of bed to see what he was doing, but he made her stay put and told her to be patient.

Yeah, that was going to happen!

"If you really want to do something, you could refill the champagne glasses. I'll meet you back in the bed in a second." He fiddled with things in the cooler, and it piqued her curiosity. Still, she did what he'd asked and filled up the glasses, dropping a couple of strawberries into each one. Quinn moved back to the bed and found her teddy on the floor. She put that back on and retied the laces so her tits were prominently displayed once again. She settled back in bed on the pillows and waited to enjoy his next surprise.

Jacob had stopped filling up the tray with dishes of food and watched her, smiling. "Why did you put that back on? You know I'll just peel it off of you again."

"Hey, I paid good money for this thing, and I'm going to wear it every chance I get. The panties are toast though. Still too wet to put back on."

"Don't you dare put *any* panties back on. I'll rip them off of you and I mean it." He was still smiling, but she knew he meant what he said. He'd always told her he wanted her to be naked and ready for him at all times. No problem there, but her stomach was really growling now, and he was taking so long to cross the room with the food.

"What do you have on that tray?"

"I remembered something you told me once. That you can change the taste of your cum with the foods you eat. So I made sure to get some of your favorite foods so we can experiment on our own. Are you game?"

He had gone all out with little dishes filled with a variety of Quinn's favorite fruits and cheeses and even some deli meats. Her stomach rumbled and growled.

Jacob laughed again. "I'll take that as a yes."

She eyed the pineapple greedily and handed him his glass of champagne when he settled in next to her on the pillows. "Where do we start?" She took another sip of the bubbly, which was fast going to her head. The lack of food in her stomach helped to make her quite tipsy. She wondered if that was another one of his plans.

He picked up a bite-sized piece of pineapple, put part of it in his teeth, and leaned over to offer it to Quinn. Now she understood where he was going with all of this, and she liked it. She liked it *a lot*. As soon as she bit down on the pineapple, he pulled it all the way into his mouth and kissed her quickly before she could protest. He had another piece that he traced over her lips, teasing her a bit before feeding it to her.

She smiled, the one he called her naughty smile, and he bit his lower lip waiting to see what she was going to do.

She picked up a piece of pepper jack cheese and start to offer it to him but then pulled it away. Instead, she placed it between her breasts. Quinn took another drink of her champagne, watching him over the top of the glass. He kept his eyes locked on hers, leaning closer until he was just inches from her lips. She could barely hold still. His gaze dropped to her chest then returned to her face before his lips found hers then trailed down her neck to the top of her breasts. His tongue found the cleft between them, trailing down to the cheese. "Mm, now that's what I am talking about, baby doll."

"The cheese or the way it was served?" She winked and reached around him for another piece of fruit. Being this close to Jacob and his magic tongue sent her whole body into overdrive, but her stomach was really complaining now. She had to eat more food before she got lost in his eyes again.

"Honestly, I don't think I tasted the cheese at all. You put anything on those tits of yours and I want it. Plain and simple."

"You've got a one-track mind when it comes to boobs." She offered him a piece of salami, and he took it between his lips, sucking on her finger tips.

"You know I'm a boob man, but the first time I saw yours in those pictures you sent me it was all over. I knew I had to have them and the woman attached to them. I was falling in love with you before that, and 'the girls' just clenched it for me."

"Aw, thank you, baby. And for the record, the strawberries that you've eaten so far tonight made your cum taste so sweet." They reached for the mangos at the same time so they fed each other the fruit. Her eyes rolled back as she savored the sweet sensation in her mouth. "That is fantastic. When did you get the time to do all of this?"

"I just went with it all and hoped you'd say yes. If you didn't, well, I would have a lot of food to take home to my sister and the kids. I had thought of our first night together over and over since we started this between us. I wanted to give you all the romance you deserved. Jack doesn't get that about you, but I do."

Quinn placed her hand on his cheek, feeling a little bit of stubble that she found so irresistible. "You do, don't you?" He turned his face to kiss her palm and then pulled her close, her lips close to his ear. "I'm so happy you finally came for me." His arms tightened around her as she pulled back to look into his eyes. "I love you, Jacob. There's not a moment that I'm not thinking of you, wishing you were with me. My soul wasn't complete without you in my life. When I thought you were lost to me forever, I just gave up."

"I, I'm so sorry, Quinn. I never, ever meant to hurt you like that. I kept denying to myself how much I was in love with you. I thought there was no way we could be together, so I just kept going through the motions in my life, but there was that nagging feeling. My life became very empty without you in it. The sound of your voice when you told me that you were in love with me and you thought I didn't feel the same way—that damn near killed me."

"Then why didn't you tell me? I remember that day all too well. You even said you were sorry for leading me on to think that. You'd just confirmed my worst fear, and it devastated me. If you didn't feel that way, why didn't you say it then? Why did you go so long without contacting me? I thought you didn't want me anymore."

"I thought it was best to let you go at that point and let you think it was over. I couldn't give you the life you deserved. Hell, we didn't even know if we would feel the same way in the real world as we did with our fantasies. I couldn't ask you to give up everything for me and then have it all fall apart."

"What changed your mind?"

"No matter what I was doing or who I was with, I kept thinking of how it would be if you were there with me. How would you like this new restaurant, or any movie I was watching? How different would it be with you in my bed curled up against me? I heard your voice in my head when I asked those questions, and I longed to really hear you and to see you, to touch you. I guess I became really withdrawn. Iris got suspicious and started switching phones with me, monitoring the computer, and the Xbox. Hell, even her kids were telling her what I was or wasn't doing. I couldn't take it anymore."

Quinn kept quiet and let him talk. She'd told him a long time ago she didn't think Iris was right for him. She was so controlling, and he'd let her do it. He'd actually created that monster whether he wanted to admit it or not, but there was no way she was going to remind him of that now. He was right here with her and not with Iris. He'd finally chosen her. "When did you break off your engagement?"

"Honestly, it was over before it even started. As soon as I let her have the ring, I regretted it. Hearing the pain in your voice after you found out about it on your own tore me up inside. But I kept telling myself that you were married and I couldn't have you, so why not eventually marry Iris. She was there and available."

Quinn settled back against the pillows and let Jacob tell the story of how he finally ended his engagement. He had agreed to go to Greenville for spring break at the end of May to help her look for a place to live, but when they returned to Chicago he was going to move out and try to figure out what he wanted. "Iris was in denial even then. She was sure I would change my mind as soon as we were in North Carolina with her family. She refused to see I was pulling away from her, even after her sister pointed it out repeatedly. Jacqui followed me around, watching my every move to be sure I didn't try to contact you.

"I'm sorry you had to go through that. You had to know her family was going to be that way. They were just trying to protect Iris."

"I guess I didn't think about it all that much until it was happening. They had more control over me than they did over the kids. Finally I had enough. I rented a car and drove back early. I called work and told them I was available to cover the holes in the schedule for the rest of the month. Iris assumed I was doing this to make extra money for the move, but her family knew otherwise. They'd sent Jacqui's husband Aaron after me under the pretense that he'd help start packing up the house.

"When did Iris get back to Chicago?"

"She got home about a week later on a tear trying to find out if I was in contact with you or anyone else. She called work to see exactly when I was scheduled and even kept trading phones with me left and right. One night, it all came to a head."

Jacob snatched his phone off of the charger before Iris could take it. "The phone switching thing stops now."

"Why? Are you expecting a call from someone?" She followed him into the kitchen and leaned against the counter. "You didn't have a problem switching phones with me before, so why now?"

"It's over, Iris. It has been for a long time."

She moved over to the kitchen table and sat in the chair next to his. "What do you mean it's over? Are you breaking up with me?"

He reached over and held her small hands gently with both of his own. "You are an amazing woman and you deserve someone who can love you and take care of you for the rest of your life. That's not me. My heart will always want to be with someone else, and that is not fair to you or to the kids."

"You don't know what you're saying, Jake. As soon as we move to Greenville, we'll have our new life together as a family, as the family that you've always wanted. Why are you trying to throw that all away for someone who's already moved on with her life? The two of you never even slept together. How the hell do you know that she is the one for you? I've been here with you all this time. Doesn't that count for anything?" Tears formed in her eyes and her cheeks turned dark red.

His heart ached for her. He knew he was hurting her all over again, but he was determined to get it all out now. "Yes, it does mean the world to me that you stuck by me through all of this. That doesn't change the fact I'm not in love with you. It's not fair for me to keep this going hoping that my feelings for you will grow into something more. You don't need another loveless marriage under your belt. You deserve so much better than that and I won't let you settle for it anymore."

He pulled off the engagement ring Iris had given to him and placed it on the kitchen table. She just stared at it with her eyes wide, not saying a word.

"Right from the very start we didn't have a chance. My heart has and always will belong to Quinn. I'm so sorry."

* * * *

CHAPTER 9

"Holy shit! What did she do?"

"She stared at the ring for a long time and then pulled hers off and threw it at me. The ring wasn't even hers to begin with."

"I don't understand. The ring wasn't hers?"

He smiled sadly. "I bought the ring to give to the woman I wanted to spend the rest of my life with. I had it locked away and safe, or so I'd thought. Iris found it and had assumed it was for her. She'd never looked at the engraving inside: 'my heart and soul.' That ring was meant for you, and I let her ruin it. It would've looked beautiful on your finger, Quinn."

"Oh, Jake." She took his hand and squeezed it tightly, urging him to continue with his story when he was ready.

"I picked the ring up off the floor and put it in my pocket. She threw a couple of dishes at me, and then she told me to get the fuck out of her house."

"Didn't it make things awkward at work after that?"

"You could say that. I went to our boss and told her Iris and I had broken up and requested that we not be on the same shifts if possible. Good thing I did too because Iris went in there the next day and tried to manipulate the schedule. She didn't count on so many of our coworkers and supervisors to take my side. Of course, she didn't let that stop her. I had to change the combination on my locker so she couldn't get into my things. It was a hell of a month, let me tell you."

Quinn could see why he didn't call her during that time. It sounded like he had gone through a lot of shit and barely had time to think, let alone a free moment to call her. She sat up and nibbled on some more meat and cheese while he continued with his story.

"Iris had called my family trying to get them on her side in this thing, and they more or less told her they were going to stay out of it and respect my decisions no matter what. That didn't go over too well with her. I guess she'd built up this fantasy they all loved her and would do what she wanted. Truth be told, my family didn't like her much and *really* didn't care for her kids. They all warned me to stay away from her, but I wouldn't listen. She'd kept up her efforts to turn them against you. Of course, Eric already knew you and pretty much told her to fuck off when she called him."

Quinn nearly choked on the piece of cheddar she had in her mouth. "What was she telling them?"

"Pretty much what they already knew. That you were married and having an affair with a known mobster. I was just going to be another notch in your belt. What's so funny?"

Quinn was practically hysterical with laughter now. "Steve, a mobster. You, another notch in my belt?"

Jacob laughed with her. "Yep. You were going to use me and toss me aside when you were done with me."

"They didn't believe her, did they?" She stopped laughing and worry crept over her. Eric knew about her love affair and ongoing friendship with Steve, but the rest of them didn't know her from Adam. The last thing she wanted was to alienate the Hartleys.

He grabbed some more of the salami for himself and fed her another pineapple piece. "Maredyth keeps asking me when she gets to meet you, so I don't think you have anything to worry about. I've never felt this much passion for anyone before, and my sister can tell just by the way I talk about you that you're my one true love. My mom will love you because I do, plain and simple. And you know Eric has always adored you. Don't worry, Quinn."

She smiled at her lover. "The only person who matters to me right now is you. As long as you love me, I can get through just about anything." She chose another piece of mango and put it between her breasts. "Are you still hungry, lover?"

He chuckled and pulled her to him so she could straddle his hips again. His cock grew harder as he sat all the way up. His hands trailed up her back and he grabbed her hair and pulled her head back to expose her neck, shoving her breasts forward. The touch of his lips on the skin of her neck nearly caused her to swoon. He let go of her hair, and he reached for something on the nightstand. Quinn opened her eyes just in time to see what he had in his hand, the whipped cream. "This will go great with mango, don't you think?"

She giggled as the whipped cream fill the cleft between her tits. Jacob removed the mango with his lips and then licked off the whipped cream. Her hard nipples chaffed against the satin of her teddy. She wanted to be free of the fabric so Jacob could suck on them again.

The man was a mind reader. He tugged at the ties quickly and pulled the teddy up and over her head, freeing her full breasts. He took the can of whipped cream and shook it. This time he circled her nipples with the cool cream, and she gasped as he took one of them into his mouth to suck off the sweet foam. Her cunt pulsed with need for him and his cock inched its way inside her. Jacob grabbed her ass and lifted her up so he could enter her all the way. Quinn tried to move, but he held her tight. "Slow down, baby, we've got all night."

"I, Jake, I can't stop." She could barely speak anymore but managed to whisper hoarsely as Jacob eased her up and down his shaft. "I have dreamt of being with you this way, but this is so much more than—ohhhh, God, baby."

He leaned back to rest on the pillows, still slowly moving her up and down his shaft. He trembled beneath her, and that triggered another orgasm to race through her body. He let go of her ass and trailed his fingertips up her back, pulling her down to kiss him. His tongue tasted of mango and whipped cream, which magnified her excitement. She moved faster against him, wanting more and more each time his cock entered her cunt.

Jacob suddenly turned them over in the bed so she was on the bottom again. "Open your eyes, baby doll."

She loved the feel of his body on hers and opened her eyes to see him watching her intently. His cheeks were flushed and his eyes dark and smoky in the candle light. "What do you see?"

"I see the light of the candles dancing in them. I see all the love I feel for you right now reflected back to me, making my heart want to jump out of my chest. I see...my entire world."

She choked back a little sob and pulled him into another kiss, holding him tightly around his neck and shoulders. His knees pushed her legs further apart as he thrust harder and faster. "Jake, Jake." She moaned and bit her lip to hold back a scream. His cock felt so fucking fantastic inside of her. The faster and harder he went, the more powerful the tremors zipping through her body.

"Mmmmmm, Quinn, I'm so close."

Her hips snapped up against him, nearly lifting him off of her. Her nails dug into his back as his body gave in completely. "Harder. Oh, yes!"

Jacob thrust twice more and collapsed on top of her. Quinn cherished the feel of him inside of her and the taste of his mouth on hers. She loved the way their bodies molded together, covered in sweat, cum, and rose petals. This was what she wanted every night for the rest of her life.

"Holy shit, Quinn. What are you doing to me?"

She reluctantly let him go and looked into his eyes. "What do you mean?"

"I want nothing more than to make love with you constantly. I don't care about eating, drinking, talking, nothing but being right here with you. "

She knew exactly what he meant. She was more than a little overwhelmed by it all herself. "So, is what you're feeling a good or a bad thing?" She had been afraid to ask, but she had to know and be sure they were on the same page. After what they had experienced so far that night, Quinn hoped he wouldn't pull away from her again.

Her worry must have been written all over her face. "Oh, no, baby doll. It's only a good thing. You can't get rid of me that easily."

"Are you sure this is what you want? To be with me forever?"

He didn't miss a beat. "I'm absolutely sure and I'll fight for you for as long as it takes. There's no doubt in my mind anymore. My heart won't let you go again."

"I won't let you go either, Jake, but you're going to have to let me out of this bed right now."

"Why?"

"I have to pee!" She pushed him off of her and left him laughing in the bed. She scooted to the bathroom to relieve herself. Her legs were a bit wobbly after making love for several hours, but other than that she was feeling fucking fantastic. Not only had her fantasies come true, they'd been more than fulfilled. Being with Jacob was everything she'd ever dreamed it could be. Unfortunately, she still had to deal with Jackson. The original plan had been to drive back with him in four days. The idea of spending any more time with him turned her stomach.

She put those thoughts out of her head. She didn't want to worry about anything at all and just be with Jacob tonight and tomorrow. Whatever came after that they could deal with together. A knock on the door brought her out of her head.

"Babe, are you okay?" Jacob pushed opened the door, but didn't look inside. "You've been in here a while. Can I come in?"

"Sure."

He slipped into the room and brought his arms around her. He kissed her neck and gazed into the mirror at their reflection. Both of them were still flushed from their lovemaking and covered in rose petals. "I think it's time for more shower fun, don't you?"

She smiled at him in the mirror. "Um-hm." She loved the feel of his arms around her but not the sticky residue on her chest from the fruit and whipped cream. The only good thing about that stuff was that it gave her an excuse to hop back into the shower with Jacob. "Do you think we can get more sheets from housekeeping?"

He chuckled in her ear again. "What? You don't want to sleep in cum-soaked sheets tonight?"

She looked into his eyes in the mirror and shook her head. "Hey, a girl's gotta draw the line somewhere."

"Don't worry, love. I've got it covered."

"You really thought of everything, haven't you?"

"I wanted to make all our fantasies come true tonight. I wanted you to see and feel how much I love you and want you in my life."

She turned around and kissed him. "You've exceeded any fantasy I've ever had about you. What I wanted the most in the world was for you to want me in your life, to love me as much as I love you and will always love you. How about you? Have your dreams come true tonight?"

"God, yes. You took my hand this afternoon and took a chance on us. You let me into your life and your heart again."

He reached into the shower stall and turned on the water. He closed the shower doors and turned to her, pulling her into a deep kiss, trailing his hands down her bare back. As her knees buckled, his embrace tightened, molding her body to his. He lifted her up and sat her on the vanity next to the sink. "I want to test our theory about your cum tasting like the foods you eat. Let's see, you ate a lot of mango and pineapple."

She leaned back as his mouth slid down her body. His hands caressed her thighs as he brought them up to rest on his shoulders. He rubbed his stubbly cheeks and chin on her inner thighs.

She purred and gasped as he treated her to his magic tongue. Her body responded the only way it could with another wave of passion. Cum flowed freely from her and into his eager mouth.

He licked and sucked and licked some more. He firmed up his tongue and thrust it deep within her pussy, all the while working her clit with his thumb.

Her thighs kept clenching and trembling around his face, but that just turned him on more, and he grabbed her ass to help him fuck her with his tongue. Quinn clutched the end of the vanity with one hand, and the other she kept tangled in his hair. He was pushing her over the edge yet again, and she didn't care. She wanted it all. "Mmmmmm, your tongue is fucking fantastic!"

Jacob looked up at her and winked. "I can't get enough of your pussy. You taste so sweet, baby. I think I'm gonna feed you pineapple, mangos, and strawberries every single day." He moved his mouth quickly up to her throbbing clit and suckled hard, thrusting three fingers into her cunt, bringing her to yet another climax. His hand was drenched in cum, and he put it up to her mouth so she could taste, too. She sucked on his fingers, licking them clean. That pushed him over the top, and he stood up, lifting her up off of the vanity and down onto his cock.

She held on to him tightly while he spun around and pinned her against the bathroom wall. Over and over again he plunged into her. "Jesus Christ, Jake. I don't know if I can take much more of this."

"It feels like we're making up for all the time we've spent apart." His voice became a hoarse whisper in her ear. Her entire body flushed. Her breasts were so tender, the lips of her cunt so swollen with need for him, to give everything she had left to him. And she did. They climaxed together against the bathroom wall and clung to each other, struggling to breathe normally again.

Jacob pulled out as his cock softened. He let her legs slide down his hips so she was standing tiptoe with her arms still locked around his neck. Quinn was afraid to let go. She wasn't sure her legs would support her weight any longer.

"Don't let go, Quinn."

She sobbed against his shoulder. "Never again, Jake."

He tipped her chin up to make her look into his eyes. He reached up and brushed the tears from her cheeks. "Come on. Let's take that shower, change those sheets, and get some sleep. You've drained every ounce of energy from me. I want to be able to spend the whole day with you tomorrow but if we don't get some rest, we'll sleep through it.

She stepped into the stall and stood under the hot shower, letting it cascade down her shoulders and back. As the steamy water washed over her body, she closed her eyes and tipped her head back to get her hair wet. She didn't hear the shower doors open up because of the water in her ears, but she knew Jacob had joined her when his hands and arms encircled her body. She smiled as he nuzzled up to her neck. His stubble was gone.

"Were you afraid that you were giving me whisker burn?"

"Uh-huh. Gotta think ahead. I don't want to put anything on your body that will tip Jackson off to where you were tonight."

Quinn felt the scrunchy on her back lathered with that vanilla-scented soap for the second time that night.

"Baby, when did you get the dragon tat? It looks like Derek's work, like the ones on my back. I saw a sketch he was working on for you the day he finished mine. Is this the end result?"

"I had it done when I went for the conference this year. Derek had designed it for me after I told him what colors I'd wanted. I was going to surprise you with it, but then things changed." That's when her world fell apart, but that didn't matter anymore. She was with Jacob now, sharing a shower like they'd fantasized about on many occasions. "What do you think of it?"

"It's beautiful, just like you. And I see you added another butterfly." His fingers traced the one on her right thigh and then the one on her left. "Derek said he'd always wanted to use you as a canvas."

Quinn smiled. "He still does. After the first butterfly, I realized that those needles weren't too bad and I could do it again, so I added the second butterfly the following week after you left to move to Chicago."

Jacob laughed. "I bet Derek and the other guys got a kick out of that. You go years chickening out and then you get two in one trip! I remember Eric mentioning it to me that you got another tat, but with everything that's happened, it slipped my mind." He turned them around so he was directly under the water and he could continue to explore and lather up her body.

Quinn grabbed the shampoo bottle, squirted a little into her hands, and reached up to wash his long thick hair.

"Mmmmmm, magic fingers on my scalp. I definitely could get used to this."

"Lean back and rinse off the shampoo before it gets into your eyes." She took the scrunchy from him and started to lather up his chest and abs while he rinsed out the shampoo. He tried to take it back from her, but she put it behind her back so he had to embrace her again. His lips found hers, teasing her with his tongue while sliding his chest over hers, getting everything all soapy.

Damn! She couldn't keep him away from her breasts if she tried. Not that she really wanted him to leave them alone, but she was finding it very fun teasing him with them. He turned her around so her back was against his chest, and he stole the scrunchy back. After he applied more soap to it, he slid it all over her chest and stomach and then down to cover her hips and thighs.

Quinn tried to move away from him a little bit, but he held her tightly against his body, gliding his soapy hands over her breasts, squeezing them together and letting them fall back to rest in his hands yet again. She took the scrunchy back and relathered her hands. She reached around to soap up his hips slowly grinding against her ass. This time they simply enjoyed the feel of their slick bodies against each other. He brought her back under the cascading water to rinse off the soap from their bodies and then he started massaging her scalp. Quinn wasn't the only one with magic fingers in that shower. She could have fallen asleep in there, but he was on to her and quickly helped her rinse out the remaining shampoo.

The water had turned from steaming to warm. The temperature change chilled her body. Goose bumps formed over her skin, and her nipples puckered to sharp points. Jacob reached behind her and turned off the water. "Come on, doll. Your eyes are drooping, and I want to fall asleep with you in my arms in bed, not the shower."

Quinn quickly kissed him once again. "Good idea."

He produced two more of those fluffy towels they'd used earlier. He wrapped her up in one, secured the second around his waist and stepped out of the shower. "You go ahead and blow-dry your hair in here, and I'll put the clean sheets on the bed."

"I can help—"

No, don't argue. Let me take care of this."

"I'm warning you. I could get used to all of this pampering."

He kissed her on the forehead and left her alone in the bathroom. She turned on the hotel hair dryer and quickly went to work on her short hair. Two days ago she'd given her hair dresser to go ahead to give her the spikey, sassy cut she'd had the first time she'd met Steve and Jacob. Not only was it so much easier to manage while on vacation, the wild style reminded her to stop living in the past and grab life by the balls. No more would she put her happiness on hold. She owed it to herself and to those she loved to make good on that promise.

Out of the corner of her eye, she noticed a flash of purple. She glanced around the vanity and noticed that Jacob had brought in her little toiletry bag from her suitcase. *He really did think of everything.*

Hair dried and teeth brushed, now she was ready for bed with her lover. Quinn kept the towel secured around her and stepped out of the bathroom to find Jacob just turning down the bedding and fluffing up the pillows. *Holy cow! Are those silk sheets?*

He caught the expression on her face and smiled. "Yeah, these are silk. Only the best for you, my love."

"You didn't have to do all of this."

"Yes, I did. I told you I wanted to give you a night to remember." He crossed the room, and this time she didn't step back from him. He grabbed the towel away and threw it back toward the bathroom. He scooped her up into his arms and carried her over to the bed.

"Good Lord, you're gonna break your back. Put me down!"

He smirked. "As you wish." He dropped her onto the bed. "Happy now?"

"Not until you join me." She scooted over to the other side of the bed and made room for him, patting the mattress next to her. Jacob didn't say a word and kept his eyes locked with hers as he climbed into the sheets. He settled back onto the pillows, and Quinn snuggled up next to him, resting her head on his right shoulder. He tipped her chin up toward him so that he could kiss her again.

"With you right here in my bed with me, I can finally go to sleep dreaming of you because when I wake up again, you'll still be here, Quinn. You have no idea how many nights I've wished for this, and now here you are."

"I think I have a pretty good idea what you're feeling right now. Goodnight, baby." Before she knew it, she was snuggled up in his arms, feeling the rhythm of his heart beating against her hand on his chest. Their breathing slowed as they both fell into a deep peaceful slumber, dreaming of each other and waking up in each other's arms.

* * * *

CHAPTER 10

The room was still dark when Quinn woke up with a start, not knowing where she was for a moment. Her heart beat wildly as she surveyed the room. The empty bottle of champagne stood on the night stand. Her teddy still lay on the floor next to the bed along with some other random clothing pieces. She smiled as she realized where she was, with Jacob. She'd indeed fallen asleep in his arms and it wasn't all a dream this time. *Holy Shit!*

She looked over to see his serene face just inches from her own. She wanted to touch him to be sure he was real, that she wasn't imagining the whole thing, but she didn't want to wake him up yet. She glanced over at the clock on the nightstand. It was just 3:00 a.m. She had thought she had been asleep for longer than the three hours the clock was telling her. She felt amazing and wanted to start the day with him, even if they just stayed in the hotel room in the bed covered in silk sheets. Unfortunately, her body had other ideas. *Damn bladder!*

Washing her hands and face, she kept thinking about all that Jacob had done to make the night sensual and memorable. Not only had he remembered all of their fantasies they'd shared with each other, he came up with a few surprises on his own to ensure she fell in love with *him* and not the fantasy. He'd definitely succeeded.

She collected the clothes she'd left in the bathroom and put them back into her overnight bag. She found the shirt Jacob wore that day on the chair near the window and put it on. The scent of his cologne lingered in the fabric, and her body responded to it immediately. Man, how was she going to get through her day-to-day life without him? She had kept those thoughts out of her head for most of the night with him, and now the reality of their situation crept back in.

Jacob was finally free to be with her, but she wasn't available quite yet. She had to call Steve to give him the go-ahead to push the divorce through even faster. Until Jacob told her that he'd left Iris, she'd thought she would go ahead with the divorce and then see where the relationship with Steve ended up. Now she had to figure out how to tell him that Jake had finally found her and they were planning their future. They'd been through so much together in the last year and half. She didn't want to hurt him, but Jake was her heart. No matter, she didn't have to think about all of that for the next few days so she might as well slip back into bed. Jacob reached out for her and pulled her close to him, spooning up behind her.

"Hey, are you wearing my shirt again?" He reached under the shirt to cup her breasts, but only after he made sure she didn't have the nerve to slip on more underwear. He moved one hand lower between her thighs and found out exactly how wet she was for him already.

"As soon as I put your shirt on and smelled your scent on it, my body prepared itself for you. Does that make you happy?"

Jacob pulled her tighter against his body, making it easier for his cock to enter her from behind. Her body shuddered and shook, but he didn't move. "What do *you* think?"

She tipped her head back a little bit so he could nibble on her neck and completely send her over the edge. "Don't stop, baby."

Jacob began to move, pulling his cock nearly all the way out of her before easing it back in. The slow, sleepy fuck they'd fantasized about was now a reality, and it was so much better than she could have ever imagined. Quinn felt so close to him at that moment, almost like they were one person and always had been.

Quinn was sure Jacob felt it, too, and he kept up the steady pace bringing her to another orgasm, with another one fast on its heels. Her pussy clenched around his cock spasmodically through each one. He moaned as he pulled out during one such clenching episode. His lips were at her ear, nibbling as he whispered her name softly over and over again.

She clutched at his arms around her chest and waist as she gave in to the passion coursing through her body. She bit down on her lower lip, holding back from crying out his name and maybe a few choice swear words. In this position, Jacob's cock caressed every inch of her cunt. Every single nerve ending inside her was stimulated beyond her wildest dreams.

She closed her eyes and held on as his thrusts slowed and stopped. She was afraid to move at all. She didn't want to break the spell between them. Her heart was nearly bursting with love for him, and she didn't know what to say to make sure he knew it. She didn't have to worry about that, as it turned out.

"Do you have any idea how much I love you right here and now, baby doll? My cock was not the only thing that exploded. Yeah, I know that sounds corny, but it's the only way I know how to explain it."

He released his bear hug, and she turned toward him so that they were now face to face, arms and legs entwined, both of them breathing heavily. She smiled, kissed his chin and then his lips. "You don't have to explain it to me at all." She took his hand and placed it over her heart. "I feel it in here every time we touch. It's almost overwhelming at times, but I don't care. I want to be with you always, Jake."

"Shhhh. No worries, love. I know we'll be together forever, and I meant what I said to you. I'll fight for you and wait for you as long as it takes. There is no doubt in my mind that we'll have what we want."

"So, until that time, what are your plans for me today?"

Jacob let her go, rolled over onto his back, and stretched his arms over his head. "Well, besides ravishing you every which way I can imagine, I guess I could let you out of this room for a bit and maybe take you out for an early dinner or whatever. When do you have to be back with Jack?"

Quinn sat up in the bed and leaned back against the pillows, watching her lover watch her. God, it still gave her palpitations! "I'm not sure. Depends on how he's feeling. If he's still going to need to sleep it all off, I'm not going to stay in that room watching him do that. I'll give him a call a little later and see what's up. In the meantime, I think we should get a few more hours of sleep in, don't you?"

Jacob laughed and reached for her hand. "I think that's a very good plan, but you know it won't last for very long. I can't keep my hands off of you."

"I never asked you to keep your hands off of me. In fact, I want your hands, lips, and tongue all over me at all times, but you've loved me into sheer exhaustion. I need to sleep before I can give any more to you. How the hell can you be so wide-awake after all that we have done to each other tonight?" She let him pull her close to him so she could lay her head on his chest again.

"Being with you has my adrenaline going on overdrive, but you're right. Sleep will do us both good, and I want you well rested so I can ravage you all over again in a few hours."

Quinn pinched his nipple, causing him to jump and laugh again. "You're so bad!"

"Yes, I am, and you love it."

"I don't know about that. I do know that I love *you*."

Jacob kissed her forehead and hugged her tightly. "I love you, too."

Quinn was curled up on her side holding tight to Jacob's pillow. He still couldn't believe she was actually there in his bed. He'd woken up an hour ago thinking that it was all a dream, but then he turned and saw her asleep next to him, still in his T-shirt. He touched her face gently, pushing stray hairs off of her forehead. She moved and started mumbling in her sleep. "Go back to sleep, baby doll."

"Okay, my Jacob." Quinn let go of his pillow and rolled over onto her back. The first few rays of sunlight peeked through the blinds and softly lit up her face. *God, she's beautiful.* His heart fluttered every time he looked at her and nearly jumped out of his chest when she smiled. Now that they'd spent the entire night making love, he couldn't imagine his life without her. He looked around the room and noticed that she'd tidied up the last time she was up and about a few hours ago. The towels were hung up on the hooks and the shower door in the bathroom, and their clothes were no longer strewn haphazardly around the room. He checked the cooler and found they'd pretty much eaten all the food he'd brought with him. *Good.* He wanted to take her out and spoil her some more. Room service would be a good way to start the day together in bed.

Jacob thought he'd left the hotel menu on the desk near the phone, and that's where he found it along with his cell. He'd turned it to vibrate several hours ago, so he hadn't noticed there was a voice mail waiting from his sister. "Hey, little brother. I hope you're lack of response means she agreed to hear you out, and I meant what I said to you when you left. I want to meet the woman who has you so in knots. I've never seen you this way. Please let me know how it went. Talk to you soon."

He looked at the time on the message. Fifteen minutes earlier. He grabbed another pair of boxers out of the dresser, put them on, and slipped outside onto the patio to call his sister. It was a bit early for the kids to be awake, but she was an early riser and would be up and having a little quiet time for herself over coffee. The phone only rang twice then her voice rang in his ear.

"So what happened? I want details!"

"She still loves me, Mare. I could hardly believe it when she took my hand and followed me back to my room."

"So did she clean your clock first for breaking her heart, or did she just jump in the sack with you?"

"Maredyth!" Her laughter rang through his phone and he couldn't help but join her. "She did make it a bit tough at first, asking me why she should trust me again. I just laid it all out for her. I didn't tell her right away that I'd called off the engagement. That came later."

"You dog! How much later?"

"I really didn't watch the clock. Time sort of stood still with her. All I wanted was to touch her, kiss her, and make love to her all night long. I was going to settle for just a couple of hours, but as it turned out, she was able to stay the whole night, and we're going to be able to spend today together as well. Mare, she's everything I've ever wanted, and last night was amazing."

"So does this mean you two have a future together, or is this just a fling?"

Jacob was a bit miffed that she called the love of his life a fling, but after his track record, he could see where she was going with this. "Quinn isn't a fling to me. She's my heart. My life. And I will fight for her for however long it takes to make her mine. She told me again last night that she'll finally divorce her husband."

126

"Well, when do we get to meet the love of your life? The kids and I will be heading out to the beach tomorrow. How about the two of you join us for the day and a cookout?"

"I'm not sure if she can get away for that, but I'll ask her. She was able to spend this time with me because her husband is really sick. He didn't want her to spend the time in the room watching him sleep all day. She'll find out later this morning what's going on, and then we can make more plans. You know, this trip wouldn't have turned out so good if you hadn't told me to just take a chance and tell her how I felt. And all the ideas on how to spark the romance, thank you! She was so surprised."

"Glad I could help. Now, stop talking to me and get back to your woman. Let me know if we can expect you two tomorrow."

He hung up with Maredyth and went back into the room. Quinn had tossed enough in the bed that the covers were all askew and his shirt was riding up. Her beautiful, round ass peeked out at him. He was just about to cross the room and take a bite out of it when she woke up with a start. "Jake?"

"Right here, baby." He got back into bed, pulling the covers up over both of them. "I didn't want to wake you up. You looked so beautiful asleep in my shirt."

"I was a little scared when I didn't feel you next to me. I thought it was all a dream."

"No. Last night was the real thing. The sun is coming up and we're still together." Quinn sat up and ran her hands through her short hair. She was so cute with her hair going in several directions and the sleepy, dreamy look still in her eyes. Jacob's heart fluttered again looking at her.

"Why are you staring at me like that?"

"This is what I want to wake up to every single day. My sleepy Quinn Lee."

"It's your fault that I'm so sleepy. The sun is barely up and you leave me alone in this big bed. Some lover you are!" She started to pout a little bit, but he knew how to fix that. He eased her back down onto the pillows and under him. Her pupils dilated and he got lost in her eyes. He swore they changed color as he pulled her close, becoming even bluer if that was possible. Her hands slid up his arms and then his neck. Finally, her fingers entangled in his hair as he lowered his head to kiss her.

Her body molded to his, and he deepened the kiss. God, he wanted to take her again, but he forced himself to slow down. "Is that better, baby doll?"

She just smiled that naughty smile of hers that had stolen his heart in Vegas. She brought both of her hands to his face, brushing the hair from his forehead, and kissed him again. "Now that's how I want to wake up, in your arms, kissing you. But there is something I would change."

His forehead creased in confusion "What do you want to change?"

"I think we're wearing too much clothing. Don't you?"

"Oh, you are a naughty one, aren't ya?" He let her go and quickly slipped off his boxers as she peeled off his shirt. God, he loved this woman! She pulled him back on top of her, wrapping her arms and legs around him. His cock was already rock-hard and throbbing. He reached down between them and felt her pussy. She was definitely wet and ready for him. That made him smile. He wanted to fuck her, but first he was going to taste her and find out if that pussy of hers still tasted sweet from all the fruit he'd fed her the night before.

She read his mind and stopped him from sliding down her body to feast on her. "I want to play with that cock of yours, too. No fair that you get all the fun driving me wild."

Holy shit! Another fantasy to check off of their list. He kept kissing her while turning their bodies so she was now on top. She pulled up and turned her body around so she was straddling his chest. Her cunt was directly over his face. Her hands encircled his cock and balls as her warm mouth covered the head of his cock. He nearly exploded right there but distracted himself by grabbing her hips and shoving his tongue deep inside of her. Her moans vibrated against his cock as he entered her with his tongue. Jacob swallowed some of the sweet fluid that rushed out of her. She did still taste like pineapple. His tongue could not get enough of her, and he kept swirling it through her lips and up to her pulsing, engorged clit. She jumped slightly when he took that nubbin into his mouth. Using the tip of his tongue, he kept flicking it and sucking it.

She bucked against his mouth. He held on to her ass tighter to keep her where he wanted her and still be able to lap up all the juices that continued to flow out of her. Quinn worked his cock at the same time. Using her tongue and hands, she brought him close to climaxing but not enough to explode inside her mouth. He thought she was having way too much fun teasing him.

She hummed and moaned while she sucked on his shaft, sending so many different sensations through him that he nearly forgot what he was doing at his end, but he kept it together enough to remember that she loved it when he fucked her with his fingers and his tongue. He shoved two, three, and then four fingers inside her clenching cunt.

She gasped, popped his cock out of her mouth, and thrust her hips back onto his hand. "Fuck me with your fingers, baby. Yes, mmmmm, Jesus Christ!"

Her body literally shook the both of them, and Jacob was gripped by her clenching thighs as another orgasm crashed through her body. He loved the noises she made during sex. They turned him on more and more. He thrust his cock up toward her mouth as her lips encircled it again. She sucked hard, drawing the cum to the surface with each pull, swirling her tongue around and around his shaft. When her mouth and tongue weren't working his cock into a frenzy, she used her hand at the top, pulling and stroking deep moans out of him. "God, Quinn, if you keep that up I'm gonna blow in your mouth."

She stopped for a second and looked back at him over her shoulder. "What do you want to do, lover? Come in my mouth or my pussy?"

He didn't need any more prodding. He grabbed her around the waist and pulled her back to the top of the bed. He shoved her legs apart and drove his cock deep inside her. This is where he wanted to be. He grabbed her arms and pinned them up over her head. Her tits bounced with each thrust and that made him want to pound her faster and harder just to see them bounce all over the place under him.

Quinn pulled her knees up, braced her feet on the bed and bucked her hips, meeting his every move. "Oh, Jake. Your cock feels sooooo good pounding my pussy. *Your* pussy. Only yours."

She could get him to come just talking to him on the phone and now she was right there with him, his cock buried deep inside her. He knew he was going to share another orgasm with her. Her breathing came much faster and her cries more urgent for him to keep pounding her. He watched as her cheeks became rosy and the blush traveled down her neck and chest. Her body shook violently under him, and her pussy clenched hard on his cock one last time. That sent him over the edge with her. They clung to each other as their breathing slowed and the spasms subsided.

He started to roll off of her, and she protested, holding him tighter. "Don't move yet, Jake. Just hold me like this for a little longer."

"I don't want to crush you, babe. And besides, you really are going to be walking funny if we don't put your legs back into a normal position."

She chuckled against his neck before kissing him there. "Well, okay. I guess I should be thankful that you're thinking about my welfare."

"Speaking of that, I was thinking of ordering breakfast from room service and then talking about what you want to do today. We're going to have to leave the room so housekeeping can do their thing, anyway. Maredyth called this morning and asked if I wanted to join her and the kids at the beach tomorrow and bring you along so she can meet you."

Quinn sat up in the bed and just stared at him with her eyes wide. "I don't know if I can go. I'm afraid to think beyond today."

"Hey, it's all going to work out for us eventually. But you don't have to think past today if you don't want to. I really want you to meet the rest of my family as soon as possible. I've talked nonstop about you, and they're beginning to think I made our relationship up."

"So what? Your Mom and sister think you're spending time in Anaheim with a figment of your imagination and Eric is in on the whole thing?"

He didn't know how she did it, but she could come up with some funny shit when she was all freaked out about something. Yet another thing he loved about her. "No, Maredyth knows you're real. She's scoped you out on Facebook, and she approves already. She wants to meet the person behind the profile and the one who has my heart."

She lay back on the pillows, looking up at him with those come-fuck-me eyes. If she kept doing that, they'd never get out of the bed "Well, if it's that important to you, I'll figure out a way to be able to go with you. If fate is on our side, Jack will be feeling better and up to spending time with other friends that are down here, too. If he's busy, he won't be wondering what I am up to all day. Even though we're not here as a couple, I don't want to cause a scene with him. If he feels attacked or embarrassed in any way, he could make things very difficult for us. "

"Well, how about we just see how things go today, and if we can do it, I'll call Mare later tonight and let her know." His stomach started to protest the lack of food in it, and Quinn giggled as her stomach chimed in. "Well, I guess we've heard from the peanut gallery now. What do you want for breakfast?"

She shrugged and snuggled back into the covers. "I'll be happy with whatever you choose, except oatmeal."

He leaned over and kissed her soundly before she could say anything else. "I'm going to order the food now before you distract me any further with your naked self. I have another surprise for you, and it'll come in handy this morning."

"What are you up to now?"

He got up from the bed, reluctantly leaving her arms, and went over to the closet. He reached inside, pulled out a gift bag, and brought it over to her. "Why don't you open it and find out?"

"More presents?"

"I'm not done with you yet, baby doll. Open it."

Quinn pulled out the purple tissue paper and peered inside. Her eyes flew open and her jaw dropped. Inside she found the silk robe he'd purchased for her yesterday. It was a deep, dark purple with two large embroidered dragons over the back, similar to the tattoos on his body. "Baby, it's beautiful."

"Put it on. Let me see how you look in it."

She knelt on the bed and wrapped the kimono-style robe around her. *Perfect fit.* Quinn jumped up off the bed and ran over to the mirror to look at herself.

He laughed. She was like a little kid on Christmas morning. He crossed the room and joined her at the mirror. "Well? Do you like it?"

"Like it? I *love* it! Thank you. I feel bad, though. I don't have anything for you, and you've showered me with all sorts of surprises and gifts."

He tilted his head and lifted an eyebrow at her. "You're kidding, right? Don't you have any idea the priceless gift you've already given to me?" She really looked confused and just goddamn beautiful. "Quinn, you gave yourself to me, and I can't think of anything else that would top that, or anything else I would want more." He lifted her up into his arms again, kissing her deeply.

"Jacob, honey, if you keep kissing me like this, we'll never leave this room, and I think I'll pass out soon if I don't eat some food."

"Okay, okay. I'll call room service and get the food ordered, and you start thinking about what you want to do today. Disney? California Adventure? Universal Studios?"

"We could go to Universal Studios and then have dinner at one of the restaurants on City Walk. Is there any place you had in mind?"

"Let's get the food up here and then we can talk about it some more. I want to take you someplace nice, dress up a little bit. Nothing super fancy, but I want to show you off."

Quinn blushed and hid her face in her hands. "Stop! I don't know if I can take all these compliments so early in the morning."

He gently moved her hands away from her face. "Well, you'll just have to get used to it. I'm not going to stop any time soon." He kissed her quickly one more time and then slapped her on her ass as she scooted off to the bathroom. He placed their order to room service and then to housekeeping to find out the maid's schedule for their room. He wanted to set up a few more surprises for her, but without knowing how much longer they could be together, it was going to be tough to do.

Quinn bounced out of the bathroom with another naughty smile on her face. He smiled right back at her. He could only imagine what she was thinking. If it was anything close to what he was thinking, they definitely were not going to be leaving the room that morning. "What's going through that pretty little head of yours, baby doll?"

She held up her cell phone. "I called to check on Jackson. He's feeling a little bit better, but still pretty weak. He's ordered some bland stuff from room service and so far has kept that down. We're supposed to leave here in four days. He doesn't think he'll be much fun at all until we leave. I asked him if he wanted to go home early, and he didn't think he could make the drive yet, so he wanted to just stay put. I offered to have a service take him home, but he still refused. Some of his buddies were flying down and he hoped he would feel up to spending a little time with them. He asked me if I was able to get another room for the last couple of days or whatever. Can you believe it? I'd already had the desk promise to inform me as soon as another room opened up. We weren't supposed to be in the same room at all but something got mixed up with the reservations."

Jacob was a bit shocked. Was she pulling his leg? Then he noticed that the smile on her lips was not in her eyes. "What's wrong with him? Why would he want to push you away like this? I'm sorry, but sick or not I would never want you to see if you could rent another room."

She just shrugged and sighed. "Things haven't been very good between us for a very long time now. My therapist thought it would be a good idea if we took this trip together as friends first to see if there was anything left at all we could salvage in our relationship. We were just kidding ourselves thinking that a trip to Disney, even with our other friends, would change anything. We argued the whole ride down and the first full day we were here. I was going to rent a car and drive back early, but several of our friends were going to join us this year. I hadn't seen some of them in over three years, and I wanted to at least spend a few hours with them. I was going to hang out at the pool with Janice and her kids when you showed up."

He hadn't realized just how badly her marriage had deteriorated because she had so much trouble leaving him. She looked a little defeated by the whole thing but was still trying to put on a happy face to be with him. Jacob reached out for her, and she rushed into his arms and finally let the tears fall. "Shhhhhh. It's okay, baby."

"I, I'm sorry."

"For what? You have nothing to be sorry for here. You told me before that you've tried over and over to save your marriage. It's not your fault that he didn't want to work on it with you. You didn't fail here, honey."

"I know that now, Jake. It's just that I wasted so much time staying in this marriage. I pushed aside my own happiness just to fulfill a promise I made to Jackson's grandmother on her death bed."

"Baby, it doesn't matter now. We have each other and you said Steve and his lawyers would help you get out of the marriage now. It's all going to work out."

Quinn looked up at him with her eyes still glistening with tears. "I don't know what I would have done if you hadn't showed up yesterday. Now I have something to look forward to, the day I can be with you and not have to hide or sneak around. You want to show me off? I want to show you off and introduce you as the love of my life. I am so tired of just going through the motions to get through the day."

"We'll have all of that. It's just going to take a little time."

Both of them jumped at the sudden knock at the door. He kissed her on the forehead and then let her go so he could answer the door. The waiter brought the food in for them, set up the place settings, and quickly left them alone. Quinn giggled.

"What's so funny?"

"Oh, like you didn't notice the wink and sly smile he kept giving you when he was setting up. He had a pretty good idea what we've been doing in here. The room is covered in rose petals, there's a pile of sheets in the corner, silk sheets on the bed now, and tons of pillows all over it. He thinks you've got game!"

"No, he sees the sexiest woman in Anaheim in the room, and he thinks I have to be the luckiest man alive."

"Oh, stop sweet-talking me, mister, and feed me! My stomach is really growling now." She crossed the room to join him at the table, peeking under the metal covers on the plates. "You weren't kidding about the omelet, babe. It's huge! And would you look at all the fruit!" She grabbed a large piece of pineapple and popped it into her mouth. "Mmm."

Mmm was right. Seeing her eating that pineapple made him remember the taste of her, and he craved it all the more. But he promised to behave at least until they got some more food into them, and then all bets were off.

They took their plates of food out onto the balcony. The sun was now up, and the day was turning out to be a warm one already even at 8:00 a.m. Being on the fourth floor, they had a pretty good view of the gardens surrounding the hotel, and very few people were moving around down there. The food was pretty good, but being with her made it all taste amazing, and he couldn't stop silently thanking Steve and the rest of his family for convincing him to be there with Quinn. "You know, I have the room reserved for the next four days. You can stay here with me if want."

"So let me get this straight. Not only did you plan all these surprises for me in hopes that I would say yes to spend even a few hours with you, you actually booked an entire week here at this hotel? What would you have done if I turned you down?"

"Well, I booked three nights, and after you said yes and told me how long you would be here, I called the desk and was able to extend the reservation. I wanted to be sure I was here as long as you were. I just wanted to be near you even if you weren't in my bed. Now as luck would have it, you need a place to stay, and I have plenty of room." Of course, the hotel staff was very accommodating since Steve told them to give Jacob and Quinn whatever they wanted. He had to find the right time to tell her all Steve had done for them.

"I don't know what to say."

"Say you'll spend the rest of your vacation here with me. Let me spoil you rotten and fuck our brains out every chance we get."

She didn't say a word but placed her nearly empty plate on the table, got up out of the patio chair, and came over to sit in his lap. He held her close as she whispered the words he'd hoped she would say. "Of course I'll stay with you. I'm yours. Now and always."

He kissed her shoulder as she buried her face in his neck. Jacob snuck his right hand under her robe, tracing her inner thigh with his fingertips, inching higher and higher until he hit the jackpot. His fingers found her pussy, all wet and ready for him again. He inserted two fingers into her, and she moaned. She tilted her head up to look into his face, and he kissed her hard, wrestling with her tongue until he won the right to suck on it, all the while continuing to fuck her with his fingers.

"Jake, please take me back inside."

He didn't need to be asked a second time. He pulled his fingers out of her and scooped her into his arms as he got out of the patio chair. Jacob kept her mouth quite busy as he carried her through the doors and over to their bed. He held Quinn close for a moment longer and then let her go so that she stood next to the bed but still in his arms. Her robe loosened and fell from her shoulders. He reached between them and untied the sash from her waist, letting the dueling dragons fall completely from her body to the floor.

She looked up at him with those beautiful eyes, and he was lost once again. He reached down around her to pull back the covers so she could lie back onto the pillows and the silk sheets. She took his hands into hers as she knelt on the bed, gently pulling him toward her as she eased back onto the pillows. Jacob followed willingly, wanting to touch every inch of her body, starting with her glorious tits.

She arched her back as soon as his mouth brushed the top of her chest. She knew how much that excited him. He held her tight against him as he feasted on her nipples, nibbling and sucking until she thrashed beneath him, her fingers entangled in his hair. He knew very well what she wanted, and he was going to give it to her.

Quinn's hands trailed down his neck and shoulders. Her fingertips were so cool against his skin but set him on fire just the same. He slid down her body, trailing kisses until he was between her thighs. He looked up at her and found her watching him, biting her lower lip. Her eyes twinkled and encouraged him to continue.

His fingers had found her even more hot and wet than when they were on the patio, and he couldn't resist any longer. His tongue teased her clit and flicked it several times. She cried out and clutched at the sheets. She closed her eyes and let the heat flash through her. Quinn rewarded him with spurt of fluid against his hand. Jacob buried his tongue inside her, taking more cum into his mouth as she shoved her pelvis toward his face. Her thighs quivered and shook against his shoulders. He held them tight as he continued to lick and suck her pussy.

"Baby, please…"

Her desperate, breathless plea was his cue that she was more than ready, and if he didn't take her that moment, his cock was going to explode in his boxers and not deep inside her as they both wanted. He let her go long enough to strip the rest of the way.

Quinn wasted no time in letting him know what she wanted next. She turned over and got on her hands and knees, arched her back, and looked back at him over her shoulder. Jacob grabbed her hips and pulled her toward him, but instead of impaling her right off, he eased the head in gently, enjoying the heat from her and the way her pussy clenched and spasmed around his shaft, trying to pull him in all of the way.

He was more than happy to oblige her and entered her fully. She moaned and tried to move, but he held her hips still. He reached around and found her swollen clit and massaged it using small circles. That sent a new round of spasms through her pussy, and his cock had become painfully engorged. He couldn't hold off any longer and moved with her then, still taking his time, nearly pulling all the way out before entering her all the way again. Over and over again; their bodies becoming slick with cum and sweat.

She lowered her body to the bed, taking Jacob with her. His thrusts became more urgent, and so did her thrusts against him. The passion built faster now and her body shook beneath him. He pulled out of her so they could change positions. He wanted to look into her eyes when they came together this time. She climbed on top of him, and he sat up to hold her close as she settled back down onto his cock, taking it all the way in. She tilted her head back and clung to him as another orgasm took over. He kissed her neck and the top of her breasts as she continued to ride his cock through her climax. His was fast approaching and he wanted to share that with her. "Look at me, baby. Open your eyes."

She moved her hands to cup either side of his face, opened her eyes, and stared deeply into his. "Promise?"

She looked so vulnerable at that moment, still riding his cock and trying to open her heart up completely. "God, yes, Quinn. I'll protect your heart with my life."

She kissed him as they both exploded together. He held her as her tremors slowed. Jacob loved the feel of her in his lap, with her legs bent around him and her tits against his chest. This by far was his favorite position with her. He felt her move, and he looked back up into her face.

"Wow. What just happened between us, Jake?"

"Exactly what was supposed to happen right from the moment we met. No more games, no more secrets, no more walls. Just you and me, loving each other completely. That's what happens when soul mates share everything with each other. Wow is right, baby doll."

Quinn laughed softly against his neck. "You know, I love when you call me that."

"Good. I'll remember that!" He turned her toward the bed and laid her back onto the pillows so he could stretch out next to her. She turned toward him and kissed him again, rubbing her hand along the stubble on his cheek.

"Does that bother you? The stubble?"

"No, I love whiskers. They turn me on when you rub them on my neck and chest, hell, anywhere on my body. So you don't have to shave at all when we're together unless you want to. Whisker burn be damned!" She moved her hand down to his chest and rested it over his heart, feeling it beat against her fingertips.

"How about we get showered and dressed—oh, now don't give me that pout—and leave the room for the maids. They'll be here in two hours. Let's go to Universal Studios for the afternoon. But first, you have to go back to your room and pack up the rest of your things if you're going to stay here with me."

"Okay, but I think we need to take separate showers. Hey, you stop pouting now! You know I'm right. It'll be faster and I can get my stuff back here before we head out to explore."

"How about we still take the shower together, and I promise to behave?" She laughed as she walked into the bathroom. Jacob stepped out on the patio to collect their dishes and nearly missed the ringing of his cell. It was Maredyth again.

"What's up, Mare?"

"I didn't expect you to pick up the phone. I was going to just leave a message. The kids really want you to come meet us at the beach tomorrow. Will your lady be joining us?"

"Things are turning out much better than I'd hoped. Yes, she will be with me tomorrow and for the rest of the week. It's a long story and someday we'll fill you in, but right now I just want to spend every moment with her."

"Okay then! I was hoping you would say she was able to join us tomorrow. I have another surprise for both of you. Eric just called from the airport. Steve gave him a first class ticket out here. He said he's got more surprises for the two of you. Anyway, I'll just let you get back to Quinn, and we'll look forward to seeing you both tomorrow around noon for burgers and dogs on the beach. Don't forget your sunscreen!"

Jacob laughed. "We won't. I'm not going to tell Quinn about Eric. I want him to be able to surprise her himself. This trip just keeps getting better and better." He hung up with his sister, tossed the phone back onto the desk, and went into the bathroom to join Quinn in the steamy shower. Now he'd have to live up to his promise to be good in there!

* * * *

CHAPTER 11

"It'll be all right. I'll go back to my room and pack up the rest of my things. Give me a half hour tops, and I'll meet you back here ready to go out for the day."

"A half hour? Relax! I'm kidding. Take all the time you need, but you call me if you run into any trouble. I mean it, Quinn. I will come over there and take you from him now if I have to."

She kissed him again. God, she couldn't get enough of those lips! "Thank you, baby. I'll be back before you know it." She slipped out of his arms and out of the shower, leaving him in there to enjoy the steam on his own. She decided to just towel-dry her hair and let it dry naturally with just a dollop of mousse to give it some body. Her hairdresser was right. This cut was so versatile! Wash and go was what she wanted right now. She didn't have time to fuss with her hair.

She dressed as quickly as she could and checked her phone. *No messages. Good.* Jackson was either back asleep, or he was in the shower. He had already talked to housekeeping, and they agreed to send over extra bedding and towels to cover him for the next few days.

She was slipping on her flip-flops when Jacob came out of the bathroom. "Make sure that you bring your bathing suit for the beach tomorrow."

"I will. I have three suits. I'll let you pick the one I wear tomorrow with your family. Oh, I do have a slinky summer dress packed. Would that be what you had in mind for me to wear tonight?"

"Perfect." Jacob was still naked and wet from the shower, and Quinn was really having a hard time focusing on getting out of there to get her things. He noticed her discomfort and laughed.

"You know, you're not making this any easier." She turned her back on him to rifle through her backpack for her room key card so she didn't notice him zip across the room before he kissed her on the neck. "Hey! You're still wet!"

He turned her around so they were face to face. "You know I can't keep my hands off of you. I want nothing more than to keep you naked with me, but you do look good in that tank, with your boobs peeking out over the top. Yum."

She couldn't resist with him that close, wet or not. She draped her arms around his neck as his lips brushed over hers several times before his own self-control broke and their tongues battled once again. Her mind was going to mush, and she had to stop. Quinn pulled out of the kiss and gently pushed him away. She had a hard time finding her voice, but she managed a throaty whisper. "Baby, please. You're killing me."

"Oh, all right. Hurry back to me. I have plans for that body of yours."

She smiled and rolled her eyes, triggering another round of laughter from him. Quinn finally found her key card with her park tickets. She turned at the door to see Jacob leaning against the desk watching her. She blew him a kiss and left before he could distract her any further. She looked at her watch and noted she had less than an hour to get her things together and back to Jacob's room before the maid was due.

It was nearly 10:00 a.m. and the tourists were really starting to get active now. Several families with small children were milling about trying to get organized for a day at the Disney parks. Quinn had to dodge a few little ones on her way to the other hotel, but all in all she made it through there in less than five minutes. This time she didn't have trouble with the key card. She opened the door slowly, not knowing what to expect. Jackson was up at the desk, using his laptop. He looked like shit, but definitely better than night before. "Hey. I was able to get another room."

He barely looked up from the computer screen. "Oh, good. You'll probably catch this thing if you stay in here with me. No point in ruining the whole trip for you, too." It seemed like several minutes before he looked up again to notice that Quinn was just standing there watching him. "What?"

"I brought your tickets for the Disney parks and Universal if you feel up to going over there with your friends for a few hours."

"I can't be too far from the bathroom yet, so I don't think I'll want to go to the parks today or even tomorrow. Were you able to hook up with any of the gang yourself?" He wasn't looking at her at all and kept playing with his laptop.

"I found someone to do things with. Heading over to Universal today, and I was invited to go to the beach tomorrow for a barbecue." She went into the bathroom and grabbed the rest of her toiletries she'd left behind, and one of her bathing suits that had been hanging in there to dry out from the swim yesterday morning. She went over to the dresser to be sure she had all of her things and placed everything in her rollaway. She opened the closet doors and grabbed her sneakers and the heels to go with the summer dress for that night. Everything fit in there without a problem. She looking around the room to see if there was anything else that she wanted to have with her. *Oh, can't forget the Netbook.* She grabbed the case and attached it to the rollaway. "So if you need anything, you can reach me on the cell. You know how loud the parks are, so I may not hear it ring at first."

"Hmmmm?" He was still engrossed in his computer.

"Jack, could you stop doing that for just a second?"

He looked up and saw her standing there with her bag packed, hands on her hips. He shut the laptop slowly and just stared at her. She had to fight to not throw something at him. It was very obvious that he couldn't care less what she did.

"Do you need anything before I head out for the day?" *Besides a swift kick in the ass?*

"Nope. I still have the Sprite you got for me last night, and I can always call for room service or drive somewhere for takeout. I'll be fine. Go on and enjoy yourself. I don't need a babysitter." He kept fiddling with the computer like he was trying to get rid of her. If he wanted her gone that badly, she was more than happy to oblige. Karla was right. They couldn't get along anymore. The marriage and the friendship were definitely over.

"Okay then. I'll just go drop my things off in my room and head out for the day. I'll give you a call later to check on things." Quinn turned and started for the door, pulling her suitcase behind her. She hadn't even left yet and he was turning the television volume up and was back to his computer shit. She could feel the angry tears forming in her eyes and it took all of her strength to blink them away. There was no way he was going to make her feel bad any more. That chapter of her life was quickly coming to an end. *Good riddance!*

The walk back to Jacob's room took a little bit longer since she had to lug the suitcase up the stairs, but it wasn't heavy, just awkward. She supposed she could have taken the elevator, but she wasn't sure where that was located and it was faster for her to take the outer stairwell. She was about three doors down from the room when her cell phone went off. "Hello?"

"Where are you, babe? Do you need any help with your suitcase?"

"Open the door and find out." The door practically flew open. He must have been standing at the door when he called her. His face lit up when he saw her there with the rollaway and her phone still at her ear. "Can I hang up now?"

"Uh-huh, and get your beautiful ass in here." He reached for her suitcase and then for her, pulling her close to him so he could nibble on her neck again. He did manage to get dressed while she was gone, but going right for one of her hotspots before she even got in the door was not fair! They were never going to leave the room if he kept that up, and lord knew how her body responded to his every touch.

"Jake, you're bad! Let me hang up my dress so it doesn't wrinkle more, and then we can get going." He groaned against her neck, not wanting to let her go but knowing that she was right. He was the one who wanted to go out and about today, and Quinn was determined to hold him to it. "Where are we going tonight that I needed my dress?"

He only smiled at her. "It's a surprise, baby doll. And that dress is perfect for where we're going. But first up, Universal Studios and maybe a little shopping at City Walk before we come back here to change for dinner. I made special reservations. I think you'll love it."

Quinn put her hands on her hips and scolded "What do you mean a little shopping? You are *not* going to get me any more presents, Jake!"

"If I want to get more presents for you, I will. Don't argue with me, woman." Jacob pulled her close to him again. "Please let me do this. You deserve to be pampered and fawned over. It makes me very happy to do this for you."

"Well, if it makes you happy, then I'll let you, but don't go overboard. All I want is to be with you. That's all I need." She untangled herself from him long enough to hang up the dress and grab her back pack off of the table. "I think I have everything. Ready?"

Jacob just smiled and took her hand. "Now I am."

"She's busy packing up more of her things now." He pushed send so the chat could continue. He didn't have long to wait before there was a reply.

"Does she suspect that you know where she's been?"

"Don't think so. She looked her usual pissed off when I was on the computer and not paying attention to her."

"I told you Jake was going to follow you to Anaheim. He's obsessed with Quinn, and he's going to do whatever he can to steal her from you."

"I really don't give a shit what she does. It's not like I haven't been fucking around on her."

"But you said that you weren't going to give her a divorce. WTF?"

"I'm not. She doesn't know it yet, but if we divorce, I can't get my inheritance from my grandmother. It's a thing she put in her will just before she died. She had a soft spot for Quinn and pretty much left her the money. Hang on. She's leaving now."

"So how are you going to keep her in line? What's stopping her from just divorcing you and keeping the money for herself?"

"Quinn is a bleeding heart. Apparently she promised my grandmother that she'd stick by me no matter what and help me get my inheritance. She's had several chances to divorce me and yet she's stayed. And why? All because of a death-bed promise. She's not going anywhere. I'm going to let her have whatever time she wants with Jake while we're here in Anaheim, and then I'm going to tell her that I know everything. Since we both fucked around, no need to divorce. If she gives me a hard time, I'll make her life a living hell. I'll ruin her reputation and her career."

"ROFLMAO. Now that's what I am talking about, lover. How about you make her pay no matter what happens? She took away my man, my kids, and made it nearly impossible for me to get another job after I moved to Greenville. I think I deserve a little payback. I'll be on the 8:00 p.m. flight tonight for Anaheim. When I get there, we can party and talk about how we're going to get even with your wife."

"Iris, you're one mean, crazy bitch! Now turn your webcam back on and show me what you can do with the dildo I sent you."

Spending five hours with Quinn walking hand in hand was just surreal for Jacob. He couldn't get over the fact that they were together, enjoying the park and the rides and then ending the day with window shopping in City Walk. He'd noticed her interest in a purple lacey shawl at one of the hand craft stores, and he went back to get it when she made one of her stops to the ladies room. Since there was a line in there, he had plenty of time to get the shawl and meet back at the bench where she'd left him.

He couldn't keep anything from her. "What did you do, Jacob Hartley?"

"Why? What do you mean?"

"What is in the bag?"

He just smiled at her. "What? This old thing? I found it and was going to turn it in to Lost and Found on the way out."

Her eyes flashed, and she snatched it away from him.

"What? You don't believe me?"

She just narrowed her eyes and peered into the bag. She looked up at him through those long eyelashes, and he couldn't help himself.

He leaned over and kissed her before she could say anything. "Do you like it?"

"I love it. I'll wear it when we go out tonight. Thank you, baby." She tilted her face up, and he kissed her again, savoring the feel of her tongue wrestling with his. He let her go after a half dozen kids walked by them giggling.

"I guess that's our cue to leave." He took her hand and they headed for the parking lot outside of City Walk. "It's just after 4:00 p.m. Our reservations are for seven, so we have some time to kill before we have to get ready. Is there anything you want to do?"

She looked up at him after wrapping her arm around his waist. "What do you think, Jake?"

"I think that we need to find our car and get back on the road. I don't think I can wait too much longer before I need to rip off your clothes and feast on you again."

"My feelings exactly. I was thinking we could try a little more anal."

"You don't have to ask me twice, baby. I love your ass, and now we had better hurry. My shorts are getting awfully tight."

Quinn laughed and pulled him toward the car. When they reached the passenger door, he pushed her back up against it and kissed her. She wrapped her arms around him tightly, resting her forehead on his shoulder. "Jake, when you kiss me like that, you make my knees weak."

He put his hand under her chin and tipped it up so she looked into his eyes. "I can't resist kissing you every single chance I get. I love you, baby doll."

"I know. I love you, too. Now take me back to our room so I can show you how much." She placed one hand on his cock, and rubbed the shaft through his shorts.

"You're killing me, woman!" He moved away from her enough to open her door and get her inside without blowing his wad right there in the parking lot. He had to get her back to the hotel fast, or they were going to have to find a deserted back road for some privacy. "Buckle up, baby. I'm going to break just about every traffic law I can get away with. I need you so badly right now."

"You know, I can take care of you while you drive. That is, if you think you can handle that and drive at the same time."

Jacob couldn't believe what she'd just said. He had to ask her to explain what she meant by that. She repeated it again. Nope, he hadn't misunderstood what she said. She wanted to give him a blowjob while he drove. *Holy shit!*

She reached into her backpack and took out the beach towel she'd bought at the park today.

What the hell is she going to do with that?

"Don't look so surprised. If you think you can handle me sucking you off while you drive, I'll use the towel to give us a little privacy. At first glance, other drivers will think I'm just asleep in your lap. You've got tinted windows, for crying out loud. We'll be fine.

Just promise me you won't slam us into another car. I don't want to bite down too hard." She laughed.

Jacob really didn't think that part was all that funny, but the idea of her mouth on his cock right now, *oh man!* It was straining so much to get out that it was becoming a little painful.

Quinn noticed his discomfort and draped the towel across his lap. She trailed her hand under there and opened up his shorts slowly, first the top button then the zipper. She eased her hand into the shorts, protecting his engorged cock with her hand from the zipper teeth. Man, he loved this woman! Her mind was always thinking one step ahead.

Once she had his shorts open, she pulled out his member so he was standing at attention, free of any binding clothing. He loved the feeling of her finger tips on his cock, tracing the whole thing at first before wrapping all of her fingers around it to squeeze it firmly, driving him absolutely insane. "Quinn, I don't know if I can do this."

"Baby, you're so hard. Let me help you feel a bit better." She dropped down across the seat with her head in his lap, all the while keeping her hand moving up and down his shaft under the towel.

He was more than surprised at how good it felt with her there in his lap and that he could actually concentrate on driving. Jacob decided to not think about it at all and just let her do what she wished while he made every effort to get them back to the hotel in record time. He wanted her in his arms again, her body quaking under him.

She lifted up the towel and got under it. Within seconds, she found the head of his cock and sucked on it, gently taking it in and out of her mouth. God, she was going to tease the hell out of him before the ride was over. Well, two could play at that game, and he had some plans for her pussy as soon as they got in the door.

The traffic slowly ground to a halt just as Quinn found a rhythm that was nearly put him into a trance. Jacob noticed the flashing lights ahead and figured there had to be an accident causing the delay. Not good. He couldn't take much more on the road. He had to get off the freeway and find an alternate route or, better yet, somewhere to park and have his way with her. Someplace very secluded where they could be as loud as they wanted.

"Quinn? I really need you to stop for a second. I have to pull over and get off the freeway. Some sort of accident up ahead." She popped him out of her mouth one more time before she sat up back into her seat, licking her lips. *That does it.*

Jacob found an opening in the traffic and made straight for the next exit. Lucky for them, there was a rest area ahead. Not the best place, but there were very few vehicles and none in the back corner of the lot surrounded by a lot of trees. *Thank God for tinted windows!* As soon as he got it into park and slid the seat all the way back, Quinn had her shorts off and straddled him. His cock was still at full attention and drove into her as soon as she was close enough. He nearly came right then and there, but somehow he found the strength to hold back.

Quinn on the other hand rolled through one climax, clinging to Jacob and grinding her pelvis into him. He reached under her shirt and unhooked her bra. He pulled one breast out of the top of her tank and sucked on the nipple hungrily.

She moved faster up and down his shaft while he sucked on her tits, first one and then the other. He reached down and found the lever to lower the seat so they were able to lie back. He let her ride him in that position, holding her beautiful tits in his hands and watching her face flush as another orgasm raced through her. He loved the fact that she could come so many times.

He let go of her tits and trailed his hands down her back to her ass, cupping each cheek as she continued to slide up and down his shaft. He parted her cheeks and inserted two fingers into her ass. That caught her by surprise and she moaned in his ear, "Yes, baby. Fuck my ass."

She rifled through her backpack for their lube. He pulled her up a little to pull out of her hot, pussy. She squeezed the thick gel out onto her fingertips and then coated his cock. He helped her ease down again, but this time his dick buried in her ass. He held her there for a second, both of them breathing hard and staring into each other's eyes. She braced her hands on his chest as he moved her slowly so he was nearly out then pulled her back down again. Her thighs clenched against his waist as her body quaked. Her moans and cries became louder as they increased speed.

He couldn't hold back any longer and slammed hard into her ass, holding tightly to her waist now as she moved to take all of his cock deep into her ass. He entangled his fingers in her hair and pulled her mouth to his as they went over the edge together.

Quinn collapsed on top of him, and he held her close. Jacob
loved the feel of her body on his, still shuddering from the
aftershocks of their lovemaking. Every single fantasy of his had come
true with her, and he was overwhelmed by how happy she made him.

"Jake?" Quinn attempted to sit up but still stay straddled over
him. "Could you help me fasten my bra before I sit up all the way?"

"I still have my cock buried in your ass and you're worried about
your bra?" The laughter was already rolling out of him before she
could reply. She was so cute when she was trying to be all sneaky.
Good thing they were still alone in the part of the rest area where
they had parked. "There's no one around now, why not just let the
girls be free so I can play with them a little longer. I'm not ready for
you to climb off of me just yet." Jacob wrapped his arms around her
and pulled her back down so he could bury his face between her tits.

She giggled and moaned again. "Baby, you said we had
reservations tonight. If we stay here any longer, we won't make them,
and you said you had another surprise for me."

"Oh, so fucking you in the ass here in the car wasn't a surprise?"
He pretended to be hurt by that, but she saw right through it. She
could always make him smile and laugh, especially when she was all
flustered trying to back pedal.

"I, Jake, you know that's not what I meant!" She eased herself
off of him and back into her seat but not before she used the beach
towel to clean herself and him off. "Where did my panties go?"

He twirled them around on his fingertips. "Do you mean these?"

She lunged to snatch them back from him, but he held them out
of her reach. "Jake, come on. We need to get going."

"You don't need your panties for me to drive. You can sit there
in your seat with the towel over you while I finger-fuck your pussy.
It's only fair since you were driving me wild with the blow job."

"How about we save that one for another drive. If you start that,
we'll most definitely get a ticket. I won't be able to control myself.
You have me so worked up now, baby. I don't want to share any part
of you with anyone else. Not even if they're just watching."

That was the answer he was hoping to hear. They had often
talked about adding a partner or two in their fantasies. He thought
that was what he wanted, too, until they'd made love the first time.
Now all bets were off. No one was going to have her but him. No
other man or woman, for that matter. Jacob had to be sure that was

what she wanted, too. "I know we had talked about bringing in another partner at some point, but after what we've shared so far, I don't want that any more. You're all I need and the only one I want." He searched her face for any clue as to what she was thinking. "Does that disappoint you?"

Quinn tilted her head to the side and bit her lower lip before answering him. "I used to think that was what I wanted, to have threesomes and foursomes. Not now. Disappointed? No. Relieved is more like it! I was thinking how I was going to react to seeing you with another woman and my mind just wouldn't go there. And I don't want any other man touching me this way again. You set my body on fire just with just the sound of your voice. How can anyone top that?"

Jacob winked at her and handed over her panties. She winked back and leaned over to kiss him before putting them back on. For the first time in ages, he could honestly say his heart was full and it was all because of her.

After both of them were dressed and presentable, they left the rest area. They had been there nearly an hour. Man, the time flew! Lucky for them, the accident had been cleared from the freeway, and the traffic moved along at posted speeds. He reached over and took her hand in his. "Quinn Lee, you've made me happier than I had ever thought was possible. One day soon, you'll be my bride."

She squeezed his hand and brought it to her lips. "I feel like I'm already your wife, Jake. You have my heart now and forever." She was quiet for a second or two, just looking at him before she spoke again. "Steve's lawyers, my lawyers, had instructions to file the divorce papers today. When I get back to Oakland, I'll move the rest of my things out of the house and away from Jackson once and for all. There's no point in delaying it any longer."

"You don't have to do all of that alone. The sooner you're away from Jackson, the sooner you'll be in my arms and my bed forever." Jacob pulled her hand to his lips as she had done and then placed it over his heart. "Will you look at that, the exit for our hotel. Time to change and head out for dinner and the first of many more surprises I have in store for you."

They parked the car in the private lot next to the hotel reserved for guests. There were trails from the parking area through the hotel garden and Jacob wanted to walk through there on the way back to their room. The gardens were beautifully arranged with flowers, plants, and waterfalls. There was even a bird enclosure where guests could go in and feed the Lorikeets. The sun was sinking fast and a chilly breeze swept through the gardens. Quinn shivered and snuggled closer to Jacob.

"Baby, we better get back to the room and warm you up. Looks like the shawl will come in handy tonight."

"Where are you taking me?" She loved surprises, but the anticipation was driving her crazy. Jacob had been so secretive about what they were doing that night. She would love to just spend the rest of the night in bed, but she guessed he had other plans.

He stopped walking and looked at her. "Do you really want me to tell you and ruin the surprise? Or can you wait just a little bit longer? I promise you'll love it. "

Now she was really intrigued. "Okay. I'll try to be patient, but I can't promise you it will last very long!" She slipped out of his arms and walked faster toward the stairwell. "If you're a good boy, I'll let you join me in the shower." Jacob started after her, and she barely made it to the door before he caught up, pinning her against it.

"Are you forgetting who has the key card?" His lips were on hers stopping any further protests from her. She forgot what he said in that moment, enjoying the feel of his tongue dancing with hers. He pulled her to him as he slid the key card into the slot and shoved the door open. They slowly backed into the room, shutting the door behind them. All packages and backpacks were forgotten as soon as they were dropped to the floor.

Jacob tugged her tank top up and over her head while Quinn unzipped his shorts, giving her access to his already swelling cock. She loved the feel of it in her hand, growing and straining against her fingertips. He chuckled in her ear and bit the lobe. "You know, two can play at that game, baby doll." Within seconds he had her bra unhooked and was sucking madly on her left nipple. She gasped and her knees weakened, but Jacob had her up in his arms.

He carried her over to the bed with her arms and legs around him, sucking on his lower lip. He turned and sat down on the edge of the bed, keeping her on his lap while they kissed. Quinn moved her hands to either side of his face, enjoying the feel of the stubble against her palm. The wetness forming in her panties was hard to ignore. She squirmed in Jacob's lap, wanting to be free of the soaked lingerie as soon as possible. .

"Are you wet again, love? I think we need to do something about that." He lay back on the bed and rolled over so Quinn was on her back. He slid down her body, trailing kisses as he went. She raised her hips as his hands unzipped her shorts and eased them off her hips and down her thighs. He was really going to tease her now, definitely payback for the blowjob while he was driving.

"Jake, baby, did you forget about the reservations?" He got up long enough to kick off his own shorts before sliding back up on top of her body. She shuddered as his cock tapped at her outer lips. "Maybe we have more time—"

His demanding lips took away any thoughts she had about stopping him. She would do anything for the touch of his lips and his hands all over her body. She wasn't disappointed either. He teased her nipples with his tongue and teeth until she practically begged him to stop, but he wasn't finished with her yet.

He slid down to rest between her thighs, spreading them a little wider with his hands as his tongue slipped between her outer lips. She arched her back and shoved her pussy toward him, causing his tongue to slip in deeper. He pulled his head back to look up at her with a smile that made her heart skip a couple beats. Jacob rubbed his whisker stubble all over her inner thighs before diving back into her cunt.

He immediately began sucking her clit hard, drawing out a long moan from her. His fingers slipped into her pussy, tickling her G-spot and triggering an intense cluster of orgasms. "Oh my God, Jake, yes, don't stop."

His tongue flicked at her clit as he fucked her with three fingers faster and faster. Her hips snapped up to meet his hand. Quinn couldn't think. She couldn't speak. All she could do was gasp and moan until her body couldn't take it any longer. She shook so violently she thought she would black out from sheer ecstasy.

He got up from between her quaking thighs and slid up her body. His gaze held hers as his knees pushed her legs further apart and his cock entered her. "I love you." He kissed her tenderly, shifting his body to hold her closer, grinding against her. The pace was nearly torture. She had to admit she loved the feel of him inching in and out, bringing her nearly to the brink, but not letting her go all the way over just yet.

She babbled a string of nonsense words. Her mind went to mush. Wave after wave of passion flooded over her. "Jake, I can't. It's too much." She closed her eyes as another orgasm took hold of her body. Jacob's thrusts came faster now, harder, more urgent. He was falling with her once again.

She locked her legs around his waist and pulled him as close as she could with each of his hard thrusts into her. Quinn braced her hands against the headboard as Jacob slammed into her, her tits bounced wildly.

Jacob clutched the bedspread next to her as they climaxed together, crying out each other's names. He rested his head on her chest and then positioned himself to look at her face.

She brushed his hair out of his eyes and kissed him. "I love you so much." There was more that she wanted and needed to tell him, but the words just wouldn't come.

Jacob kissed her back and moved to lie on his side next to her. "Baby, what's wrong?"

"Nothing's wrong. You showing up when you did down here was such a shock. I didn't know whether to hear you out or just punch you in the mouth and walk away. Now after the last twenty-four hours, I can't imagine my life without you."

"That's good, because I won't let you. I'm not going anywhere, Quinn. I know I have a lot of work to do to make it up to you for all the pain I caused you. If you'll have me, I'll spend the rest of my life making you happy."

"If I'll have you? I think I've *had* you several times since yesterday and there's no way in hell I'm going to let you go. Not now and not ever." Quinn got up off the bed before he could pull her back down under him. "Come on, I need some help getting ready."

Jacob rose, took her outstretched hand, and held her still for a moment. "Will you tell me what happened to you after I—?"

"Shh. I'll tell you all of it. I promise. It's just a very painful time, and it's hard for me to talk about without falling apart. I don't want to ruin the evening you have planned." She pulled him toward the bathroom. "Come on, baby. I'll let you play with my boobs while I wash my hair."

Jacob smiled. "Oh, you are a devious woman! Using the girls to distract me. Well played!" He turned on the water and turned his attention back to Quinn. He nuzzled her neck and whispered in her ear, "I'll be here when you're ready to tell me. I wish I could take away all that pain."

His gorgeous blue eyes filled with tears. "It's okay, baby. We're together now, and that's all that matters. You can't change what happened any more than I can."

"I know, but it kills me when I think about how I hurt you. You had every right to punch me in the mouth and tell me to fuck off, but you didn't. "

"We belong together. It just took us longer to get there. No turning back now." Quinn stepped into the shower and under the hot water. "Come on, the girls are really lonely in here without you, and so am I."

"Well, since you put it that way, how can I refuse?" He stepped in and pulled her close, allowing the water to cascade over both of them before he reached for the soap. His hands moved over all of her curves, finally settling on her tits. The nipples were still tender from their last lovemaking session, but Jacob was very gentle, gliding his soapy hands over them, squeezing them together as he lifted them and gently let them fall back into his hands. "Do you have any idea how often I've fantasized about touching you this way."

"I think I have some idea." Quinn turned around so that she could tip her head back under the water and wash her hair. Jacob's hands continued down her back lower and lower until he was finally cupping her ass. "Now it's my turn."

They shifted positions so they could rinse most of the soap off of her body. Jacob grabbed the shampoo while she started lathering his chest and arms. Quinn loved the feel of his muscles under her fingertips. They tightened up a little as her soapy hands traced all over them, flexing and pulsing. She continued lower and lower, lathering everything in her path. His cock waited for her. She enjoyed the feel of it slipping and sliding through her hands. Reaching under his balls and between his legs, she soaped up every single inch of him. Quinn looked up to see him watching her, his eyes smoky with desire. Jacob pulled her up his body, keeping her tight against him. His mouth crushed hers as his tongue thrust inside, possessing her completely.

No one else existed in that moment. They held each other close while rinsing off the remaining soap from their bodies. Not bearing to lose contact with each other for more than a second or two, they kept touching and kissing even as the water started to get cooler. Jacob turned off the water, keeping his lips on Quinn's. She shivered against him, and he broke off the kiss. "Baby doll, we did it again."

She laughed. "Yes, we did. I can't help myself when I'm with you. I forget everything and just live in the moment. Let's get dressed and see if we can still make those reservations. I'm starving!"

"Good. The reservations are at Steakhouse 55 at the Disneyland Hotel. I expect you to eat and not just pick at a salad." Jacob stepped out of the stall and handed her another of those large, fluffy towels. "I hate it when I'm trying to impress my lady and she just picks at the food and pushes it around the plate."

"You don't have to worry about that with me, honey. You don't get curves like these eating like a bird!"

Jacob nuzzled the back of her neck while his hands trailed down to rest on her hips. "I've obsessed over them from the first time I saw you in that killer red dress laughing with your sister, and now they're all mine."

"I have to get them into my new dress so we can get to the restaurant on time. If you keep kissing my neck and rubbing your whiskers on my shoulders, I'll never be ready."

Jacob kissed her shoulder one more time then let her go. "Okay, but I'm only doing it because my stomach is starting to protest, and I want to see you all decked out in that dress."

* * * *

CHAPTER 12

He left Quinn to finish up alone in the bathroom while he used her blow-dryer at the full length mirror near the dresser. Normally he would just let his hair dry naturally, but they were in a time crunch to make the reservations, and he wanted everything to be perfect. He now wished he would have done the room service thing again tonight. He really wanted to keep her all to himself a while longer, but taking her out and showing her off would be fun, too. Hopefully he could get her to open up more and let him know what had happened to her when they were apart. He needed to know, but he wouldn't push her if she wasn't ready to share it with him.

He slipped into his black dress pants and flipped through the shirts in the closet. He decided to wear the dark purple shirt that Maredyth picked out for him. Quinn loved purple, and her dress had multiple shades of the color splashed throughout the fabric. He traced the skirt with his fingertips. It was soft and silky and would cling to her body, showing off those killer curves.

"Wow, don't you look tasty." She'd stepped out of the bathroom naked and looked quite tasty herself. She'd dried her hair and kept it soft and sleek. She had put a little makeup on, not that she needed any, but her eyes appeared even more blue-green if that was even possible. She walked over to her bags and pulled out light purple matching lacey panties and bra. "Looks like we're going to match all the way around." She slipped on the panties and attempted to put on the strapless bra. "Wanna give me a hand with this?"

He didn't need any prodding for that one. He took in a deep breath at her neck. "Good lord, Quinn. You smell fucking fantastic."

She smiled and reached for her dress. "Sorry to bother you again."

"Baby, it's no bother zipping you up as long as I get to unzip you again later tonight." Jacob moved his hands over her arms, straightening the spaghetti straps on her shoulders. "You're so beautiful. You take my breath away."

She looked back at him in the mirror. "I feel beautiful when I'm with you. The way you look at me at times, like when I got up this morning, hair all this way and that. I felt how much you wanted me in your touch, and I saw it in your eyes. You have no idea what that means to me. I take your breath away? You do the same to me and you always have."

She turned to face him and placed her hands on his chest as she stepped into her heels. She'd grown four inches and now was nearly standing eye to eye with him.

"I forgot how much I love you in heels."

Jacob started to pull his hair back into a ponytail, but Quinn stopped him. "Don't tie it back. I love it when you have it loose and a little wild." She straightened his collar and kissed him softly.

"Wait, I have something for you." He went over to the mini-fridge and reached in for a plastic container. Inside was a small purple orchid. He took it out of the container and placed it behind her left ear. "Wearing a flower behind your left ear means your heart is taken. Will you wear it for me?"

Quinn's eyes glistened. "Of course I'll wear it for you."

His phone rang. It was the call he'd been expecting. "Hello. Thank you, we'll be right down." Jacob draped Quinn's shawl over her shoulders. "Your chariot awaits."

"What's going on?" Quinn was a little hesitant but put her hand in his as they walked out of their room. "I thought we were going to take your car."

"It's another surprise." She held tightly to his hand as she navigated the stairs in her heels. When they got to the bottom, he told her to close her eyes and let him lead the way. In front of the hotel was a horse-drawn carriage. Just as they neared, the horses whinnied and her eyes flew open.

"Jake, you didn't!"

The footman stepped forward, opened the carriage door, and placed steps down for her to enter. "Ma'am? Can I help you aboard?"

She was speechless and just nodded to the man as she placed her hand in his and he eased her up the steps into the seat. Jacob got in after her and put his arm around her shoulders. "Well, I had to find another way to spoil you." He leaned over and whispered into her ear, "Don't worry. I got a great deal on it thanks to a family friend and the Magic of Disney."

"Holy shit, Jake! I feel like one of the fairy-tale princesses." Her face just lit up as they rode through Downtown Disney and toward the Disneyland Hotel and the restaurant. There were several little kids with their parents waving at them in the carriage. Quinn smiled and waved back. He loved watching her and hearing her laugh. He almost wished they could ride around a bit longer, but at this point he was absolutely starving, and if he knew Quinn, her stomach was nearing a revolt.

The hostess seated them right away in a quiet corner near the windows. Jacob had requested a booth so they could sit close to each other and not feel like they had to talk over the other diners to hear each other. He wasn't disappointed. After the hostess left them at the table, Quinn slid closer to him in the booth so they could share a menu and figure out what to order. Jacob was too busy taking in her scent to concentrate on the menu, but somehow they managed to get the food ordered with the help of their waiter and a glass of wine. Of course he made sure that they had some fruit as an appetizer.

They ordered different entrees so that they could share and try a bit of everything. They had fun feeding each other, laughing, and just being together. He looked around the room at one point and noticed that other diners were watching them and smiling. One table actually sent over a bottle of champagne. They thought Jacob and Quinn were celebrating an anniversary or something. They smiled and accepted the generous gift. One day they would be celebrating an anniversary together.

As they were leaving, they heard music coming from Downtown Disney. Quinn looked at Jacob and smiled. "Why don't we walk back to the hotel? We could cut through Downtown Disney and enjoy the music on our way back."

"Whatever you want, baby. As long as I have you on my arm, I'll go anywhere and do anything." He kissed her before taking her arm, and they headed toward the music. When they got closer, their ears were treated to a variety of tunes from various decades. By the looks of the large crowd dancing around them, the band was quite popular. As they approached, the lead singer asked if there were any requests.

Just as they got closer to the stage, the band launched into the opening strains of one of Jacob's favorite songs, "Unchained Melody." Several couples were already dancing together as Jacob guided Quinn out to the center of the group and held her close. Everything else melted away. He only saw her eyes looking into his. He only felt her body melting into him as they moved to the music. At the end of the song, he surprised her and put her into a dip. It wasn't until that moment they noticed no one else was dancing. They were all watching them and clapped when the song was over. Even the band clapped.

Quinn laughed and hugged Jacob tightly before she curtsied. The crowd chanted for them to do one more as they tried to beg off and move on. The lead singer of the band asked what they wanted to hear. Since they had a female singer as well, Jacob asked if they could perform a song by Faith Hill and Tim McGraw, "Let's Make Love." He nodded and winked at him, "You got it. Great choice."

As the first few bars started to play, he took Quinn back into his arms. Now they were cheek to cheek. "You are my heart, Quinn. I can't live without you."

"Shh, don't talk like that. I love you. We'll be together, I promise." Quinn gazed into his eyes as she touched his face. "You've always been my heart, and now I'm whole again." She felt so good in his arms, dancing to a song talking of making love all night long, just what he planned to do with her when they got back to the room.

He kissed her again just as the song ended. She slid her arms up around his neck and deepened the kiss. The crowd once again applauded and a few catcalls erupted before he let her go. They waved to the band and started off down the way toward the hotel. Jacob could hear the band launch into their rendition of "Hey Ya." The crowd cheered wildly once again.

She rested her head against his shoulder as they walked. "This has been the most amazing day with you, Jake. From sun up to sun down there has been one surprise after another. I hope you don't think you have to do this sort of thing for me every day. The best surprise of all was when I looked up to see you watching me at the pool."

"You deserve to be happy and loved. I want to be that person for you. I meant what I said. I need you in my life and not just sporadically. I want the day-to-day stuff. I want to go to sleep with you in my arms and wake up the same way. My life is nothing without you in it."

"Let's enjoy the time we have this week and then we can plan for our future together. It's going to be a rough road ahead once we leave Anaheim, but if I have your promise to hold on to, I can get through it."

He could hear the hint of pain in her voice, and it pierced his heart. "I won't leave you this time, not ever."

"I know baby, and I'm counting on that." She was quiet for a moment and then she asked a question out of the blue, "Would you be willing to relocate to the Bay Area?"

They were at the crosswalk, waiting for the light to change when her phone rang. He recognized the ringtone as Jackson's. *Fuck!* The man's timing was just uncanny.

"Hold that thought. Hello? Just finished dinner at the Steakhouse. How'd your day go? So are you feeling better? A little bit? Well, that's good. Yeah, tomorrow I have plans to go to the beach for most of the day. All right then. I'll call you tomorrow later in the day." Quinn shut her phone off and slammed it back into her purse.

"So I take it he's still sick?"

"Jackson's not sick. He's just being a fucking asshole. He may have been sick earlier yesterday, but he got through that overnight. He was screwing around on the computer when I went in there this morning. He was being all sneaky. He wanted me out of the room so he can do whatever he wants with whoever he wants. I heard sounds in the background that tells me he's at the airport right now, probably meeting up with one of his 'friends' from the games he plays on the Xbox. Well, good for him. I don't give a shit anymore."

She wrapped herself up tight in her shawl and walked quickly toward the stairway of the hotel. He didn't think she could move that way in those heels. She sure as hell was sexy when she was pissed, though. She pulled off her heels and practically ran up the steps. She was really fuming when they reached their door.

"Wow, what has been going on with you two over the last few months?"

She stormed into the room and sat down on the bed. "Oh, let's see. I packed my things up at least five times since February. When he found out you had proposed to Iris and I had nowhere to go, he laughed in my face. He said I was stupid to think someone else would ever want me. Stupid to fall in love with someone who was just stringing me along for hot phone sex."

He was stunned. "Wait. Jackson knew about us and how you felt about me?"

"Yes. I told him flat out I was going to leave him for you. But when I found out you'd proposed to Iris, I snapped." She searched his face for a moment and reached out to him as he sat down next to her on the bed. "I thought Eric would have told you what happened in February when I went there for my conference."

Now Jacob understood why Derek had cracked his jaw had nearly fulfilled his promise to kill him. "Quinn, tell me."

"I was going to surprise Derek and take him out to dinner as a thank-you for my beautiful dragon tattoo." She explained how she was so happy at that point in the trip because she was in love with him and making plans for their new life together, and she couldn't wait to share the news with her brother. Unfortunately, she overheard a very angry Eric ranting and raving about how Iris had posted on his Facebook page that she was engaged.

"I waited outside the work area a few minutes, listening to Eric say he couldn't believe you would marry that conniving cunt. Sorry, those were his words. I guess Derek had his laptop out and pulled up your Facebook pages. That's when I walked in, just as Derek said he wanted to try to keep all of it from me for as long as he could."

He kept quiet even though he was dying inside. This had been when she'd found out he'd betrayed her after months of telling her he loved her and wanted her forever.

"I walked in and made them tell me. Then I made them tell me again. And again. I kept shaking my head and said it had to be a mistake. I had just talked to you on the phone and told you that I was going to leave Jackson when I got home from Vegas. It had to be a cruel joke."

She told him everything she remembered about her collapse in the Tattoo Parlor and how she turned to Steve for comfort. "My mind wouldn't completely accept that you'd dumped me, so I pretended it didn't happen. Steve let me do that. He didn't push me to accept what you did. He got me through that week by showering me with presents and keeping me busy with dancing at the club, shows and gambling, amongst other things." She looked down at her hands in her lap and seemed a little uncomfortable telling any more of her story.

He brought her hands to his lips. "It's okay, baby. I know he's been there for you whenever you've needed him. You don't have to hide any of it from me. He's a big part of your life."

Quinn nodded. "I don't know what I would have done without him. Hell, I was still battling with my decision to leave Jack or not."

"You said before Jack would've been okay with you leaving him for Steve, but not for me?"

"He kept throwing it in my face that you picked Iris over me. He was actually *insulted* I would leave him for you. He said he could understand if I left him for Steve, but not you. He was more than happy for me to just keep seeing Steve as long as we stayed married. My mind kept battling with my heart and I didn't know where else to turn."

Jacob put his arm around her and held her. He knew there was a lot more to her story and he hoped she would share it all with him. And she did. Quinn told him about the Bay House and agreeing to move in there with Steve. She told him all about the sleepless nights, the dreams of their island and longing to be with him even though he was engaged to Iris and out of her reach. Finally she told him all about her breakdown, from finding out that Jackson was using her bed to entertain his girlfriends, dreaming of Danny and him on their fantasy island, to waking up in the hospital in Steve's arms.

"When I found out how long I'd been in the hospital and why, well, I just gave up trying to run away from my problems. I arranged for a medical leave from work so I could get myself back on track."

"How the hell did you get through all of that in such a short period of time?" Jacob brushed the hair off of her forehead and kissed her there again.

"It's still a work in progress Jake, but with the help of my therapist and daily sessions, I was able to get back to me again. I learned that I had never dealt with the losses I suffered in my life. My brother Danny. My Dad. My career and partnership in Michigan. My personal life, what a mess there. She helped me understand that just because I've made poor choices in love doesn't mean I'm not worth being loved by someone. My ex, Brad, and then Jackson both made me feel like I wasn't worth loving, that I wasn't worth the trouble to find out what made me tick. They took all that I could give them and then gave me nothing back." She got really quiet and looked at Jacob. "I thought you were different. That's why I broke when you left me."

"I'm so sorry to make you think I didn't love you. I thought it would be easier for you if I let you go. I thought I could give you up and we both would go on in our separate lives. I was so wrong. I put you through so much pain."

She stretched out and settled back against the pillows. "Well, with all the miles between us and the only way we had to talk to each other was to sneak through texts, phone, and e-mail, there was no way you could have known. I couldn't just pick up the phone any time to call you. I wrote you e-mails that you never were able to read. I was cut off completely from you, and I didn't know why. I suppose I could have just called you or sent you texts knowing Iris would intercept them, but I couldn't do it. Even though you were hurting me, I couldn't bring myself to hurt you like that.

"My therapist helped me to let you go. She told me to remember the old poem about loving something and setting it free. It would come back to you if it was meant to be." She pulled him down beside her. "Here you are. We *are* meant to be." She snuggled up and laid her head on his chest before she went on with her story. "Jack and his family have been controlling my life since day one. I've had to move to the Bay Area away from my family and friends so he could be close to his family. We were over his parents' house every single week, and we couldn't do anything on our own. His parents were consulted about everything, even when we were planning a family. Of course our inability to conceive was my fault. Never mind the fact that I had full workups and I was pronounced healthy and fertile."

"I remember you mentioning that you had miscarried early in your marriage. Didn't Jack go to the doctor to see if he was the problem?" Another painful memory that Jacob made her suffer through. He had told her before that he would give anything to be able to get her pregnant with his child.

Quinn snorted and shook her head. "No Hollis had ever had trouble conceiving, so it couldn't be his fault. Month after month his mother called to see if I was pregnant yet. She bought me super-sized packs of pregnancy tests from Costco and would have waited outside the bathroom when I took the tests if I would've let her."

"I gained a lot of weight during the first half of our marriage and so did Jackson. That didn't seem to matter at first. We still had an active sex life with each other and enjoyed it for the most part. Being overweight didn't make it any easier getting pregnant, and my doctor encouraged me to drop the weight. I tried back then, but month after month of not being pregnant really wore me down. After I miscarried, I just wasn't going to put myself through it anymore. I think that was when Jack started to pull away from me. We went longer and longer in between times we had sex. Nothing I did made a difference. I finally shed the extra pounds, started to really look good and feel good. Jackson lost weight, too, so I thought we had something in common again. He couldn't care less.

"I met Steve, and he gave me what I needed each time I went to Vegas, friends with benefits at its best. I knew he genuinely cared for me, and yes, we did fall in love with each other, but at the time I didn't think we had a future together. It was just different with him. He gave me everything else I wanted in my life, but still there was something my heart was missing." Quinn sighed as Jacob hugged her tighter.

"You shouldn't have to go back to that. Stay with me down here. My sister won't mind at all."

She sat up and looked him in the eyes. "I wish I could, Jake. I would love nothing more than to stay here with you and never go back to the Bay Area, but I have a responsibility to the people I work with. They gave me the time off to heal. They're my family, and I can't just leave them. I've talked to my boss about possibly transferring to one of our hospitals in the South Bay area or even to our new San Francisco specialty practice. I think either would be a good place for me and far enough away from the Hollis family and most of their friends. We could start over, just you and me."

"I like the sound of that." He kissed her forehead and traced her cheek with his thumb as he eased the orchid out from behind her ear. "I'll follow you anywhere Quinn."

She sat up and took the orchid from him. "I want to save this for a few days." She got up off the bed and went into the bathroom to fill a glass with some water. Quinn walked over to the nightstand next to her side of the bed and placed the flower in the glass on it. She stood there looking down at Jacob on the bed. He reached out to her, and she took his hand but didn't get back on the bed. "You would leave your family to be with me?"

He knelt up on the bed and took her other hand. "I would go anywhere to be with you. Stay or go, doesn't matter, as long as we're together."

She tightened her grip on his fingers and moved his arms around her waist. Jacob found her zipper and slowly pulled it down. He looked up into her eyes and felt the love between them grow stronger. "I'll put you first, baby doll. Now and forever."

He slid the straps down her shoulders as her dress fell away from her body.

She stepped out of it and back into his arms. The pale purple color of her bra and panties was in stark contrast to her tan skin. The lingering scent of her perfume heightened his desire for her.

He eased her back onto the pillows with him and held her close with her head on his chest. Her right hand moved over his chest and then down his abs to his belt and stopped. She looked up at him before trailing lower to find his cock already swelling for her, eager for her touch and to be inside of her. He lowered his lips to hers as she loosened his belt and started to undo his fly.

She tugged his shirt out of his pants and sat up, taking him with her so that both of them were kneeling on the bed. Her fingers quickly unbuttoned his shirt while he unhooked her bra and let it fall away. She pushed his shirt open and he pulled her tight against him. She kissed him and whispered in his ear, "Make love with me, Jake."

His jaw muscles tightened against her cheek. He moved his head back to look into her face. His deep blue eyes danced, pulling her in. His hands moved up and cradled her face as his mouth devoured hers. She wanted him so badly at that moment. She couldn't think of anything else but his eyes, his lips, his hands roaming over her body and holding her tight to him. She felt his need bulging through his boxers.

She pushed his shirt back and all the way off of the rippling muscles of his arms. Her hands moved around to his back and traced the muscles there and the dragons battling over his shoulders and almost his entire back. He rose from the bed so he could step out of his pants and boxers, all the while keeping his eyes locked with hers. Quinn's chest rose and fell faster, the excitement and the need for him building. "Jake, please."

He came back toward her, and she sank back down on the pillows. He traced his fingers along her foot, up her calves and her thighs, and hooked his thumbs in her panties, inching them down and off. Quinn watched him as he made his way back up her quivering body, trailing kisses as he went. He stopped just a moment to kiss each inner thigh and then took one long, slow lick of her swollen outer lips. The sensation was almost unbearable, so slow and deliberate, drawing out the anticipation.

He slid further up to nuzzle her breasts. Her fingers ran through his long, silky hair, coaxing him further. He circled first one and then the other nipple with his tongue. She wiggled and squirmed under him, trying to thrust her pelvis up to take him in so she could share her orgasms with him. She wanted to enfold him deep inside of her so he'd experience firsthand how her pussy clenched and spasmed because of him.

Finally he slid up, covering her whole body. The head of his cock throbbed against her pussy, wanting to be inside where it belonged.

But instead of entering then, Jacob rolled them over so Quinn was on top, sitting in his lap and impaled on his cock. "Oh my God, Jake!" He pulled her legs around him as he sat up and kept slowly sliding her up and down his shaft. She arched her back and ground against him while he was deep inside her, hitting her G-spot with each and every stroke. Wave after wave ran through Quinn's body, and yet they were still moving against each other and enjoying each and every orgasm together.

His hands moved up and down her back as her body took over their rhythm. He pulled her mouth down to his, sliding his tongue over hers, inviting her to do the same and still keep up the pace of their thrusts against each other. Finally, when she thought she couldn't take any more, Jake's whole body stiffened. He grabbed her ass and moved her faster, literally bouncing her wildly up and down his shaft. "Quinn, Quinn, uuhhhhhh." He brought her to him one last time hard as he erupted inside her.

He held her in his lap while the climax took over both of their bodies, draining her completely. She didn't realize she was crying until Jake brushed the tears from her face. "Honey?"

She smiled at him, her lover, her life. "Nothing's wrong. Everything is as it should be. I love you. So much so that sometimes I just can't express it in just one emotion. They all hit me at once and overwhelm me."

He rolled them over so she was under him again. "I'm not quite done with you yet, baby doll." He pinned her hands next to her head, keeping his fingers laced with hers. He moved his hips in a circle as he thrust inside of her, flooding her body with new sensations.

She wasn't sure how or why he was still hard after what they'd just experienced together, but hell, she wasn't complaining. She didn't think she had more to give him, but somehow her body kick-started again and gave in to him completely. He teased her mouth with his as he fucked her, driving her wild once again. He released her hands, and she immediately pulled him down on top of her so they could roll over. Quinn braced her hands on his chest as he thrust harder and harder. He held her hips in place so she couldn't move with him but just feel him glide in deeper and deeper.

"Ohhhh, baby, you're going to make me come again."

"I'm almost there with you, Quinn. Come on, baby doll, make me come with you, mmmmmm. That's it, honey."

She buried her face in his neck as he finally released. She couldn't move even after he softened and slipped out of her. She giggled against Jacob's neck.

"What is so funny, baby doll?" He didn't seem to mind one bit that she was still on top of him. In fact, she thought he wanted to keep her that way for a bit longer, but she needed to move, and she needed his help.

"Honey, I can't move. My legs are jelly."

Jacob held on tighter. "No problem. I have you right where I want you."

"As much as I love being on top of you, you have to help me out of bed." Quinn moved her head to look into his face and whispered why. "I have to pee."

He started to chuckle then laughed really hard.

Her bladder threatened to empty right then and there. "Jake, you are not helping!"

"I'm sorry, but you have to admit, it is funny." He rolled over and helped her up off the bed. He held onto her for a few steps to be sure her legs could hold then she pushed him back toward the bed.

She shuffled quickly toward the bathroom. "I got it from here, mister. You just wait until I get back!"

He fell back on the bed and watched her scoot off to the bathroom, still a little wobbly. He didn't know if he could take all the credit for that, more like a combination of the wine, the champagne, and her emotional revelations, combined with the mind-blowing sex. He couldn't get enough of that woman. He wanted to hold her, kiss her, and protect her from everything and everyone, especially that fucking prick Jackson. He would beat the shit out of him right then if he knew it wouldn't come around and hurt Quinn in the long run. He didn't want to do anything that would get in the way of her divorcing him quickly.

Besides, he had already put her through more than anyone should have to bear. He'd let his fears get in the way, and he'd damn near destroyed the best thing that had ever happened to him. He *had* read all of the e-mails she'd sent to him eventually, and he'd cried with each one. But one of the last, the one where she'd said good-bye because she thought he didn't love her, that he'd lied to her all those months about how much she meant to him, telling him her heart was shattered. *Oh, man.* Jacob could still feel the vice grip that took hold of his heart that day. He would never let her feel that way again.

Quinn came out of the bathroom with her new robe on. Jacob preferred her naked, but she did look really hot in that deep purple with her tan. "Come here, sexy woman."

She just smiled, went over to the mini-fridge, and took out two bottles of water. "Thirsty?" She slipped into the sheets next to him, handing over one of the bottles.

He chugged half of it down in a couple gulps. "Thank you, baby doll. That was exactly what I needed, besides you." He leaned over and nibbled on her neck a little, causing her to giggle. He loved her laugh. He used to imagine her eyes sparkling when she laughed, and they did. He couldn't help but laugh along with her because her eyes drew him right in. He pulled her close so she could snuggle up on his shoulder. "Thank you for sharing all that you went through. I know it was painful for you." Jacob took a deep breath and confessed one more thing to her, "I did read all of the e-mails you sent to me, Quinn. Every single one of them when you were in the hospital those four days."

She sat up and looked him in the eyes and smiled. "You did?"

"Yeah. Pretty heartbreaking stuff. Ma read them first because I was afraid."

"That I hated you for trying to make me believe you never loved me?"

Jacob nodded. "I kept telling myself you were better off without me, but if I would've read those e-mails, I would have known you weren't, that I'd caused your breakdown. I think deep down I knew it. But my mother was right. I had to know what I did to you so I could make it right with both of us."

Quinn snuggled back down hugged Jacob tighter. "It's over now. You came back for me and that's all that matters."

"I promise you that I'll never let you feel worthless ever again. You deserve to be loved and cherished every single moment of your life. I want to do that for you. You're my reason for living, Quinn. I want to keep the sparkle in your eyes and the laughter in your voice. No more heartaches, baby doll."

She sat up to look into his eyes again as she placed her hand over his heart. "Jake, you already make me feel loved and cherished. When I'm with you, my heart is whole. I'm not going to make you feel like you have to constantly make amends for hurting me. You thought you were doing what was best for both of us. I know that now. I know you didn't do anything to hurt me deliberately. We found a way back to each other through all of that pain, and we're stronger for it."

"You're one amazing woman. I'm so blessed to have you back in my life." He kissed her softly. "I can't wait to introduce you to my sister tomorrow. She's been rooting for us to get together ever since she found out about you."

"Really? I can't wait to meet her either. I want to learn all about you and the best person to find out all the dirt from is your big sister. She won't gloss over all the gory details!"

"Oh, is that so?" He pulled her down into the covers so he could pin her under him. "I don't have anything to hide from you, but you're right. Maredyth will give you her spin on things, and some of it will be a tad embarrassing. But if it makes you laugh then I am all for it."

She traced his jawline with her fingertips. "Shut up and kiss me."

Quinn didn't wait for him to respond but instead lifted her head off the pillows so her lips touched his, gently teasing him with the tip of her tongue.

He let her lead, teasing, tasting, and drawing out the desire they shared for each other until he could no longer stand it. He reached between them and undid the sash of the robe. He wanted to feel her body next to his as they continued to kiss, tongues slipping and sliding over each other, neither one taking the lead this time, just giving and taking equally.

They had enjoyed each other so much over the last two days, trying to cram it all in to the short time they had left to be together, but right at that moment something changed. The desperation vanished. They were no longer afraid they were going to wake up to find it was all a dream. They were finally where they both belonged.

He pulled back from her soft lips to gaze into her eyes, so sleepy now. She'd given him everything she had that day and then some. As much as he wanted to keep loving her all night long, he had to let her rest and let himself rest as well. "We have a long day at the beach with my family tomorrow. I for one don't want to get yelled at by my sister for keeping you up all night."

Even sleepy, her laugh was sexy as hell. He remembered when he'd heard it the very first time. It was in Las Vegas just before he moved to Chicago and met Iris. So much would have been different if he would have ignored his brother and asked her to dance. Maybe they would be married by now, without all the pain they both went through.

"Jake, what are you thinking about?" He helped her out of the robe the rest of the way, and she settled back down into his arms. "You looked miles away just now."

"I was remembering the very first time I heard your laugh and saw your killer curves."

"Oh? When was that?"

"Las Vegas last year."

"I remember watching Derek finish up your dragons. I was so enthralled by the artwork and the fact that you just lay there all relaxed."

"It was before that. The night before you and Randi were at the bar of the nightclub in your hotel. You wore that red mini-dress and men were falling all over themselves to get close to you. At one point you looked at me while you were dancing, and our eyes locked." Quinn's face lit up. *She remembered!* "Eric said I was thunderstruck, and then he got me the hell out of there. If only I would have stayed. You could have been mine already."

She pulled him tighter to her so that his head rested on her breasts and he could listen to her heart beating in sync with his own. "I'm yours now and I'll be yours forever. We have to let go of what could have been because now we have what was meant to be. It wasn't our time to be together then. It is now."

Quinn gently rubbed his neck and shoulders as he started to drift off in her arms. The scent of her perfume still enticed his senses and his desire to take her over and over again, but now it carried over into his dreams of their island and making love in the moonlight on the beach.

* * * *

CHAPTER 13

They were at the Studio Café having an early breakfast while discussing Steve's plan to get Jake and Quinn together. He wasn't sure how Derek was going to react when he originally told him about it, but since her stay in the hospital in Oakland, he'd had a change of heart. Derek was still mad at Jacob for hurting her in the first place, but he also knew the love they felt for each other couldn't be denied.

"Eric called me this morning from his sister's place. They'll be spending the day at the beach with Jake and Quinn. God, I still can't believe I am saying that again. Jake and Quinn. Just when I was really getting used to the idea of you and my sister, you do everything in your power to get Jake back into her life. I know why you're doing this, but I just don't understand it." Derek waved the waitress over for more coffee.

"Yeah, well, Quinn never understood it either. She kept asking me why I was always pushing her toward Jake, but deep down she knew I was right. Her heart has always been his, not that she didn't share it with me, too, but she could never give it all to me no matter how much she wanted to. I could have asked her to marry me and made a life with her in California, but eventually she would hate me for keeping her away from Jake. I couldn't take that. This way I'll always be in her life. What we had will stay with both of us forever."

"You became a totally different person after she came into your life." Derek smiled at Steve and shook his head. "She's with you one night and you're sitting in my shop having her portrait inked on your chest. I never would've thought you'd do that. It's like you found yourself again through Quinn's eyes, and I have to say everyone liked the changes. You'd cut yourself off from everyone, always in business meetings and locked in your office. Now you're enjoying your casinos again. It's great to see."

"I'm enjoying *life* again, Derek. That was Quinn's gift to me. I was just going through the motions most of the time after my illness ten years ago."

Derek dropped his fork onto his plate and looked up at him with shock. "What illness? You look like a picture of health to me."

Steve guessed it was time to come clean with his new family. He would have to work up to telling Quinn about it, and he hoped Derek will help him with that, too. "It was a couple of years after you opened your shop at the Mandalay Bay, so I'm not surprised you didn't know. Not too many folks do, just my old assistant Anthony and Darryl and, of course, a few of my partners. Just after I got rid of wife number two, I was diagnosed with non-Hodgkin's lymphoma."

Derek paled. "Jesus Christ, Steve. That's what we lost Dad to six years ago. Are you...?" He swallowed hard and seemed to be having trouble speaking.

"I've been in remission now for the last ten years. I go in every three months for checkups and the last one was just before I went to stay with Quinn at the Bay House. Anthony has been pushing me to tell her, but I've held off. She had too much on her plate. I didn't want to add to her stress and finding out that I have the cancer that took her Dad from her. It just didn't seem like a good thing to do."

"I agree with Anthony. You have to tell her, but you were right to wait. You were and still are her rock. You're the only one she has ever asked for help when she was feeling overwhelmed. You made her feel safe and loved and you asked nothing from her in return. If you would suddenly be gone out of her life—"

"That's not going to happen, Derek. Now that we've made it possible for her to be with Jake, I think she'll be in a better place emotionally for me to tell her about it. I won't keep it from her, but I have to find the right time to tell her."

"I'll help you any way I can. You just let me know what you need me to do."

They got up from the booth and headed out to the casino floor. "Right now, we need to fly to Oakland and get Quinn's things moved into the Bay House. By this time tomorrow, Jackson will be served with the divorce papers in Anaheim, and Quinn will be one step closer to being free of that asshole once and for all. Sarah has an extra set of keys for the house and she'll meet us there with a few of my friends from OPD. I don't want to have any trouble going in there to get her things. With the police presence, I hope to avoid having any confrontations with the Hollis family. I also don't want them tipping Jackson off. I want him to be knocked on his ass when he's handed those divorce papers."

"How long do you think it will take to get it all finalized?"

Darryl had already pulled the car around and was loading up their luggage when they stepped out into the casino's private garage. Steve waved him off and got the door himself. He knew Darryl would yell at him for that later. The man knew he wanted to get to California as fast as possible to help Quinn. He was sure Darryl would forgive him eventually. "Our lawyers tell me that Jackson can try to hold things up, but the way they have the settlement worded, if he contests in anyway, Quinn will claim half of his grandmother's estate instead of letting him have all of it. She doesn't know about that part. I had them add that in there as extra insurance against him trying to drag the divorce out longer than the six month waiting period."

"I still can't get over the idea that she stayed with that spineless prick all this time because of something she promised a mean old bird on her death bed, but it really is exactly what you'd expect her to do. She's always trying to please everyone else, even at the expense of her own happiness and mental health."

"Now it's our turn to make sure that all her dreams come true. While Jake proves to her that they deserve to be together forever, we'll help to remove the rest of the obstacles in their way. Eric will talk to Quinn about staying there a little longer and then move into the Bay House permanently if she wants to stay in that area. Sarah has already sent her an e-mail about the two of them transferring to their new San Francisco Specialty group where they can also teach new interns and technicians. It's all of the things Quinn loves to do: surgery, emergency medicine, and teaching. Apparently the merger with the San Francisco group was Quinn's idea. She'd drawn up the proposals, presented the merger idea to both sides, and had won them over during that very first meeting."

Derek smiled and laughed. "That's exactly how Quinn was when she was partner in the specialty practice in Michigan. Tenacious! It's good to hear that she has that spark back again. Now it looks like she may be finding happiness in her personal life."

Steve finished off his coffee and grinned. "From your mouth to God's ears and whatever I can do to move it along, I'll do it."

You've thought of everything, haven't you?"

"When it comes to Quinn getting everything her heart desires, you better believe it! But honestly, the only person who can do that is Quinn herself. She has to choose which path in life she is going to take, and who will or won't be by her side for the journey."

They'd fallen asleep in each other's arms the night before, remembering when they'd first laid eyes on each other. Quinn didn't know it was her laugh that had grabbed his attention first. She assumed it was the red dress. That's why she'd bought the thing in the first place. She'd loved the attention she'd received wearing it. That night brought her two of the best things that ever happened in her life: Steve and Jacob. It was meant to be that she was to fall in love with both of them. She knew that now, but Steve had been right all along.

Even though they loved each other deeply, Steve and Quinn could never make a marriage work because it was Jacob who was her everything, her heart and soul. She had to go through hell and back to figure all of that out, but it was Steve and his love for her that showed her the way. She didn't know how she could ever repay him for what he had done for her. She could only hope he would continue to be in her life as he would always be in her heart.

Jacob was still sound asleep, and by the look of the rapid eye movements under his lids, he was dreaming. She wished she could go inside his head and join him there, like he had for her when she was in the hospital. She knew he was really there when they'd made love the last time. It had been different than the other moments she shared with "dream" Jake. Besides, Danny said she would have her time with him then, and they had. Quinn hadn't remembered until last night that she had told Jake to promise her he would find her and make her listen to him. It took him a while, but he finally came for her.

Quinn slipped out of the bed as easily as she could. She didn't want to wake him up just yet. His cheeks were starting to flush and he wore a soft smile. She had a good idea what he was dreaming about. Hopefully she was there with him sharing it! The clock on his nightstand said 6:30 a.m. *Damn!* For not being a morning person, she was sure getting up early the last few days. *What the hell, might as well take care of the bladder situation before it started to demand it.*

She went around the room picking up their clothing from last night and hung them up in the closet along the way. She loved the purple shirt he'd worn to dinner. When she saw him standing here all dressed up with his long, sun-streaked brown hair and blue eyes smiling at her, he'd absolutely taken her breath away. Who would've thought they would be together this way or they would fall in love with each other at first sight? Not the two of them. They'd fought it all along the way and let other things and other people interfere.

Quinn looked at her reflection in the mirror after she brushed her teeth. She had finally found the love of a lifetime and she was never going to let anything stand in their way again. Maybe she should just stay there with Jacob and his family a bit longer and let Jackson go back to Oakland alone. There really wasn't any reason to prolong it any longer. After they got back from the beach that evening, she was going to go get the rest of her things she'd left in the safe. Jackson probably wouldn't notice anyway.

She peeked out of the bathroom to see he was still asleep but had rolled over onto his stomach. He had kicked off all of the covers and he took her breath away once again. His tanned skin was even darker when compared to the pale blue silk sheets he'd stretched out on. The sun was starting to peek through the curtains, and it made the dragons on his back shimmer. Quinn wondered if the pair on her back did that as well. Damn, her man was hot! She made her way back to the bed as Jacob began to stir.

"Baby doll?" Jacob reached for her, but she wasn't there. His eyes flew open, and he sat up fast.

"I'm right here, honey." She slid back into the bed and he pulled her close again. Jacob struggled to keep his breathing controlled as they settled back down onto the pillows. His heart was pounding. He guessed it would take some time before he was able to not wake up in a panic that it was all a dream. Quinn held him just as tight. He didn't have to explain to her what he was thinking, she just knew.

"What the hell has you out of bed so early?"

"The usual. I had to pee." She looked up at him and he kissed her for the first time that morning. Her lips yielded to his completely, letting him possess her one more time. Oh, that scent again! Jacob inhaled deeply and his cock responded. "Okay, where did you get your perfume? I've never, ever smelled anything like it. As soon as I smell it on you, I have this irresistible urge to make love to you over and over again." She smiled and giggled. "Not that I'm complaining at all, but I want to make sure that you never run out of the stuff."

"It was developed for me. It's called 'For the Love of Quinn.' It's from an aroma shop on Pier 39 in San Francisco. One of Steve's friends owns the place, and he developed my scent using a combination of different fragrances based on my personality and what impressions he got while talking to me and to Steve. His shop can then take that scent and make it into body wash, potpourri, lotions and a variety of other items. You name it he can do it."

"You'll have to take me there after we get settled into our own place together, just you and me."

"That I will. Did you ever in your wildest dreams think we would be here at Disney talking about setting up our own place together?" Her fingers slowly trailed up and down his chest and abs, almost absentmindedly, but he knew differently. His woman knew exactly what to do to turn him on without even trying. He decided to just go with it and see what surprises she had in store for him that morning.

"I remember that we used to fantasize about meeting up here and I would steal you away from Jack. Oh wait, that's really happening now."

Her hand encircled his erect cock.

"So, what are your plans for me this fine morning, Dr. Quartermarsh?"

She smiled again. "I just got a serious case of déjà vu. Are you going to keep calling me by my maiden name?"

Quinn was right. It felt like they'd had this same conversation before. "I will keep calling you that until you—"

"Change it to Hartley?" Her eyes flew open wide, and she bit her lower lip.

"We've had this conversation before. It was on our dream island. Baby, how can that be?"

"I have no idea, but my vote is to just go with it."

"You got it. Now come here woman!" He turned the both of them over and pinned her under him, pulling her legs up to wrap around his hips. Jacob's hands moved up her arms to pin her hands next to her head. *More déjà vu.* They just went with it, over and over again. This time they weren't saying goodbye. They were welcoming the dawn of their new life together.

"Can I ask you something?"

He reached for her after he settled back on the pillows once again. "Ask away." He kept nibbling and kissing her neck and trying to distract her.

"How is it that you're able to come with me so many times and still stay rock-hard? I have to say, I'm loving it, but there have been moments during the last couple of days that I was like, seriously?"

"Quinn, sometimes you say the funniest shit!" As soon as he was able to talk without laughing he answered her, "Remember what I told you about the motorcycle accident?"

"Yeah, that you had nerve damage and that caused it to be harder for you to ejaculate normally, so you were told it would be difficult for you to have kids." He nodded, and Quinn went on, "But you never told me that you could have marathon hard-ons. Isn't it painful for you to be erect that long?" Her hand slowly trailed down his stomach and gently caressed his cock, which at that second was drained and not ready to impale her at a moment's notice. She loved the feel of him in her hand. Hard or soft, he felt wonderful to her.

"At times it's been painful, but not ever with you. Not even when we were having phone sex. It was the weirdest thing. I was able to come each and every time I talked to you and now that we have actually been together, I've had no problem coming right along with you over and over. After meeting you, I finally believed the doctors who told me that the damage was more psychological than physical. Looks like you've cured me."

"Well, I'll be damned! I guess we were meant to be together right from the start."

"Definitely looks that way, baby doll. I've never been with anyone who could do that to me." He nuzzled her breasts with his stubbly chin, starting another round of giggles from her. "Anything else you want to ask me?"

"What's for breakfast? I'm starving!"

Jacob looked over at the clock. It was almost 8:00 a.m. "Room service will be here in about ten minutes. I had them send up the same thing we had yesterday. Does that meet with your approval, Dr. Quartermarsh?"

"Sounds wonderful, baby." She pulled him down on top of her to kiss him one more time before they had to untangle from each other and start their day. "And don't think I don't know what you're doing keeping me eating all this fruit."

Jacob smiled and kissed her quickly again before he got up to put on his boxers. He helped Quinn with her dragon robe and held her. "I thought you liked to eat a lot of fruit, and you know how much I love eating you."

Before she could give him one of her trademark smart-ass remarks, there was a loud knock on the door. Jacob crossed the room, opened the door, and they were greeted by the same waiter from yesterday. This time he had a bright smile on his face and a huge bouquet of flowers along with the food. "The front desk said these were delivered this morning and asked that I bring them up with the food for the happy couple."

Quinn rushed forward for the flowers. "Thank you so much. Hang on a second." She went for her purse to give him a tip, but the waiter waved her off.

"No need, miss. It's all been taken care of. I hope the two of you enjoy the rest of your day as well as the rest of your stay here with us. You just let the front desk know if there's anything else you need." He had everything set up and was out the door before she could take another breath. She looked at Jacob, and he shrugged and smiled again.

Quinn sat the flowers down on the dresser and pulled the card out to read it. She started to cry and handed the card to Jacob.

Jake and Quinn,
IT'S ABOUT GODDAMN TIME!!

This has been a long time coming, and we just wanted to tell you that we're so happy the two of you finally are able to be together. You've both been through so much in your lives, and all of it has led up to this moment and planning your future together. We have a few more surprises planned for you both, so sit back and enjoy!

PS: Just go with it, woman!

"It's signed from Eric, Derek, all the tat shop boys, the guys from Quarter to Three, the club bartenders, your sister, and mine. And you know the most important person in our corner, Steve."

The flowers their friends and family sent were beautiful. The vase was filled with purple roses, lilies and orchids. All of them were Quinn's favorites and his. Jacob was speechless himself, but it felt really good to know they were all behind them. He really loved the PS from Steve to Quinn, perfect. Just a few short months ago he would have been paralyzed with jealousy over it, but not now. Jacob thought it was time he told Quinn just how much help he had getting back to her.

He looked over at his lady love, and she was wiping the tears from her eyes and smiling. "I can't believe they did this. They're so beautiful. How did they know I was here with you?" She sat down at the table and looked under the covers of the dishes.

"I've sort of been texting them and letting them know what's been going on."

She smiled and rolled her eyes like she should have expected this sort of thing to happen.

"They've all helped me find my way back to you. Especially Steve. He never gave up on me. He's the one who told me you would be here now. In fact, he helped me put all of it together. I was really wary of it all at first. I couldn't understand why he'd do this for me and why he'd ever give you up. If the roles were reversed, I don't know if I could've done the same for him."

Quinn made up a plate for Jacob and then started on her own. "He always told me you and I would have the love of a lifetime if we would just give in to our feelings for each other and stop second-guessing them. He knew right from the start there was something between us, but he wanted me, too. He just took a chance, and well, we did fall in love with each other. It was different for me. He told me that I am and will always be the love of his life and he just wants me to be happy, and the only person who could make me truly happy was you."

Jacob knelt next to her after she sat down at the table and cradled her face in both of his hands. "Is that true, baby doll? Am I the only person who can make you happy?"

She smiled and nodded. "She crossed her heart and held three fingers up. "Scout's Honor."

He kissed her softly then let her go. At that point, both of their stomachs started rumbling. "I guess we had better eat before it gets cold."

He sat down opposite her at the table and dug in. The food was stellar, as it has been every day, but this morning it was even better. Things were finally working out for them, and their friends and family were behind them one hundred percent. Life couldn't get much better. He had a few more surprises for Quinn and having Eric at the beach today with them would just be the start of it.

Hunting Beach was only twenty minutes from their hotel, but it was well over an hour before they'd finally got on the road. Jacob had tried really hard to keep his hands to himself when Quinn put on her bikini, but the strings were just too hard for him to resist. Her body still tingled from head to toe when they reached their destination. They'd picked up more ice, bottled water, and sodas to put into their cooler for everyone. They had offered to bring more, but Maredyth told Jacob she had the rest covered. Quinn made sure she purchased two extra bottles of her favorite sunscreen. Jacob liked the smell of that, too, and kept smelling her skin whenever he was close to her.

"Are you going to be doing that all day? Your sister is going to think you're insane."

"Oh, she already knows I'm bonkers. She won't bat an eye that I keep smelling your skin. Hell, she'll probably keep doing it, too. That sunscreen smells good, fruity." He winked at her as they unloaded the car and headed down the walkway to the beach. "You know how much I love the combination of you and fruit!" He nodded to a group of people up ahead of them on the beach. "There they are right now."

Quinn looked over to where he was talking about, and she saw three kids running their way and two adults. "Who's that with your sister?"

"Another surprise for you. Look again." He was grinning ear to ear now, and he dropped the cooler just as the kids came flying up to tackle him. "Oy! You three monsters are going to be the death of me yet!"

Quinn turned from Jacob and the kids and was nearly knocked over by the mystery man. "Eric!" She threw her arms around him as he lifted her up and spun her around. "When did you get into town?"

"Late yesterday morning. I'm on a two-week vacation before I start my new job as Steve's assistant. Are you surprised?"

"Am I surprised? If you weren't holding me right now I would have fallen over from shock. I'm so happy to see you. I've missed seeing your smiling face and talking to you online. Now that you've been promoted you won't have time for our chats anymore."

"Oh, like hell! I'll always have time for you. You're family."

"A little help here, brotha." Jacob crawled out from the bottom of a nephew and niece pileup. Nine-year-old twins Kyle and Mark and four-year-old Cassie held on to their uncle, making it very difficult for him to get up off of his knees, let alone walk down the sand. "Stop flirting with my woman and grab a rug rat or the cooler."

"All right, you three, let Uncle Jake get up so we can get back to your Mom. How about you say hello to our guest before she thinks we're all a rude bunch."

Kyle and Mark each took a handle of the cooler and said hello to Quinn in unison before walking a bit unsteadily down the beach back to Maredyth. Cassie walked right up, put her hand in Quinn's and beckoned to her to bend down to her level so she could whisper in her ear, "You're very pretty, like a princess."

"Thank you, Cassie. I think you're very pretty, too." Her long, curly blonde hair blew wildly in the breeze, and she kept brushing it out of her eyes. She beckoned to Quinn again and kept looking back and smiling at Jacob before she started whispering again.

"Uncle Jake loves you and wants to marry you."

"Is that so?"

She nodded and giggled.

"How do you know?"

"I heard him tell Mommy when he came back to live with us. Can I call you Aunt Quinn?"

"I would like that very much."

She got up on her tiptoes and kissed Quinn on the cheek before she bolted down the beach after her brothers with Eric hot on her little heels.

Jacob took the beach bag from Quinn and then held her hand as they made their way across the sand toward the area Maredyth had staked out. "What did the little pixie say to you that had her all giggles?"

"She said, and I quote, 'Uncle Jake loves you and wants to marry you.' She wanted to know if she could call me Aunt Quinn."

"Well, you know what they say, out of the mouths of babes." He stopped and pulled her close to him. "Cassie is usually very shy around new people, to the point where she's hiding and literally clinging to Maredyth, just sobbing. You're the first person I have ever seen her talk to right off, let alone kiss on the cheek. Just that alone is going to make my sister fall in love with you." He looked down the beach and smiled. "And that would probably be why she's coming this way now."

Maredyth jogged toward them with a huge smile on her face. "Oh my God, oh my God! You're finally here!" She threw her arms around Quinn and squeezed her tight. "You have no idea how excited we have been to have you join us today, especially Cassie." Her eyes fill with tears. "She's like a totally different little girl. Welcome to the family, Quinn!" Maredyth let her go long enough to pull Jacob into the bear hug with them. "Did you see her, Jake? She was laughing and giggling when she came running back to me. She said Uncle Jake's gonna marry a princess."

Eric and Jacob took the boys out into the waves while Quinn and Cassie stayed in the shallow water splashing and building sand castles. Maredyth supervised it all under her umbrella-covered beach chair. She looked the happiest Jacob had seen her in a long time, and so was he. Here he was with his family and the woman who loved him and would be his wife as soon as they could make it happen. He caught Eric watching him, looking back at Quinn with Cassie. "What's on your mind, little brother?"

"I was remembering something you told me right after you moved to Chicago."

"That one day Quinn would be mine?" Jacob smiled at him and tossed Kyle over his shoulder into the next wave. Both boys were having a blast riding waves into the shore. "Sorry, what else did I ever talk about then?"

"You still want to try to have kids with Quinn? She's simply amazing with Cassie and the boys. I bet she'll be an awesome mother, and you would be just like Pop, spoiling your kids rotten!"

"I want kids with her more than ever now. Look at her face when Cassie takes her hand. She's glowing. She told me she'd given up wanting to have kids because of all the shit she's been through with Jack. Maybe now she's ready to try again."

"Speaking of Hollis, he'll be served with the divorce papers tomorrow morning."

"In Anaheim? Holy Shit! Steve's lawyers work fast. Does Quinn know?"

"No. That's another reason why I'm here. Steve asked me to help you keep Quinn down here with us for at least the next week or two so that they can get her all moved out of the Oakland Hills house. Derek and Steve are flying there today to meet up with Sarah and a few others. Quinn will never have to go back to that house or anywhere near Jackson again."

"Wow. This is all happening so fast. I'm not sure how she's going to take all of this news. Hopefully, she'll do what Steve told her in the card that came with the flowers this morning."

Eric laughed. "Oh, I can hear him now. 'Quinn, just go with it, woman!'"

"Exactly! The flowers and the card made her cry. She was so surprised. Nice touch, Eric."

"How did you know it was my idea?" He waved back to Maredyth on the beach. She was standing up and waving both of her arms in the air. Apparently she wanted to get the grill going.

"That's the sort of thing Pop always did for Ma, and having it signed by all of you really meant a lot to me, too." The twins were already riding the waves back up to shore, and Quinn was carrying a very sleepy Cassie back toward the shade. "Thank you for believing in me when I was ready to give it all up. Without all of you in my corner, I would never have found my way back to Quinn."

"Yeah, well, it was a lot of work all the way around. Both of you are so stubborn! No worries now. Everything is going the way it is meant to be. I'll even wager that you two will be parents sooner than you think."

Maredyth wrapped the twins up in their towels and scooted them up toward the shade. "Why don't you both read a story to your sister so she can take a nap? Oh. Now I didn't say you had to take one with her, but you could if you wanted to. It's your choice." Kyle and Mark ran up to Cassie wrapped up in Quinn's towel. They got on either side of her and started reading one of the books they'd brought with them. Quinn kissed Cassie on her forehead, and then, shocker of all shockers, the boys asked her for one, too.

"Uh-oh, Jake. Looks like the boys are putting the moves on Quinn."

"I see that." Both of them looked out at Jacob and grinned from ear to ear. He gave them the I'm-watching-you sign, and they launched into a round of giggles before settling back down to read to Cassie. Quinn met him with another beach towel in hand. He pulled her close and kissed her. "Looks like you have some more fans."

She looked back at the kids, watching them as they started to sing the kissing in a tree song. "Little heartbreakers, that's what they are." She turned back to Jacob and touched his face softly with her fingertips. "Just like their Uncle Jake."

"Not anymore. You've officially taken him off the market. Thank God!" Eric gave them both a bear hug. "Now it's up to me to carry on the bad boy Hartley legacy. What do you think, big eagle tat on my chest? Tongue piercing?"

"Nooooo. Don't you dare change a thing, Eric. You're perfect just the way you are."

"Thanks, hot stuff!" Eric took her hand and kissed it. "It's time for the Grill Master to get to work. Now if only someone could keep Maredyth out of my way. Woman! Put down the tongs and the spatula, sit your butt down at the table, and relax for a change!" Eric gently pushed his sister away from the grill. "Go on. You know you are dying to ask Quinn more questions, have at it."

"Is that a dragon tat on your back?" Maredyth's eyes widened. "Can I see?"

Quinn lifted up the bottom of her tank so Maredyth could see the whole thing. "My brother did this for me in February. He designed it the year before, but I wasn't ready to sit for something this intricate at that time. Hell, I nearly passed out with the first butterfly."

Her fingers were cool on Quinn's skin as she traced over both of the mating dragons. "It's beautiful. Derek does amazing work. When I first saw Jake's back, I couldn't stop touching it. It looks like they could just jump out of his skin and fly around. I'm going to have to visit this boy's shop myself one day."

"You should. He would love to design one for you, too. My sister ended up getting a second one from another artist in his shop, and my friend Sarah had a stalking tiger put on her lower back." They sat down at the table, and Eric brought over some bottled waters and a soda for himself. Jake sat sideways, straddling the bench so he could hold Quinn closer to him. She loved the feel of his hand rubbing her lower back. "So, what do you want to know?"

"Did you feel thunderstruck the first time you saw Jake, too? Eric has told the story a hundred times or more since that night, and Jake's given his side of the story. What's yours?"

"I was dancing with my sister at the club waiting for Steve to rejoin us when I caught Jake watching me. I have a soft spot for bad boys, so I was smitten right off."

"Didn't I tell you? Classy chicks have a thing for bad boys. Maybe you *should* get a couple piercings and grow your hair out a bit." Jacob and Eric laughed harder when Maredyth rolled her eyes and gestured for Quinn to keep going with her story.

"It was his deep blue eyes that rooted me to the spot." Quinn told Maredyth all about the physical reaction she had every time she was in the same room as Jacob. She confessed that she could barely breathe when she talked to him the first time in the Tattoo Parlor.

"You know, your brother called you to the back of the shop on purpose. He was having a grand old time torturing me. He made me promise to only look and not touch. I should've grabbed you in the shop and kissed you right then and there."

"Oh and then you would have had your skull cracked open a year earlier."

Quinn looked up at Eric. "What are you talking about, a year earlier?" Was this what she saw in her dream?

Maredyth smacked Eric on the arm. "Didn't I tell you she didn't know about that?"

"Jake? Tell me." Quinn quickly glanced over at the kids. All three of them were sound asleep. She squeezed his hand. "Derek hurt you because of me?"

"He told me if I ever hurt you, he would kill me. I went to Vegas the first week of April to talk to Eric. I saw the portrait that Derek had painted of you outside the club, and all the feelings I had for you came flooding over me. I kept hearing your voice on the phone crying, asking me why I'd lied to you all that time. My heart couldn't take it, and I realized that I didn't want to live anymore without you. I felt trapped with Iris and everywhere I turned you were there. I basically went into the tat shop begging him to make good on his promise."

Eric nodded slowly and looked at his brother with sad eyes. "I couldn't get you to leave. Mike and I both tried to shove you out before Derek flew out of the back. I have never seen him so angry. I thought he broke your jaw for sure. There was so much blood, and Iris was screaming. Damn, it was a mess. Derek would have kept going if Steve hadn't come in and stopped him."

Quinn trembled and her hands shook. Jacob put his arms around her and held her tight to his chest. "It's okay, Quinn. I deserved everything Derek could throw at me. Steve, on the other hand, I couldn't figure out. He knew right away I was trying to hurt myself and told me I had to think long and hard about who I wanted to spend the rest of my life with. He said he would help me win you back. I just had to take a chance. What did he say?"

"He said take a chance and let it all ride. It is Vegas after all." Eric did a pretty good impression of Steve, and Quinn smiled. All along he was working both sides to get them together. Quinn's heart was just overflowing with love for Steve at that moment.

Maredyth reached across the table and took her hand. "Honey, don't be too upset with Derek for wanting to protect you. When you were in the hospital, he was the one who called Eric to beg Jake to fly to Oakland to bring you back from your dreamland. I guess that's what you would call it. You were dreaming, right?" Quinn nodded, and she went on, "He said you were there in your dreams with Jake, and he was afraid they would lose you forever if something or someone didn't bring you out of it. He was absolutely sure Jake was the only one who could."

"I don't know how it happened, but I kept wishing to be on the tropical island that Jake and I used to make up fantasies about, and I just woke up there. Jake was right there telling me he missed me and we didn't have a lot of time together."

* * * *

CHAPTER 14

Jacob's pulse quickened. "Honey, I *was* there with you. The night I stayed at Ma's, I went to sleep hoping to find you on our island. It was so real. You told me to just go with it even though it didn't make any sense that we could be there together."

"I know. I made you promise me you wouldn't let your fear take over again, that you would find me and make me listen to you even if I told you to—"

"Fuck off," Jacob whispered so the kids didn't hear it. "I thought I'd finally found the way to be with you forever. I begged you to stay there with me and never go back. You started to cry and said we had to go back or we would die in the real world."

"I came back for you, Jake. Danny said if I didn't go back you would finally find a way to kill yourself. I couldn't let that happen. I loved you too much, even if it meant that you would be married to someone else."

Maredyth and Eric stared at them with their eyes wide. Eric was the first to regain his voice. "Holy shit! Ma used to talk about sharing dreams with Pop. You two are freaky!"

Maredyth agreed, "That's good enough for me. Quinn, you're not going back to Oakland. You're staying down here with Jake and the rest of us. You two have gone through hell and back. It's time you enjoyed life together."

Quinn shook her head. "I have to go back at least to San Francisco. I got word this morning that my transfer has been approved. Sarah and I will be taking over the mobile surgical unit for the new specialty practice our group opened up in January."

"How much longer are you on medical leave, baby doll?"

"I'm supposed to go back right after Labor Day and finish out that month in our Oakland hospitals then start the mobile unit traveling between the two cities with Sarah. My bosses want to ease me back into my surgery schedule and then I'll take over teaching the new techniques to the interns and technicians."

Jacob looked at Eric and nodded. He thought it was a good time to tell her about the divorce papers. "I have another message for you from Steve. Tomorrow morning, Jackson will be served with the divorce papers here in Anaheim."

Quinn took a deep breath and closed her eyes. "How? They just filed the petition yesterday. How can things move that fast?"

Eric smiled at her. "Steve pulled a few strings and called in a few favors. When it comes to you, he'll do just about anything to get you what you want. You know that. As we relax here together, he's in Oakland with Derek, Sarah, and some of your friends from work and OPD to get you moved completely out and into the Bay House. I'm supposed to remind you that the house was remodeled specifically for you, especially the kitchen. He wants both of you to consider it your home now."

"I, I don't know." Quinn looked to Jacob for his input.

He could guess what she was thinking. She was worried that he wouldn't want to move into a house that she had planned on sharing with Steve. "Would you want to live there with me, at least for a little while?"

"Baby doll, I told you I'd go anywhere to be with you. From what I hear, the place has a killer view. How could I say no to that?"

Eric clapped his hands together. "That's settled then. Steve will be thrilled."

Jacob smiled and kissed her on the forehead. "Quinn? Are you all right?"

"I'm just a little stunned. Everything is starting to fall into place for us, and I guess I'm just waiting for the other shoe to drop."

"This time you have all of us to help you get through whatever comes your way. You're part of us now, sweetie. The Hartley clan sticks by each other through everything, even when one of us tries to go it alone." Maredyth's eyes softened and she squeezed Jacob's hand.

He squeezed back. "I won't do that again. I promise."

Quinn kissed his cheek and placed her hand over theirs. "I promise too."

"With so many people helping to get the two of you together, there is no way in hell anyone or anything will be able to stop it." Eric placed his hand on top of all of theirs. His eyes blazed with determination he hadn't seen for months. His heart swelled with pride for his family.

"This is all happening because of Steve."

"You know he helped me find you again. I still can't believe all that he's done to make this happen." He bit his lower lip a little and smiled again. "I have a confession to make. He's the family friend who helped arrange the carriage ride last night. When I told him what I wanted to do, to make it all a fairy tale for you, he told me about the carriage rides and to leave it all up to him. Whatever I wanted to do, he made it happen. He helped me get away from Iris and her family and back home to mine and to you."

"I've asked him over and over again why he kept pushing me toward you, and he said that he just wanted me to be happy."

The kids were starting to wake up, and Quinn was sure they were starving by now. Eric got up to take the food off of the grill while Maredyth prepared plates for the boys. Cassie climbed up into Quinn's lap, put her head on her shoulder, and snuggled up a bit longer. She was still a little sleepy-eyed. Quinn kissed her forehead and brushed her curls out of her eyes. Jacob embraced both of them, squeezing tight.

"I know the feeling. For the longest time I thought you would be happier with Steve. Hell, he more than staked his claim on you that first night, but he ended up knowing your heart better than I did and mine as well."

Maredyth sat down across from them after she got the twins settled with food. "Go on with your story, Quinn. This is better than any romance novel I could get my hands on. Sounds like Steve has become a guardian angel for the two of you."

Eric, Jacob, and Quinn burst out laughing. "Oh, he would be the first to admit he's no angel, but you're right. He's definitely watched over all of us through everything. I can't imagine my life now without him in some way. He's seen me through so much, and he's always made sure I did what I wanted to do. Steve's never pressured me in any way. He told me that night after Derek's first concert that he was falling in love with me, and he didn't expect me to feel the same, just let him love me whenever we could be together. That's all he ever asked of me. Steve made me feel safe and he has been my rock. And, yes, I do love him. It's just not the same love I feel for Jake."

Eric nodded as he gulped down his soda. "Steve has that way about him. He tells you like it is and gives you the chance to decide what to do, good, bad, or indifferent. I do know one thing, Jake. If you hadn't finally come to your senses, he would have done everything he could to make her life with him a happy one."

Quinn looked up at the man she loved. "Steve has done everything to make me happy, and he's still doing it. He brought me you. He told me you were my heart and soul and I would always wish for you until we found each other again. He was right."

"Sounds like Steve loves you very much, and Jake should be grateful to him for that." Maredyth brushed a tear off her cheek. "I know I'm very grateful to him for giving us our brother back. We missed you so much, Jake." She passed a small plate of food over for Cassie. Quinn picked up the hotdog for her and she perked right up and started to eat. She reached up and rubbed her tiny hand over Jacob's stubbly cheek and giggled. *Girl after my own heart!*

"I *am* grateful for everything he's done and all the time he spent with me. I can never repay him for it all. How can you repay someone who's given you your life back?"

Quinn looked into Jake's eyes, and he cradled her face with his right hand before he kissed her.

Cassie giggled again then slipped off Quinn's lap to chase after her brothers.

Eric tossed his empty plate into the trash can and looked his brother square in the eye. "I'll tell you how you can repay him, by doing exactly what you're doing. Love each other and be happy. That is all he ever wanted for you both." He helped Maredyth up from the bench so they could chase after the kids. "Now who wants to play tackle beach volleyball?"

All three kids squealed and ran circles in the sand trying to avoid being tackled by Eric. Finally they worked together and ganged up on him.

"Oh! So that's how it is!" Eric dodged them expertly for a couple minutes and then pretended to give up. All of them collapsed on the sand in a heap. Their laughter carried out over the beach.

Jake held Quinn close for a bit longer. "Quinn, if it wasn't for Steve and my Ma, I would've just gone on barely existing with Iris and her kids."

"I heard Steve's voice telling me to tell you in my dream to fight for me. He told me to make you hear me and then come back."

"I saw the hesitation in your eyes when Eric told you Steve wanted us to live in the Bay House. I don't want you to think you have to cut him out of your life, Quinn. I know you mean a lot to each other, that you love each other. I can accept that now, although I'm a bit jealous that he got to have you in his bed first, or against the wall as the case may be!"

"Jake! You're so bad! I can't believe you remember that."

"Baby doll, I remember everything you've ever told me."

"Aunt Quinn! Uncle Jake! Come on and swim with me!" Cassie was standing in the waves with her hip out and her arms crossed over her chest.

Quinn giggled at the sight of Jacob's niece. "Uh-oh. Looks like my mini-me has picked up another one of my mannerisms."

"Hold your horses there, Squirt! What would you say to spending the rest of the week in our current room and then another week with Eric, Mare, and the kids at one of the Disney hotels? After that I'll pack my things and move up to the Bay House with you."

"Sounds like fun! Is this one of the surprises that was mentioned on the card with the flowers this morning?"

"Uh-huh. Eric will tell the kids tomorrow that they'll be spending the next ten days at Disneyland. Derek and Sarah will join us for at least a couple of those days. Steve wants to give us some alone time, but he invited us to stay at the Mandalay Bay for the Fourth of July week as his guests. Would that be all right with you?"

She got up from the bench and held her hand out to him. "As long as we get to be together, I don't care where we go. I'm going to take the advice of a very dear friend. I'm going to just go with it!"

She let go of his hand and bolted for the water. Cassie screamed with laughter. "Run, Aunt Quinn! Uncle Jake is gonna catch you!"

Quinn's laughter made his heart sing and was just as infections as the first time he'd heard it. Maredyth, Eric, and the kids all laughed when Jacob did catch her and threw her over his shoulder. He dove into the waves, taking them both under the warm water.

Quinn was still in his arms as they broke the surface together. "I love you, Jake."

"I love you, Quinn Lee Quartermarsh. And yes, I'm going to keep calling you that until the day you become Quinn Lee Hartley in front of all of our family and friends, with Cassie as our flower girl and the boys as our ring bearers. I want the whole fairy tale with you, and I want to do what we need to do to see if we can start a family of our own."

"You want babies with me?" Her eyes filled with tears. "Are you sure?"

"Yes, love. I want to try. If we can't have our own, I want to adopt. You deserve to be a mother, and I want more than anything to hear a little rug rat call me Daddy. A little girl with your eyes, holding my hand, building sand castles at the beach, or a little boy learning to ride a bike for the first time. Am I sure? You better believe it, baby doll."

"I need to get the rest of my things, Jake. I forgot to check the safe the last time I was up there and I want to drop off my room key. It'll only take a minute. Jackson isn't answering his cell or the room phone. He's obviously out."

"I don't think you should go over there tonight and definitely not alone. What if Jackson's family told him about what's going on at your house? He could do something to stop you from leaving. "

"And that's exactly why you can't go over there with me. If you're there, he'll definitely start something, and I don't want to be bailing you out of jail."

All of the muscles in Jacob's arms tensed, and he ground his teeth.

Quinn knew if he was anywhere near Jackson right now he would beat him to a pulp. "I'll be all right and back here before you know it."

"I'm going to wait for you by the pool. If you take too long, I'll come up there after you, and God help Jackson if he tries anything."

He held her hand tight until they got to the pool area then he pulled her to him and kissed her.

"Honey, you can see the room from here and anyone coming and going. Relax. I'll be back down before you know it."

He let her go but kept shaking his head. Quinn sprinted across the small parking area to the stairs that would take her up to Jackson's room. When she got to the third floor, she looked back out over the railing and saw Jacob watching her, but he wasn't alone. The waiter from that morning was there with him in his street clothes along with one of the security guards. All of them were watching her and waved when they saw the smile on her face. It looked like she had her own cavalry if need be. *Smooth move, Jacob!*

She put the key card in the door and went right in. All of the lights were on, and the room was a mess. *Typical Jackson!* Both beds were tossed, and she didn't want to know what the hell he'd been doing in there or with whom. She went back into the closet to access the wall safe. She pulled out her keys and half of the cash they had placed in there. It looked like he hadn't gotten into it at all yet. He probably couldn't remember the access code. She decided to just leave it open for him. She went through the closet and all the drawers one last time to satisfy herself that she indeed had everything this time. She dropped her key card on top of the desk and turned to leave.

"Well, well, well. I was wondering how long it would take you to get back here to get the rest of your things."

Jackson! Where the fuck did he come from? "Where the hell were you? I've been calling you for the last half hour." She noticed the door between this room and the one next door was open. *Fuck!* She'd forgotten about the adjoining room.

His gaze followed hers. "Yep. I've been fucking the chick next door while you've been with Hartley. Care to find out who?"

"Not really." Her intuition had been spot on. He'd known where she was the whole time. What the hell was going on with him? "I just want to leave. I'm not going back to Oakland with you, and I don't care who you're fucking now. Move out of my way, please." She started to move around him and detected the unmistakable odor of booze oozing from his pores. Her stomach dropped. Jackson could be a mean-ass drunk when provoked.

Christ! I have to get the hell out of here.

She'd left her phone back in the other room. No way to get a message to Jacob or the police. She forced herself to remain calm and not do anything to set him off.

Jackson sat down hard on the bed. "This is not the way I wanted this trip to go, you know. I had hoped that seeing our friends down here again would help you with your recovery and help start mending things between us."

She wasn't sure what to believe at that moment. The man sitting on the bed in front of her reminded her of the person she'd married, but the condition of the room they were in put her on high alert. "A lot has happened between us that we can't change. We both need to decide what we want out of life and stop letting other people influence our decisions."

He laughed. "You are so naïve, Quinn. Did you really think it was all just a coincidence that I was Grandmother's date the night we first met?"

"What are you talking about?"

"The charity auction when she introduced us? It was all arranged by her. She *picked* you for me. Grandmother wanted to control everything in my life. She couldn't stand the fact that I was still single. She never approved of anyone I dated, so she took matters into her own hands."

Quinn knew Miriam had been controlling, but she was always kind to her. "She wanted you to be happy, Jack. She loved you and wanted nothing more than to see you succeed."

"Bullshit! She wanted to control me and thought by marrying me off to someone respectable, I'd settle down. Well, it didn't work."

Quinn sat down on the bed next to him. "We never should've married each other. We were doomed right from the start."

Jackson snorted. "I was doing what I was *told* to do. I wanted my inheritance, Quinn. I wanted to be free of my parents and my grandmother once and for all. You're supposed to be my free pass. Now, you've ruined everything." He downed the rest of his drink in one gulp. "If you would've just done what you were supposed to do, we wouldn't be in this mess."

The hair on the back of her neck stood on end and her stomach churned. "I tried to make our marriage work. What else was I supposed to do?"

Jackson glared at her. "Be a good wife. Keep paying the bills. Ignore my extracurricular activities and basically just keep your fucking mouth shut!"

She had to get the hell out of there, now. Quinn got up off the bed and tried to maneuver around him, but Jackson grabbed her wrist. "Where the hell do you think you're going? Did you really think I was going to let you out of here without celebrating our ten years of wedded bliss?"

Quinn struggled to break free of his grip. "Let me go. We've got nothing to celebrate anymore."

"You know, you're not the only one who hooked up with an online lover here at Disney, Quinn. She'd be here to officially rub it in your face, but she made a booze run. How about you just hang out for a few more minutes and you can say hello to her?" He swayed and barely kept upright.

She realized she'd made a big mistake not having Jacob or one of the security guards come with her. She didn't think she had anything to worry about. She'd been sure Jackson was out of the room. Now she was face to face with a drunken monster. This was so unlike Jackson that Quinn was frozen with fear, giving him the upper hand.

He tossed her on top of the bed. "You know, it's been a hell of a long time since I fucked that Grade A pussy of yours. As I recall, you like to be pounded until you scream after my tongue laps up the never-ending gusher of cum squirting out of you. I bet you're dripping right now thinking about it. How about you let me have a taste before you go? No? Or how about I ram your ass until you scream for more?"

"Get off of me, Jack!" Bile rose to the back of her throat and she gagged. His breath was horrible with all the booze he'd consumed and whatever food he had eaten that day. She kept kicking and punching, but he had her pinned so she couldn't do that much damage.

His lips brushed over her neck and trailed down to her breasts, coating her skin with foul smelling drool. His right hand grabbed both of her wrists and pinned them above her head, while his left hand reached up under her sarong and tried to tear away her swim suit bottoms. Quinn screamed with everything she had welled up inside. "No! Jackson, stop it!"

There was a pounding on the door. "Is everything all right in there?"

Jackson tried to cover her mouth with his hand, but Quinn bit him hard. "You fucking cunt! You're going to be sorry you did that!"

Quinn screamed again. The door crashed open, and the security guard was now next to the bed in a flash. A police officer was right behind him with his gun drawn. Three other guards filed in immediately after them.

"Get off of her, and put your hands up! Now!"

Jackson did as he was told but kept grinning at Quinn. "What's the matter, officer? Can't a guy have a little rough sex with his wife of ten years? She's into all that stuff, and I thought I'd finally give it to her as an anniversary present." He kept rubbing his flaccid cock in his shorts.

Two more Anaheim police officers came into the room next. The male officer handcuffed Jackson and made him sit on the other bed. The female officer came over to Quinn and helped her to stand. "Dr. Hollis? Are you all right?"

Quinn nodded to her but couldn't speak just yet. Seemed like all hell was still breaking loose, and a major screaming match seemed to be going on outside the door.

"You get your hands off of me! I didn't do anything to be manhandled by the police!"

"Ma'am, I'm not going to tell you again! No one is going anywhere until we sort this entire thing out! Mr. Hartley, please just give me one second to see what's going on before I let you go in there."

"What's the matter, Jake? Can't stand the idea that your precious Quinn is in there having sex with her husband? You know, Jackson is twice the man you ever were in bed. I bet now that she's had a taste of you, she went to him tonight to beg him to take her back!"

"Get the fuck away from me, Iris! Quinn!"

What the hell was Iris doing here? She looked back to Jackson, and he smiled again. "Surprised? You shouldn't be. We've been in contact with each other from the moment she found out about the two of

197

you. If you think for one minute that I'm going to sit back and just give you a divorce so you can be with Hartley, you're out of your fucking mind!"

Jacob was suddenly at the door. All color had drained from his face. "Quinn?"

She rushed into his arms and buried her face into his shoulder. "I should have listened to you. I'm sorry, baby." He held her tighter to him and kept whispering in her ear that everything was going to be all right.

The female officer approached Jacob and Quinn again. "Dr. Hollis, do you need to go to the hospital and be checked out by a doctor?"

Quinn looked into Jacob's eyes. "No. It didn't get that far. He may have to go, though. I bit him pretty good." Jacob noticed the bruises that were starting to form on her wrists, and his face flushed scarlet. "Stay with me, Jake. Please don't give him the satisfaction of you going to jail, too."

"That's right, Mr. Hartley. Let us take care of this. Don't worry about what will happen to Mr. Hollis. He'll have his hand looked at once he's been booked for assault and attempted rape."

"What? She's my *wife*! If I want to fuck her, I will!"

Quinn rounded on him then. "Listen to me, you piece of garbage. I filed for divorce yesterday morning. You and your family won't have me to kick around any longer. We're done! The only reason I came on this trip with you was to see if there was any ounce of humanity left in you that I could at least have a civil conversation with, and you attack me! You can rot in jail for all I care! Better yet, why don't you have your new girlfriend bail you out?"

"Who do you think you are, telling me what to do?" Iris flew into the room and tried to clock Quinn with the bottle of vodka she had in her hand. Big mistake. The female officer had her disarmed and flat on the floor with her wrists zip-tied behind her back before she could say another word.

"Ma'am, I'm going to tell you this just once. You have the right to remain silent."

Jacob pulled Quinn out of the room while the officers finished reading both of them their rights. A third person approached them, and Quinn immediately knew why help had arrived so fast. "Frank?"

"Hey, Quinn, honey. Fancy meeting you here!" He winked at her before she hugged him. "Steve thought you may need a little help down here, and I have friends in the Anaheim Police Department. They're going to help me serve the divorce papers tomorrow morning. Looks like that plan is moving on up!" He shook hands with Jacob. "You must be Jake Hartley."

"I'm sorry, Jake, this is Frank Samuels, one of my friends from the Oakland PD and, as it so happens, a good friend of Steve's from the days they worked in construction together."

"Ah. You're the one Steve said volunteered to come down here to serve the papers." Jake slipped a protective arm around Quinn's waist again. His muscles relaxed a bit, but he was still shaking, and so was she.

"Oh, yeah. Anything to stick it to that piece of trash."

They stepped out of the way as the officers escorted both Jackson and Iris out of the room and toward the stairs. Thank God both of them kept their mouths shut this time. "Steve got a call from the private investigators watching Jack last night that one Iris Moore had checked into the room right next to this one. Seems he'd reserved both rooms and had the desk hold the keys for the second one until he gave them further instructions. Since you've been staying with Jake, these two yahoos have been partying all day in both rooms."

"Is that why the security guard came over to stand with me at the pool? They were watching them?"

Frank nodded. "They were watching the two of you to keep you safe. Jackson was seen leaving with Iris for that last run to get more liquor, but he obviously slipped back unnoticed. When Iris was spotted walking across the parking lot alone, security knew he had given them the slip. That's why you saw them rush up the stairs."

Jacob hugged Quinn tighter. "I panicked when I saw them rush the room. I had a bad feeling from the moment she said she wanted to go up there alone."

"Well, it's all over now. Come back inside and get the rest of your things. I'm going to help security pack up Jackson's shit. He's officially made it to the 'you're-no-longer-welcome-in-Anaheim' club. After spending a night or two in lockup, he'll get his own escort out of town and all the way back to Oakland." He touched her arm gently. "You can give your statement to one of the officers tonight, or come by the station in the morning."

"Thank you, Frank. Can you give us a minute? We'll be inside in just a second." She waited until they were alone, sort of, considering the officers zipping in and out of the room. "I promise that I'll always listen to you when you have a bad feeling about anything." Jake just held her close to his chest. He didn't say a word. "Honey?" Quinn pulled back and looked into his eyes, still filled with fear. "It's over. Except for a couple of bumps and bruises, I'm fine. If he hadn't been drinking so much, I have to believe he never would've attacked me. I'm so sorry. This whole thing is my fault."

He had trouble catching his breath. "When all those guards and police officers flew up the stairs, I thought the worst. I thought you were, that he had taken you away from me forever." Jacob lost all composure and let the tears fall. "You know the waiter, Tim? He kept saying to me, 'Don't panic don't panic. She's all right. You'll have her back in your arms in a jiffy. Hold on.'"

She wiped the tears from his face. "I think Tim is actually one of the people Steve has watching over us." She pointed over to him standing with Frank. "He's got an earpiece in that matches Frank's and the other security officers'." She took a deep breath and let it out slowly before she went on, "I never, ever thought he would do something like this to me." She wrapped her arms around his neck again and held on tight. "I just want to go back to our room and forget this all happened."

"Well, let's get your stuff, give your statement to the police, and get the hell away from this place." They walked back into the room, and he was floored. *Who the hell did this sort of thing to a hotel room?* It was trashed. There were empty bottles of liquor thrown all over the room. Both beds were torn apart with the bedding half on the floor. The second room didn't look any neater. This was definitely a side of Iris that he'd never seen before. *Holy Shit!*

"Quinn? Was the safe open when you were in here?" Frank stood next to the closet, packing up the rest of Jackson's clothes. Quinn went over to give him a detailed list of what was left in there and what she'd taken out of it before Jackson attacked her. She came back to Jacob with her items from the safe in a small shoulder bag she'd dropped to the floor when she was attacked. "The two of you drove down here in his Mustang?"

"Yeah. My car is back in Oak—at the Bay House. I don't think I have anything left at the house in Oakland Hills. At least nothing that's important to me." Jacob took her bag from her, and they headed out the door. "I've got all I need right here." She tilted her face up toward him, and he kissed her.

After Quinn and Jacob gave their statements to separate officers, they walked hand in hand through a sea of people gathered out in the parking lot, including the group of couples Quinn and Jackson were supposed to be vacationing with one last time. He knew who they were because they kept asking why Quinn and Jackson weren't together. She held her head high as they made their way through all of them. They overheard whispers of other guests wondering what really happened in those rooms in the third floor, and a few of them had it right. He didn't care. He just wanted to get her away from there and back into their safe haven. He wanted to make her feel safe again, the only way he knew how.

They made it to the stairwell of their hotel and she froze. She shivered uncontrollably. "I need a moment."

He dropped the bag and held her close. "He's gone. I won't ever let Jack or Iris come between us again. Remember what Eric said this afternoon? We won't ever have to fight them alone." Jacob's phone buzzed at his hip. "Speak of the devil. Hello?"

"Jake? Are you two all right?"

Jacob picked up on the sheer panic in Steve's voice. He knew exactly what he was feeling.

"I haven't been able to reach anyone since Frank called me to let me know Jack and Iris were arrested."

"He was hiding out in an adjacent room, waiting for her to come in there to get the rest of her stuff. He fucking attacked her, Steve. She has bruises on her wrists—"

Quinn took the phone from him and put it on speaker. "Steve? I'm okay. Jake and your security got me out of there before he was able to try anything other than twist the shit out of my wrists. I should've known better. Both of us had a bad feeling about Jack right from the start, and I ignored it. I made Jake stay downstairs while I went up there alone."

"Goddamn it, Quinn! You're the most stubborn woman I've ever known. Will you please promise me you'll stop doing everything on your own? Let Jake help you, for Christ's sake!"

Quinn smiled and stuck her tongue out at Jacob.

"And don't think I don't know you're sticking your tongue out right now!" All three of them laughed. It felt good to do that after all the tension of the last hour. "Do you have any idea how frightened we've all been on this end? God, I think my heart stopped twice before I was able to finally get through to you."

"Steve, honey, I'm sorry I had you so worried. I just want to go back to our room, take a shower, and curl up and watch a movie or something."

Steve chuckled. Jacob kissed her neck and rested his forehead against hers.

"Thank you for calling to check up on us and for everything. It means so much to me that you never gave up on us. And I find out today that you and the gang are moving all of my stuff over to the Bay House. It's just too much!"

"Nothing is too much for you and Jake, darlin'. And I'm glad that you could convince him to move in there with you. Well, I feel more than a little relieved talking to you both after all the excitement with Jackson and Iris. I'll let Derek and Sarah know what happened so you won't get swamped with any more calls tonight. Go on and get some rest. You know the kids will want to hit the parks early!"

Jacob hung up the phone, stared at it for a second, and smiled. "I never thought I would say this, but thank God Steve is on our side. He is one hell of a powerful man." He picked up her bag and took her hand. "Come on. Let's get you upstairs and start that hot shower. You're chilled to the bone."

* * * *

CHAPTER 15

Quinn silently thanked the Goddess they'd thought to bring the cooler and the rest of their beach stuff up to the room before she made the bad decision to go to the other hotel. They were both exhausted from playing all day at the beach, and now she was really feeling everything they'd gone through with Jackson and Iris. Jacob led her into the room and made her sit down while he went in to start up the shower. Of course she didn't sit still, and he rolled his eyes when he came back into the room to see her standing up trying to strip out of her tankini. Her arms hung like limp noodles. She didn't have one ounce of energy left to lift them up over her head to get her top off.

She took one look at him leaning on the desk quietly watching her struggle, and she giggled. "A little help, please."

"Oh, you want my help now, do you?" He winked, slid his hands up under her top, and guided it up over her head. He kept his eyes locked with hers as his hands moved down her arms, brushed past her breasts. Hooking his thumbs in the elastic of her bottoms, he inched them down her legs.

She placed her hands on his shoulders to steady herself as she lifted one foot and then the other out of the rest of her swimsuit.

Jacob stood and scooped her up into his arms. "Shower is ready, and so am I."

"Jake, I—"

He had his mouth on hers, so soft and tender, as if he was afraid she was going to break if he was too rough.

"Put me down, baby. I'm not going to fall apart."

"No, but I just might." He let her stand up on her own once they were in the bathroom, but he kept his arms securely around her. "After all we've been through to get to back to each other, I never thought I could be so scared to lose you as I was tonight. When they rushed the stairs, my knees buckled."

"I know. I felt it, too. But it's over and we're together right here and now." She stepped into the shower and let the hot water wash over her. "So are ya' gonna just stand there all night, or are you going to get naked so I can run my hands all over your body?"

He smiled and dropped his swim trunks to the floor. His tank top quickly followed, and then he had her in his arms again.

The water flowed over their bodies, rinsing away the sand and residue from the salt water. Jacob's hands roamed over her entire frame, his lips never leaving hers. Their tongues danced and swirled around each other. He lifted her up into his arms, pinned her against the shower wall, and entered her. His arms covered her back, protecting her from slamming into the wall as he took her over and over again. His lips left hers and trailed down her neck to her shoulder and back again. Quinn's arms were still tight around his neck, and her hands entangled in his hair.

"Don't ever let me go, Quinn. I don't know if my heart could take it."

She smoothed his hair back away from his face. "Look at me, Jake." He slowly opened his eyes, and her heart damn near burst with love for him. "I never gave up on you. I knew you would come find me again. You promised me on our island, and I believed you. I just had to wait until it was our time to be together." She slid her legs down his so that she could stand again. "My heart won't survive without you, either, so I guess we're stuck with each other."

He smiled and his lips caressed hers one more time. "We had better lather up before the hot water runs out on us again." He moved her away from the shower wall and under the full stream of water. "Steve is right. The munchkins will want to hit the parks early, but I think they'll be just fine without us for one day."

"You don't want to spend the day with the kids tomorrow?" She'd been looking forward to helping Cassie dress up in a princess dress, and maybe dressing up in one herself.

"We'll have plenty of time over the next ten days with them. Besides, we have to give Eric a chance to spoil them rotten on his own." He nuzzled her neck with his stubble that she loved so much. "And I want to spend the rest of the night making love with you over and over again."

"Can't do that if we have to get up at the crack of dawn to meet *our* family at the park entrance." He loved the sound of that, "Our family. Has a nice ring to it, don't you think?"

Quinn smiled. "Uh-huh. I also love the idea that you want to keep practicing making a family of our own." She reached between them and took his hard cock into her hand. "I guess your marathon hard-on 'problem' is going to come in handy tonight."

"You better believe it, baby doll." He enjoyed the feel of her skin all soapy, slipping and sliding against him. He didn't want to stop touching and exploring every inch of her. Jacob knew she felt the same. Her hands, lips, and tongue explored just as eagerly as his. Quinn tenderly massaged his scalp as she washed his hair. She wasn't kidding about the orgasmic shampoos. *Holy shit!*

She reached behind him and shut off the water after they rinsed all the remaining soap from their bodies. "You know, we're going to have to let go of each other at some point, just for a little while. How about you let me pamper you this time?"

"What do you have in mind?" He reached for the towels, but Quinn beat him to it. She wrapped one around his waist then reached out for another one.

"Well, I thought you would let me dry you off, dry your hair, and don't make a face. I love your long hair, Jake. Maybe give you a full-body massage."

Jacob kissed her neck.

"You've done so much for me I do have a few surprises for you, too, you know."

"Now you have me intrigued. What do you have going on in that pretty little head?"

She snaked her arms around his waist and smiled slyly. His heart skipped a couple of beats every time she treated him to the smile that had haunted his dreams for so long. "You keep looking at me like that, and I'm going to pin you against the wall again."

She pulled him out of the bathroom and made him sit down at the desk after she rubbed his skin dry with the fluffy towels.

Oh, man, she's killing me!

She turned on her blow-dryer and massaged his scalp once again. "Honey, you keep doing that, and I'm going to be so relaxed you will have to pour me into bed."

"I'm not through with you yet, Hartley." She nibbled on his ear after she finished with his hair. "Go stretch out on the bed on your stomach."

Oh, this ought to be good! He stood up, and she tugged the towel away from around his waist. *Yep, really good.* He tried to grab her on his way to the bed, but she shook her finger at him and pointed to the bed.

"Go!"

"Aye, aye, Captain." He stretched out on the bed, on his stomach as she requested and rested his head on his arms. "Eyes closed or open?"

"Closed." She giggled, and he heard her rustling around in one of her suitcases.

"Just what are you doing over there?"

"Just keep your eyes closed. You'll love this, I promise."

A silk blindfold slipped around his head and covered his eyes. He smiled. She knew him well enough to know he wouldn't be able to keep his eyes closed for long.

"Do you trust me, Jake?"

"Absolutely." He heard a soft snapping sound, twice, and then the unmistakable aroma of vanilla and cinnamon. He grinned as her warm hands rubbed over his back and down to his ass. Another one of their fantasies checked off his bucket list, and he was going to love every single minute of it.

Quinn thoroughly enjoyed herself watching Cassie model the little princess dresses. Maredyth had tears in her eyes for most of it. She told Quinn she couldn't believe how much her little girl was enjoying herself with all of them that day and talking to so many new people. Derek had been absolutely smitten with the little minx and had grinned from ear to ear when Cassie wanted to hold his hand standing in line for the Pirates of the Caribbean ride. Sarah took lots of pictures of them together with their Mickey Mouse ears. Quinn thought she'd be able to show the guys back at the Tattoo Parlor just how much of a big softy their tough-as-nails boss really was at heart. Not that they didn't already know it, but it was nice to have some proof to blackmail him with later. It would be a fun change of pace to have someone else the focus of friend and family harassment instead of her.

Derek, Sarah, and Jillian had arrived late the night before and checked into the Grand Californian. They all had rooms on the same floor along with additional private security teams hired by Steve. Quinn thought it was overkill since Jackson was still behind bars, but she wasn't about to argue with Steve or Jacob after what had happened. From now on, she deferred to them when it came to their safety.

Sarah sat down next to her and flipped through the pictures she had taken of Cassie in her various gowns so far. "Well, I think she looks absolutely adorable. How about we get them all for her?"

Maredyth wasn't having any of that. "Oh now, I agree with you that it'll be hard to choose one dress for her, but I won't have her being spoiled rotten by all of you on this trip, although it does warm my heart to see her like this. She's a whole new little girl!"

Sarah winked at Quinn then put on her charms. "Well, how about we let her pick out two? One from Jake and Quinn and one from Derek and me. But you have to let us get all the accessories that go with each one. If you don't say yes, I'm going to have to call up Steve and—"

"Sarah! That is so unfair! You know how he is. He'll just buy out the shop for her and have it sent to their house. I'm surprised he hasn't already done just that." Quinn sorted through the little tiaras and shoes that went with the dresses so they would be all set when Cassie picked out the two she wanted. Out of the corner of her eye, she noticed a flurry of activity at the counter. Then she saw the sales girls rushing around in another part of the store and whispering. "What the heck has their panties in a bunch?"

"Since you brought up how Steve loves to dote on the ones he loves..."

"What are you trying to say?" Quinn moved toward the back of the store to see what was going on for herself, but Maredyth blocked her path. "Are you in on this, too?"

She nodded and laughed. "This is all part of Jake's plan to give you a fairy tale, honey. I was asked to deliver this message to you if you started to fuss, and I quote, 'just go with it, woman!' I'm told you know exactly what that means!"

"Yeah, I've heard it a few times." She smiled and wondered what other things Jacob and Steve had planned for her this trip.

Jillian came out dressed in a beautiful floral gown with Eric following close behind her in a tuxedo. He looked so handsome and something else, maybe a bit thunderstruck with the Aussie beauty on his arm. "Well, don't the two of you make a handsome couple!"

Sarah took several pictures, capturing Jillian's cheeks blushing perfectly. She turned to Quinn and winked. "The magic of this place seems to be in full force, or maybe it's just the irresistible charms of the Hartley boys?"

She bumped shoulders with her friend. "You hush."

"Well, you know I can't resist a man in a tuxedo, and there he was all dressed up with no place to go. What was I supposed to do? Leave him alone like that?" Jillian rolled her eyes to stress her point. "Honestly, Dr. Hollis, I mean Quinn. You know my grandma would tear me a new one if I left him stranded like that."

"Hmmm. You two aren't fooling anyone. What the heck is going on?"

"Now who has their panties in a bunch?" Derek rounded the corner in time to see his beautiful sister with her hands crossed over her chest and her hip out. Someone was about to get a tongue lashing, and he thought he might as well take one for the team. *Man, Jake owes me big for this!* This was the second time this year that he'd had to put on a monkey suit for Quinn. He wasn't thrilled about it, but seeing her eyes and Sarah's light up when they turned toward him was all the encouragement he needed.

"Derek! You too? Is someone going to explain?" She tapped her foot, and it was clear she was getting more than a little agitated. She appeared to be channeling Miranda.

Time to come clean.

"Honey, this is all part of a big surprise Jake has planned for you. Trust me. You're gonna love it. We're all part of the parade this afternoon and riding in front of the princess float. You, Sarah, and

Maredyth still have to get changed. The twins and Jake are already done and waiting for the rest of us."

Her smile brightened up the whole room. Derek knew how much she loved to dress up, and Sarah chimed in right on cue, "Come on, doll face. Our gowns are hanging up in the back dressing rooms. We have to hurry or we're going to hold up the whole parade. Now you don't want to disappoint all of those people do you?"

"Oh, I'm going to get even with all of you for this one day, but right now I'm just gonna go with it and have fun. Now show me my dress, girl!"

That was much easier than Derek had thought it was going to be, but if he knew Quinn, and he did, she'd make good on her promise and everyone would pay for it later. He turned his attention over to Jillian and Eric. He'd seen that look before. What the hell was it with those Hartley boys? *When they fall for a woman, they fall fast and hard!*

Speaking of falling hard, Jacob peeked into the store. He was also all decked out in a tuxedo. "So how did it go?"

"Well, let's just say we need to watch our backs for the next week. She'll get even with us eventually. How did things go on your end? Did you remember to put the ring in your pocket this time or do we have to send another bellhop to go fetch it?"

Jake patted his jacket. "I got it. Steve had the jeweler put a rush on it and sent it here this morning. You don't think she suspects what we're up to? That this isn't just the afternoon parade down Main Street?"

Now it was Eric's turn to calm his brother down. "Will you relax? It's all going to work out and she'll be surprised. You're giving her the whole fairy-tale proposal, Jake, the stuff dreams are made of. What better place to do it than at Disney, her favorite place in the world besides Vegas?"

"I just want to give her everything she's given me and more."

Derek had a feeling he was still worried about Iris and Jackson ruining the whole thing. "Frank personally drove Iris to the airport after she was released this morning. As for Jackson, he's got at least another day or two as a guest of the fine city of Anaheim. Frank made sure he was served with the divorce papers just before they booked him. I wish I could've been there to see his face when it happened."

Eric smiled at Jillian. "Well, we're all getting our wishes thanks to Steve."

Yep. The man was definitely smitten and then some with Jillian.

Jacob glanced at them and then grinned broadly. He'd noticed it, too.

"You two can wait here for the ladies. We will meet you at the float. Come on, Jillian. Let's go show off how great we look all dressed up!"

"Where is our little brother running off to with that gorgeous young lady?" Maredyth appeared radiant dressed in a pale yellow gown that matched the Princess Belle dress Cassie had on. "He promised to keep track of the boys while we were getting ready."

"Don't worry. The four of them are heading over to the float now, and we should get moving, too. Are Quinn and Sarah ready?"

"Are you looking for us, Mr. Hartley?" Sarah came out first in an emerald green off-the-shoulder gown that set off her dark red hair beautifully. Derek simply beamed when he saw her. *Maybe another proposal will be coming around sooner rather than later?* Jacob heard some more rustling, and his heart nearly leapt out of his chest. There was his Quinn in a dark violet strapless ball gown. She was absolutely stunning, and he couldn't take his eyes off of her.

"I take it you approve of the dress?" Her eyes locked with his, and he could only nod. She floated over to him and took his hands into hers. "How about I take your arm so I don't fall in these heels or trip on the hem of the dress? Wouldn't want to make a fool of myself and ruin one of the Disney parades now, would we?"

"No, baby doll. We wouldn't want that." In her heels she was once again nearly eye to eye with him. The sense of falling into and getting lost in those blue-green pools nearly overtook him, but he managed to regain his composure and smile. "You're the most beautiful woman I've ever seen. Cassie was right. You really are a princess, *my* princess."

"You don't look so bad yourself, hot stuff. I knew you'd look fantastic in a tux." An impish smile formed on her glossy lips. "So how long will I have to wait to see you *out* of it?"

"Oh, good Lord! Quinn, you have a one-track mind! Get your ass moving so we won't hold up the whole production." Sarah took charge now and pushed them out the door of the shop. She was going to keep this surprise rolling and on time even if they fought her all the way.

Jacob looked at Derek, and he smiled and shrugged. Better to go with it than have to deal with Sarah later on, too.

The first surprise for Quinn was waiting right outside the shop. The horse-drawn carriage that had taken them to dinner the other night was waiting for her once again. The driver was in place, and this time there were two footmen to help the ladies on board with their dresses. A second carriage stood in front of them with the rest of the gang. Quinn laughed when she caught sight of Cassie practicing her princess wave to the crowd which had already lined up along the route.

Before they could blink an eye, the carriages were in their places in front of the Princess float, and the parade was underway. The park-wide music started to play, and Quinn settled back against Jacob, taking his hand in hers. "This is amazing! It's too much. You didn't have to do all of this."

Derek put his arm around Sarah as the parade came up to Cinderella's Castle and stopped. The footman jumped down and put the steps out for them to exit the carriage, helping the girls once again. Eric, Jillian and Maredyth were already in place with the kids at the top of the steps, waiting for everyone to join them. The trumpets sounded off, the music in the park stopped, and the announcer took over the show. "Ladies and gentlemen, thank you all for coming to Disneyland today, and we hope that all of your dreams come true."

Jacob couldn't hear anything else the announcer said. His eyes locked on Quinn's surprised face as the footman assisted her to her seat at the end of the white carpet. Another Disney cast member approached and turned on Jacob's wireless microphone. The crowd seemed to melt away until all that remained was the two of them.

"Quinn, from the first moment I heard your laugh, I was smitten. When I first looked into your eyes, I knew I was in love. When I saw your smile, I knew I wanted to be the one to make you smile every day for the rest of my life. It's been a long, rough road for us to finally be together, but I never stopped wanting you. I never stopped loving you with all of my heart." The footman dropped a pillow to the ground for him just as Jacob started to kneel. The crowd cheered. "Quinn, will you be by my side in sickness and in health, during football and hockey seasons?"

That made her giggle, and she winked. She mouthed the words *déjà vu*.

He nodded and winked back. "Will you let me love you forever and ever? Can we fall asleep in each other's arms and wake up making love every morning? Quinn, my heart, my soul, will you marry me?"

The entire park was silent for just a moment, but Quinn didn't miss a beat. "Yes, my love, my life, I will marry you." She jumped up out of her seat and threw her arms around him as the crowd and their friends and family cheered wildly.

Jacob stood up and held her tight in his arms for a moment before he set her back on her feet. He reached into his pocket and pulled out the ring Derek helped him design for Quinn. He'd made the center stone a blue sapphire surrounded by smaller diamonds all set in a platinum band. He'd had it engraved once again. *My heart and soul now and forever.* When she read that, she started to cry, and so did he.

Leave it to Eric to break the spell. "Well, put it on her finger and make it official already!"

"You got it, brotha!" Jacob slipped it on her finger and raised her hand to his lips. "I love you, Quinn Lee Quartermarsh."

"I love you, Jacob Michael Hartley."

"More déjà vu?"

"Uh-huh, but I'm just gonna go with it." She threw her arms around his neck and kissed him, causing the crowd to erupt all over again. Disney had done what it advertised. It made all of their dreams come true and then some, thanks to Steve.

"Look at these pictures, Darryl. Have you ever seen such a beautiful engagement?"

"They do raise the bar for the rest of us, that's for sure."

Steve laughed. "Oh please. I know for a fact you're a hopeless romantic. When you finally decide to make an honest woman out of Kat, I have no doubt you'll pull out all the stops to sweep her off her feet."

Darryl snorted. "She's too much like you. She buries herself with her work and leaves little time for herself."

"That bad, huh?"

"No, just not now. She knows I love her and she's my one and only. I know she feels the same for me. When she's ready for the quieter life, she knows where to find me. Don't think I don't know what you're doing bringing her up. You can't fool me."

"I don't regret letting her go, Darryl. She belongs with Jake. There's no denying it. One look at these photos and anyone would agree with me."

"I'm not disagreeing with you at all. The two of you had your time together as it should be. Both of you came out better for it."

"Then what am I trying to hide from you?" He reached into his desk and pulled out a bottle of Vitamin C and cough suppressants. He tossed back a couple of each and gulped down half of his bottle of water.

Darryl pointed his finger at the bottles of pills. "That. You've been coughing up a lung since yesterday. I thought you said you were getting better. This doesn't look better to me."

He waved him off. "It's the crud going around. It's hanging on longer than I expected but it's nothing you need to be worried about. I feel fine."

"Bullshit. You're up all hours of the night and still up at the crack of dawn. You can't keep up this pace and stay healthy."

"I'm fine."

"If you keep going like this, you won't be able to hide it from Quinn when they come out for the fourth. You are a huge part of all of their lives now. Please, go in for another checkup."

"As soon as I have Eric ready to roll, I promise I'll go in. Happy now?"

Darryl glared at Steve over his reading glasses. "Not in the least. I'm going to hold you to your promise. You break it and I call in reinforcements."

"You wouldn't."

"Try me. I stood by when you almost died once, and I don't want to go through that again. You have even more to live for now. You can't allow all these people to welcome you into their lives and their families and then leave them."

He swallowed the lump that had formed in his throat. His friend was right. He couldn't preach to his friends and family to go out and grab their happiness if he was taking his health and life for granted. "I'll set up the appointment for next week"

Next week came and went and Darryl let it slide as Steve appeared to rally in time to host Jacob and Quinn for a fun filled week of laughter and celebrations in their honor. Eric stepped into his role as his assistant with ease, allowing him to spend time with the couple. Seeing them together reinforced his original impression that they were meant to be. Their happiness together dulled the small pang of jealousy remaining in his heart. He knew over time, that would melt away but he'd always have the memories of his time with Quinn to ease the ache.

The week flew by far too fast for his taste, but it wasn't like he wouldn't see them again. They promised to visit at least one more time before Quinn had to go back to work. Jacob had interviews with three of the leading physical therapy centers in the Bay Area. Their lives were moving full speed ahead.

While his was grinding to a screeching halt.

The morning after they'd left, he'd woken up with his head in a vice. He'd had migraines before, but nothing like the pain that had gripped him. He'd managed to crawl to his bathroom and spent the better part of an hour hugging the toilet as the contents of his stomach flew out of him. When he'd been able to stand and look at his reflection in the mirror, he'd been shocked by his appearance.

Darryl is right. This isn't the flu.

Somehow he'd managed to pull himself together and drive himself to the hospital. He knew Darryl would've driven him there if he'd asked, but he didn't want to worry him more. He had to do this on his own. He'd fill them all in when he had something to tell them.

Never one to sit and wait around for news of any kind, let alone his health, he busied himself on his phone texting Eric with his instructions for what he'd wanted to accomplish for the day.

"Where are you?"

"I had a meeting with an old friend that had slipped my mind. I should be back this afternoon."

"I got everything covered here. Why don't you take the day off? You could use a break."

"Might take you up on that. You need anything, best to send a text. I won't be able to talk on the phone here. The reception isn't the greatest."

"Will do. Talk with you later."

He smiled at the message. Eric was the best choice to be his second in command but if his suspicions were correct, the young man would have a hell of a lot more responsibility thrown into his lap. He hoped it wouldn't be too much for him to handle this soon.

"Stephen, what took you so long to see me?"

He tried to smile at his doctor of over fifteen years, but could only manage a shrug. "Denial I suppose."

Dr. Carroway pulled up a chair close to his bedside. "Your test results are as we expected."

"And?"

"All your cell lines are low. Platelets, red cells and white blood cells."

His stomach dropped. "Because of the flu?"

The doctor shook his head. "That sure as hell didn't help matters but it wasn't the cause. I put a rush on the aspirates of your lymph nodes. It's back and it's angry."

He closed his eyes. The faces of all of his new family flashed through his mind in a whirlwind. He tried to memorize every detail of their faces, smiling and laughing. He didn't want to imagine how they'd look when they found out about his illness. He inhaled deeply and let the air out of his lungs slowly. "What do we do now?"

"We finish staging this thing and that will tell us what options are available for you now. We've had this discussion before. Your best chance at getting this back into remission now, would be a stem cell transplant."

"Bone marrow?" He shook his head. He didn't have any living relatives left and the chances of finding a donor that matched him would be slim. With the chemo he'd had before he wasn't sure his own stem cells would be a viable option.

Dr. Carroway gripped his shoulder and waited until Steve was able to look him in the eye again. "We'll start the search through the bone marrow donor registry now to look for a match. If we find one we'll be ready to roll at a moment's notice. Where are your friends

215

who were here with you the last time? You shouldn't be dealing with this alone. You have family now. How about you let me call them or at least call Darryl so he can contact everyone?"

"I need time to process all of this. I have to get things in order with my assistant and…"

The words caught in his throat as the sobs tore through him. *This isn't fair! I need more time. Please don't let it all end now.*

The doctor's expression softened. "You beat this before and you *will* do it again. We'll have to move fast to get your body ready. You know the routine. We can get started today with it and you can be back at your penthouse tonight. You'll have to come in weekly until we get your numbers up. At this point, your cell counts are lower than I like to see for the start of this kind of chemo."

He zoned out as the doctor outlined his treatment plan. He knew it all by heart. He wasn't fond of giving himself the injections, but he'd do it. He'd follow everything to the letter this time and keep on fighting until his last breath. This time he had so much more to live for and he'd be damned if he would give up now.

He scrolled through the contacts on his phone, debating who to call without freaking everyone else out before he knew exactly what he was facing in the coming weeks to months, if they found a donor. He pushed the button on the screen to connect him. It only rang twice but it seemed to him time stood still until the familiar voice sounded in his ear.

"Steve! I just got off the phone with Eric. He said you'd be out all morning. I have those sketches for the new artwork ready for you."

"I can't wait to see them, but I have something else I need you for if you're free."

"The guys can hold down the fort here at the shop. I'm all yours. What's up?"

"I'd rather not go into all the details on the phone, but I'm at the hospital. I…I hate to ask this but you're the only one besides Darryl and Anthony who know…" He swallowed hard and tried to continue.

Derek's sharp intake of breath echoed through the speaker of the phone. "I'll leave now."

He gave Derek his room number and swore him to secrecy. "I know I'm asking a lot of you, but I feel like I've been blindsided here and need a calm head to help me figure out the best way to tell the families."

"You don't have to explain. I'll be there in less than thirty and we can talk more about all of this then. Don't worry. Together we'll come up with a plan. I know I speak for everyone in saying we're not ready to let you go out of our lives yet."

"I promise I'm not going to give up without a fight."

The sounds of his casino filtered through the phone. He could tell Derek had run through most of it before hanging up with him. He didn't want to scare his friend like that, but there was no way around it. Thoughts of the last time they'd raced through the casino to make their way to the hospital flooded his brain. Together he and Derek had been through the scariest time in their lives because of a woman both of them loved. Now here he was the cause for all of them to relive it again. *I can't think of that now. Quinn got through it and is now so happy with Jake. I have to beat this thing again. I won't be the cause of anymore grief for these families.*

The nurses came and went throughout the morning, checking his vitals while he received two units of packed red cells. They'd wanted to place a PICC line in, but he'd convinced Dr. Carroway to agree to hold off on that until he was ready to start the longer chemo sessions. Steve wanted to be able to tell everyone about his relapse before he had catheters and ports coming out of his body. Knowing Helen and the rest of the Quartermarsh family had gone through all of this before with her husband made him even more sensitive to how they'd take the news. Derek had been hard enough. How the hell was he going to tell his mother and sisters?

Good to his word, Derek sat by his bedside through it all. He'd asked the doctor questions about the chemo protocols that Steve had been too shocked to think of when he'd first arrived. He assumed that having been present during his father's treatment, Derek had soaked up a lot of the medical jargon. He'd even promised Dr. Carroway that he'd be the one to be sure Steve made all of his appointments even after the rest of the family were told.

"How long does the bone marrow donor registry keep the information active?"

Dr. Carroway tilted his head and crossed his arms over his chest. "Depends on where you're registered. Why?"

"When my adoptive father went through his battle with Non-Hodgkin's, all of us were tested and placed in the registry while we were in Michigan. His sister was found to be his match, but Dad never was stable enough to receive the transplant. A couple of years ago, I registered here in honor of his memory. I'm sure once we let the family know, they'll volunteer too."

Tears filled his eyes. He knew the chance of finding a donor would be slim, but it meant the world to him Derek wanted to help.

The doctor smiled. "One of my old college roommates happens to run the Michigan registry. Let me see what I can find out. In the meantime, how about we see about getting our patient released. I'm relying on you, Mr. Quartermarsh to be sure he follows my instructions to the letter."

Derek saluted. "Will do, Doc."

One hurdle down. Now he had to find a way to tell Quinn without sending her into a tailspin.

* * * *

CHAPTER 16

They officially moved in together at the Bay House after they returned from their trip to Las Vegas. The place was simply breathtaking to Jacob, and surpassed everything he'd heard about it. They were still unpacking things and getting settled at the end of that month when Quinn complained of feeling fatigued all the time and couldn't keep any food down for a few days.

He'd gone into panic mode and begged her to go to the doctor. After all they'd been through to be together, he'd been afraid something would take her away from him. She'd done her best to calm him down, but he could tell she'd become a little worried herself. He'd called the one person he knew who could talk some sense into Quinn when she was being stubborn.

Sarah had come over right away with soup and another package she said was for Quinn's eyes only. She'd made Jacob stay out of the bedroom while the two of them were alone together, and if he wasn't mistaken, giggling a hell of a lot. He was glad someone could find something funny in all of this. He'd been nearly out of his mind with worry.

Finally Quinn had come out, and her cheeks were all rosy. She'd looked radiant, and the twinkle in her eyes was there again. Jacob didn't realize that he'd been holding his breath until Sarah touched his arm and the air rushed out of his lungs. "You had better sit down, honey. Quinn has to tell you something."

"Baby doll? What's going on?" Quinn's hands were behind her back so he couldn't tell what she was up to, but Jacob did what Sarah told him to do. As soon as Quinn had moved close enough, he pulled her onto his lap. "What are the two of you up to now?" Jacob had to smile even though his heart beat wildly with fear.

She absolutely beamed. "Jake, we do have to go to the doctor. I have an appointment for this afternoon and I need you to go with me."

His heart stopped. "What's wrong?"

She moved her hands out in front of her. She held not one, but four pregnancy tests...all positive.

"A baby? How?" He was stunned. They'd dreamed of having a family together for such a long time. Now it appeared it was really happening.

Sarah laughed. "Don't look so shocked, Hartley. Do I have to go over how you make babies yet again?"

Quinn cradled his face in both of her hands. "I've missed my period for the last two months now. I thought it was stress, and then I thought I was getting the flu. Nope. We did it. We got our miracle, Jake. We're gonna have a baby!"

"So, the Magic of Disney did it once again, huh?"

She nodded, held him close, her cheek against his. She whispered in his ear, "Say something."

Sarah rolled her eyes and chuckled. "Jesus Christ, Jake. The two of you were at it constantly. The odds were definitely in your favor to knock her up!"

"A baby?"

Quinn pulled back and searched his face. "Jake, are you all right?" Her eyes flew open. "You look really pale."

He couldn't speak. His emotions swirled through his body at warp speed. He was going to be a father. Quinn was carrying his child. Would he be a good parent or fail miserably? Could all of their dreams really be coming true so fast? Jacob finally placed his hand on her rock-hard, flat stomach and smiled. "I'm gonna be a dad!"

Sarah wrapped her arms around both of them. "I'm gonna spoil this kid rotten! Let me go get my car ready. I'm driving the two of you to the doctor. I can't wait for you two to confirm the test results officially. We have so much to do and so little time!"

Quinn gazed into his eyes and could tell he wanted to ask her something. She understood his concerns and she wanted to put his mind at ease. "I had my period last at the end of May, a week after I was with Steve. This is *our* miracle Jake."

"I was told for so long that I probably wouldn't be able to father children unless I had a lot of help from a doctor. Hell, Iris was more fertile than a wild rabbit and she never got pregnant with me. You can't blame me for wondering, baby doll. You and Steve were sleeping together the month before we found each other again. I'm not complaining about it at all, just going over the timeline in my head.

"Well, you can stop wondering. Even if my last night with Steve fit the timeline, it wouldn't be possible this baby could be his. He told me he's been shooting blanks for the last ten years. The first day that I spent with you, I prayed that if I couldn't have you I would at least get to have your child. This little five-week-old bun in my oven is yours. Our love for each other created this baby and I couldn't be happier if I tried."

Sarah had come rushing back into the house. "Car's ready. What did I miss?" She looked between them, clearly worried.

Jake kissed Quinn again. "Don't worry, Aunt Sarah. You didn't miss a thing. Now let's get to the doctor and confirm that everything is all right with the Momma to be and your little niece or nephew."

Quinn got up off of his lap and locked her fingers with his. "I'm scared, Jake. I don't want to get too excited. I'm forty-three now and things could go wrong and I could end up losing—"

"Stop. Let's take one thing at a time and see what the doctor says."

"You're right. No sense worrying about anything until we talk to the doctor. By the way, you'll like her. She's down to earth and doesn't sugar coat things."

"Sounds like my kind of doctor. We better get moving. Traffic this time a day can be rough."

Sarah sang with the radio while Jacob sat in the back seat, holding Quinn close and smiling. "I don't want to get too excited yet either, baby doll, but goddamn, I just want to shout it out for everyone to hear. We're having a baby!"

Sarah started laughing all over again. "You know your sister had twins, Jake. Maybe Quinn will surprise you with one of each!"

"Oh my God, Sarah! I totally forgot about that. Maredyth said there are multiple sets of twins in your family."

He smiled and kissed her forehead. "I know!"

"Don't you think you should have shared that little tidbit with me?"

"I thought I had that covered since my sister told you the entire Hartley family tree. Since that didn't scare you off, I figured I had it made."

She laughed and snuggled back against him, enjoying the music and the banter between him and her best friend. She placed her hands over her abdomen and said a silent prayer. *Goddess, thank you for this blessing. Boy or girl, or both, I will love them more than life itself. I ask they be healthy and strong and that my father and brother, Danny watch over them. Blessed be.*

"I hear your prayer, my child. Your children will carry on your legacy of love and light for years to come, and in each and every lifetime." The Goddess Fate watched the monitors before her. All of the Guardians charges were on full display. All but two of them were on the right paths. That had to be remedied and quickly.

Guardian Michael Hartley stood next to her with tears in his eyes. "It's good to see them so happy. My family is growing as we speak and yet there is another hurdle they have to get through."

"They'll have one another to lean on and will be stronger for it. This has to happen for our angel on earth to find his true path."

"He needs all of the Hartley and Quartermarsh families to survive this. I take it we've been given permission to intervene again."

She nodded. "Yeshua has consented to allow you free reign to nudge or fully intervene if necessary. It worked the last time we had Quinn and your Jacob on the Island."

"So Steve is to make that journey now?"

"If necessary. Although, I think you and Daniel will be able to help him here in this realm through your families. It's not Stephen who may be spending time with us in paradise, but one who is closer to him than either of them realized. Another will also have to choose between life and death in this realm."

He nodded and kept his expression neutral. He'd learned to expect the unexpected with his charges. "Lucius will want to intervene Himself on her behalf and leave the others to us.

"He too has to abide by her free will and allow her to choose. But you're right. I would expect nothing less from him. As much as I've taken interest in your families, Lucius has an even greater stake in how all of this plays out."

He watched all of his charges on the screens. So many of their lives had become interconnected because of his son and his soul mate. He hoped he and his fellow Guardians had the strength to keep all of them on the paths that led to their promised destinies. If he learned anything since he'd become a Guardian, it would be to expect the unexpected. Humans were created to be an unpredictable bunch.

After Quinn's exam, Dr. Goldman had them wait in her office for the test results. She put a rush on them, considering Quinn was nearly forty-four. She walked in with a huge smile on her face, and Jacob was immediately relieved. "Well, how does it feel to be expectant parents?"

Quinn screamed and jumped up out of her seat to hug her doctor. "Are you serious? It's not a mistake?"

"No. Quinn, you're definitely pregnant. Your estimate is right, a few days over five weeks."

Jacob shook the doctor's hand at first then hugged her. "You have no idea how happy we are. We both gave up hope this could happen for us."

Dr. Goldman had them both sit back down again. "Oh, I know. Listening to your story, Jake, I wasn't at all shocked that this could happen. Sometimes the old saying is true. Time does heal all wounds whether they are physical or psychological. Quinn, you're in the best health of your life. The complications you had before shouldn't happen this time, but we'll monitor you closely. We need to get you started on your prenatal vitamins and set up a schedule for your checkups and the very first ultrasound. Will you want to know the sex?"

Both of them said yes at the same time. Jacob squeezed Quinn's hand again. "Doc, Quinn and I have been through so much to be together that we want to do everything we can to make sure everything works out. But if there is any question between her health and the baby—"

"Jake, don't."

"No, Quinn. I won't lose you again. If this pregnancy will be dangerous for you, I don't want you to go through it. We'll find another way."

Dr. Goldman smiled. "That's something we agree on. Don't worry. Quinn and I have had this conversation before. She agrees with you, too."

He looked at his lover and the relief washed over him. "Really?"

She nodded. "I don't want to lose you either. Having children would be a blessing, but I wouldn't want to do that alone, and I couldn't do that to you either."

"Sounds like the two of you are on the same page and you didn't even know it. Bonus all the way around! On a personal note, I couldn't be happier for you, Quinn. I've never seen you this way. Pregnant women really do glow, and I can tell you two deeply love each other. I, for one, am going to enjoy taking this journey with you both." She took Quinn's left hand into hers. "And does this mean there is a wedding in your future?"

"As soon as the divorce papers are finalized, we're going to make it official, and you are invited!"

"I'd be honored to share in all the fun. How about we start the party off with an ultrasound in two weeks. At that point you'll be just over seven weeks along. We can confirm that and make sure all is progressing normally."

"Would we be able to tell if we're expecting more than one?"

The doctor nodded. "It will be too soon to know the sex of each in the case of multiples, but if we find that you are carrying one, there are blood tests we can do to confirm. Either way, we'll have more information and you'll be able to tell your friends and family about the good news. I guess you'll want to know if it's safe for you to travel in your condition."

Quinn smiled and nodded. "Besides Sarah, no one else knows. I'd like to tell everyone in person. That means travel to Vegas, Michigan and Indiana."

"Not if we get everyone to one place. We can make a party out of it. You know my brother will take care of all the arrangements."

"The two of you met in Vegas, right?"

He grinned and turned his eyes back to Dr. Goldman. "Yes. I can't think of a better place to celebrate our new life together. Plus, it won't be long before we'll have to stay put until the baby arrives."

"I'm supposed to go back to work after Labor Day. I'll have to sit down with Sarah and our hospital managers to discuss surgery schedules. Will I need to take special precautions?"

"To answer your first question, you can travel safely during this stage of your pregnancy. We will monitor you every step of the way, and if there are any concerns or restrictions that come up, we can talk about them at that time. As for work, you know your body. Don't do those marathon surgery sessions. Make sure you take your vitamins and eat well. You do need your rest but that doesn't mean you can't be an active participant in your surgical practice. If you don't need to be in the room while they are taking x-rays, stay out. Make sure all the anesthetic machines are well serviced. You know the precautions other doctors and your staff have had to take during their pregnancies."

His mental check list grew by the second as he listened to the women discuss how the pregnancy would change their lives. At the top of the list was not worrying about every little thing that could possibly go wrong. No matter what came their way, he knew they'd get through it together. Both of them had been through hell and back in their lives and managed to find their way back to each other. He'd be damned if anything would threaten their happiness ever again.

* * * *

CHAPTER 17

August 15ᵗʰ McCarran International Airport
Las Vegas, Nevada

Eric paced in front of the monitors in the baggage claim area waiting for them to update. "I don't know how you can stay so calm, Darryl."

"It's my job to be the calm in the middle of the chaos, Mr. Hartley."

He rolled his eyes. "Stop calling me that. I'm not your boss."

Darryl chuckled. "Quinn gets almost as riled up as you do. You both make it too damn easy to get a rise out of you. I promise to call you by your first name when we're not on official business. Does that make you happy?"

"Picking up my brother and Quinn at the airport isn't official business."

The older man shrugged. "It is to me. I'll be damned if I'll let anyone else do it. She's become more than family to me and I need to ask her a favor."

"What kind of favor? Is it something I can help out with?"

Darryl nodded. "Maybe. I'll let you know. I'm expecting a call from an old friend this afternoon. Between him and Quinn, I might be able to pull this off and I won't need you to intervene too."

"Dude, you can't leave me hanging like that. Spill."

Darryl sighed. "It's Steve. He's been running himself ragged the last month and as far as I can tell, he's refused to see his doctors. I'd be lying if I said I'm not worried."

"He has looked rough around the edges lately, but when Jake and Quinn told him they'd be back here one more time before she went back to work, he seemed to rally. What's going on that you're not telling me?"

"It's not my place—"

"Bullshit. We're a team. If there's something wrong with Steve, we have to take care of him together. He's done so much for all of us."

Darryl glanced up at the monitor. "Well, looks like we have a little time. Their plane is set to land in twenty minutes. Must have been a hell of a storm in San Fran to delay them this long."

He waved Darryl over to a quiet corner away from the other passengers milling about looking for their luggage. "What are you not telling me?"

"It may be nothing, but I don't want to take any chances. Steve has Non-Hodgkin's Lymphoma. He's been in remission for over ten years, and just had a clean bill of health from his docs in April. With all the new projects he's been working on here on the strip and working to get Jake and Quinn back together, he's not been paying attention to his own health. He thinks it's just the flu that's hanging on."

"You think it's more than that?" His chest tightened. He'd come to see Steve as more than a boss. He considered him not only a close friend, but part of his family. If anything were to happen to him now, after all he'd done for all of them, he didn't know how any of them would make it through.

"I think he needs to get his ass to the doctor to check his blood counts. He could be coming out of remission. Since he's been fighting me on this, I called Anthony. He's supposed to let me know when he can get a flight out. If anyone can get him to get to the doctor, it's Anthony."

"And Quinn."

"She doesn't know about his cancer, Eric. He'd kept it from her up until now because he didn't want to cause her more worry. Now that she and Jake are on the right path, maybe it's time she finds out."

He rested his elbows on his knees and clasped his hands together. "Anthony is definitely the big guns. We'll wait until he arrives before we tell Quinn and Jake. There's no need to worry anyone else until we find out if Steve's relapsed."

Darryl nodded. "Sounds like a plan. With you running things, it will be easier to gang up on Steve and drag him to the hospital if necessary."

He sat back in the chair as his mind raced. He'd managed to coordinate all the travel plans for his mother and sister as well as Quinn's family in less than a week. All of them would arrive on separate flights that afternoon and the following morning. The plans for the private party had been finalized in record time and he hoped all of it met with Quinn and Jake's approval. They had shared their secret with him so he could plan the perfect setting for the party. It had been hard not to pass out a bunch of cigars in Jake's honor, but he'd managed to keep mum.

Maybe hearing about the pregnancy will get Steve to see he has to take care of himself. If anything happens to him, Quinn will be devastated. Can't these people ever catch a break?

Jacob stared at the prints of the ultrasound for the hundredth time. They weren't much more than little blips on the screen, but they were his children just the same. Twins. Not only had they been given a miracle with the pregnancy, they'd been doubly blessed. It would be a couple more weeks at least before the doctor could tell them the sex of the babies, but in his heart he knew they'd have a boy and a girl.

Quinn stirred against his shoulder where she'd been napping, her body curled against his. "Are we there yet?"

He kissed her forehead. "We're still over forty minutes out. The delay at SFO set us behind schedule and now the captain says we'll have to circle McCarran until we're cleared to land. Even Steve can't pull strings to get us in faster."

She giggled. "Who says I want to get to Vegas sooner? I like napping at thirty thousand feet with you."

He rolled her under him. "Is that going to be our code word in front of the kids when we want to have some adult time?"

Her fingers moved up and down his bare back. "Probably not. Can you imagine the amount of therapy they'd have to go through if they walked in on us 'napping'? We'll have to come up with something else."

He rested his forehead against hers. "I don't care what we call it, as long as we get it."

"One baby is hard enough but two at once will be exhausting. We're going to need a village to help us with it all. Are you okay with that?"

"I don't think that will be a problem after we tell everyone. We may end up having to hide away just to get alone time with our babies. I know what you're asking and yes, I'm more than okay with asking for help raising these two."

She kissed him as they rolled to lie side by side facing each other. "We should probably get dressed and take our seats."

He groaned. "You're right, but can't blame me for trying to keep you all to myself for as long as possible. As soon as we land, our lives won't be our own. This party is just the beginning. There's the wedding to plan and if we're lucky, we'll tie the knot before the twins join us. The Bay House is going to be full with family all the time."

She tossed the covers aside and helped him gather their clothing. "Casa del Hartley has a nice ring to it don't you think?"

He smiled. "Perfect."

She chattered on about asking Jillian to be their nanny and having her cousin, Brigid perform their blessing ceremony, and asking Steve to be their godfather. He agreed with it all, especially about having Steve as godfather. He was the most logical choice and would take the job seriously. The twins would want for nothing. Jacob knew he wouldn't have to compete with Steve for their affections because he'd proven himself time and time again to be a dear friend. It had taken him far too long to see that and accept Steve's help and friendship.

As they made their way back to their seats and fastened their seatbelts, he vowed to embrace his new life and everything that came with it. He'd been offered the chance to head up the new physical therapy center for California Pacific Medical Center. The hours would be perfect as he'd be on the road before the major traffic backups would occur and drive home after the evening rush hour wound down. Best thing about the job was the location—within walking distance of Quinn's hospital. They'd be able to commute together on most days. He couldn't have asked for a better opportunity.

He was about ready to burst with excitement over being able to share the news of his new career path and then surprise them all with the news of the twins. He'd literally dreamt about how he'd tell them. Having them all in one place made it easier to do it, especially for Quinn who needed more time to rest when they traveled. Just a drive along the coast had exhausted her. Dr. Goldman had assured them that was to be expected. Even so, he'd taken to make sure any of their travel plans involved time for the mother to be to rest and concentrate on enjoying her pregnancy.

Of course the nap times usually ended up with the two of them naked and in each other's arms. That too was normal according to his new best friend, Dr. G as he liked to call her. She'd given the all clear for Quinn to fly after their last appointment. Both of them literally glowed with joy since finding out about the twins and anxious to share the happy news with their families. Keeping the secret from everyone so far had been difficult, but they'd managed with the help of Eric and Sarah. He'd asked both of them to not tell Derek as he'd wanted to be the one to tell him, but something in his voice the last time they'd talked put Jacob on edge. Normally open and a talker, especially when it came to what he was up to with his art and music, he'd become a little subdued. Derek had given some lame ass excuse about being under deadlines for a special project with Steve, but something didn't feel right.

Quinn had been disappointed that both Steve and Derek weren't able see them when they'd checked into the MGM. Of course, Steve had them up in the best suite on the floor below the penthouse and had stocked the kitchen with all of their favorite foods. She'd hoped to be able to host an informal dinner party that night so they could tell them about her pregnancy, but both had begged off citing their secret project.

Two, or three as the case may be, can play at that game. If two of her favorite men could have secrets, so could she. Lucky for her Eric had cleared his schedule to spend the evening with them. Eric was thrilled to go over the final preparations for the party at Saints and Sinners that would take place the following night. By that time, all of their friends and family would be in town and ready to party.

"Everything looks fabulous, Eric! You've outdone yourself. How on earth did you do all of this and hide it from Steve?"

"He's been really preoccupied the last month. He and Derek go off all day together once or twice a week. They say it's for some project, but I don't know what it could be. Steve hasn't filled me in on that one. Everything else he put in my hands. Honestly, it's great to have all this responsibility, but the casinos pretty much run themselves. The new construction projects are on track and little left for me to do. This one thing, though, bothers me. I'm worried about him, Quinn. Something isn't quite right."

She sat down on the sofa next to him in the living room of the suite. Jacob had volunteered to go with Darryl to pick up more of their guests. This would most likely be the only time she would have to speak with Eric alone, so she pounced. "I've noticed a change in his voice when we've talked. He's definitely hiding something from me. I don't want to have a repeat of last year, so please just tell me what the hell you think is going on."

He bit his lower lip and sighed. "I don't know what's happening. That's the truth. Darryl is worried about him too and he'd planned on asking you to help him get Steve to go in to see his doctors."

"I know he's been fighting a bug for some time now but he told me he was doing fine and his meds were helping. I assumed he was under a doctor's care. Are you saying that's not the case?"

Eric visibly paled. "I don't know how to say this."

Not again. Not again. She grabbed his hand and held on with all her strength. "I can handle whatever you have to say. Please don't keep anything from me. Not now."

"Steve has Non-Hodgkin's."

She shook her head. "That's impossible. He's in great shape and in perfect health."

"You don't understand. He's lived with it for over a decade. He's been in remission all this time, but with him burning the candle at both ends lately...well, Darryl is afraid he's relapsed."

Her vision swam and she had to blink rapidly to clear it. This was the secret Anthony had kept bugging Steve about. He'd begged him over and over again to not keep her in the dark. She'd never dreamt he'd kept something this devastating from her. Of course, she'd been in no shape to hear her knight in shining armor could be taken from her life at any given moment.

Just like her father.

She squared her shoulders and let her medical mind take over. "Well I guess we'll all have to gang up on Mr. Eischer. Until I hear otherwise, I'm going to believe he can beat this."

He leaned over and hugged her. "I'm sorry to hit you with that when all you guys wanted to do was celebrate."

She laid her palm against his cheek. His forlorn look tugged at her heart just like Jacob's had when he'd come to find her in Anaheim. She wondered if their father had the same expression. Both of his sons showed their deep emotions through their eyes. "How long have you known about his cancer?"

"I found out at the airport waiting for you and Jake. All I could think about was that this wasn't fair. He's done so much for so many people and this town. Then I remembered everything you and Derek went through with your dad. When is it all going to end?"

"I thought the same thing when the pregnancy tests came back positive. Everything was finally going our way. In the back of my mind, I've been waiting for the other shoe to drop. This is it, but you know what?"

"What?"

"We'll get through this too because we're family. My heart wouldn't let Jake go and it sure as hell isn't going to let Steve go either. So as soon as that brother of mine and Steve are back here, we're going to confront them both."

"That may be a while. Brigid flew in this morning and she's been with them all day. Something about a blessing?"

She laughed. "I thought you knew. She's a Wiccan priestess. She'd promised Steve that she'd perform a ceremony at one of the construction sites."

"Oh yeah. He mentioned that he'd invited clergy from multiple religions to Nevada. I didn't realize it was happening this week. It's not in the schedules he'd given to me."

"Maybe it's something he wanted to handle himself? Can't expect him to turn everything over to you in one swoop. That wouldn't be our Steve."

A breaking news banner on the muted television caught her eye. Bile rose to the back of her throat. She scrambled for the remote and punched the volume button with enough force to break it.

"Just in. Casino Mogul Stephen Eischer and two companions were transported to the hospital after the vehicle in which they were traveling was broadsided by a delivery truck. Police report the driver of the truck has been arrested on suspicion of DUI. We'll keep you updated as soon as we have more details."

She dropped the control on the coffee table, grabbed her purse and ran for the door with Eric on her heels. She fumbled with her phone, only to find that Eric had beaten her to it. "Jake, meet us at the hospital. There's been an accident."

"Derek? Come on, cousin. We have guests who want to talk to you."

He rubbed his eyes and sat up in the bed. The sound of gulls and the ocean reached his ears. "What the hell?"

Brigid laughed. "Give yourself a moment to adjust and meet me outside."

She darted through the curtains covering the opening of a sliding glass door he presumed led out toward the water. Confusion clouded his brain. The last thing he remembered was singing along to a song on the radio with Brigid. Steve had cranked up the tunes and had been smiling. His blood counts were up and his body appeared to be tolerating the high dose chemotherapy he'd started the week before. He'd promised after the party, he'd sit everyone down and tell them about his illness.

Then the horrible sound of screeching tires and busting glass. Brigid's screams rang out as a damn truck blew through a stop light and hit his side of the mustang. He should be in a hospital now unless...

He bolted through the curtains and came face to face with the one person he'd prayed to when he thought he'd lost Quinn. "Pop?"

Danial Quartermarsh wrapped his arms around him. His large hand cupped the back of his head as Derek sobbed against his shoulder. "It's okay, son. You're gonna be okay. You just need a little break."

He looked up to find Brigid standing next to another man, covered in tattoos and body piercings. One he'd recognized from his dreams. "Danny?"

The younger man smiled. "In the flesh, sort of."

He brushed away his tears with the back of his hand. "I don't understand what's happening. Is this where Jake and Quinn were able to find each other?"

Brigid nodded. It's called the Island. It's the realm between Heaven and earth. Some come here on their way to their next life, while others come here so their mind and body can heal. You're here in part because of the accident we were in and we needed a way to help you on your path."

"My path? Have I taken a wrong turn or something because life is finally pretty damn good. Well, except for Steve's cancer coming back."

His father pointed toward the deck chairs. "You're going to want to sit down for what we have to tell you."

The four of them settled into the chairs and Danny started off. "I'm one of the Guardians who watch over our family and the Hartleys, as well as others who are connected to them. Steve is one of those people. We've used him to help all of you move toward the destinies chosen for you at the beginning of time. Now it's his turn."

His throat constricted and his saliva seemed to dry up in an instant. He licked his lips and forced the words to come out. "He's going to leave us?"

Brigid shook her head. "His will to live is strong, but his body has gone through so much with his relapse and treatment. He needs a blood relative to come forward to give him the gift of life."

"He doesn't have anyone left. His brother died years ago. His parents passed before that."

Danny held his gaze. "Dude, listen to your heart. Haven't you been drawn to Steve since the day you met?"

His mind fired in a thousand directions at once. "How can I be related to him? I was given up for adoption after my mother died in childbirth. I don't know who my birth father is. As far as I'm concerned, I've always been a Quartermarsh."

Daniel smiled. "We feel the same about you too but your bond with Steve is strong because your mother loved both of you. She never meant to leave you. Unfortunately, her death shattered her husband's world. He couldn't take care of the boys he had let alone a newborn so he gave you up."

He slumped in his chair. "Why are you telling me all of this now?"

"When you go back, you'll find out that you're the donor match who will save Steve's life." Brigid knelt before him and took his hand into both of her small ones.

"I already signed the paperwork to agree to do it if I'm a match, so I'm not sure why I'm here. Not that I'm complaining about spending time with the three of you, but what's the catch?"

His father cleared his throat. "You sustained a severe head injury in the car accident. As we speak, you've been taken to surgery to stop internal bleeding. As per your instructions, they will collect the needed stem cells from your bone marrow. You have a choice before you now. Go back and deal with weeks of recovery, or choose to stay here and wait for your next life cycle."

"It's that bad?"

Brigid squeezed his hand tighter. "You'll have to go through intensive therapy like Jake went through with his motorcycle accident. At times you'll want to give up, but you'll have all of us and of course Sarah with you every step of the way. You'll still be able to do your art and perform with the band but there will be moments where you think it's all gone."

"As beautiful as this place is, I can't stay here. I need to go back."

"I knew you'd choose wisely, dear heart."

He turned in his seat to find a beautiful woman with dark auburn hair cascading down her back. If he didn't know better, he'd have thought Sarah had joined them. "Lady Fate?"

She placed her hand on his shoulder. "I know this is all a lot for you to take in. Please rest here a while and spend time with your family. When you're ready, I will take you back to the earthly realm and to those who love you beyond measure."

Sarah bolted through the doors of the ICU waiting room and straight into Eric's arms. Quinn got up from her chair and embraced both of them. "Derek's in surgery now. We won't know more until it's over, but he was thrown through the windshield."

"Wasn't' he wearing his seat belt?" She wiped the tears from her cheeks and searched Quinn's eyes for any hope.

"The police said all of them were but the truck hit them with enough force to snap the restraints. He's bleeding internally and around his brain. He was unconscious when they brought him in. All of them were." Jacob brought over the box of tissues.

"I came right here from the airport. When I didn't see one of you or Darryl, I knew something was wrong. I think I scared the hell out of that poor driver. He kept telling me his instructions were to get me to the hospital ASAP and he'd take care of my luggage. I thought something had happened to the babies."

"Babies? What babies?" Helen Quartermarsh dropped her cup of coffee on the floor.

Quinn hugged Sarah again and led all of them back to the chairs in the corner of the waiting room. "We wanted to wait to tell all of you tomorrow night at the party. Jake and I are expecting twins. So far they're doing well and so am I. Jake and Sarah have made sure of that."

Miranda smiled through her tears. "You're going to be a wonderful mother, Quinn. Now it's payback time for spoiling my boys."

She laughed. "I wouldn't have it any other way."

Eric cleared his throat. "There's something else all of you have to know. Apparently the secret project Derek and Steve have been working on has been coming here."

Helen voiced her confusion again. "What do you mean? Has one of them been sick and keeping it from us?"

Anthony spoke up this time. "Against my better judgement, Stephen has kept his illness from all of you except myself, Darryl and most recently he told Derek. We nearly lost him to Non-Hodgkin's ten years ago. He's come out of remission and has been preparing for a stem cell transplant. It's the only thing that can save him now."

"Like my Daniel?"

Anthony draped his arm around Helen's shoulders. "Yes, love but we do have hope. As one of Stephen's medical advocates, Dr. Carroway called me this afternoon to let me know they'd found a donor. It's Derek. He's a perfect match."

Quinn's heart beat wildly. Here they all were faced with the very real chance they could lose not one, but two of the men they all loved. One part of her brain shouted for joy that Steve could have the chance her father never had. Derek would be the one to save his life. Another part of her mind kept conjuring up the picture of the doctors coming in to tell them they'd lost her brother on the surgery table, his life ended before he could build a life with Sarah. Yet another part of her mind screamed it wasn't fair their families had to relive the worst times in their lives. Her eyes found Maredyth's and she instantly knew she'd been lost in her memories of when Jacob fought for his life. Her sister clung to her husband Robb as they too remembered when they'd lost Danny and their father.

Then there was Brigid. She'd been tossed around the back seat and had sustained multiple of lacerations and bruises as well as a concussion. The doctors wanted to keep her overnight for observation and had given her pain medication to help her sleep. Her parents were out of the country and unable to join them for a couple days. Quinn promised she'd watch over Brigid until they arrived. She'd sat at her bedside while she slept. It wasn't long before she figured out that her cousin was on the Island with Derek. She'd asked her to keep him safe until both of them were able to return. "Love you, girlie. Hurry back. We have so much to do to get ready for the wedding and the babies. I can't do it without you."

* * * *

CHAPTER 18

Quinn walked into Steve's room and stopped short. The man before her in the bed didn't look like the same person who had fought to bring her through her hell. Dark purple bruises bloomed over his forehead and right cheek. The doctors had assured her his injuries weren't as bad as he looked, but seeing him this way still shocked her.

She climbed into the bed next to him, expertly maneuvering her body around all the tubes and wires attached to his body. She laid her head on his shoulder and cried. "This is not the way I'd pictured telling you I'm going to be a mother. Jake would come in and hand out cigars while I shared the picture of our first ultrasound with you. We had to tell Sarah and Eric first, but it was all part of the plan to surprise you. You are the reason we are where we are now and here you go keeping a huge secret from me all this time. I understand why, but damn it! I will not lose you too, do you hear me?"

She placed her hand over the portrait tattoo of her on his chest. "Please keep fighting. We all need you. I need you. You told me that you couldn't imagine a life without me in it, well that goes double for you, Mr. Eischer. There is a waiting room full of people who love you unconditionally. Don't you dare even think of checking out on us now."

A deep rumble tickled her hand and her ear. "I wouldn't think of it, darlin'."

She sat up and to find his eyes open and staring back at her. "How much of that did you hear?"

"Every single word. I should've told you about the cancer before and most definitely should have told you once I knew I'd relapsed, but I couldn't do that to you. I didn't think it was the right time."

"Promise me you won't keep secrets from us again."

He raised his arm slowly and crossed his heart. "I promise. So where's this ultrasound picture you wanted to show me?"

She grinned and pulled the print from her back pocket. "I wanted to have this blown up and used as one of the decorations at the party, but I think it's only fair you get to see it first."

He held it up close to his swollen face. "Those tiny blips are mini you and Jake?"

She nodded. We won't know their sexes for a while yet. When we spring you from this place, I have a video of the sonogram the shows their heart beats. Jake cried when he saw them for the first time. I cried through it all."

His right arm pulled her closer to his side. "Happy tears of course."

"Of course. You know, you've scared the hell out of all of us tonight but we do have some news for you. Brigid will be released tomorrow morning and Derek made it through surgery."

He exhaled slowly. "I was afraid to ask. That truck came out of nowhere. We were in the middle of the intersection and the next thing I knew we were airborne."

"Shh. You don't have to think about that now. They arrested the driver at the scene. Apparently, his blood alcohol level was three times the legal limit. Enough of that. I have one other bit of good news for you. They've found you a donor."

"What? How is that possible?"

"Derek is a match. They were able to collect his stem cells during surgery. Once you're stable again, you'll be able to have the transplant."

"It must be the pain medications, but I thought you just said Derek is a match for me."

"Can't blame it on the meds, honey. Your hearing is just fine. You will have your transplant and you'll beat this thing."

He kissed her forehead. "That appears to be the plan, darlin'."

She kissed his cheek gently trying not to cause him any additional pain. The little ache in his face was worth it to be able to have this time with her, and have the truth out in the open. Now he could concentrate on his recovery. He'd worried himself sick over how Quinn and his family would handle his diagnosis when he should have come clean right from the start.

The news that they'd found a donor for him had come as a shock, but not as much as finding out Derek had been the one to match. The odds of that happening for him had always been slim if at all. As his pain medications kicked in all the way, he vowed to find out how closely related he and Derek were in order to have this miracle. *Could I have had family near me all this time and never knew it?*

"I'm sorry to ruin your surprise. I want all of you to still have the party. I don't want you fussing over me in the hospital." His words came out slow and slurred. He had more to tell her but his body cried uncle.

Quinn settled back down against his shoulder. "Hush now. You get some rest. I'll stay with you as long as you need me."

He drifted off to the sound of her softly singing their song. "I'll always love you…"

Helen left Derek's bedside as Jacob entered the room.

"Don't go. I'll just be a couple minutes."

She placed her hand on his arm and rubbed over his tattoos there. "I'm going to check in on Quinn and Steve. You need to be here with my boy now. His doctors say he'll need months of rehab and I hear you're one of the best physical therapists in the country."

"I've been right where he is so I know how to help him get back on his feet. I'll do everything I can, whatever he needs…"

She hugged him and kissed him on the cheek. "He'll get through this because of you and all of us. He's a fighter and I know for a fact he loves you too."

She let him go and left him alone with his best friend. He sunk down into the chair next to the bed. "Jesus Christ, D."

Derek's head had been covered with bandages. A tube had been placed through his skull just behind his ear to help keep fluid and blood from reforming around his injured brain. His eyes appeared to be swollen shut and his entire face the darkest shade of purple he'd ever seen. He recognized all the tubes and wires as well as the machines connected to them. He went through the list of injuries the surgeon detailed for all of them while Derek had been in recovery. Multiple skull and jaw fractures, five broken ribs, lacerated liver and a ruptured spleen had been the main concerns along with a broken collar bone and pelvis.

"Red?" Derek stirred against the pillows.

He placed his hand over his friend's. "She'll be back in a couple minutes. Your mom made her grab something to eat before she passed out. Don't try to move around too much yet. You're body has been through the ringer."

Derek moved his hand up toward his face. His fingertips brushed against the bandages. "Tell me the truth. I need you to be straight up with me."

"Remember when Eric told you about my accident?"

Derek closed his eyes. "That bad, huh?"

"It could've been so much worse."

"I know. I was on your Island with my Dad, Danny and Brigid."

The hairs stood up on both of his arms as goosebumps covered his skin. "I'm glad you decided to come back to us. I don't know what we would've done if we lost you too."

Derek's eyes snapped open and he struggled to sit up. "Steve and Brigid? Are they okay? They said I'm a match. Steve's supposed to beat his cancer now. Brigid walked off with some tall smoking hot dude, who I thought Pop called Lucius. She wasn't supposed to stay there, Jake. She promised me she would be right behind me when they brought me back."

"Whoa. Calm down. You're gonna spike your blood pressure. Brigid is back asleep in her room. She'll be released tomorrow morning. Steve will have to be here a couple more days but so far his doctors are happy with his progress too."

Derek eased back down against his pillows with Jacob's help. "You don't understand. There was something going on between this Lucius guy and Brigid. I think he was trying to convince her to stay there with him."

"Well he failed. She has been awake off and on. Randi sat with her last before she fell back to sleep."

"Wait. You didn't react when I said I was a match. Does everyone know now?"

He nodded. "Quinn was a little miffed that the two of you kept Steve's illness a secret but she's determined to get both of you healthy. You really didn't think a thing such as a car accident would get you out of wearing another tuxedo for the wedding did you?"

Derek snorted, or what was supposed to be a laugh and then winced. "I guess not."

"You two weren't the only ones with a secret." He pulled out the ultrasound print from his front shirt pocket.

"I'm going to blame the double vision on my head injury, but looks to me like I'm going to be an uncle again."

He nodded and beamed. "Twins, D. We're gonna have twins. Can you believe it?"

"With what's gone on between the two of you, I've learned to believe in miracles."

"Now you get to give one to Steve. I'm here to help continue with yours."

"What do you mean?"

"You've got a long road ahead of you, but if you'll let me, I want to help you through it."

A sob broke through his chest. "You'd do that for me?"

"Damn straight. Try to keep me away. You're my best friend and a brother to me. Of course I will be with you every step of the way." In his mind he'd worked out his travel plans from California each week. He'd already been in touch with his new bosses and they'd agreed with his proposal to split his time between San Francisco and Las Vegas.

"Promise you won't cut me any slack, not even when I want to give up. You keep pushing me to get better." Derek held his hand up and clenched his fingers together.

He bumped his fist against Derek's. "You got it, brotha. How about you let your pain meds take over and get some rest. Sarah and your mother will be back soon. I don't want to be accused of wearing you out before anyone else gets to talk to you."

Derek nodded. "I am feeling a bit fuzzy around the edges. They've given me some good shit. I should enjoy it while I can."

He laughed. "Yes you should." He fluffed the pillows and helped him to reposition. Within five minutes Derek's breathing had slowed. He could tell the broken ribs prevented him from breathing deeply, but it appeared sleep had come over him again. He sat back in the chair and watched his friend rest. *You have so much to live for, D. I'm going to give to you what you gave to me—a second chance.*

"Wipe that smirk off your face, Lucius."

"I told you I still had it. Just because I spend all of my time testing Our creations, doesn't mean I don't like to feel appreciated for my charms once in a millennia." The God of Trials and Tribulations rocked back and forth on the balls of his feet with his hands clasped behind his back. "Maybe Derek could put in a good word for me with the priestess."

Fate arched one eyebrow and shook her head. "What did you expect her to do? Her family is in crisis and you ask her to leave them all to stay with you. How did you put it?" She cleared her throat and mimed his voice perfectly. "Just say the word and I'll give up all that I am to spend eternity with you."

He scowled. "I don't understand why she's so stubborn."

"She's right. You don't know her at all if you thought for one instant she'd ask you to give up your immortality for her. You're far too important to Us. We are and have always been The Three. We've worked together since the moment Yeshua created Us. We are the foundation of their belief systems and you'd toss it all away on a whim."

"She is *not* a whim."

Fate slipped her arm through his and sighed. "No she is not. None of them in this group are. That's why I asked for your help. It was never my intention for you to lose your heart to her again."

He patted her hand. "You were right to intervene, but you can't protect me forever. What have you preached to me time and time again?"

"The heart wants what the heart wants. Eventually, in this life time or the next, love always finds a way."

"My heart was created to love as well, Sister. My immortality doesn't change that. She is who my heart wants."

Together they walked to stand at Derek's bedside. Her fingers touched his chest over his heart. "It's because of the love you have in your heart that Derek lives. You are the reason that Brigid and Steve live as well."

"I didn't do anything you wouldn't have done."

"I beg to differ. You snapped their seat belts to throw them from the vehicle. If you hadn't done that, all three would have been killed. Other lives would have been lost if you hadn't prevented the car from exploding."

He shrugged. "I promised you I wouldn't continue to test them. This is their time for happiness. I was simply honoring my vow to you."

She kissed his cheek. "Come. Yeshua has asked We return for now and let the Guardians continue to watch over all of them. It won't be long before We are asked for Our help again.

He smiled. There was still so much to do for these two families and their friends and he looked forward to interacting with them again. Never before had he taken an interest in mortals other than to test them so they proved worthy of the gifts from Heaven.

These mortals had proved worthy and so much more.

* * * *

CHAPTER 19

February 14ᵗʰ, eight months after Anaheim

Finally a moment alone! Quinn swore, between her mother and Jacob's mother, she had not had a moment to herself for the last week. Not that she was complaining because she loved them both, but it was nice to have a few moments to herself to think and just relax before the ceremony. Sarah and Miranda had helped her into her dress and stood behind her crying over the way she looked. Quinn had to threaten them with bodily harm if they didn't stop. There was no way in hell she was going to redo her makeup one more time.

The dress had been made for her by one of Steve's favorite dress makers in Vegas. She'd designed the dresses Quinn wore to the different functions with him over the past couple of years. This one turned out to be her finest piece. It was a very pale lavender off-the-shoulder number that showed off her breasts beautifully. The neckline was simple with four small lavender roses at the center. The bodice fit snugly, and the dress fell softly over her very large baby bump. She cradled her belly in her hands and smiled. "Hey, pumpkins? Are you ready to party?"

"If they're anything like their mother, they're already dancing."

Quinn smiled and looked back into the mirror at those green eyes she knew and loved so well. "How long have you been there, Mr. Eischer?"

"Long enough to have trouble breathing. You're stunning in that dress, darlin'. And I was just remembering when you told me you were carrying those bambinos of yours."

She turned around and held out her hands to him. "Will you sit with me for a bit while I relax before the ceremony?"

"I wouldn't miss a chance to have you alone for a few more moments on Valentine's Day. Oh, don't give me that look. I have no regrets losing you to Jake. You two belong together, and I loved having my part in making that happen. Man, so much has changed for all of us during the last eight months, hasn't it?"

"I'll say. You helping Jake and me find each other again. Finding out about the twins the week before we almost lost you and Derek. I never thought I could get through all of that emotion again, but I did. We all did. And I'm still a bit mad at you for not telling me about your cancer sooner."

Steve cringed a little before smiling broadly. "I know, I know. Anthony is still ripping into me about it. One great thing that came out of it is that I found more family. Was a bit of a shock, to say the least, to find out Derek was a match for me and agreed to donate his bone marrow. It seems like I was bound to be a member of the Quartermarsh family one way or another!"

Quinn squeezed his hand. "You will always be a part of our family, and of my heart. From what I heard, you are now a member of the Hartley clan as well."

"All of these years he's worked for me and Eric never noticed the picture I had on my desk at the club. When he got a good look at it, he told me he thought his mother had one just like it. The picture is of my mother and her cousin, Karina, when they were teenagers in Poland. The women had lost track of each other after they'd immigrated to America. Spending time with her has helped me remember so much about my mother." He squeezed her hands tighter in his before he went on. He was fighting tears. "Darlin', you're the reason I've been blessed this way. It was meeting you and your sister that set this all in motion. I have the Quartermarsh and Hartley families adopting me. I couldn't be happier. I went from being a loner workaholic to someone who jets around the country to be at a soccer game for his nephews. I never would have seen this coming!"

She smiled at the man who still had a piece of her heart and always would. "No regrets?"

"None." He leaned over and kissed her softly. "You'll take Jake's breath away when he sees you. I'm happy to see this day finally get here."

Anthony knocked and strolled right in. Quinn knew she'd made the right choice picking him to plan her whole wedding. Nothing was going to go wrong if he had to say anything about it. "Oh, there you are! Stephen, you need to get out there and keep the mothers occupied. You know they'll be in here hovering over our Quinn and making her a bundle of nerves. Can't have her mess up that makeup again! Now out!"

Steve kissed her one more time. "I am on it! Save a dance for me, darlin'."

She blew him another kiss as he left the room. "You got it, babe!"

Anthony rolled his eyes but smiled. "I still think that the two of you would make a great couple, but your Jake is absolutely divine so I'll forgive you for not marrying Stephen when you had the chance."

He crossed the room to the refrigerator and pulled out her bouquet, a beautiful arrangement of cream and violet roses. "Here you are, love." He looked at her one more time in the mirror and scowled. "Oh, there's something missing. Let me see." He reached into his pocket and pulled out a jewelry box.

"What do you have there, Anthony?" He opened the box, and she nearly fell over. It was a diamond and sapphire necklace. "Where did that come from?"

"It's a gift from both of your families. Something old, new, borrowed and blue."

"What do you mean?"

"Look at the diamond in the center. That's the new from Jake. The blue are all the sapphires, one from each member of your families. The old are those two matching diamonds on either side, one from Katrina and one from Helen. And here is the borrowed." He pulled out two teardrop diamond earrings from his breast pocket. "These belonged to my mother, and I would be honored if you would wear them today."

Quinn threw her arms around him. "If you were not already my gay husband, I would walk down that aisle with you right now."

247

"Oh, don't I know it, love! We would be the best-looking cake toppers around. Now let's get you out of here. Derek is waiting for you at the end of the hallway to walk you out to Jake."

Derek paced as he waited to walk Quinn down the aisle. Sarah had to come back twice to make sure he hadn't worn a hole in the carpet. "Will you stop all the pacing? For Pete's sake, you would think you're the one getting married!"

"This is a big job, Sarah. Maybe Robb should walk her down. He's been in her life longer and has earned the right to give her away."

"Stop it. Robb is performing the ceremony, and you're the only person that Quinn would want to give her away. You've known both her and Jake all this time and have seen them through it all. It's your blessing that she needs for this. Both of them do."

Tears stung his eyes. "I don't deserve this."

Sarah wrapped her arms around him and whispered softly in his ear, "Yes, you do. You're her brother and always have been. Your pop would be very proud of you both right now. I know Helen is beside herself with pride. You're the one who brought Quinn out of her shell and into both Steve and Jake's lives. You got all of this started. Jake and Quinn love you very much, and so do I."

Derek pulled back from her and kissed her softly. "I love you, too, Red." She smiled and left him alone for a few more minutes before he caught glimpse of Quinn and Anthony approaching. She was stunning in that dress. He remembered taking her to a couple of the fittings. They'd had to do a lot of work on it the last month since the twins were growing so fast. He was beginning to wonder if they were going to make a surprise appearance today. That would definitely be par for the course for Jake and Quinn.

She took his hand and squeezed it before leaning in to kiss him on the cheek. "Hey, handsome. You ready to give me away?"

"I am, if you are, that is. You can still change your mind." Derek leaned on his cane and winked. She blessed him with that loud, bawdy laugh of hers. He tapped his cane on the floor in mock protest. "You think I'm kidding? I have a signal worked out with Nathan. You just say the word and he'll have the limo fired up and ready to go in less than a minute."

"Do you know how much I love you, Derek?"

"Uh-huh. As much as I love you."

"That's why I wanted you to give me away. What we feel for each other keeps me grounded and connected to Dad and to Danny. You worked so hard to recover from your accident and I couldn't be more proud of you if I tried. You are my best friend as well as my brother, and I need you here with me on the most important day of my life. So stop trying to get out of the job of walking me down this aisle, bucko."

He should've known she would know exactly what he'd been going through. That, and he was damn sure Anthony had tattled on him. "All right, doll. I'm honored that you want me to give you away today. Helps me practice for my own wedding day."

Quinn's eyes flew open. "Are you thinking about asking Sarah anytime soon or just gonna keep that bit of information to yourself?"

"How about we get through one wedding and the birth of twins before we start planning the next big shindig?" He kissed her on the forehead before he pulled her arm around his. "Come on, Doc. Jake has been waiting his whole life for you and those babies. We don't want to keep him waiting any longer now, do we?"

"Well, Jake, it's now or never. You have any second thoughts you better speak up." Eric grinned from ear to ear and hid behind Robb. "This is your last chance to run for the hills. Once you say 'I do,' Quinn will have you forever."

"You know, if anyone else would've said that to me today I would've put my fist through their teeth. But you, you earned the right to question me."

"Well?" Eric was still safely behind a now laughing Robb.

"I'm right where I want to be, waiting for the moment that Quinn is finally my wife."

Both Robb and Eric pretend to wipe their foreheads and give huge sighs of relief. Robb patted him on the shoulder and excused himself to go over his notes one last time. "I want everything to be perfect for our Quinn. Oh, and for you too of course, Jake!"

Eric burst out laughing again, and this time Jacob joined him. It took a little time to get Robb to warm up to the idea that he and Quinn were going to be married, but once he saw how happy they were together, and that Steve was really all for it, he got on board along with the rest of the family. It meant a lot to Quinn to have him perform the ceremony today, and Jacob was all for giving Quinn her fairy tale that she deserved. She more than did that for him when she'd forgiven him and taken him back into her life after he'd pushed her away. Now that was behind them, and they had their whole lives ahead of them. His entire world centered on Quinn and the impending arrival of the twins.

They had been really active over the last week, and Quinn was worried they would try to show up during the ceremony. Just in case, Jacob had asked Steve to be sure to have a doctor on call at the vineyard at all times. No surprise he was already on that and then some as he made sure Dr. G would be able to join them in Napa for the wedding.. He had Nathan plot out the fastest routes to the hospital in advance and programmed all of the GPS units in the limos with the information. Definitely was a bonus to have a billionaire in the family. He still couldn't get over the fact that their mothers were cousins and had grown up in Poland together. Saying it's a small world really didn't cover their situation at times.

The music started, indicating that Robb and Miranda's boys were seating the guests and it was nearly time for Jacob and Eric to join Robb at the front of the chapel. Right on cue, his little brother stepped into his role as best man with ease. "All right then. Let's not keep our Quinn waiting any longer." He fussed a little bit with Jacob's lapel and the lavender rose bud pinned there. "I had been trying to think of what Pop would say to you on your big day, and it finally came to me last night." He cleared his throat and lowered his voice a few octaves to sound exactly like their father. "See, boy. I told you that you were not a screw up. Here ya are about to marry the woman of your dreams and become a daddy. You're all grown up now, and I am so very proud of you. Love you, Jakey."

"Love you, too, Eric. Pop would've been very proud of you as well, running several of Steve's casinos already. You're a dynamo, and I'm proud to call you my brother."

Maredyth peeked her head around the corner and smiled. "Hey, you two. Time to get up front so Quinn can walk down the aisle. You know pregnant women have to pee every ten minutes. Now get a move on, will ya?"

The first few notes of "Unchained Melody" floated through the doors. The band from Anaheim was there performing it for them once again. They'd been thrilled to do them the honor of playing for the ceremony and the reception. The fondly remembered Quinn and Jacob's dance together in Downtown Disney.

Quinn held on to Derek's arm as they walked down the white walkway strewn with purple rose petals. Little Cassie did her job well. She smiled broadly up front with the rest of the wedding party, still dropping the rose petals.

Quinn's eyes locked on Jacob's, and she didn't see anyone or anything else from that point on. This was where she wanted to be. This was where their lives had been taking them all along. Her heart pounded, and the babies kicked madly in her belly.

Derek felt them, too. He chuckled softly and whispered to them. "Hey, you two, let's get your parents to say 'I do' before we start the party, shall we?"

Anthony and Steve heard his comment and laughed, too. She couldn't help herself and smiled at her husband to be. He winked and pointed to his abdomen. She nodded, and he laughed and told Eric and Robb what was going on. By the time she got up front, the entire place was giggling and the twins were kicking wildly, obviously loving being the center of attention.

Derek kissed her quickly, placed her hand in Jacob's and then took his place next to Eric. Robb looked so handsome in his monkey suit. This time he'd volunteered to wear one. That made Miranda happy as a clam. Quinn glanced over at her family sitting in the front row, all dressed in their finest and smiling back at her. Jacob glanced toward his family and beamed. Quinn didn't think she could be any happier than at that moment, until Jacob turned back to her. Their eyes met and she fell in love with him all over again.

Robb cleared his throat and got down to the business at hand. "On behalf of Quinn and Jacob I want to thank you all for coming and sharing this day, one that has been a long time coming. The road they took to get here was a hard one, to say the least."

Anthony snorted. "You got that right." That set off another round of chuckles from everyone.

"And no one knows more about the hell they went through to find each other again than their friends and families who have cheered for them all along. But it took one special friend to make it all come together. One special person who means the world to them both, and who we recently found out was actually family. Quinn and Jacob have asked that we all take a moment to give thanks to God, the Goddess Fate, or whoever you hold dear for bringing us all together today. We offer thanks for giving Derek the chance to save Stephen's life in August with the bone marrow transplant. We are thankful for blessing the happy couple with their miracle, twins no less. We give thanks for letting true love prevail and for the unselfish, unconditional love that only friends and family can give each other. We also want to ask that Heaven continue to watch over the ones we have lost before: Michael Hartley, beloved husband and father. Rose Eischer, beloved wife and mother. Daniel Quartermarsh Senior and Daniel Junior: beloved husband and father, and beloved son and brother. We know these loved ones are watching over Quinn and Jacob today."

After a few moments of silence, he began again, smiling. "Everyone here knows their story, so there really isn't a need for me to rehash any of it." He tossed his cards over his shoulder, and the place erupted into laughter again. "Quinn and Jacob would like to say their own vows to each other, and I think this is the perfect time for them to do so."

Jacob squeezed her hands and began the first verse of the poem they'd had written for them entitled "Heart and Soul."

"Never thought I would feel at peace. Always seemed a large part was missing from my restless Heart and Soul."

She smiled and continued the next verse, "Thought my career would fill the void, but it only made the yearning stronger: to find and complete my Heart and Soul."

"From the moment you first smiled at me, the pull was there...strong and bold. But it scared me, too. Could you really be my Heart and Soul?"

"I let the old childhood fear of rejection rob me of the time to see if it was true, if the electricity zipping through me was real, or just a fantasy to complete my Heart and Soul." Tears threatened to fall, but she held them back.

His eyes glistened, but his voice stayed strong. "Thoughts of you, your smile, your laugh crept into my thoughts and dreams at times. When I felt lost and alone the call went out to find my Heart and Soul."

Now she couldn't hold the tears back, and she let them fall. Happy tears this time. Jacob smiled, encouraging her to continue with their vows. "Would things have been different? Would we feel the same now as then? Would we still be bound Heart and Soul?"

"Both lived separate lives, had separate loves, but something was always missing, always pulling and drawing us back together. Can we really ever deny our Heart and Soul?"

Now the tears rolled down Jacob's face as well, and she reached up and brushed them away. She continued on, "One day, shy no longer; a leap of faith was taken. No rejection, only laughter and love, a love that's been there all along." Quinn squeezed his hands tighter as she felt the twins kick again. They were really getting restless now.

"Finally at peace. Restless no more. Once again whole with you, My Heart and Soul." Jacob let go of one of her hands to put his on her belly, immediately calming their children to just a wiggle or two.

Robb asked Eric for the rings and continued with the ceremony. Quinn barely heard the words and kept her eyes locked with Jacob's. They finished the rest of the vows as required by law in the state of California, and then Robb pronounced them husband and wife.

"Well, what are you waiting for, Jake. Kiss her already!" Eric gently poked him in the arm, but Jacob was already moving in for his prize. Quinn's eyes stayed locked on his until their lips touched, and then it was all over. He pulled her close as they deepened the kiss, tongues dancing with each other as their guests erupted into cheers. "I love you, Quinn Lee Hartley."

"I love you, too, Jacob."

"Come on, all of you beautiful people! Let's move into the ballroom and get the party started!" Anthony led the guests out after Quinn and Jacob made their way down the walkway. It was such a beautiful day, without a cloud in the sky, perfect for the ceremony at Steve's vineyard. The band was already set up and ready to roll for their first dance together as husband and wife. Of course it would be the same song that started the ceremony. It was their song, after all.

Jacob looked over at Quinn as he removed his tuxedo jacket and touched her belly. "What's wrong, baby doll?"

"Jake, this is surreal. I have seen this all before."

"Déjà vu again?" He was feeling it himself and just going with it.

"Uh-huh." She looked down at their hands entwined over her stomach. "How about a dance, pumpkins?" Four swift kicks against their palms were her answer.

"Come on, Mrs. Hartley. Can't disappoint the bambinos now, can we?"

Jacob held Quinn in his arms for their first song and then several more. Their guests had joined them out on the dance floor and soon everyone was having a wonderful time. Cassie even had found herself a new best friend, Steve, who was just beaming to have the curly-haired moppet giggling in his arms while he twirled her round and round.

The evening flew by with great food and more dancing. Jacob didn't think he would be surprised anymore that night until Derek's band took the stage and asked Quinn to join them. As soon as the first notes rang out, Jacob was thrilled. There she was in her wedding gown, pregnant with twins and belting out Pink's "Trouble" once again for him. This time she was only singing to him. This time he was the one to greet her at the edge of the stage and hold her tight. They had definitely come full circle.

Even though she'd been dancing and mingling for hours, Quinn wasn't tired. Just carrying the twins was exhausting enough on any other day, but today she was filled with love for Jacob, for their families and friends, and she was so happy. She felt that she could keep going and going. She saw Nathan standing just off the dance floor watching her closely and she went over to him. "What? Do I have something on my dress?"

He laughed and shook his head. "Oh, no, Quinn. You look amazing. I was just wondering how you can keep going like you've been all day. Where do you get that energy, and can I have some of whatever you are having?"

"Well, how about you dance with me instead? Maybe some of it will rub off on you and you will be part Energizer Bunny tonight, too."

"It would be my pleasure, Mrs. Hartley." He took her into his muscular arms and held her with ease, twins and all. Quinn felt like she was floating along on a dance floor on a cloud. Of course the twins had other plans and started up a ruckus once again. But this time there was no quieting them down. With each spin with Nathan around the floor, the babies kicked harder and faster.

"I noticed you dancing with my cousin, Samantha."

"She's a looker like you. How could I resist?"

She laughed. "You do know my mother and sister have been working behind the scenes to hook the two of you up, right?"

He smiled. "Do you hear me complaining?"

"I think if you feel a connection, you should jump on it. Life is way too short to let it pass you by. You seem to always be working. I know from experience you can't keep that up indefinitely. Besides, if you snatch her up now, you'll have a connection to Randi's cinnamon rolls."

"How's that?"

"Sammi's best friend, Kate is going into the restaurant business with Randi, Robb and Brigid. You'll be set for life with all your favorite baked goods. All I'm saying is think about it."

"I'll let you in on a secret. I've been thinking about it all evening."

The laughter died on her lips. Quinn clutched Nathan's lapel as a contraction hit and nearly took her breath away. "Is the limo ready to go?"

Nathan stopped dancing and held her tight. "How far apart?"

"Not sure, but my water just broke." She clutched him again, and he swooped down and picked her up into his arms and made a beeline for the exit.

"Jake! Steve! Come with me! Derek, Plan B!"

"What the hell is Plan B?" Quinn looked up in time to see Jacob and Steve racing across the room to meet them at the door. "Do you know where the hospital is?"

"Honey, Jake and I have had this planned from the very moment you two decided to get married here. Derek will make sure that your doctor and the rest of the family get to the hospital in time to welcome the babies, but for now, it's my job to get you safely to the hospital."

Steve helped Jake get Quinn settled in the back and then got into the front with Nathan just as he hit the gas pedal speeding them out of the vineyard's long driveway.

Jacob was pale as a ghost. "Baby doll? Are you okay? Is it too early?"

"I am fine now that you're here with me." Quinn settled back into his arms and closed her eyes. "The doctor told us that they might try to come before the wedding, so they actually waited until their parents were married before coming to us. I think everything will be fine as long as we deliver in the hospital. I don't want to do it alone in this limo. No offense, Nathan!"

"None taken, sweetie! You just concentrate on breathing and let me do the driving."

Steve had spent the last six hours listening to Quinn swearing up a storm in the other room. Good thing the kids were all back at the bed and breakfast with Jillian who'd graciously volunteered to watch them while their parents waited at the hospital. He was about to ask a nurse to check on them when Jacob burst through the door with another hospital gown in hand and threw it at him. "What the hell, Jake?"

"Oh, do you really think I am gonna be in there alone with her in all of this pain? You gown up and get your ass in here with me. She's calling for you, too, and I wouldn't piss her off right now. You know how she is." Jacob's eyes flashed, and he laughed a little. "Seriously, I need some moral support in there. I can't take away her pain, and help the doctor with the delivery. Please?"

He quickly put on the gown and followed Jacob. She was curled up on her side, clutching her belly, trying to get through another contraction. "Oh, Holy Hell! These two are taking after their father, stubborn as mules and bull-headed!"

"Oh, and look who's calling the kettle black, darlin'." Steve took one of her hands, and Jacob took the other as she bore down again. He looked up at Jacob and could tell he was thinking the same thing. "Jesus Christ, Quinn, both of us are gonna need these fingers later. Care to loosen up a little bit?"

"Mr. Eischer, you ain't felt anything yet. They have been beating the shit out of my gut all day to make an entrance and now they're refusing to come out. You think your fingers hurt now, wait until one of them starts to get through the birth canal…" She bit down on her lower lip and then his fingers went numb. "Like right now."

Steve met Jakes eyes. There was nothing more either one could do for her but hold on and let nature take its course. It was much easier said than done in Steve's opinion, but he wasn't about to leave her side now.

Quinn's body finally relaxed as the last contraction eased up. She looked so exhausted. "I don't think I can keep this up much longer." A sob escaped her lips. "How the hell do women get through twelve-plus hours of this?"

"No two births are the same, Quinn, and it looks like your first child is about to arrive. Jake, let Steve hold her hand and you get over here by me so you can cut the cord when it's time."

Quinn closed her eyes and curled her head toward her chest.

"Now, Quinn, push hard. You have to get the baby's shoulders out." Dr. Goldman put gentle traction on the head of the baby and eased her out and into the arms of the nurse. Quinn fell back against the pillow to rest before the next baby made its entrance. "Cut here, Jake. That's it. Now go over with the nurse and help her clean up your daughter."

"I knew she would come first. Just like her mother, stubborn and bull-headed." Jacob looked back over at Quinn and Steve, smiling and crying at the same time. "She's beautiful like her mother, too."

Quinn sat up, and Steve got behind her to help support her through the next several contractions. "Jake, I think you better get over here and watch your son come into the world, too." Steve could see everything with Quinn in the mirrors they had set up. He was overwhelmed with the whole thing and so in love with Quinn and now her babies. Steve felt his bond with Jacob grow now, too. He could die a happy man at that moment.

Jacob took his son over to the nurse this time and helped clean him up as well. "All fingers and toes and other parts accounted for. Oh, and will you listen to those lungs! Definitely takes after his mother!" He brought him over to place in Quinn's arms then went back for his daughter and brought her over to Steve. "Want to meet your namesake?"

He was momentarily confused. "What do you mean?" Steve looked down at the rosy, red-faced bundle of joy in his arms and immediately fell head over heels.

Jacob cleared his throat before going on in a soft voice. "Steve, meet Stephanie Rose, your first godchild."

He looked up at both of them just stunned, unable to speak. Stephanie for him and Rose for his mother.

"And here is Daniel Michael, your godson. That is if you would do us the honor."

"I, I'm overwhelmed." He kissed Stephanie's little forehead and she smiled. "Overwhelmed and in love. You just try and stop me from spoiling these two. I'd be honored to be their godfather." He chuckled and handed Stephanie over to Jake so he could hold Daniel for a moment or two. "I never would have seen this coming a few years ago. My life is full and happy thanks to you, Quinn."

"No regrets?"

"None at all. Everything brought us here to this moment and these two. Who can ask for anything more?"

Steve placed Daniel back into Quinn's arms and excused himself to let the new family have some alone time before the rest of their clans invaded their space. He looked back one more time at them and caught Quinn's gaze. She blew him a kiss and smiled, the one that would always have his heart, the one he would still do anything to see over and over again. Now he felt his life was complete. He had his family once again and people who loved him for him and not his money. He'd been able to bring two people together who were always meant to be, and he was alive and well thanks to Derek's bone marrow.

Steve walked toward the waiting room to give the news to the rest of the families. He caught Derek's eye and smiled. That was going to be his next project. Get him and Sarah down the aisle by the end of this year. It was going to be a tough one with his touring and her surgery schedules, but with a little luck, and the fact that Steve had bought the company she worked for, he could get her to move to Vegas without a problem.

Nathan appeared to be falling for another of Quinn's family, Samantha. Steve had only recently met her himself and had been tickled to learn she was a veterinarian and an author. She'd helped Jacob and Quinn with the poem for their vows. She'd listened to how they'd met and all they'd been through to find each other and the words flew out of her pen and onto paper. He made a mental note to look into getting her work published. Talent like that had to be nourished and released out to the world for all to enjoy. By the looks of the two of them together, he was positive Nathan had finally found his match.

Then there was his protégé, Eric. Steve noticed that he was more than smitten with Jillian. That was another promising match. Time would tell, and now he had all the time in the world and the resources to make it all happen.

But first things first. "Who wants to meet Stephanie Rose and Daniel Michael?"

THE END

ABOUT THE AUTHOR

Tammy Dennings Maggy is a best-selling, multi-published poet and erotic romance author with Siren Bookstrand and Sassy Vixen Publishing. Her writing explores many facets of romance from ultimate betrayal to finding your soul mate. Her poetry serves as a companion to her novels and has inspired entire series of novels all on their own. Tammy and her alter egos Lia Michaels, Stephanie Ryan, and Tawny Savage make up the core authors of Sassy Vixen Publishing, and together they've created the shared world series, Temptations Resort. Look for the first books of that series to come out late 2018.

Now happily married to her own Muse and soul mate, she continues to live her dream and act as secretary to all her characters demanding to have their stories told.

Connect with Tammy

www.authortammydenningsmaggy.com

www.sassyvixenpublishing.net

Other Tales by Tammy Dennings Maggy

Now and Forever Series

For the Love of Quinn (Now and Forever Part 1)
For the Love of Quinn (Now and Forever Part 2)
The Island (Now and Forever 2)
The Surrender of Julia (Now and Forever 3)
Bound in Paradise (Now and Forever 3.5)

My Love, My Friend (Now and Forever 4) coming in 2018

Kayne Legacy Series

The Courtship of the Vampyre (poetry)
Course of the First Born Cain (Kayne Legacy 1)
Legacy of the First Born Michael (Kayne Legacy 2) coming 2018

Immortal Siblings Series

Karma in Blue Jeans (Immortal Siblings 1) Coming Christmas
2017

Poetry

Follow Me: Poetry from the Heart and Soul
The Courtship of the Vampyre
Suffering in Silence: journal based on the poetry of Tammy
Dennings Maggy
Suffering in Silence (non-journal version with additional poems)
Coming late 2017

Sassy Vixen Publishing Anthologies

Sweet, Sultry, and Oh So Taboo
Season of Sun and Sin

www.ingramcontent.com/pod-product-compliance
Lightning Source LLC
Chambersburg PA
CBHW020556180626
46810CB00007B/2524